DISHONORED
THE CORRODED MAN

DISHONORED

THE CORRODED MAN

ADAM CHRISTOPHER

TITAN BOOKS

DISHONORED: THE CORRODED MAN
Print edition ISBN: 9781783293049
E-book edition ISBN: 9781783293070

Published by Titan Books
A division of Titan Publishing Group Ltd
144 Southwark Street, London SE1 0UP

First edition: September 2016
10 9 8 7 6 5 4 3 2 1

Editorial Consultants:
Harvey Smith
Paris Nourmohammadi

A CIP catalogue record for this title is available from the British Library.

Printed and bound in the United States.

DISHONORED
THE CORRODED MAN

PROLOGUE

SOMEWHERE NEAR UTYRKA
Month undetermined, 1849—1850

"Contrast this with the prisons of Tyvia, located in the tundra at the center of that nation-state. At some of the labor camps in Tyvia, there are literally no walls. A prisoner exhausted from hard labor and without tools is unlikely to survive the harsh climate or the hungry packs of hounds that rove the frozen wastes. In fact, Tyvian prison authorities make it known that any prisoner is free to leave at any time. In all of recorded history, no one has made the remote walk across the snow and ice to the nearest city."

— PRISONS OF THE ISLES
Extract from a report commissioned
by the Royal Spymaster

The Prisoner stopped at the edge of the precipice and gazed out over the land ahead, the trailing edge of his heavy black woolen greatcoat flapping in the stiff wind that screamed out of the glacier valley in front of him. The gale was so loud he could barely think, let alone contemplate the complexity of the task ahead.

There was no time to dally, no time to waste. There was work to be done.

He had come this far—too far to fail, too far to give up—but at the same time, not far enough. Too close to his captors, to his *tormentors*. He knew he had to keep going and he knew that there was nobody in the world who could stop him, except himself.

The Prisoner adjusted his black traveller's hat, pulling the wide brim down tight over his face to stop it cartwheeling away in the wind, and he looked out at what lay before him. This was the howling wind and the snowy wastes and the cold sun that burned with a flat, dead light.

This was the tundra.

This was Tyvia.

The Prisoner turned, letting the chains he carried over one shoulder slip off into the snow. At the other end of the chains was a bundle of black cloth, curled into itself, shaking in the snow. If the shivering thing was whimpering, or crying, or begging for forgiveness, the Prisoner couldn't hear it over the wind.

This *thing* had once been a guard at Utyrka, the labor camp. Now the Prisoner's own captive, he was numb—numb from the cold, numb from the journey, numb from the knowledge that his story was coming to an end and that soon he would be one with the Void. Because the guard had not been a good man, and he knew it. He knew also the fate that would befall his untethered self once the Prisoner had finished his cruel business in the hard snows.

His end would come soon, but not yet.

The Prisoner still had need for him. He hefted the chains in his gloved hand, twisting, pulling, just a little. The shivering wreck rose to his knees but no further, and shuffled forward but remained bowed, his head buried in a dozen orbits of his scarf, the huge collar of his black greatcoat upturned. It was the same kind the Prisoner wore, the standard issue of the Tyvian military, designed for unpopular tours in the harsh icebound interior of the country.

The Prisoner had taken his coat from another guard at the camp—one of three captives and the first to die, there in the camp, before they had even walked out onto the snowy plain. The second had died two days into the trek, and the Prisoner still had that captive's chain bound around his waist, the thick steel collar now hanging from his belt.

The Prisoner had needed three men, so he had taken three. The first, for his clothes—the heavy winter uniform of the Tyvian army supplementing the ragged wardrobe the Prisoner had worn for years and years without ever taking off. Now he wore the fur-lined greatcoat, the hat with the wide brim to shade from the glare of the dead winter sun, the scarf woven from the pelt of the tundra's saber-toothed black bear. And over his eyes, the first guard's snow goggles, two discs of polished red glass nearly as big as the saucers off which the guards at the camp sipped their hot, imported Gristol tea.

That first guard was dead. It had been necessary. He hadn't wanted to surrender his uniform, so the Prisoner had taken it by force. It was of no consequence. There was no one else alive at the camp for the man to guard.

Not anymore.

As the Prisoner had picked over the dead guard's clothing, the other two he had captured—chained at the neck, shackled like the pigs they were—had knelt on the hard ground and watched in silence, their minds spinning over distant horizons as their new master got dressed for the long journey ahead. Then the Prisoner had yanked the chains and led his two captives away, their heads bowed, their lips moving as they murmured deliriously, stumbling through the snow behind him.

The second guard had been taken for another purpose altogether.

Food.

Not food for the Prisoner, nor for the third captive, but for the wolves the Prisoner knew would be tracking them as soon as they left the safety and light of the camp's outer perimeter. After crossing that boundary they had walked for two days through snow that was sometimes hard-packed, other times waist-deep. The going was slow.

The wolves were fast. In the hard winter, in the Months of Darkness, of High Cold, of Ice, this was their world, their domain, and outside of the Tyvian prisons that dotted the frozen plains, man was a trespasser—though, for the wildlife, not an unwelcome one.

On the contrary. Those trying to escape—the fools

who thought they could make it, who took the mocking invitations of the guards to just walk out—were most welcome indeed. Food was scarce, and in this frozen world the wolf packs were hungry.

In the trek from the camp, the Prisoner found evidence aplenty of previous flights of freedom. Such dreams, such attempts were all the same—ill-conceived, desperate. *Impossible.* Because the prisons of Tyvia were all the same. Each was a labor camp in the wilderness, in the tundra.

They varied in size, ranging from small camps of a few dozen convicts to prisons that were more like small towns. They varied in function, too. Those convicted of lesser offenses were doomed to nothing more than the harvest of lumber—still a task that would break most men, for the wood of the forests was as solid as Dunwall granite. The trees themselves were petrified by the cold, becoming nothing but tall, vertical shafts of permafrost.

But the lumber camps were not penitentiaries, not in the mind of the Prisoner. They were something far lesser— merely "correctional" facilities, the inhabitants of which might even one day return to the warmth of civilization, albeit as shadows, as ghosts of their former selves, their fight, their rebellion, worked out of them.

The other prisons were different. Quarries for rock-breaking or, as at Utyrka, mines sunk deep into the tundra, where salt was wrested from an impenetrable, frozen darkness in the earth.

To be sentenced to those camps was to disappear. Death would be preferable, but there was no such statute in the Tyvian law books. Indeed, to be sent to prison wasn't even considered a punishment, according to the twisted logic of the High Judges, the quasi-military tribunal who ruled over the isle with an iron fist. To be sent to the camps was, in their words, to be granted *freedom*.

Because the prisons had no walls.

They had *guards*, certainly. The Prisoner pitied the poor bastards who were themselves sentenced to long tours out in the frozen wastes, but at least the guards could go home again when their time was up. The guards were there to run the camps—to keep order, to keep the work going, to punish those who did not fulfill their quotas, whether it was lumber or salt or broken rock. But they were not there to prevent escape.

Escape, the High Judges said, was impossible, because the camps were not prisons. There were no walls, no gates, no fences. The "prisoners" were not shackled or manacled or locked in, at night or in the day. In fact, the prisoners were free to leave—everyone in the camp was a free man, pardoned by the state, permitted with full authority to return home, to their families and their towns and their villages and their causes.

Of course, escape *was* impossible. The prisoners knew it. The guards knew it. The High Judges knew it, but their hands were clean, their consciences clear.

Because every man was a free man.

The Prisoner and his two remaining captives came across the first body just a mile from the lights of the camp. Half of it was missing. It lay face down in the snow, arms outstretched, the thin cloth covering the back torn wide open, exposing perfect, unmarked flesh as white as Morley alabaster and just as hard, frozen forever.

What had become of the lower half of the man could not be known. This close to the camp, the would-be escapee would have died of the cold rather than been killed by wolves. Although, if the winter had been particularly bad, it was possible his legs had been taken by a desperate animal venturing closer to human habitation than it would normally risk, probably scared off by the lights and the guards before it could do more than gnaw off the lower limbs. The cold had preserved the rest of the body perfectly. He could have been lying there a day, he could have been lying there fifty winters.

The body was just the first. Indeed, it was said from the top of Utyrka's north tower, on a clear day you could see frozen cadavers lying even closer to the camp than this one. But the Prisoner had never climbed the north tower to see.

Now there wasn't a tower to climb. Not any more.

Soon after they found a second body. Then a third. Then more. For a time, the Prisoner and his two chained companions followed a virtual trail of corpses, each as cold as the ice, each looking as though the walker had just lain down for a while in the snow and had not gotten up again.

Some were intact. Others were just parts.

At the end of the second day, the Prisoner slaughtered the second captive and butchered the body with a knife that had a golden hilt and a wicked, double blade. As he did so, the last surviving captive sat in the snow at the end of his chain and watched with glazed eyes, such was the magic that held him. Then the Prisoner laid out the red meat and wet bones for the wolves. It didn't look like much, spread out on snow stained crimson under the cold sun, and the bones were a waste, but it would be enough. Free from the threat of wolves, he and his last captive would have time to reach the glacier valley.

To reach his *escape*.

*

The Prisoner had examined the first three frozen bodies, just to be sure in his own mind that they weren't suitable. While he had expected to find the frozen cadavers, he hadn't expected that any of them would fit his needs. His examinations confirmed this. The flesh was hard, though pliable under his twin-bladed knife, but the bones beneath were unusable, the matrix of ice crystals within disrupting any reservoirs of power they may once have held.

Useless.

What he needed was the bones of a man—*living* bones, from a *living* man. To escape the tundra, to return to the world, he required a very particular sort of magic. This was why he had brought the third captive. The second had been brought for his flesh. The third had been brought for his *bones*.

The Prisoner looked out at the glacier valley before him. The precipice on which he stood was a sheer drop of a thousand feet or more, the cliff-face a shocking black scar of bedrock in what had been, so far, an uninterrupted wasteland of blinding white, ground and sky alike, the horizon merely a dirty gray smudge that flickered and moved in the corner of his eyes.

Beyond the precipice was a deep, wide valley, the floor hard-packed snow, the walls a jagged jigsaw of giant blocks of ice, their sides vertical and a deep, translucent blue, as if the glacial crags were made not of ice but of sapphire.

It was, some said, one of the wonders of the world, a landscape of untold beauty. The ice field had been explored and illustrated for hundreds of years, but even the engravings that could be found within the precise geographical tomes housed at the Academy of Natural Philosophy in Dunwall could never do justice to the sheer, breathtaking majesty of the landscape.

The landscape that was the *key*.

His fur scarf pulled high, the wind tugging at the wide brim of his hat, the Prisoner turned his red-glassed eyes from the valley to his last captive, bundled behind him in the snow. The wreck of a man lifted his head. Maybe he could sense that the moment was *now*, even as his addled mind swam in a sea of confusion, of madness. Another effect of the Prisoner's magic—the magic that allowed him to walk out of the camp, and would allow him to walk out of the tundra, to walk back to the world, to civilization.

To revenge.

As the last captive stared at his own reflection in his master's snow goggles, he moved his mouth as if to say something, but no words came out. Kneeling in the snow, the captive, the former camp guard, swayed, from side to side, as if held in the thrall of his own distorted image. But his eyes were unfocused, his pupils small, the bare skin of his face worn red raw by the cold and by the wind that screamed and howled and screamed again.

Behind his scarf, the Prisoner smiled.

The magic, the aura, was holding.

His escape was near.

With his free hand, the one not wrapped in the end of the chain leash, he reached across his body, sliding his gloved hand beneath the heavy flap of his greatcoat. Even before he touched the knife he could feel the warmth radiating from the twin blades. Indeed, he thought, perhaps the greatcoat, the hat, the scarf, perhaps they were all unnecessary. Perhaps he *hadn't* needed to kill that guard, just to take his clothes.

No matter. And besides, he had enjoyed the first guard's death. There was a satisfaction there—a small one, but a satisfaction nonetheless. Perhaps because it was the first tiny sliver of revenge, the first act of war against his oppressors.

The first death of many more to come.

The Prisoner pulled the knife from his belt, and immediately the swooning captive's eyes found the blades and focused keenly on them, watching as they shone with a golden light, taking the cold light of the sun and spitting it back as something else entirely—an electricity that sparked behind the eyelids, the reflection of a fire, of a Great Burning that ended one world and started another, uncountable years ago.

The knife was warm in the Prisoner's hand and that warmth spread up his arm, through his body. It felt as if he was sinking into one of the rare, natural volcanic springs that periodically interrupted the tundra, the springs that provided the camps with their heat and their power.

Then he lifted the golden knife, placing the tip of the twin blades in the hollow of his captive's throat.

"The people of Tyvia thank you for your service," he said.

The captive looked at him, all understanding absent from his glazed eyes. And then the Prisoner pushed, and the white snow was stained with something hot and red.

SOMEWHERE IN THE CITY OF DUNWALL
7th Day, Month of Rain, 1851

"Young Lady Emily is undisciplined, I'm afraid. Here within Dunwall Tower, she receives instruction from the finest tutors known in the Isles, yet her mother spoils her and she spends most of her time lost in imagination, wasting her time drawing, or asking Corvo to teach her to fight with wooden sticks. The girl might rule the Empire some day; every moment spent at play is a moment wasted."

— FIELD SURVEY NOTES: THE ROYAL SPYMASTER
Excerpt from the personal memoirs of
Hiram Burrows, dated several years earlier

As she pushed off from the rooftop ledge behind her, three thoughts ran through her mind.

One, that the ledge opposite was much farther away than she had estimated, and that there was a more than fair chance she was going to fall short and tumble to what was most likely a painful and unpleasant death, dashed against the cobbles of the street four stories below.

Two, that the Month of Rain was not only the most depressing time of the year—*give me the Month of High Cold anytime*, she mused—but the waterlogged, rain-soaked nights were probably the worst to be out running the rooftops of the city.

Three, that her impending and quite clearly unavoidable death wasn't the most regal end for the Empress of the Isles, and that her father was going to be very, very disappointed.

A fourth thought—of Corvo standing over her broken body, not sad, but annoyed that she hadn't managed what should have been a simple jump—was quickly knocked out of Emily Kaldwin's mind as she hit the flat roof of the building, feet first. Her body, lithe and athletic, driven by reflexes honed and trained over the last decade, absorbed the impact of this misjudged jump by falling into a forward roll, the tails of her black coat catching in the puddles and flicking a spray of water up into the air.

Finishing the roll, Emily paused, kneeling on the rooftop, balanced on her hands, the rain pouring off the peak of her hood and down into the puddle underneath her.

One breath…

Two breaths…

Three.

Well, that wasn't so bad, she thought. *Better to overshoot than miss entirely. And not just in the dark, but in the rain.*

Emily allowed herself a small smile under the hood.

Not bad, Empress, not bad at all. Perhaps her father wouldn't be so disappointed with how she was doing, if only he could see her now.

She pivoted on her heel, then stood and walked back to the edge. The smile vanished from her sharp, angular features, replaced with a frown as she told herself to *bloody well pay attention!* Otherwise the next mistake really would be a fatal one.

Yes, it was a *long* way down, and that was a stupid, stupid thing to try. She'd made it—just barely, thanks to her father's training and her own endless hours of practice leaping around the castellated ramparts of Dunwall Tower, keeping herself well out of sight of the watchmen on patrol.

Lightning flashed ahead, casting the silhouette of that tower into sharp relief. A moment later the thunder rolled, as loud as cannon fire as it echoed around the stone of the city. It was late—actually, *early*, the hours very small indeed—and with the constant downpour Emily suspected she was the only person who was out and about.

Certainly she was the only person in the entire city commanding a view like this. Turning from the edge, she jogged up to where the building joined the next, the neighbor higher, its roof a jumbled collection of tiled surfaces assembled with all the precision of a child who'd had too much Serkonan honey cake.

As she approached, Emily accelerated, then jumped to plant one foot on a windowsill, propelling herself up, bouncing against the angle of the wall opposite to go higher, reaching the next portion of roof and pulling herself up with her arms. She continued, using the planes and angles of the building—its windows, overhangs, ledges, gables—to push up and up and up, until after a few minutes she was standing on top of a small, square tower, the highest point, apparently, in this part of the city.

She stood tall. Despite the deep hood of her tailcoat, her raven-black hair was still soaked. She sighed and pushed the hood back, rain washing over her face as she looked out over the thousand labyrinthine streets and alleys crammed with tall, narrow buildings built of dark Gristol granite or weathered brown brick, their gabled roofs reaching like jagged fingers toward the night sky. This was Dunwall, and this was *her* city, though that still didn't sit easy with her.

Then the lightning flashed again and she ducked down, wary of being seen. Her covert journey—from Dunwall Tower, across the rooftops to skirt the Boyle Mansion, then across the bridge named after her family, and finally over the narrow buildings that crowded the southern shoreline of the Wrenhaven River—was an exercise in secrecy and the state of mind that such stealth required.

But she hadn't been seen. The darkness had helped, and the rain, too.

And she had been trained well. Ten years of hard work, of toil in the small hours when she wasn't bound by her Imperial duties. Ten years of pain, of cuts and bruises and… well, quite a lot of blood, actually. For ten years she had been trained by the best, in fact. Trained by the Royal Protector himself, Corvo Attano.

Royal Protector, and her *father*. Even though the years were creeping up on him, he was still the best spy, the best agent, and the best hand-to-hand combatant in the Empire.

The rain pounded the rooftop and Emily hunkered down, allowing herself a moment to think about her father. She was grateful for his presence in her life. Not just for his protection—the protection he offered her as Empress, offered her as *daughter*—not for his friendship and love and guidance, official and otherwise. But for his skills in the subtle arts of subterfuge, espionage, surveillance, and, of course, stealth and combat.

Skills he had been instilling in her these past ten years—more, even. Emily smiled again. It was coming up to fifteen years since her coronation. Had it really been that long? Fifteen years since Hiram Burrows, self-appointed Lord Regent, was thrown from power.

Fifteen years since Emily was restored to the throne left vacant by the murder of her mother, Empress Jessamine Kaldwin I. Her mother, murdered on the orders of the Lord Regent himself, part of a conspiracy that had run deep in Dunwall aristocracy, a secret circle that had finally been broken by Corvo himself.

It felt like longer to Emily. A lifetime, really—and that's exactly what it had been. She had been ten when her mother died. Now she wasn't yet twenty-five, and she could still feel the pain of her mother's absence, if she allowed herself. Most of the time, she allowed those memories of Empress Jessamine to sleep in her mind— she had to, because despite the tragedy she had to live her life and do her job.

And what a job it was. Fifteen years now she had ruled the Empire with a firm and just hand, working hard to reverse the damage done by the Lord Regent to Dunwall and the rest of her domain. At the same time, she and Corvo had embarked on another, less public, project—the result of which allowed Emily to be here, now, crouched on a rooftop in the dead of night.

With no palace walls to keep her prisoner, no protocol, no etiquette to bind her actions, her thoughts, out here in the open air, the city was *hers.* Here, now, alone, she felt she could go anywhere, do anything, and nobody would know a thing about it.

Not even Corvo Attano, the Royal Protector.

Because as far as he knew, as far as everyone at the palace knew—from the guards on the gate to the members of her inner court deep inside the ancient keep—the Empress was enjoying blissful slumber in her private apartments.

Emily laughed, and though the rain lessened slightly she pulled her hood over her head again.

Getting out of the Tower had been the easiest part. In her bedchamber there was a hidden door which led to a secret room, one she had discovered when still a child, before the death of her mother and before everything changed. She had kept the knowledge to herself, although she knew some older members of the court were aware of the Tower's secret rooms and hidden passageways.

In the large room beyond her bedchamber, Emily had built up an armory all of her own—not just weapons and protective clothing, hooded cloaks and caps and coats, but gold, too. Anything that might be useful on her new adventures.

Her new adventures *outside* the palace walls.

Although, truth be told, she hadn't needed much of it. Ropes, grapples, crampons—they just slowed her down. She had taken to using a pair of fingerless gloves, the palm and the tops of the fingers padded, giving her an excellent grip while sparing her hands from the battering they would otherwise have taken as she traveled across the rooftops, leaping from ledge to sill.

As Empress, it was her hands—perhaps surprisingly—that she felt most self-conscious of, but for good reason. Because as Empress, they were forever being kissed, or held reverently, or otherwise brought to close examination by friends and strangers alike.

It was a strange life, and it wasn't one to which she was quite accustomed, even after all this time.

Emily glanced up, but this seemed only to encourage the skies to open more. Renewed, the rain poured down as heavy as a wool blanket. Yet even above the roar, she heard the Clocktower of Dunwall, over by the Estate District, chime the second hour of the morning.

Emily turned to face the sound. The Clocktower was the tallest structure in the city, save for Dunwall Tower itself. For two months Emily had been exploring the city at night, crossing to the southern bank of the Wrenhaven River and then mostly keeping to this part of the city. Perhaps that decision had been subconscious, an effort to avoid being spotted by members of the aristocracy who mostly occupied the more fashionable quarters north of the river.

But the Clocktower—now, the view from there would be *spectacular*, even in the rain. It would make a good climb, too.

Another test to pass.

Decision made, Emily paused, willing the downpour to ease, if even a little. To her surprise, the elements appeared to obey her royal wish, the torrential downpour lightening again to a shower. Nevertheless, the rooftops would be treacherous, and she would need to take care. But there was time to get to the Clocktower and then back into the palace before anyone knew she was gone. In her mind she

ran through her official schedule for the following day—
no, for *today*—but there was nothing much on. She could
afford to be tardy.

Steeling herself, Emily stepped up the steep incline,
her mind already plotting a route across the jumble of
buildings and streets ahead.

And then, with a smile, she drew her hood down and
ran for the edge of the rooftop...

PART ONE

THE SLEEPING CITY

1

THE GOLDEN CAT, DISTILLERY DISTRICT, DUNWALL
1st Day, Month of Darkness, 1851

"There is an establishment within Dunwall called the Golden Cat. A bath house, I believe, though some say it's a brothel."

— MISSING WOMEN, GOLDEN CAT
Excerpt from a crime story, revolving
around the Golden Cat

Galia Fleet was having a good night, which was more than could be said for the drunken oaf rolling in the gutter in the alley out the back of the Golden Cat.

Taking a swig from the bottle of Old Dunwall Whiskey, Galia looked down at the... what *was* he, exactly? His black velvet jacket had gold embroidery around the edge, which had looked fancier a few moments before, when it hadn't been wet and caked in... well, in whatever it was the man had fallen into.

The waistcoat under the jacket—unsullied by the gutter but stained with a tracery of vomit—was a rich, royal purple. It stirred something in the back of Galia's mind. Did the purple mean something, signifying some high office? Or was her memory playing tricks?

She shrugged to herself and sucked on the whiskey, then gave the man a kick with the toe of her boot. The moaning imbecile might well have been a royal ambassador from a far and distant land, for all that it mattered here. Because at the Golden Cat, names weren't used, identities and ranks were not discussed. Everyone was as equal as the coin in their purse.

Galia shoved the man again and he rolled with the movement like a bundle of linen just unloaded from a Horizon Trading Company skiff. He moaned and gurgled in the gutter.

His weapon—a swordstick he so foolishly unsheathed while inside the pleasure house—lay in two pieces over by the back door of the Cat. That was a shame, she thought. It looked as if it had been a good piece, a vanity accessory for an aristocrat, but one that actually made for a serviceable weapon. Galia would have liked it for herself, had she not snapped it in two before picking the man up by the front of his purple waistcoat and throwing him into the muck.

That stick would have made a good trophy, a nice addition to the collection of weapons she kept in her office. Being security chief at the Cat gave her a lot of leeway with Madame Steele, but even she, daughter of the old proprietor, Madame Prudence, might have raised an eyebrow at the small armory Galia kept locked away out of sight.

As Galia eyed the broken stick, the alley swayed pleasantly in her vision as the effects of the whiskey started to take hold. Maybe she could give the weapon to her assistant, Rinaldo, to see if he could get it fixed.

Ah, never mind. Too much effort, and she wasn't entirely sure Rinaldo much approved of her little collection.

The man in the purple waistcoat moaned again, tried to scramble to his feet, but all he succeeded in doing was getting his ass up into the air while his face was still planted in the gutter shite. Galia grinned, unable to resist such an invitation, and with a swift jab of her foot, the man went sprawling.

"Maybe next time you'll think twice before trying to impress our girls with your mighty weapon, eh?" Galia said, but she wasn't sure the man was listening. He was puffing like a whaling ship, apparently unaware that he hadn't yet attained an upright position.

Galia sighed, hands on her hips, the buzz of the whiskey wearing down to cold melancholy.

Is this really what it's come down to? she wondered. Throwing anonymous noblemen out of the Golden Cat when they tried to get frisky? She was just thirty-five years old, and she liked to think herself in pretty good shape, but when the fog of the alcohol settled over her like a shroud—and settle it did, most nights now—she felt a good deal older.

Sighing again, she swigged at the bottle held in one hand while she ran the fingers of the other through her short, greasy blonde hair.

Where had the time gone? What had *happened* to the old days? The days when she was young; the days when she yearned for adventure—and for coin. The days when she wore the mask of her gang, and did so with pride. The days when she traveled at the side of her leader, doing his bidding, following his orders, helping him clean the city of cretins and collecting a profit in the process.

At least that's what Daud had told her, and that's what she had believed. Back then, as a twenty-year-old novice assassin, she would have followed him to the ends of the world.

There was a moment, too, when it seemed as if her luck had come in. Billie Lurk had vanished, and Galia had never been happier. She had never liked Daud's little enforcer, and with her out of the frame, the chance arose for Galia to step in and show Daud what she was made of. To show him who really deserved to be his right hand, instead of that gloomy hardass.

But then he disappeared, too.

Soon enough, they all had. Sure, Thomas had taken over leadership of the Whalers, what was left of them anyway, gathering the stragglers and members of a few other minor gangs to form his own, new group, but—

The man in the purple waistcoat sighed and slumped face down into the gutter. Her train of thought broken, Galia stepped over to him and, although thinking twice about it, bent down and rolled him onto his back. A drunk aristocrat was one thing. A dead nobleman, drowned in two inches of gutter water, was something else altogether. Attention the Golden Cat could ill afford.

Not that the establishment was illegal. Far from it. The Golden Cat was part of Dunwall history—an entertainment palace of great renown, home to theater and burlesque, and the best tavern in the Isles. What went on between the patrons and the hostesses in curtained-off rooms was nobody's business at all.

The man in the gutter had passed out, so Galia, ready to give him the standard line about being barred, saved her breath and instead just killed the bottle of Old Dunwall. Maybe it was for the best. He'd wake up, feel embarrassed and ashamed, and hide himself at the court for a few days before desire and need got the better of him, and he came back. Only when he did, Galia would be ready and waiting. She'd be sure to extract payment *before* any transactions took place.

Turning around, she headed back inside.

It was late, the usual evening festivities winding down,

the quiet murmur in the Cat punctuated by the occasional laugh and shriek of delight as the last remaining patrons sat and smoked and drank and spent some quality time with the hostesses. Walking through the main parlor, the walls festooned with gilt-framed mirrors and acres of deep-red velvet drapery, Galia counted the men passed out on the various pieces of sumptuous furniture, pipes hanging from unconscious fingers, the fronts of their trousers undone, their purses far lighter than they had been when they had arrived.

This, she thought. *This is what life is, now.* And it wasn't bad, not really. Galia was the first to admit that. Head of security at the Golden Cat sounded like a cushy job and, actually, it was. Things had been changing over the years as the city rebuilt itself. How long had it been since the Flooded District had been drained and reconstructed, becoming once again the throbbing financial heart of the Empire?

A long time, anyway. That was the problem.

Time moved on, but inside the Golden Cat it was like time sat still, caught in amber, never to move again. Business was good—it always had been. Before, when she had been a Whaler, the Cat had been... well, unsavory, really, the haunt of the Lord Regent's officers and guards, travelers from other islands in the Empire drawn to the temptations offered within its walls.

The fortunes of the Cat had improved along with those of the city. With the Rat Plague a distant memory, and free movement reestablished throughout most of the Empire, trade resumed, and with trade came travelers, foreigners, dignitaries. They brought money, and that wealth flowed through Dunwall, refilling the coffers, not just of the Imperial Court, but of the citizens, too.

Freed from the oppressive yoke of the Lord Regent, the city was revived, rebuilt, and was once again prosperous.

This prosperity found its way to the Golden Cat. Business couldn't be better.

Yes, life was good, her job was easy. *Wonderful. What a joy.* Galia lifted the empty bottle of Old Dunwall and peered at it with disappointed eyes, then headed over to the bar, ducking behind to extract another, unopened bottle. This she took with her as she disappeared through a curtained door, back to her office.

The room was small, spare, furnished with rugs and a table and a chair, all old and battered and worn, unlike the fittings out in the parlor. In here, it didn't matter. She had all she needed, and that included a window that looked out onto the main street.

Yes, this was what it had come to.

A highly paid job throwing drunks out of a bar.

She missed the old days, when the Golden Cat was… well, it wasn't, had never been *dangerous*, exactly. But it had been… *interesting.* And now the gentrification that was spreading across Dunwall had reached the famous Golden Cat. The clientele had grown richer, but softer, too.

Head of security. It felt like overkill. Galia was a trained warrior—no, more than that. Galia Fleet was an *assassin*.

Or… had been. *Once.* Once, when Daud led the Whalers.

She sat behind the table, put her feet up, and began to work on uncapping her new bottle of whiskey.

She'd tried to track them down, but the Whalers were masters of deception, of slipping undetected across the city, the freedom of which was theirs thanks to the power Daud had allowed them all to share.

The only one she'd actually been able to find had been Rinaldo, and he'd come to *her*. What was it… five, no, *six* years ago? He'd come into the Cat, his dark features hidden behind a beard, his wild hair streaked with gray, matted into thick, dirty dreadlocks. But there had been no mistaking the glint in his eye, the way his mouth curled to one side when he smiled, and the scar over his left eye, an echo of a past life, a past battle—one in which she, if she remembered rightly, had saved Rinaldo's skin.

She took every opportunity to remind him of it.

Had he tracked her down to the Golden Cat to reminisce over old times, or come in to partake of the pleasures of the establishment without realizing she was there? Galia had never found out, but they had talked and laughed and drank, and at Galia's request the proprietor had given the former assassin a one-time discount. After that she offered him a job, one he sorely needed.

Galia and Rinaldo, united again, keeping safe the courtesans of the Golden Cat.

Rinaldo might not have expected to find Galia working at the Cat, but he admitted that he, too, had been looking for old friends from time to time, without much luck. Some had gained employment on trading vessels, others on whaling ships, or in the whale oil processing factories. They'd laughed at that. "Whalers" becoming whalers, changing jobs but not their masks.

The bottle cap finally came loose, and Galia took a long gulp of the fiery liquid as she glanced over to the bookcase on her right. The shelves, like most of the room, were bare.

Save for the Whaler's mask, pride of place in the center of the bookcase.

Gathering dust.

Not a day went by when Galia hadn't wished Daud were here. It had been years—fourteen, at least, Galia thought, pretending not to have counted the days one by one by one. And in that time, the itch had not faded away. If anything, it had grown stronger and stronger, the itch becoming an ache becoming a burning agony in her mind. The drink helped, of course, dulling the pain along with the rest of her senses.

That itch, that ache, wasn't a pang for adventure, or for danger, although Galia knew she craved both of those things. Her new life was easy, it was safe—two things Galia always thought she would abhor. There was no pleasure in life if you took it for granted. Life was to be fought for, to be risked, in order to be truly appreciated.

But the ache, it was more than that. She'd worked hard at burying it in her mind, but recently it had bubbled to the surface more and more. It didn't matter how much she drank, how much she trained, alone in her apartment at the top of the building, trying to keep herself in condition even as nothing more than the simple passage of time took it away from her.

What she wanted was what Daud had given her, as he had given to all his Whalers.

Galia closed her eyes, and there, *just there*, as she squeezed her eyelids closed and watched the darkness moving and sparking blue like a shorting whale oil tank, she saw the memory, and she imagined herself transversing, the turning of the world stopped for just a split second as she pulled herself across the rooftops of the city, crossing an alley, a street, as she came up behind an unwitting target, the blade in her hand already sinking to the hilt in the victim's side before they even knew she was there.

That was power—Daud's gift. To move in the blink of an eye, the geometry of the world unfolding just for her, for his Whalers, allowing them a freedom of movement that was beyond the imagining of most people. That kind of movement, transversing, that was *power*.

She hadn't missed it at first. To be free of Daud's thrall was like waking up on a cold morning, sober, alive, aware. *Energized*. A reaction, perhaps, to the withdrawal of Daud's gift.

It got worse after that, becoming a pain that was almost physical, driving her first to despair and then to hard liquor. At first, working at the Cat provided an outlet, something new on which to focus, but soon enough it became—like everything in life—merely ordinary. A routine to be repeated every single day.

It had taken years to realize how far she had fallen. One day Galia woke up and the city looked different, and she realized she had lost weeks, months, *years* to her misery, to the pain—a pain she had grown to love.

So she embraced it. She used it. She began training again, returning to the life of a Whaler, if not to the old job. The world had moved on and had left her behind, and now she raced to catch up.

The drink helped, of course, as it always had. Rinaldo didn't approve. Galia wasn't sure she'd ever seen that man taste a single drop—

There was a thump from outside the office door, heavy and wooden, ending with a rattle. Galia blinked out of her reverie and cocked her head, listening. She recognized the sound. Someone had thrown open the front door, with quite some force.

Another drunk—

No. The same drunk. That bloody oaf with the sword stick. He'd probably been found by his friends, and now they were coming back to cause a little scene. Young aristocrats were all the bloody same. Thought they owned the bloody place.

Fine. If that's the game they want to play, then so be it. It was time to show these young idiots who was in charge, no matter the lineage of their birth or the amount of coin in their purses.

Galia dragged her feet off the table and made her way to the door. She paused there and listened. She could hear talking, murmurs really. Nothing that sounded out of the ordinary.

She relaxed. Maybe they'd gone on their way. Maybe Rinaldo and the other guards had seen them off.

Good. She turned from the door, her eyes back on the bottle of Old Dunwall Whiskey on her desk.

Then there was a crash from the parlor, and shouting. Lots of shouting. The surprise helped to sober her up. She wheeled around and yanked open the office door, then ripped aside the curtain that hid it from the parlor. She pulled the knife from her belt.

"What in the High Overseer's *balls* is going on here?" she shouted.

The parlor was in chaos—courtesans and their clients, most half-drunk or worse, most half-*dressed* or worse, were running to the back of the room and beyond, clothes hastily grabbed, veils held high. A couple even stood behind one of the big velvet curtains, the drapery pulled around their bodies for protection.

In the center of the room stood Rinaldo and three of the Cat's minders, knives out, standing to protect the clients and keep their new visitor at bay.

The visitor didn't move from the doorway. He wore a dark woolen greatcoat with red epaulets and brass buttons. The collar of the greatcoat was pulled up so high that it formed a black fan behind the man's head. Under the collar, his neck was wrapped in a woven fur scarf that was pulled up over his mouth and nose. The upper part of his face was likewise hidden behind two great red circular glass eyepieces, each nearly as big as the saucer of a fine Morley tea set. The outlandish, heavy outfit was topped off by a black hat with a huge circular brim which pushed against the top of the overturned coat collar. His hands were encased in thick leather gloves.

He stood, motionless, like a mannequin from a Drapers Ward fashion house.

Rinaldo rolled his neck and lifted his knife toward the intruder.

"I don't know who you are, *friend*, but this ain't no way to go about it. You either show yourself and show your coin, or we throw you into the gutter out back, and deduct a fee for our services."

The intruder didn't speak. It looked as if he was just standing, staring, but Galia knew he was likely scanning the whole room and those in it, his eyes completely hidden behind his goggles. His gloved hands were curled into fists, and there was no way to know what weapons he was hiding underneath the huge coat. It might have been the Month of Darkness, but it was hardly *that* cold outside, even at this time of night. There was no reason for the strange getup.

Unless he was hiding something.

"Okay, that's enough—" Galia said, taking a step toward the man, her own knife held out in front, but the words caught in her throat as the intruder turned his face toward her. It was unnerving, the way she couldn't see it. In fact, all she could see was her own distorted reflection in his goggles.

She glanced down at his hands. He wasn't reaching for anything, and the buttons of his coat were fastened up to the neck. If he was hiding something underneath, there didn't seem to be any way of getting it out quickly.

Galia frowned, then nodded her head at the security detail.

"Rinaldo, show our friend here the exit and use your knife on his purse strings."

Rinaldo grunted a reply and took a step forward.

That was when the intruder sprang into life. His elbow

came up and out, and he swung backward, catching Rinaldo in the chest. Rinaldo staggered, but only briefly. Recovering in an instant, he and his men rushed toward the interloper. Galia, too, her knife heading straight for the man's scarf-wrapped neck.

Suddenly she stumbled, then stood, nearly tripping over Rinaldo and the others.

The man had gone. Vanished, between the blinks of an eye.

There was a gasp from the Cat's patrons, most of whom were still cowering at the back of the parlor. Galia spun, her knife out, searching, not quite believing what she had seen. Behind her, Rinaldo and the others recovered and fanned out, creeping forward, each of the three men facing a different corner of the room.

It was impossible. *Impossible.*

Galia stopped.

No, not impossible. Improbable, perhaps, but she had seen something like that before. In fact, she had been able to do it herself, many years ago.

Before Daud had slipped away, leaving it all behind, taking the magic with him.

"Show yourself!" she yelled, and the patrons gasped again in fright. There was a crunching sound. Galia and the others spun to face it, and saw the intruder standing on the other side of the room.

No, he wasn't. It was his reflection in the huge mirror with baroque gold frame, one of many that hung all over the parlor walls. Galia spun away from the mirror, her instinct telling her the stranger was standing behind her.

But… he wasn't.

She turned back, just in time to see the man's reflection move *out* of the mirror and into the room, his own reflection becoming visible behind him.

Galia gritted her teeth.

"That's some trick," she said, "but you picked the wrong parlor to show it off in." She rushed forward, Rinaldo and the others behind her.

Now this—*this*—was a good night. She hadn't had to cut a patron open in a long, long time.

But the intruder was fast, even under the heavy winter clothing. Expertly he blocked Galia's attack, parrying with an arm and riposting with the other. Rinaldo and the other two security guards joined the fray. Together they surrounded the intruder. They were trained. Ready and able to fight.

So, it seemed, was the intruder. At the center of the fray he was a dervish, the tails of his coat whirling as he blocked, attacked, counterattacked. Galia's knife—and Rinaldo's, too—made several palpable hits, but their sharpened blades were unable to penetrate the thick cloth of the coat.

Within moments one of the security men was down, blood arcing from his face as he careened backward, eliciting more screams from the patrons. Galia saw it out of the corner of her eye, and yelled as she redoubled her efforts. As she fought, she saw Rinaldo grin on the other side of the intruder. He was enjoying it as much as she was. Just like old times.

The intruder staggered under the attack. Galia pressed the advantage, forcing him back against the wall. Against another of the large mirrors.

There was a crunching sound, like boots on snow.

The man was gone.

A shadow-shape out of the corner of her eye. Galia turned, and saw the man stepping out of another mirror, among the huddled patrons. They screamed and scrambled away, but the man ignored them.

The last of Galia's men charged, but was knocked down

almost instantly. At Galia's side, Rinaldo tensed, but she reached out and grabbed his shirt.

"No, wait," she said.

The two of them faced the intruder who, apparently, was none the worse for wear, his scarf, hat and goggles still in place. He did not move.

Galia stepped forward. She looked up into those goggles, tossing her blade end over end in her hand. Then she caught the handle and returned the weapon to its sheath on her belt.

"Hey, Galia, sweetness," Rinaldo said, "what are you—"

"Shut up, Rinaldo." Galia cocked her head. She felt…

Actually, she felt *good*. Light-headed, and not just from the whiskey. She had enjoyed the fight—okay, so that wasn't quite why she was in this job—but more than that, seeing the stranger, the intruder, had rekindled a fire within her that was many, many years cold.

This stranger, who wore a strange outfit more suited to the snows of Tyvia. Who fought like a soldier. Who could move in the blink of an eye, traveling through, it seemed, mirrors.

It wasn't transversal, the ability to stop time and pull yourself across two points in space, the gift that Daud had shared with the Whalers.

But it was… close. It was a *power*, too.

She looked into the stranger's red eyes and was overcome with vertigo, the sensation of falling, falling, falling…

She saw,
Men. Lots and lots of men, their heads covered with hoods, their faces obscured by large masks with glass eyes, respirator cans bouncing as they slaughtered the enemy, the City Watch, the Wrenhaven River Patrol falling before them.

In front, a Whaler in a dark-red coat. A leader. The best of the best. The leader called out, and Galia recognized the voice.

It was her voice. These were her men. She was a leader. She was the best of the best.

And then Galia the leader vanished in a swirl of inky nothing, and then her men followed…

Galia swayed on her feet, the room snapping back into focus. She felt the itch, the ache, burning inside her. For just a moment, just a *second*, Galia wanted to scream her desire, her demand for a share of that power to the strange intruder.

And then the feeling was gone.

She pursed her lips. She had to know. Had to know who the man was, why he was here. He wasn't Daud. He was too tall. But then again, the disguise, the clothing… the *power*. Maybe he *knew* Daud.

Maybe he—

"Galia Fleet," the intruder said, and Galia gasped and took a step backward. The voice was loud but muffled. Male, deep, resonant, but… rough. Dry. She would have thought he sounded sick, if it wasn't for the fact that he had easily bested four security guards.

She opened her mouth but no words came out.

"I'm not here to fight you, Galia," the intruder said. "I'm here to rescue you."

2

NEW MERCANTILE DISTRICT, DUNWALL
8th Day, Month of Darkness, 1851

"At times I have ventured beyond the city walls, meeting in forgotten graveyards and the outlying ruins frequented by those of ill means."

— RUMORS AND SIGHTINGS: DAUD
Excerpt from an Overseer's covert field report

Emily peered over the edge of the building, which stood on the western side of the large square. She peered down, and for a moment held her breath, wondering what in all the Isles was going on.

It was late, later than she would've liked, but she'd come a long way—perhaps too far. Out of Dunwall Tower, over Kaldwin's Bridge and, skirting the Boyle Mansion, up to the tall Clocktower on the northern border of the Estate District. At the Clocktower she'd paused a while, considering her next route of exploration.

It was a cold night, but a calm one. The rains and winds that came with a dreary inevitability over the last couple of months had given way to short days and long nights as the chill swept in over the city. Tonight the drizzle was merely irritating, and between the broken clouds above there was a moon that shone, full and bright.

North. She would go north, up to the edge of the city, where there was a lot of new construction, whole new districts slowly growing up as the walls of Dunwall were extended outward, in the only direction the city really could expand. It was an area she didn't know well, but to her, that was part of the reason for these nocturnal excursions. This was *her* city, legally speaking, and it was a city she wanted to know as well as the inside of Dunwall Tower itself.

From the Clocktower she followed a broad avenue that took her not directly north, but northwest. She traveled for perhaps an hour, stopping to watch, to observe. The streets were quiet and Emily had taken the usual precautions, sticking to the shadows and eaves, keeping out of sight of windows and doorways and the streets themselves, as much as possible. She'd seen a few people moving around—a couple of patrols of the City Watch, a couple of couples making a damp journey home from whatever evening's entertainment they had enjoyed.

That was one benefit of exploring at this time of the year—it was cold, but not *that* cold, so she could move around unnoticed. The early call of winter was enough to keep people inside when the hours grew small, but without freezing her to death in the process.

Eventually she found the old city wall and, skipping through the shadows past a patrol of the City Watch, she crossed over. This was new territory, the city growing to absorb the small towns and villages that had once been separate. Here she crouched in the high gables of a tall house, one of a dozen that surrounded the old square.

Except… it wasn't a square, not quite. As Emily looked down, it took her a moment to realize that the streets in this new district were more than quiet—they were *empty*. Literally so. The district appeared to be mostly residential, the houses pressed tightly against each other in rows like most other parts of the city, although here they were bigger, with narrow alleyways separating the buildings at regular intervals. It looked like a nice area, but, Emily realized, these large, lavish homes were, in fact, completely unoccupied.

Perhaps that wasn't such a surprise, she told herself. The Rat Plague may have been a decade and a half gone, but the city had been hit hard. In some areas, residents had been forced from their homes as their streets became too dangerous, as household after household succumbed to the disease, transforming neighbors, family, friends, into weepers.

That, in turn, became an open invitation for the gangs to move in—the Bottle Street Gang, the Dead Eels, the Hatters, and later the Parliament Street Cutters. Areas of the city that once provided happy homes for happy families became derelict badlands, areas that even the City Watch left to their own devices.

But that was before. History, ancient. Dunwall had changed. The Rat Plague was a footnote in the past and, with Emily's guidance, the city was rebuilding itself—which included expansion north, beyond the city walls.

Places like this.

As Emily looked closer, she could see that the homes here were not derelict, although they did show signs of neglect. The square, and the buildings that orbited it, had most likely been part of a large village or small town, once hit hard by the plague and abandoned. Then, as the city rebuilt itself, the whole place had most likely been bought up in one job lot by a developer. That wasn't uncommon.

So for now, the houses slept, patiently awaiting repair and restoration.

For now, they were empty.

The square in the center was *not*.

Emily ducked down, crawling forward on her elbows to the lip of the rooftop to get a better look. Reaching the edge, she pulled her hood up. Water trickled from its peak down her nose, and she wiped it away. She shuffled on her stomach and brought out her spyglass, a short, ornate tube of dark metal and brass fittings. She placed it against her right eye, and adjusted the geared wheels with both hands, bringing the scene—the men at work, far below— into sharp focus.

The square was perhaps one hundred yards along each side, and was bordered by high black iron rails. It appeared to be a private park of some kind for the residents—overgrown now, the grass long, the twisted metalwork of pergolas and ornate bench seats scattered around it, once a scene of reflection and relaxation, now choked with weeds. At the far corner stood a gnarled tree, its bare branches reaching for the night sky like skeletal fingers silhouetted in the moonlight.

There was something else in the park, aside from the ironwork and the seats. Pale in the moonlight, there was a series of standing stones, some nearly covered by grass that was waist-high. They were arranged in crooked rows, the stones themselves keening at odd angles. Some had fallen altogether.

This wasn't a park or a private garden, Emily realized with a start. She lowered the spyglass to look with her own, unaided eyes.

It was a cemetery.

Which made the people who were working in it, under the cover of moonlit darkness, grave robbers.

Emily looked again through the spyglass, twisting the mechanism to zoom out as much as possible. There were five of them. Each wore a long coat against the cold, heads covered, like Emily's, with a hood. But unlike her, each of them appeared to be masked. They worked by the dim yellow light of hooded lanterns, the weak illumination hardly adequate for any kind of labor, Emily thought. Occasionally that light caught their faces, but from her high vantage point, even with the spyglass, Emily could see nothing but sharp glinting, as though they were wearing eyeglasses or goggles.

Over on the west side of the cemetery stood a pair of big iron gates that hung permanently open, their metalwork caught in thick branches of shrubbery that had grown through them over the years. Next to the gates was a covered wagon. The horse shackled to the front was silent and unmoving, its breath steaming in the cold night as they continued their work.

Continued their *digging*.

The cemetery looked old. One man leaned against one of the taller, more upright stones as he watched two of his cohorts, the pair standing waist-deep in an open grave. They continued to mine beneath their feet. Beside the hole stood another pair.

A moment later, they stopped digging. Emily couldn't hear any of them speak, but the three who had been watching sprang into action, waving and gesticulating at one another. One of the diggers climbed out of the grave with some help, while the second digger bent down, disappearing out of Emily's sight and into the earth.

The remaining group gathered around, bending down, some kneeling, reaching into the grave. Slowly, awkwardly, a long box was brought up and shunted sideways onto the embankment of freshly dug earth. Emily twisted the spyglass to get a closer look.

The man still standing in the grave climbed out on his

knees and shuffled over in the mud. He felt around the edge of the exhumed coffin, like he was checking for something, then, apparently satisfied, he braced himself on it to push himself to his feet. He waved at the others. Two men grabbed the coffin, one at either end, and lifted, carrying it swiftly across the cemetery and through the open gates. Two others jogged in front to peel back the canvas cover of the wagon in preparation to receive the sarcophagus.

Emily zoomed out again and then gasped, heart racing, as she saw what was in the back of the wagon.

More coffins.

Four, perhaps five, with the new addition slotted in next to the others.

Emily turned her attention back to the small cemetery, scanning it through the spyglass. The group had been busy. Several graves had been disturbed, apparently dug up, the burials dragged to the surface. She had missed them before, the piles of dark earth melting into the shadows of the overgrown burial ground.

What in all the Isles is going on? Emily thought.

Were they clearing the site? Maybe the whole area, houses and all, was going to be demolished, which meant relocating the cemetery so work could take place. That was logical… but she knew that wasn't the answer.

There was something about them and their work that turned her stomach. If their activities had been legitimate, they would hardly be doing the work in the dead of night, would they? Anything like this would be done during the day, the work supervised by the City Watch, or at least a city planning official. Emily didn't know the minutiae of everything that was going on in Dunwall as it was being rebuilt—that was impossible, and unnecessary—but she could easily check.

No, there was something… *sinister* about it. The way

the people were not just hooded but *masked*, the way they worked in silence, in the night, under the greasy and flickering sickly yellow light of their lanterns.

There was nothing normal, nothing official about it. They were grave robbers, plain and simple. Perhaps the remnants of one of the old street gangs, looking for a new source of income, plundering the riches buried with the dead.

The thought brought a cold, hard lump to Emily's stomach. She slid back along the flat roof, back into the shade of the gable behind her, thinking the situation over in her mind.

She came to a decision. An obvious one.

There were five masked strangers. They were preoccupied with their grisly task, and they thought they were alone.

Five robbers. And one of her.

The answer came easily. She could take them on. She could *stop* them, put an end to their night work of horror. She *knew* she could.

She crawled forward again, scanning the cemetery, the thieves, the surrounding buildings.

She could take them. She *knew* it. Corvo had taught her well, and this was the perfect opportunity to put that training to a practical use. This was *her* city.

Emily slipped the spyglass back into her jacket, then looked around the cemetery and the houses. She calculated positions, rehearsed movements in her mind as she watched them head back into the cemetery, moving to the next grave. It occurred to her they were more than likely armed, if this was a secret, hidden crime.

That was fine. Just fine.

She looked up, assessed her surroundings, calculated that if she moved across to the eastern side of the square, where one building had an elaborate porticoed balcony that jutted out over the street below, practically hanging over the railed edge of the cemetery itself, she could pick a route down to the ground, using shadows and vegetation to hide her progress until she was in striking distance. The robbers would be busy digging. She would have an easy advantage.

She could do this.

She *knew* it.

She lifted herself from the damp roof, then glanced to her right, checking her path.

Up to the roof of the neighboring building, which stands half a floor higher. Across the top, down to the window ledge of the building at the corner. Up the heavy drain of the building, then across that roof, out onto the overhang. Drop down onto the balcony, hide in the shadows behind the pillars and check the situation.

Reassess, choose the next path.

The thieves would never see her coming.

Emily turned and ran in a crouch toward her first obstacle, and then she stopped and ducked down, dropping herself nearly flat onto the rooftop. Heart thudding in her chest, she lifted her chin and glanced across at the balcony that was her intended destination.

There was someone already there. They were hiding, and hiding well, but Emily's trained eye saw the movement, and now she saw the man as clear as if he was standing out in the open. He was nothing but a shadow, but he was wearing a hood and... yes, a mask, too. Of course. A lookout. He hadn't signaled yet, which meant he hadn't seen her.

Emily breathed a sigh of relief.

Well, no matter, she thought. He could be taken out, too...

Although...

She re-examined her proposed route. It was no good. While it would keep her well hidden from the cemetery and the men working below, she would be in plain sight of the high balcony and the lookout.

She'd be seen.

In fact—

Emily froze, slowing her breathing by instinct, willing herself to vanish into the shadows, to become just part of the roof, hidden in the night, a bundle of nothing.

The lookout stood behind a pillar, but he appeared to be—no, he *was*—looking straight at her, the moonlight betraying his presence as it glinted off his mask.

Now she'd been seen. He would alert his friends any second, the element of surprise a fading memory. They'd be ready and waiting, and even though she was up for the fight, the addition of the lookout—and who knew how many others might be lurking in the empty buildings, unseen—the odds didn't feel quite as certain any longer.

There was nothing for it. She had to leave. She was Empress of the Isles. She shouldn't have been here in the first place, and she certainly couldn't *die* here.

As soon as the lookout turned…

The seconds felt like minutes as they ticked past in Emily's mind as she lay on the rooftop, not daring to move, watching the lookout. He hadn't moved either. Nor had he signaled his friends. Perhaps he was unsure. Perhaps, like her, he was waiting, counting time, wanting to be sure.

And then he was gone, having retreated into the shadows in a blink of an eye. Probably on his way down to his friends, through the empty house, to tell them about the spy on the roof.

Emily let out a long, hot breath, and decided to call it a night. There were other ways of investigating the grave robbers. More official ways. She felt suddenly stupid and suddenly afraid of the terrible risk she'd been prepared to take.

She made a new decision—to retreat to the safety of Dunwall Tower. In the morning she'd send a patrol of the City Watch out to investigate, and she'd ask Corvo if his spy network had heard or seen anything strange.

Backing up on her elbows, she edged into the shadowed gables, the cemetery and the grave robbers vanishing from her eyeline as they continued their silent, criminal work. She expected an alarm, a shout, but none came.

Yet.

Emily turned, and headed for home.

3

"Restrict the Restless Hands, which quickly becomes the workmates of the Outsider. Unfettered by honest labor, they rush to sordid gain, vain pursuits, and deeds of violence. Of what value are the hands that steal and kill and destroy?"

— THE THIRD STRICTURE
Excerpt from a work detailing one of the Seven Strictures

Corvo Attano slid into the deep shadow cast by the wide fluted columns that formed the front of the balcony. He watched the rooftop to his right, waiting patiently as Emily Kaldwin slowly crawled backward on her belly, disappearing out of sight. If all went as he hoped, she'd decided to be cautious and head back to Dunwall Tower.

She'd done well—Corvo was the first to admit that fact. In the last few months, Emily had started exploring the city by night, sneaking out of Dunwall Tower to watch her citizens go about their business, watch as the city was rebuilt, restored, repaired. Every night, she'd pushed farther and farther out. Tonight was the first time she'd come so far north, crossing the old city wall and entering the New Mercantile District.

Good, he thought. This was all very, very good. No—better than that—she was *superb* as she put to practical use a decade and a half of training, their sessions hidden behind the Tower walls.

During her nocturnal outings, Corvo had followed her, keeping his presence a secret as he trailed the young Empress, watching as she darted around rooftops with a speed and agility even he found impressive.

The way Corvo saw it, he was *obliged* to follow her, two separate, individual duties calling on him to keep her in sight, to keep her safe. As Royal Protector, it was his official duty—the Empress sneaking out, alone, into the city at night would give the Imperial Court a fever fit.

And as a father he had another duty—one to keep his daughter safe, while allowing Emily to stretch herself, to find out what she could and couldn't do, to explore the limits of her abilities, her ingenuity.

She was safe enough, of course—he'd seen enough to prove that. Yet he could never really relax while she was out. The tension of being constantly alert, ready to step in but hopefully never needing to, made the nights exhausting.

He'd trained her well, though, even if he said so himself. There was no mistaking it. In Emily he had the perfect pupil, willing not just to learn, but to be *pushed*. Nearly fifteen years they'd been training—fifteen years of study and practice in the subtle arts of stealth, of hand-to-hand combat. Of protection and defense. They'd come a long, long way since the old days, when Jessamine was on the throne. When he and Emily, so young, had dueled with wooden sticks in those long, glorious Dunwall summers.

How times change. And now the Empress had what she wanted—the skills and abilities she craved in the determination to cut her own path through history, not just as Empress, but as defender, protector.

Of that, Corvo couldn't have been more proud.

As for the fact that Emily remained entirely unaware, oblivious to the fact that her protector was shadowing her... well, indeed, she *was* good. There was no denying it. It was just that he was *better*, a trained assassin with years more experience.

Not to mention a certain set of skills that Emily could never *dream* he possessed...

But tonight he had let himself be seen. Just a little, just enough—not to scare her off, but to force her to take a more cautious approach. Except she *had* been scared off, which in a way was a shame, because Corvo wanted to see what she was capable of.

There were five intruders down in the cemetery, and Corvo was sure she could have taken them all on, and won. *Except...*

Except he wasn't quite so sure, was he?

Or... actually, no, scratch that. It was *he* who wasn't ready, not yet. He was still Royal Protector, she was still the Empress, and while she was clearly eager for action and adventure, an escape from what he could plainly see were the stuffy, occasionally suffocating duties of state, he wasn't ready to let her risk herself to that great a degree.

Not quite yet.

Pleased that Emily was out of the picture, Corvo returned his attention to the cemetery below. The porticoed balcony on which he hid was an extravagance, more like a platform from which official proclamations would be made, rather than just a cool place to sip hot tea in the afternoons when the square would have been full of life.

He'd been up here before, several times in fact. This had

been a small town, clinging to the side of Dunwall so closely it was practically a part of it, despite the separation dictated by the cut of the city wall. It was a town—now a district—of merchants, rich old middle-class families not really part of Dunwall's aristocratic society, and probably quite happy to stay independent, plying their trades and building their family fortunes up here, just outside the walls.

And then the Rat Plague had come. As in the city proper, the Rat Plague changed everything. The town had emptied, the houses here in the square and in the surrounding streets abandoned. What had become of the traders and their families, Corvo wasn't entirely sure. Most probably shipped out of Dunwall as soon as the Lord Regent had taken power, wary of his plans for the city's close—but separated—neighbors.

Good for them. There were plenty of other, safer, places to make a living, make a life.

The merchants had gone, but their dead had remained. The garden cemetery, a place of quiet contemplation and remembrance, had been abandoned along with the houses, its deceased inhabitants oblivious to the slow creep of decay that surrounded their final resting place.

The gang was working on the sixth grave now. The rain had settled into a mist-like drizzle which did little to hide the sounds of their shovels and picks as they sliced into the damp, stony ground.

Grave robbers. The thought sickened Corvo. Given the wealthy merchant families who once lived here, the private cemetery was likely rich pickings. Theft from the grave, from the dead, was desecration, a total disregard for the families, for relatives and lovers taken away too soon. This wasn't something he could let pass.

Corvo readied himself. The task looked like an easy one—easier now as one of the thieves, apparently bored of the labor in the cemetery itself, wandered back to the covered wagon. He would be the first. All Corvo had to do was blink to the wagon, behind the thief, and strike. From there, the overgrown cemetery would provide plenty of cover, allowing him to reach the others without needing to call on his powers again.

It would require just a few moments to take the rest of the gang out—all, he hoped, without a single shout that might attract Emily's attention as she scampered away over the rooftops.

Corvo concentrated. He felt the familiar pins-and-needles sensation crawl over his left hand, on the back of which the Mark of the Outsider glowed with the electricity of the Void. Corvo focused, picked his target, was ready to step swiftly across the impossible distance between his present location and the street, when—

He ducked down, the tingle in his hand flashing into a hot, harsh burn as he was forced to release the gathering power. Hiding against the front of the balcony, he peered out between the small, sculpted pillars in front of him.

The grave robber by the wagon, restless and bored, had moved into the moonlight and turned around, and was facing Corvo's direction. Corvo had caught himself just in time—if he had blinked then, the man would have seen him instantly.

But there was something else, something that made Corvo's pulse thud in his throat, his own breathing suddenly loud behind his mask.

The grave robber was a *Whaler*.

There was no mistaking it. High black boots strapped with brown buckled leather, heavy black gloves with cuffs folded back at the elbow. A form-fitting leather coat with characteristic short sleeves, the front crisscrossed with a wide belt from which hung pouches. At the hip, a long knife, the gloved hand hovering just a few inches from the handle.

Over the head, a tight hood that shone damply in the moonlight, and covering the face, the mask—two large, circular eyeglasses set in thick rubber. Below, the nose and mouth covered by a protruding, cylindrical respirator designed to protect the wearer from the noxious fumes of a whale slaughterhouse.

Corvo shrank down into the shadows, willing himself to vanish into the darkness, all the while, a single thought running through his head.

Whalers. Whalers. *This man is a Whaler, this man is a Whaler, this man is a Whaler.*

Could it be possible that they were back?

Corvo wracked his brain. The fortunes of the Dunwall street gangs had waxed and waned since the fall of Hiram Burrows, the Lord Regent. Some gangs had been taken down, worn away by a newly organized— and reinvigorated—City Watch. Word was that others had relocated wholesale and intact, trying to establish themselves elsewhere in the Empire, out on islands and in cities where things might be a little easier for them. Over the years, Corvo had even heard whispers that some of the Dunwall gangs—or members of them, anyway—had set up shop as far away as Karnaca, the capital city of the southern island of Serkonos. Corvo's birthplace.

Some gangs had vanished altogether, their membership evaporating. That included the Whalers, although the group hadn't been just any street gang. They were different—they were *assassins*. Highly effective, highly trained killers. They had a special gift, granted to them by their leader, Daud. A man who, like Corvo, had been marked by the Outsider, the brand granting them both the ability to call on the power of the Void, and wield the supernatural.

Daud. Assassin. *Murderer.* The man who had killed Jessamine, forever changing the course of the Empire. Forever changing the course of Corvo's *life.* Jessamine had been his lover; Emily was their child. Daud had destroyed it all, and it had taken all the willpower Corvo had been able to muster not to kill the man outright. Instead, Daud had been banished from the city, on pain of death should he ever return.

Fifteen long, long years ago.

Fifteen years Corvo had spent wondering *why* he hadn't given in, hadn't killed Daud when he'd had the chance. Perhaps he should have. Daud's crime deserved it—but then, perhaps there was a part of Corvo that wanted Daud alive. Living in fear of the Royal Protector's terrible wrath, should they ever cross paths again.

Because perhaps living in fear was a fate worse than death.

Perhaps.

Afterward, Daud's group had splintered. One of his former aides, Thomas, had apparently taken control, at least for a time, until he too disappeared. Dead, most likely. Whatever became of the rest of the gang, nobody knew, despite the best efforts of Corvo and his ring of royal spies to try to track them down.

Now, a decade and a half later, here he was, watching a group of Whalers as they robbed a graveyard. Corvo peered again at the one by the wagon—despite the clarity afforded by the lenses in his own mask, it was a little too dark to quite see the color of the Whaler's tunic. As far as Corvo could tell, it looked gray—a novice. If they were all of that class, perhaps it wouldn't be so hard to take them all out.

He shifted his attention to the others, watching as they worked in the weak yellow lamplight. They were hooded, yes, but...

Corvo frowned. The others weren't wearing the respirators. Instead, they merely had their faces hidden by kerchiefs tied behind heads, and while they were all hooded, their clothing wasn't a *uniform* as such. Which meant they *weren't* Whalers.

He raised himself up to get a better look, glancing cautiously over at the wagon. To his surprise, the Whaler—the *actual* Whaler—had gone.

Corvo ducked around a pillar, careful to keep himself in the shadows as he cast his gaze around the square. The other men continued digging, oblivious to the fact that their leader had gone—but where?

He had a good view of the wagon, and the Whaler wasn't anywhere near it. He wasn't walking back toward the cemetery gates either. There was plenty of cover beyond, but the space between the gates and the wagon was open and well lit by the moon.

There was a sound from behind Corvo.

Infinitesimally small.

A *tick*, a click, metal on metal.

The sound of a switchblade.

Corvo spun around. Impossibly, the Whaler was standing *behind* him on the balcony, knife in one hand, the other outstretched, fingers splayed. Now spotted, the assassin lost no time and darted forward, feinting to the left with the blade, then cutting right. Corvo jumped, curving his body away from the blade as it sliced through the air.

Then he stepped forward, his hand already pulling the unique folding sword from his belt. With a flick of the wrist, the blade snapped open. Corvo brought it up, ready to parry the next attack.

The next attack didn't come. Corvo lowered the sword, just a little, as he stared at the empty space in front of him.

The Whaler had gone, again.

Corvo turned, running on instinct, sword swinging. Behind him, the assassin moved easily out of reach before flipping their knife around, holding the blade parallel to his forearm, then lunging in for the attack.

Adrenaline coursed through Corvo's veins. He took a half step backward, then focused ahead, beyond his attacker. There, on the other side of the square, was a building with big, black windows and heavy stone ledges.

Corvo closed his eyes, felt a wind that didn't exist in his world, then opened his eyes again.

He'd made it… just. He was hanging from the window ledge by his fingertips, his folding sword awkwardly gripped against the building's stone. He pulled up, lifting himself onto the narrow ledge, then turned, figuring out where he was, what his routes and his options might be.

From the corner of his eye he saw the assassin vanish from the big balcony in a swirl of black shadows caught in the moonlight. Corvo glanced down, and blinked to a lower balcony located to his left, on another side of the square. Then he did it again.

And again…

And again, up to a rooftop, down to a wide copper gutter that creaked under the sudden materialization of his weight.

Down again, on the street now, behind the wagon, hidden from view of the cemetery robbers, then back up to the columned balcony from which he had started.

He dove into the shadows in a forward roll, then spun, flattening himself against the cold stone by the archway that led inside the empty home. He crabbed toward it and slipped inside, the darkness there like a black liquid. His chest heaved with effort. So many blinks in such a short space of time was draining, and the Mark of the Outsider throbbed on his hand.

Corvo hadn't brought any vials of Addermire Solution with him, the magical blue elixir that—according to its maker, Dr. Alexandria Hypatia of the Addermire Institute in Karnaca—revitalized both the body *and* the mind. It was an improvement on the old health elixir developed by Sokolov and Piero's Spiritual Remedy, if only because the Addermire Solution had the same restorative qualities as both of those potions combined. That meant less to carry but, if he was honest, he hadn't thought he'd ever need to use the stuff again.

Perhaps it was time to rethink that.

Keeping to the edge of the arch, he peered around it, his strength slowly returning. He needed to rest, if he could.

He was in luck. There was no sign of his pursuer, no movement, no swirling shadows on rooftops, on ledges, in doorways.

He had lost him.

Moving back to the balcony, Corvo ducked down, ears straining for any sound. There were voices now, from below, in the cemetery. Reaching the balcony edge, he peered again through the small columns, and breathed a sigh of relief.

The Whaler stood in the middle of the cemetery, pointing with one hand, the switchblade in the other, still glinting in the moonlight. Around him, the robbers were starting to hurry, pulling the last coffin out of the ground and racing it over to the wagon, shoving it carelessly into the back with the others. While they did that, the Whaler remained where he was, looking around, knife ready. Corvo ducked down a little more as the Whaler turned in his direction, but there was no indication that he had been seen again.

One of the others called out. Corvo couldn't make out the words, but the meaning was clear. Confirming his suspicion, the Whaler ran over to the wagon and, finally putting the switchblade away, was helped into the back. At the front, one of the men mounted the seat and took up the reins. He gave them a flick, and the wagon jerked into motion, the horse protesting as it was forced to speed away from the scene of the crime. The wheels rattled harshly on the cobbles.

Corvo watched them go. He should have followed them. He *wanted* to follow them, but he couldn't—not tonight. He'd worn himself out with the blink chase, and even if he got back to the Tower to grab a supply of Addermire Solution, it would be too close to dawn to head back out.

And besides, where would he go?

Corvo sighed in frustration. Already, a thousand thoughts crowded his mind.

The Whalers are back, they are active, they are planning something—*why else would they rob graves, carting coffins off to who knows where?* More important than that, if the Whalers were back then so, apparently, was their leader— the man Corvo thought was gone forever.

The way the Whaler moved, transversing around the square to attack him—there was only one way to get power like that. There was only one man who was able to share it with the gang.

Daud.

He was back, gathering his forces.

But the assassin who had been supervising the operation at the cemetery, who had attacked him—he *wasn't* Daud. Corvo was sure of that. The assassin had been smaller, slimmer. The body language, the movements, they were different from what Corvo remembered.

Then again, it had been a long time. Fifteen years. Memory had a way of playing tricks.

Corvo stood. The cart was gone, the sound of the wheels, and of the hooves of the horse, slowly fading in the city. Then he glanced to the east, where already the sky was bruising orange and purple in a gap between the patchy rain clouds. Dawn approached, and with it, his duties to the Empress. He only hoped she had gotten back to Dunwall Tower and hadn't stuck around, perhaps witnessing the events of the night.

Corvo headed back home, already running a plan through his mind. In the morning he would send out his spies and begin the search. He would find Daud, and he would discover what he was doing back in Dunwall.

4

GREAVES AUXILIARY WHALE SLAUGHTERHOUSE 5, SLAUGHTERHOUSE ROW, DUNWALL
8th Day, Month of Darkness, 1851

"With this lucrative turn of events, the number of slaughterhouses quadrupled, and the demand for fresh whales increased proportionately. Many districts immediately adjacent to what was suddenly known as Slaughterhouse Row began to change as families moved away to avoid the industrial fumes and offal runoff produced by the processing plants. Crime grew overnight, forcing the City Watch to redouble its efforts against Dunwall's gangs."

— *SLAUGHTERHOUSE ROW*
Excerpt from a book on Dunwall city districts

As soon as the wagon clattered through the street-side loading doors, Galia jumped from the back, pulling back her hood and lifting her Whaler's mask up and off her head by the respirator. The bloody thing was hotter than she remembered, but the rubbery, chalky smell of the air filter, the feel of the seal around her face sucking at her skin, were long-dormant memories brought instantly to mind, like a long-forgotten song from childhood suddenly remembered word for word, as though no time had passed at all.

Galia smiled. Those were memories—*feelings*—she very much enjoyed having back. Because she was a Whaler once more—and more than that, she was now the *leader*.

The loading door crashed shut behind her as she walked past the wagon, out onto the vast factory floor of the old whale slaughterhouse. She thought to rebuke her men for the noise they were making, but there was no time for that now. Mask swinging in one hand, the fingers of the other running through her damp, greasy hair, she headed past the big, empty oil vats set into the factory floor in a series of long, parallel rows, and made for the iron stairway that wound up to a series of platforms and galleries overlooking the main workspace.

The job had been a success, but there was a problem—a problem the boss needed to know about.

"Hey, hey, Galia, my sweetest! You're back in good time. You bring back the goodies?"

She paused and looked up to see Rinaldo rattling down the stairs toward her, a grin plastered wide on his face, his yellowed teeth bright against his dark skin. She frowned. She wasn't in the mood for conversation. Galia glanced at her old friend, his thick, curly black hair chopped so roughly it stuck up in great tufts all over his scalp, but didn't answer him, instead heading straight up the stairs, brushing past his shoulder.

Rinaldo turned, hands outstretched.

"Hey, did we get what we wanted or did we not?" The grin on his face flickered then went out as he watched Galia's back.

She paused at the point where the iron stairway turned ninety degrees, curling up to the next level. She leaned over the rail and pointed down at the wagon, where the others were milling around, watching the other two.

"Tell the men to unload the wagon," she said, then she lifted her eyes up, indicating the control room above. "Is he still up there?"

Rinaldo dropped his arms and laughed, but the laugh didn't reach his eyes. "Ah, yeah, the Boss? He hasn't moved a muscle since you left. Been staring out the windows this whole time. I tell ya, I haven't been in there, but I've felt him watching me the whole bloody time."

"Fine," Galia said. She turned, heading up the next round of stairs. "I need to talk to him. Nobody is to disturb us, do you understand?"

"Hey, hey, my girl," Rinaldo said, "trust me, *nobody* wants to go near that guy, and that includes yours truly. Is he even a *man* underneath all that?"

She could hear it in Rinaldo's voice, buried in the humor and loud, confident tone. Something else. Something wavering, cracking. His last question wasn't entirely a joke.

Galia licked her lips and said, "Just get the wagon unloaded." And then she disappeared up the next flight of steps, taking them two at a time. As she reached the control room door, she could hear Rinaldo heading down, clapping his hands at the others, his voice echoing up from the cavernous factory floor.

"Okay, you heard her. Get that wagon unloaded!"

She reached for the door handle, and found herself pausing, her fingers brushing the cool brass of the knob. Then she shook her head, opened the door, and went in.

Galia dumped her mask on one of the rusting, dirty consoles that lined the walls of the control room, and began peeling off her gloves. As Rinaldo said, the Boss—

capital *B*—was still standing exactly where he had been when she left the slaughterhouse, what, *hours* ago. He stood with his back to the door, at the far end of the room, looking out through the plate-glass windows at the vast factory floor below.

It seemed appropriate for the Whalers—the *new* Whalers—to be using an old slaughterhouse as a base. Galia liked the connection. The city was full of these factories, most located here, in Slaughterhouse Row. It wasn't an individual street, despite the name, but a small district all of its own, nestled in a bay of the Wrenhaven River, where the stench of the whale oil refinement could go on without disturbing the city's residents. Some of the slaughterhouses and refineries were still operational, but like large parts of the city's industrial heart, a huge number had been mothballed, condemned to years of slumber as they lay in wait for new owners and new work to bring them back to life.

This particular slaughterhouse was an auxiliary facility, designed to handle overflow from other factories in the Greaves Lighting Oil company empire. Located at the far eastern side of Slaughterhouse Row, it was separated from other factories by a couple of streets of warehousing, and had been shuttered by the company a couple of years after the restoration of the Empress, the company focusing efforts on new, more modern facilities closer to the harbor mouth in the west.

As a result, the auxiliary slaughterhouse was intact but, without maintenance, subject to slow decay. The roof leaked, which meant that at this time of year particularly, the factory floor itself was practically ankle deep in water. As Galia walked up to the Boss, she glanced down at that floor through the picture windows, the water as still as glass, mirror-like.

Getting into the slaughterhouse hadn't been a

problem. Galia and Rinaldo still had plenty of contacts, and finding a facility large enough to meet the Boss's exacting requirements actually hadn't been that hard. Surrounded as it was by tall warehouses—themselves likewise closed, disused, abandoned—the reformed gang of Whalers practically had half a square mile of the city all to themselves. The chance of discovery was slim, and there was ample space for their operation.

Whatever that operation was. The Boss hadn't exactly been clear on the matter—not yet. He outlined tasks one by one, as they came up. For now, Galia was happy to obey, and Rinaldo was happy to follow her orders and pass them on to the others.

Altogether, the new Whalers numbered eight—Galia and Rinaldo the only members of the original gang, the only ones who had actually known Daud. The others they had recruited from the docks and the nearby taverns—the Lucky Jim, the Seven of Bells. Some claimed to have been members of other street gangs, back in the day, but Galia suspected that people said a lot of things late at night in the dockside watering holes. With the Boss funding the operation, however, money bought loyalty.

But for Galia, loyalty was a more… *complex* concept. The Boss gave the orders, and Galia followed them, but she wasn't paid in money. She was paid in something else entirely. Something far, far more valuable.

Something she had yearned to have, for fifteen years…

Except now it was time for answers. Whatever the Boss was doing, it was time for him to trust her, to fill her in on his plans. She was the leader of the Whalers, after all. The Boss depended on her to carry out his tasks. True enough, he paid her with what she most desired, but, after the little encounter at the cemetery, things were becoming more complicated.

He needed to know about what had happened, and she needed to know what the plan was, the endgame. So Galia walked up to the Boss and stood, legs apart, arms folded, cocking her head and regarding his back.

He was still wrapped in the heavy military greatcoat, the edges caked with dried mud, the wide-brimmed hat, the thick scarf, and snow goggles still firmly in place. It was hot and stuffy in the control room, the evaporation of the rainwater down on the factory floor making the whole building humid and covering the control room walls with condensation. The liquid streaked large red-brown Vs down the filthy walls. The Boss had to be baking inside his strange getup.

"Listen, Boss," Galia said, "we have a problem."

She waited for a response, but none came. He didn't move, didn't even appear to be breathing. Rinaldo was right—it was like there was nothing there, underneath the heavy clothes. It was no wonder the others didn't want to come near him. The Boss was like something out of a children's bedtime story.

Beware the monster, the bogeyman.

Galia sighed and moved to one of the consoles. She idly trailed the fingers of one hand over the switches and buttons, through the dust, flicking a couple, pulling a larger lever. Nothing happened, of course. The console—like the rest of the slaughterhouse—was dead. Just to the side of the console there was a socket where a whale oil tank would normally be inserted, providing power. The socket was empty, the shutter hanging by one hinge, the magnetic coupler inside, designed to hold the tank in place, missing entirely. The slaughterhouse had been empty for a long time, and chances were, thought Galia, that her gang weren't the first people to break in. There probably wasn't even any wiring left underneath the consoles, the valuable metal stripped out of the cables and sold on the black market years ago.

Galia steeled herself as she moved along the console, then she turned back to the Boss. She stood beside him and watched for a moment, her eyes drawn to his red glass goggles. There was still no sound, no movement, not even the rise and fall of his chest.

"I *said*, we have a problem…"

Then the Boss cocked his head, the movement tiny but enough to make Galia jump. Immediately she cursed herself for being startled so easily. She stepped toward him, her hands curling into fists on her hips.

"*Listen!* We were seen—"

"Did you get what I wanted?" the Boss asked. He spoke slowly, as if he was taking a moment to choose the exact words to use, like he was speaking to someone from a distant land who knew another tongue.

Galia paused, and then she said, "Yes. We got six. The men are unloading the wagon now."

The Boss turned his face to her. She raised an eyebrow, and found herself staring at her own reflection in the huge, red glass goggles.

"I asked for seven."

"Yeah, well, six is what you've got." Galia took another step forward. "But will you *listen* to me? We were *seen.*"

The Boss's head tilted the other way.

"Seen?"

"Yes, thank you, *seen*. I chased him off."

"Then it is no matter."

"No," Galia said, "it matters all right. Listen, he was, I don't know… Void-touched. He could use transversal, like me. Back in the day, that was a power that Daud gave to me, and now you've given it back. How did this other guy have it? How is that *possible*? Who else knows secrets like ours?"

"It is no matter," the Boss said. "He is just one man, and one man can do nothing."

"That doesn't answer my question. And how do you know he's just one? There might be more of them, out there."

The Boss turned to Galia, and she found herself taking a step backward.

"Tell me, Galia Fleet, are you happy? Are you satisfied?"

"I… what? Happy? What kind of question is that?"

"A simple one," the Boss said. "I have promised you power. I have given you a taste of that which you desired the most. The gifts you once had, the gifts granted to you by the man Daud. You have these again."

"Yes, but…"

"You speak of him often, this Daud. He was a great man, was he not?"

Galia felt the heat rise in her face. "Yes. Yes he was. He was a great leader." She paused. "Though," she said, "I think he was troubled, in the last days I knew him."

"And what of the others?"

Galia shook her head. Over the past few days she had got used to the Boss's tendency to go off on tangents— but here? Now? This wasn't the time or place. She had a feeling they were in trouble, surely, and yet the Boss seemed unconcerned.

"What others?" she asked.

"You were once a formidable force. Yes, the *Whalers*." The Boss nearly hissed the name of the gang. "Led by Daud, followed by Billie Lurk and by Thomas and by Rinaldo and by… you. Galia Fleet, the novice, the acolyte. The *learner*."

Galia gulped down a breath. How did the Boss *know* all this? Yes, it was true, she had been a novice in the Whalers. But… so what? She'd been the only one who'd tried to keep the gang alive, after they'd all gone, vanished or dead—Daud, Billie, Thomas. All of them. Now it was just her and Rinaldo. When she told this to the Boss, her voice was louder, harder than she had intended.

There was a pause, a beat, and then the Boss laughed. It was harsh, somewhere between a cough and chuckle. Galia wondered again what was beneath the coat and hat and goggles. The Boss was a big man.

And he sounded… sick.

"And now the learner is the leader," he said, his laugh fading. "Remember that, Galia. Remember what I have done for you. Remember what I have promised you."

He turned back to the plate-glass windows. Galia moved to his side and looked down at the factory floor. The wagon had been unloaded and moved, the grim cargo sitting in a line between two of the huge whale oil vats.

"I'm… I'm sorry," Galia found herself saying, hardly realizing she was saying it all. She felt hot, dizzy. "We could only get six. We were interrupted before the seventh could be raised." She glanced sideways at the Boss.

He gave a small nod. "Six will suffice. You have done well, Galia."

Praise. A tiny, tiny scrap of praise, but it was enough. Galia felt her heart thud, her head grow light.

She had done well. She had pleased him.

Which meant… payment. Another taste of power.

The Boss seemed to sense her anticipation. He nodded again.

"Soon," he said.

Galia nodded, and turned back to the window. The hunger gnawed at her stomach and she wanted to be sick, but she focused instead on the view of the slaughterhouse, pushing aside the craving, the desire. The men were gone, she noticed.

"According to the map you gave us, that cemetery was in the heart of an old town that used to be outside the city walls—an enclave once populated by merchants and bankers." She nodded at the line of coffins far below, sitting on the wet factory floor. "The graves belonged to rich families. They'll be missed. We didn't have much time to clean up after ourselves. Someone will find the disturbance, and then we'll have the whole City Watch after us."

"It is not important."

Galia shook her head. "You keep saying that, but it's not just the City Watch." She turned to face him, the heat rising in her chest, in her neck. "I told you, we were seen by someone else—someone who can transverse, like I can."

And then... the boss laughed again, this time his shoulders shaking. Galia could only stare at him. What could he find so funny, so amusing? They'd risked a lot to drag six coffins to him—not to mention the hours of labor it had been for the men, working in the wet and the dark.

Enough!

"What are we doing? What's it all *for*?" she asked. "You want our help—no, you *need* our help! For what? To rob graves? Is that all?"

The Boss turned again to Galia and this time it was he who took a step forward. To her credit, Galia didn't move, her feet firmly planted on the floor. And one hand hovering over the knife hanging from her belt.

"And I ask you again, Galia Fleet," the Boss said. "Are you not happy? Are you not pleased?" He spread his hands. "I have given you what you wanted, haven't I? You have the power you crave, the power to transverse the geometry of the world, to *blink* from one place to another. This is what you wanted, what you desired, what you *craved*. Ever since your old master, that man Daud, abandoned you."

Galia pursed her lips, but relaxed the hand over her knife.

"I have helped you," the Boss continued. "This is just the start, Galia, just the start. With my help you can rebuild the Whalers—look, you have started already. And with my help, the city will learn to fear you again. It is *you* who command them. Small steps, small steps, but ones that will lead soon to great things."

Galia's lips parted, her breathing fast, shallow, as she took in the vision the Boss was sharing. Yes, small steps... but it was just the start. The Whalers were back.

And she was in command.

She found herself lost in his red eyes, the world spinning around her as she fell...

The Boss reached out a gloved hand and touched Galia's chin. She felt a spark, like static, and when she blinked she saw blue light dance across her vision. Her mind cleared.

She felt the *power* surge within her.

"And there is more to come, Galia," the Boss said. "Much, much more."

He turned away, leaving her standing, breathless, on the tips of her toes. He moved back to the plate-glass window and looked down at the factory floor.

"You have talents, Galia," he said. "Wild talents. They have been growing, nurtured inside you. With my help, we can bring these talents to the fore."

Galia found herself nodding.

"You have been *sleeping*, Galia Fleet. Years have gone by, years burned at the Golden Cat." The Boss raised his arms, as if to embrace the view. "Isn't this better than guard duty at a brothel? Trust me, Galia, you are destined for great things—and I can help you realize that destiny."

Galia rocked on her heels. Yes. He was right. She had been asleep. No, worse. She had been *dead*. Fifteen years—

fifteen years had passed since Daud vanished, and over those years she had done nothing. Nothing but *rot* at the Golden Cat, pickling herself with Old Dunwall Whiskey, or sometimes Orbum Rum if a shipment came in from Karnaca, pretending Daud would just walk in the door, one day, one day...

So yes, he would help her. He would give her what she wanted—

No. What she *deserved*.

Power. She wanted it, and she would have it.

Now.

Galia's head felt light, and she felt hot, hot in the stuffy, humid factory office. Yet the Boss just stood there, ridiculous in his heavy winter clothing, clothing more suited for the snows of Tyvia than the damp of Dunwall.

Yes. *Yes.* The Boss was a fool. A fool who spoke in riddles, who thought he could tell Galia what to do.

Well, *no more.* If he wouldn't talk, then he would give her all the powers he promised.

And if he didn't, then he would bleed.

Galia tightened her grip on the handle of her long knife, the knife she didn't even remember pulling from its sheath. The blade was light, well balanced, the perfect assassin's tool. And she was the same—older, yes, but as balanced as her blade, as ready to do the work for which she had been born.

Lifting herself onto the pads of her feet, she lowered her head, ready to spring. As ever, he stood, his broad back to her, his peripheral vision obscured by the ridiculous hat.

Let's see what riddles he will speak, with the edge of my blade hard against his windpipe, she thought. He would yield. She would *make* him.

There was a moment, a pause between heartbeats, where Galia saw herself reflected in the plate glass of the factory office, even as she moved forward, silently, ready to force the madman to his knees. The Boss was there too, in the reflection, but… something was wrong.

It happened in an instant, in the blink of an eye, as Galia found herself groping for thin air. Suddenly his reflection was *behind* her in the window. She wheeled around, all hope of surprise gone, and swung the blade. It was a clumsy move, but usually an effective one—one born of instinct, of years working as one of Daud's Whalers, in the hope of moving from novice to master, to be closer to him, to share more in the power he held.

Again Galia stumbled forward, expecting to meet a body with a blade embedded in its neck. But the knife sliced through air.

She turned. The Boss was on her other side, standing a yard or more away.

With a growl of annoyance, Galia moved again.

And met air.

She looked up. Now the Boss was *behind* her, on the other side of the factory office.

Transversing, of course! Two could play at that.

Galia focused and picked a new position, transporting herself the short distance nearly instantly, appearing three yards behind where she had been standing, ready to take the Boss by surprise.

He was gone.

There was a rattle from outside, beyond the windows. Galia turned to look, and saw her target out on the iron latticework of the platform that circled the control room. She focused, blinked, reappeared where the Boss had been, but she was alone again. She looked around, looked down. *There.* Below. He was on the slaughterhouse floor, striding toward the line of coffins.

Galia vaulted the iron rail, still gripping the knife. As

she fell, she transversed, and reappeared on the factory floor in a crouch.

Alone. *Again.*

She stood and moved forward, glancing around. The factory floor was a huge space, empty save for the whale oil vats and the six coffins. The gang had gone back to their makeshift quarters at the back of the building. Ahead of her stood the tall set of double doors, as high as the slaughterhouse and nearly as wide, big enough to make room for the precious cargo from a whaling ship, docked on the river outside. The frame holding the whale would be swung in by crane arms located high up in the slaughterhouse ceiling, until it was suspended over the huge vats.

Galia spun around. The need for caution was gone. She kicked at the inch-deep water, sending a plume of spray into the air.

As it fell back to the floor, the Boss stepped forward, appearing out of the air. He was close—too close, and Galia knew it. He struck her with a fist in her stomach. She doubled over, heading for the floor, then she transversed again to appear behind him. Winded, she summoned her strength to strike out—

Only she had no target. Instead, a boot caught her thigh, sending her sprawling sideways. She splashed in the water, the sudden cold shocking. Quickly she stood, swung right with the knife, but the Boss was out of reach. She lunged forward, dropped to one knee, and punched out with her left fist. This time the punch connected, but it had no effect. The Boss swung down, striking her forearm.

There was a crack, pain shooting up Galia's arm. Quickly, she transversed to the other side of the factory, as far away from the Boss as possible, and fell to the floor. There she lay on her side, the pain in her arm and her leg almost too much to bear.

There was a splash. She looked up.

The Boss was in front of her.

She raised herself up, but she was slow, too slow. Aside from the pain, she felt… weak. Her limbs, her whole body, felt like lead, her head filled with cotton wool and whale blubber. He stood in front of her, looking down with those red glass eyes.

Galia coughed and climbed to her feet. Then her thigh shot through with pain and she fell forward, back to the wet floor, her knees singing in agony as the joints slammed into the concrete. She coughed again, and dropped to her haunches, then to her backside, sitting in an inch of water, cradling her left arm across her chest, her thigh throbbing, her head spinning.

"Enough," she said, although she could hardly hear her own words over the ringing in her head. "*Enough*. I yield."

The Boss laughed, or maybe Galia just thought he did. Her head spun and she felt tired, so very, very tired. It was as though the more she used the power—the power that the Boss had granted her—the weaker she became. It wasn't just the powers she couldn't use, but her whole *body*, her strength evaporating with the slow rise of steam from the floor.

Her gaze fell to the pooled water around her. She saw her own reflection, gently rippling, and that of the Boss towering above her.

Of course. The reflections—first up in the control room, then down on the factory floor. *Exactly as it was at the Golden Cat.* The Boss could transverse, too, but his power was different. He traveled through reflections—mirrors, glass, the shine of water on the floor.

And his powers didn't seem to drain him.

Galia tore her eyes from his reflection, feeling as if the red glass goggles were burning into her mind. There was a roaring sound in her head. Her lifted gaze came to rest on the row of six coffins that were lined up, near to where she had fallen. The men had brushed the earth from them, but they were still dirty, the grime of the ages clinging to their wooden frames. They hadn't bothered to record who the graves had belonged to, or how long they had lain undisturbed. The Boss hadn't specified that they should.

All he wanted was the bodies.

Seven of them.

He had six.

"What do you want them for?" Galia asked weakly, nodding at the boxes. At this, the Boss walked over to the row, his boots splashing in the water. As he reached the first one, he bent over and ran a gloved hand across the surface, first brushing the dirt away, then tracing the contours of the lid with his fingertips. He leaned in, bringing his hidden face close to the top of the box, a few inches of wood the only thing separating him from the mummified cadaver within. Galia thought she heard him sniff, loudly, but then she thought this was merely her imagination, too, so loud was the rush in her ears.

"They are essential to me," the Boss said, then he straightened up. "They are essential to us, my dear Galia, to *us*."

She sighed, dragging herself to her feet. Her leg throbbed from where he had kicked it, but it wasn't broken. Nor her arm, but she knew it would hurt for a long time. More important, she wouldn't be able to fight as she had been. She would need time to rest, to heal.

"But what are we *doing*?" Galia demanded, practically yelling the question. "*Who are you?*"

The Boss laughed, then he lifted his right hand. With his left, as Galia watched, he pulled his glove off. Beneath the heavy leather, his hand was wrapped in black, dirty bandages.

Tossing the glove to the wet floor, the Boss began to unwrap the bandage, spiraling it around and around his hand and forearm until he held a long ribbon of mottled fabric—stained with blood or some kind of ointment, Galia couldn't tell. Then she gasped as she realized that the blackened, charred bandage was entirely free, and what remained wasn't more cloth, but the man's skin—blackened and charred as well, flakes floating down like ash and drifting in the sticky air to rest on the water like tiny dried leaves.

She had been right. He was sick, or injured, or both. The Boss curled his fist, sending more ash-like flakes drifting to the ground. Then he turned the hand around, showing Galia the crusted, burned back.

Galia's eyes went wide. The skin was black, but there was something else on it. It was like the echo of ink that remained on paper when a sheet was thrown into a fire—a delicate, black-on-black outline. A symbol, like an emblem.

A *mark*. Two semicircles, bisected by a ray which sprang from a smaller circle at the center of the emblem. She knew that mark, that symbol. Daud had had one, and it was drawn on the weird shrines they had found scattered through the city. A relic, an echo of another time.

The Mark of the Outsider.

"My name is Zhukov," the Boss said. "I am the Hero of Tyvia, and I am here to save the world."

$\overline{5}$

DUNWALL TOWER
8th Day, Month of Darkness, 1851

"In the capital city of Dunwall, each new Emperor is allowed to appoint a Royal Protector. This is far more than a trusted bodyguard. Much more revered than the hand-chosen guards defending Dunwall Tower or the food tasters, the Royal Protector is a court figure, given enormous latitude, who keeps constant company with the highest ruler in the known world."

— THE ROYAL PROTECTOR
Excerpt from a historical record of
government positions and ranks

Corvo entered the throne room to find the others already waiting for him. As one, the group turned to watch as he entered, Emily herself sitting on the throne up on the dais, one leg crossed over the other, her chin resting on one hand while the fingers of the other drummed on the seat's dull silver arm.

As he reached the group, he gave the bow that was customary. Behind him, Corvo heard the great doors of the chamber slam shut. Glancing over his shoulder, he saw that even the palace guards who were assigned to permanent duty on this side of the door had left, most likely at the express orders of the Empress herself.

It was just the four of them. Corvo cast his eye around the group as they each bowed to him in return.

Closest to the steps of the dais stood High Overseer Yul Khulan, the big, barrel-chested man with a shaved head, resplendent in his long red-velvet coat with high collar. Corvo hadn't spent much time with Khulan, but he seemed a good man, even a kind one, and one fiercely loyal to the Empress while, at the same time, keeping his own position independent. After the fall of the Lord Regent, Khulan had been quick to form an alliance with the restored young Empress. He and Corvo had helped guide the young ruler on matters of state for nearly a decade, until Emily had reached an age where they both thought she was more than capable of striking out on her own.

If only the High Overseer knew what a capable young woman—not to say, formidable duelist—the Empress truly was.

Next to Khulan stood Jameson Curnow, young son of Geoff Curnow, the former Captain of the City Watch, now enjoying a long and happy retirement with his wife, thanks in no small part to Corvo himself, and Geoff Curnow's niece—Jameson's cousin—Callista, former caretaker for the young Emily.

Jameson was smartly dressed in a brown jacket with black brocade across the front, the collar high, as was the current fashion among the aristocracy this season. His long bangs sat curved across his eyebrows, and as he gave Corvo a stiff nod, he brushed the hair to one side, out of the way. Then he glanced sideways at Emily—a look that wouldn't be noticed by either the High Overseer or the Empress. As far as they were both concerned, Jameson was a young member of her inner circle, barely a year or two older than she was, and, thanks to the strong bond forged between Callista and Emily, a trusted advisor.

Little did they know that Jameson Curnow fell under Corvo's direct command. For Corvo was not only Royal Protector, he was Royal Spymaster, as well—the first to unify the two roles.

And Jameson Curnow was his chief agent.

Emily stood from the throne and stepped down onto the long red carpet, an elegant figure in a slim, formal black trouser suit, the white ruffled collar of the shirt beneath pulled high around her neck. Corvo gave her a nod and a smile, and locked his hands behind his back. She gave a tight-lipped smile back.

He knew the meaning well, and having received the summons early that morning—shortly after he had returned to the Tower—he knew exactly what this meeting was about.

"I believe I know what concerns you, Empress," he said, giving a small bow. "The Captain of the City Watch reported the discovery to me this morning." This wasn't really a lie—when he'd got back, he had had one of his agents report to a City Watch patrolman, who had in turn informed his Captain, who then came to Corvo. "And," he continued, "I've already sent out a couple of agents to take a closer look. I expect their report presently."

"Dark deeds in Dunwall!" Jameson said with a smile. He folded his arms and raised his eyebrows dramatically, pushing his bangs up his forehead. "Grave robbers at work, and it's still seven months to the Fugue Feast. Somebody is getting ideas."

Corvo pursed his lips while High Overseer Khulan drew in a gasp, the big man clutching the lapels of his velvet coat in what appeared to be shock. Emily looked at Jameson with an eyebrow raised, then turned and led the way over to the side of the room, where a large table had been set out.

"I only hope you are right, Mr. Curnow," she said as the others followed. "But robbing the dead is still a heinous crime. Here."

The group gathered around the table, on which was spread a large map of Dunwall, secured at the corners with the ornate jeweled gold fish statuettes that normally graced the display cabinet on the other side of the room. Corvo allowed himself a small smile—the statuettes were periodic gifts from a place he knew well, a collective of smaller villages in Serkonos, the country of his birth. Although he'd grown up in Karnaca, the capital of Serkonos, until the death of his father he'd spent many happy hours wandering through the more rural areas between the cities along the coast, a region rightly famous for the quality of its fishing.

As Emily spoke she pointed to a sector of the map, up north, just outside the line of the old city wall. Corvo nodded, tugging at his bottom lip, feigning quiet contemplation as she described what she had seen with her own eyes, but which, covering her nighttime activities, she now attributed to the Captain of the City Watch.

When she was done, the High Overseer shivered, his olive skin coming out in gooseflesh, the knuckles of both hands bleaching white as he squeezed his lapels tighter and tighter.

"Disgraceful business, Your Majesty," he said. "Simply disgraceful. Who would do such a thing? To desecrate the graves of those who've faded from the world—those who have earned their escape from existence? *Disgraceful.*"

Jameson nodded and leaned over the map, arms outstretched as he scanned the schematic of the city. His bangs fell across his face and through them he glanced again at Emily, and lowered his head.

"I apologize for my earlier levity, Your Majesty," he said, and Emily nodded in return. Then Jameson turned back to the map and stood tall. He pointed out several locations. "The city has many cemeteries and gravesites—some very public, like the mausoleum at the Abbey of the Everyman, and the main city cemetery, *here*." He tapped the map at the corresponding locations. "But there must be, oh, a dozen others much like the old garden cemetery in the New Mercantile District… *ah*! Here, and here, that I know of, anyway."

Corvo watched Jameson as he pointed out the approximate locations. Emily grabbed two more fish statues from the side of the table and slid them across the map, marking the spots.

"We need to find out who is behind this," the Empress said. "I can't—I *won't*—have this happening in my capital city."

"Agreed," Corvo said. "Let's see what my agents bring back from the scene—perhaps the robbers left some clues. If the intention of the gang is to plunder graves for coin, or other valuables that may be buried, then it's possible they'll strike again. I'll liaise with the City Watch—they can send patrols out to keep a close eye on every cemetery and graveyard."

"But then they'll know we're onto them," Jameson said. He pointed again to the location of the crime. "They seem to have left quite a mess at the garden cemetery. This district is largely empty, but they'd have known somebody would spot it sooner or later."

"Fortunate that it was so soon, my friends," the High Overseer said. He was looking at the map with a grimace on his face. "That area is, I understand, undergoing heavy restoration work. It could have gone unnoticed for days—*weeks*, even." Then he shivered again, and clutched at the lapels of his coat. "Let us hope," he said, in a quiet voice, "that these acts are being carried out by thieves seeking coin, as you say. Otherwise, I shudder to think at their purpose. Some cult of the Outsider, perhaps—though I hesitate to say his name aloud here in your company, Empress—enacting part of a foul plan. High heresy, indeed."

Khulan sighed and recomposed himself, then turned to Emily and gave a small bow.

"Your City Watch should be praised for their diligent surveillance." At that Corvo licked his lips and glanced up at her, gauging her reaction, but she was good, showing none. Instead, she simply bent down to peer at the map.

Corvo turned to Jameson. "You're right," he agreed. "They will be alerted, but if we're careful…" He nodded to the High Overseer. "Khulan, if you could spare some Overseers to help with the Watch, then if anyone notices the activity, they'll assume the Abbey is preparing for funeral rites."

Khulan bowed. "Certainly, Royal Protector, the Abbey is at your disposal."

"Good idea." Emily looked up. "We can focus our attention on these, the smaller plots." She pointed out more locations on the map. "They're unlikely to hit the Abbey Mausoleum or any public tombs, but we should still watch those as well."

Corvo nodded. "Yes, and I'll send my agents out into the city, see if anyone is talking about grave robbers."

And more besides, he thought.

"We should reach out to the families of those whose graves have been disturbed," Emily said. "I can write to each, or grant an audience if they are in the city. I can promise them we will find the culprits, and have them punished."

"That may be difficult," Jameson said. "I did a little digging myself—ah, pardon the pun—and it seems most of the houses in the New Mercantile District have been empty for years. I believe a small number of the families are still in Dunwall. Some went to Potterstead and Baleton, but I believe most headed up to Arran. The majority were of old Morley stock, so I'm told."

Emily looked toward her council. "Understood, Jameson. Do your best." Then she looked up at the others. "Thank you, gentlemen, for your assistance. We need to keep a watchful eye over Dunwall. Even after all these years, parts of the city are *still* in recovery after the terrors of the Rat Plague. It can be a slow process, but while we are rebuilding these areas, nothing must interfere. The people need confidence in the Empire, and—I'm sure you understand—confidence in *me*. This crime may seem a minor one, compared to what this city has faced in its past, but I *cannot* and *will not* let it pass."

The others agreed, including Corvo, who watched Emily with careful eyes. The plan was a sound one—keep watch on the city while working to find the grave robbers. Of course, it wasn't just going to be the City Watch or Corvo's agents out looking. He knew that Emily herself would make this her new task.

He only hoped she didn't get herself in too deep.

Emily walked back to the throne. Standing in front of it on the dais, she lifted her hands and clapped, three times, the staccato sound echoing loudly around the chamber. A moment later the double doors of the throne room were swung open by two members of the Imperial Guard, letting in bright sunlight from the terrace beyond.

There stood a young noble, about the same age as the Empress, wearing a high-collared jacket in a deep velvety green, with heavy blue brocade ornamentation. As the doors opened, the newcomer straightened and locked eyes with Emily. Corvo couldn't resist a grin, and when he turned to Emily he saw that she, too, was smiling at Wyman.

He was pleased that she had managed to somehow find love, despite her hectic schedule as Empress and, in secret, as Corvo's pupil.

Jameson turned to the throne and gave a theatrical bow, then bade farewell to Corvo and the High Overseer. Then, to the Royal Protector he gave a slight, discrete nod, which Corvo returned.

They would continue this meeting in private.

"Your Majesty," Khulan said, giving a deep bow before the throne. "I shall keep you informed of all developments."

"Thank you, High Overseer."

"Your Majesty," Corvo said, "if I may have a moment with the High Overseer. There are some arrangements to be made with the Abbey that I want to go over."

Emily smiled at her Royal Protector. "Of course," she said, then she descended the steps of the throne and took the High Overseer by the arm, leading them toward the double doors. Released from her grip, Khulan turned and gave a bow, first to Emily, and then to Wyman, still waiting patiently. Wyman returned the bow, then winked at Emily.

Emily turned, trying—and *failing*—to hide the smile on her face.

"Well, yes," Corvo said, clearing his throat. "I'll leave you to it. High Overseer Khulan, would you come with me?"

Emily nodded and turned. Wyman gave Corvo a mock salute, then entered the throne room behind her. The two guards who were supposed to be on duty inside the chamber returned to their customary positions, leaving two more stationed out on the terrace. As the double doors closed, Khulan nodded and straightened his velvet coat.

"Royal Protector?"

Corvo stood for a moment outside the doors, tugging on his chin as he considered. "Ah, give me five minutes. Join me in my chambers, if you will."

Khulan bowed, and headed for the lift that would take him down into the body of Dunwall Tower. Corvo, meanwhile, turned back to the throne room doors, thinking things over.

Until now, Emily's nocturnal adventures had been innocent enough. True, if her secret had got out, they would scandalize the court, if not the entire city, but Corvo was confident in her abilities, and in his own.

Following her out at night was his duty, and it was part of her training. Real-world training, outside of the safety of Dunwall Tower. But now, there was a risk. True enough, there had been before—risk of injury, of discovery—but the city was relatively safe, the spread of the gangs having mostly been contained years ago.

Besides which, Emily could look after herself in a tight spot.

But this… this was different. Emily had seen the grave robbers and now, clearly, had got it into her head to investigate further, to solve the mystery and catch the miscreants. He didn't blame her. She craved adventure. Being Empress of the Isles was both a curse and a blessing— she knew her duty, and embraced it.

Her restoration to the throne had been a chance to honor her mother, Jessamine, and to undo the damage the Lord Regent had wrought, not just to the city of Dunwall, but to the Empire of the Isles. Emily's foremost goal was to be a just, fair ruler. And to do this, to really understand her empire, and the people within it, she explored Dunwall.

She had to do it on her own terms, in her own way, and Corvo approved. So long as he was there to keep an eye on her, Emily would be fine.

But the grave robbers—they were more than just another gang who had discovered a new way of getting rich. Emily had only observed a part of the picture.

Corvo had seen the rest.

The man in the Whaler's outfit—and with the Whaler's power.

The power of the Outsider.

That made the situation far, far more dangerous—not just for Emily, but for everyone. And Whalers didn't snatch bodies in the dead of night. Not without another reason.

He could watch her, but only so much. He needed a little backup.

Corvo rolled his neck, and gestured at the guard on the left side of the throne room door, his insignia marking him as a lieutenant in the City Watch, his companion only a corporal.

"Lieutenant?"

The young officer snapped to attention, his sword rattling in its scabbard as it knocked against his leg.

"My Lord!"

"I want a special watch kept on the Empress," Corvo said. "She is not to be left alone, day or night. I'll talk to the Captain of the Watch and make out an official order, but in the meantime, do you understand my command?"

"Yes, sir."

The officer lifted his chin just a little more. Corvo nodded, then turned and walked toward the terrace lift. Giving Emily an escort wouldn't stop her going out at night, but it might slow her down a little. It might even make her think twice, especially if he doubled the guard around the Tower.

It was ridiculous, really. Here he was, attempting to keep the Empress safely locked away in Dunwall Tower—

an Empress who was on her way to someday being as skilled a combatant as he was.

Nevertheless, he had a bad feeling about the grave robbers. Something strange was happening in Dunwall. And he had to find out what.

Corvo found the High Overseer waiting in the Spymaster's office, admiring a painting. Khulan turned as the Royal Protector entered and shut the door behind him.

"Corvo," Khulan said, all trace of formality gone now they were out of Emily's company. The High Overseer shook his head, his hands already reaching for the lapels of his coat. "A miserable business this. Disgusting. Quite disgusting."

"You'll get no argument from me," Corvo said. He walked around to his desk, looked at it, but didn't sit down. Instead he stood and pulled at his bottom lip.

"I'm sensing trouble, Corvo," Khulan said, raising an eyebrow. "What have you discovered that you don't want the Empress to know about?"

Corvo paused. He looked the High Overseer in the eye, then smiled. He tapped the desk with his fingernails.

"Perceptive as ever, old friend."

Khulan's mouth turned up at the corner. "All this cloak-and-dagger is your department, not mine. Just tell me what you want, and I'll do it. You know that, I hope."

"You'll organize for the Overseers to help out the City Watch?"

"As I said."

"Right," Corvo said, lowering his voice. He could take no risks. "I also want Warfare Overseers equipped with Music Boxes."

Khulan blinked, a smile blooming across his broad face. "I'm sorry, Corvo, for a moment there I thought you said Music Boxes."

Corvo answered only with a steely look. The smile quickly vanished from Khulan's face.

"Music Boxes, Corvo? If you mean for the Ancient Music to be heard again, that can only be because..."

Corvo just nodded.

"But... *sorcery*?"

"Yes, High Overseer. Black magic in Dunwall."

"But... oh my, this is serious." With one hand, Khulan reached to lean on the chair that sat in front of the Royal Spymaster's desk, as though he needed support to stay standing. With his other hand he rubbed his forehead. "Magic," he said again, shaking his head. "Who would open the bowels of the black worm and bring this heresy to Dunwall?"

"That's exactly what I'm going to find out," Corvo said.

"But can you do it?"

The High Overseer hissed between his teeth. "Yes, but it will take time. We haven't had need of such an enclave of Overseers for a long time. I will consult with my Vice Overseers and see what can be done. And we haven't used Music Boxes since, well, since the days of the Lord Regent. I'll need to order them out of the Abbey's armory, but after all these years, they will need to be retuned, their suppression of magic tested.

"That won't be easy, especially as no one has had need to even look at them in all that time. Truth told, many of the younger Overseers scarcely believe the tales of those touched by the Outsider. Despite the whispers from our Sisters of the Oracular Order, who get glimmers from time to time, and despite the abandoned shrines we find in abandoned apartments and condemned buildings. But even these are often not proof enough. Most simply wave them off."

"Quite." Corvo frowned. "Does that mean you can do it, or not?"

The High Overseer nodded the affirmative, but his expression was far from pleased.

"Okay," Corvo said, "get them out and start work. Let me know how you progress. I need the boxes operational as quickly as possible."

"Very well, I will arrange it," Khulan said. "But I fear the operational boxes may only be few in number."

"Raise what you can, and arm the rest of the Warfare Overseers with grenades and pistols. There should be ample supply in the Tower armories, if not at the Abbey. I want them all set and ready to go, at my command, should the need arise."

"It will take time, but we can do it."

"Thank you, Yul," Corvo said. "And thank you for your discretion. Once we have more information, we can form a better plan, and then we can take it to the Empress. In the meantime, these are just precautions, trust me."

"Precautions, Corvo?" The High Overseer tutted. "It sounds more like preparation for war."

Corvo sighed.

"I really hope it isn't, Yul. I really hope it isn't."

6

"I've known four people in my time who carried the
Mark of the Outsider, but I've known dozens more
who wanted it, who stood at night in stagnant ponds
or begged with the dust blowing through graveyards.
People who gutted farm animals or burned the flesh
of men, thinking it would call forth the Void. I met
a dying man once who had collected runes and
charms for years. He crushed them all into powder,
made a paste and ate them, thinking he could gain
whatever magic was in the things. His death was
long and painful."

— COBBLED BITS OF BONE
Excerpt from a journal covering various occult artifacts

Still kneeling on the wet factory floor, Galia stared at
Zhukov's hand, stared at the dark insignia burned into
his blackened skin—the same mark that Daud had on
his hand, only his had shone with a blue light that, even
all these years later, still haunted her in her dreams.

The Mark of the Outsider.

Galia hadn't believed Daud at first when he had told her, and even now, she had doubts. The Outsider was a myth, a story spread in the back of taverns—a creation of the Overseers, most likely, part of some great conspiracy to keep the populace in check while allowing the Abbey of the Everyman their studies of forbidden arts—forbidden *magics*—for their own purposes.

So some people said, anyway.

But Galia had felt the power of the Outsider. Daud had given it to her—given it to all of the Whalers. It was what made them the greatest assassins in the world. Nobody and nothing could beat them, could stop them.

Zhukov had given that power back to her. It felt different, yes, somehow, but Galia didn't care. All she cared about was the fact that it had come back to her, and that this stranger, the man who said his name was Zhukov, who said he was a hero from a distant land, had promised her more.

She took a step forward, her eyes locked on Zhukov's hand. Then he turned his hand around, denying her, and he began to wind the stained bandage back in place.

"You recognize the symbol," he said. It was a statement, not a question.

Galia nodded. Then she ran her fingers through her greasy hair.

"Who *are* you?" she asked.

The man laughed. "I told you. I am Zhukov, Hero of the State of Tyvia."

Her eyes narrowed "Hero?" She didn't know much about how Tyvia worked, only that it was a very different place to Gristol. Didn't it have princes, or some kind of council? She wasn't sure. "You don't *look* much like a hero."

Zhukov paused as he wrapped the bandage, then

resumed again in silence. When he was done he picked his glove up off the wet floor and slipped it back on.

"I was betrayed," he said. "But they cannot take my status away from me. A Hero of Tyvia I remain, no matter what they did to me."

Galia shook her head. "I don't understand."

"To be named a Hero of the State is the highest honor of my country. Do you know Tyvia? It is a beautiful land, full of wonder, but it is also a strange, difficult place, a country ruled by its people, but not always *for* its people. A people I was sworn to help, fighting for their rights, for their way of life. Where there was injustice, I fought it— even when the authorities turned a blind eye. I took my struggles to every city of the country—Tamarak, Caltan, Dabokva... even Samara and Yaro in the north. And the people loved me."

"You said you were betrayed?"

Zhukov inclined his head. "I was. I said Tyvia was a strange place, and it is the truth. Once ruled by princes, there is now a council, assembled from representatives, elected by the citizens from every region. That council is itself governed by a triumvirate—the High Judges, the head of which commands all.

"It was for the High Judges that I was working, in secret. As a Hero of the State I was merely a tool. My purpose was to maintain *balance*. To keep the citizens happy, thinking that there was someone who existed *outside* of the system, fighting for them, making things right—and, maybe one day, my struggles would lead to the return of the Princes of Tyvia. Whatever thoughts kept the people happy... and kept them in check. But everything I did, I did for the High Judges."

"And, what, they turned against you?"

Zhukov paused again, and he nodded slowly. "My

usefulness had come to an end. I was their tool—and their property. With my task complete, I was an inconvenient fiction. They could not allow me to remain among the people, so they removed me—they sent me to their camp, at Utyrka, in the frozen heart of the country."

Galia felt a smile appearing on her lips. She folded her arms and cocked her head at the stranger.

"You're saying they sent you to prison? In *Tyvia*?"

Zhukov nodded.

Galia's mouth curled up at the corner—she couldn't help it. "But that's not possible. Everybody knows that nobody has ever escaped from a Tyvian prison. The prisons are in the middle of the tundra, in the middle of all that snow and ice. Nobody gets out. *Everybody* knows that."

"And yet," Zhukov said, spreading his hands, "I am here."

Galia lifted an eyebrow. "Then you're lying."

Now it was Zhukov's turn to cock his head. He lifted the hand he had bared to her, covered again by the thick black leather glove.

"Am I lying about this?" he asked. "About the mark I possess? About the powers I have granted to you?"

Galia felt her nerve waver, even at the slightest mention of the powers. She bit her bottom lip, and gave a slight nod.

"So you're the first—and only—man to ever escape Tyvia," she said. "How did you do it?"

Zhukov turned his hand, looking at the back of it—although it was impossible to tell for sure, with the large red goggles still in place. Slowly he lowered it.

"The labor camp at Utyrka was a cruel place," he said. "There were guards—military personnel, stationed there to run the camp. They were not called guards, of course. We did not need them, or even walls. The snow and the ice were our jailers."

Galia glanced down, watched Zhukov's rippling reflection in the puddles of water on the slaughterhouse floor.

"The work was crushing," Zhukov continued. "It was… *lethal*. You are right to say that no one had ever escaped. None have ever been released, either—not from Utyrka. Even the shortest sentence there is one of death. The work will kill you before your time is due.

"But at night, I dreamed," he continued. "I saw stars that spun, shining with a blue light. I dreamed every night. As the years went by that blue light changed, darkened. It became yellow, then orange, then red—it was a fire, a vision of a great burning. And—"

"Wait, *the* Great Burning?" Galia's eyes widened.

Zhukov paused, then continued, apparently content to ignore Galia's exclamation.

"And from that fire stepped a man. He spoke to me and I listened. He told me many things, secrets out of time, the secrets on which our world was built. That night, when I awoke, I had the mark."

He held up his hand again.

"This mark is *power*, Galia. It was my escape. It allowed me to cross the tundra and the great fields of blue ice as clear as glass. It was here I discovered how to use my ability—I could transpose myself with my own reflection, then project that reflection into another, and another, and another. I could cross the ice, stepping between reflections. Then I was free."

He turned back around to Galia. Her eyes moved from the reflection in the water to her own reflection in his goggles.

"But you aren't in Tyvia now," she said, unable to tear her eyes from his face. "You still wear the clothes from the camp? The snow goggles, the coat—"

Zhukov's laugh, a low bass echoing from his broad chest, was muffled beneath his scarf.

"It was the ice of the Tyvian glaciers. They are famous throughout the empire, a wonder of the world. But their depths are not perfect—far from it. And the reflections within were likewise fractured. The more I traveled, the more *I* became fractured. *Corroded.*"

Galia lifted her chin. "Show yourself. I want to see your face."

Zhukov laughed again.

"I am a shadow of my former self—my blood burns in my veins, but I cannot bear the cold and the light of Dunwall. You will forgive my attire, but I feel as though my very soul is corroded. Every moment is a painful reminder of my betrayal."

Galia found her fingers floating near to the knife on her belt.

"I asked you to show yourself."

"My face is not the face of the hero I once was, Galia."

Then she stood, moving in one swift movement, balancing on her toes as she looked up at Zhukov. Finally she lowered herself, stepped back, and folded her arms, trying to control her frustration.

Trying to keep the knife out of her hand.

"So this… dream you had?" she asked. "You think that was the Outsider, come to say hello?"

"Perhaps. I cannot remember the vision clearly, but I have been marked. Nothing else matters."

"Nothing else matters? Why would the Outsider appear to you? What did he want? Why give you his mark?"

Zhukov didn't move, didn't speak.

"Answer me!" Galia felt the blood rise in her face, her temper flaring.

"The Outsider's plan and his reasons are his own,"

Zhukov said. "He is not a man. How he thinks, how he operates—these are beyond our understanding. All that matters is that I now have his power, which I used first to escape from Utyrka, and then from Tyvia." He took a step toward her.

Galia refused to move, instead lifting her chin higher as Zhukov bore down on her.

"I have traveled the Isles for months," Zhukov said. "Once out of Tyvia, I traveled to Morley, to Karnaca—I even saw the shores of Pandyssia. I was gathering intelligence, information. I was following a light, and finally that light led me to Gristol—to Dunwall, and to you, Galia Fleet."

"But what *for*? You have to tell me. What are you saving the world from?"

"From *itself*, Galia. My betrayal was just the start of something much, much larger—a great *unbalancing*—not just of Tyvia, but of the world."

Galia shook her head. "I don't understand."

"Then maybe you can understand this. I was betrayed by Tyvia, and I will get my revenge. I plan to go back, and take what is mine by right."

"But *how*?" Galia sighed and flapped her arms against her sides. "What do you need all this for? What do you need *me* for?"

Zhukov spun on his heel and walked across the slaughterhouse floor. He paused, turned, and gestured for Galia to follow him.

"Come with me. I will show you."

Rinaldo slid out of the shadows up on the iron gallery by the control room, and watched as the black-coated wraith they were now calling the "Boss" led his old friend

Galia across to the other side of the slaughterhouse, where there was a railed stone stairway against the wall, leading down into the bowels of the factory.

Rinaldo let out a breath he'd been holding for a long time. Galia and the Boss hadn't heard or seen him up here, he was sure of that, but it had been close, the damn rusting stairwell and platforms creaking and rattling with the slightest movement. Rinaldo's calves ached from balancing on his toes in the shadows, frozen in place so he could listen in.

Now he stood, walked over to the platform rail, and leaned down. The floor was empty, Galia and the Boss heading down into the cellars while the rest of the gang slept off their night's work in the back of the factory. Rinaldo was alone.

He whistled, just quietly, but it still echoed more than he would have liked, then he stopped and shook his head as he thought back over the conversation.

It wasn't true, of course. None of it. *Escape from Tyvia?* Yes, of course, no problem. That happened all the time, right? It was nothing more than a nice little holiday in the snow, getting a little light exercise in the health camps before walking off into the sunset once you'd had enough.

Rinaldo sniggered. It was ridiculous. The whole thing. Okay, so he'd escaped from Tyvia… with, what, magical powers? After being visited by some kind of supernatural benefactor, in a *dream*?

It was worse than a child's bedtime story. Beware Zhukov, the monster from Tyvia, the only man in history to have ever visited the prisons of Tyvia—and returned to tell the tale! Add music…

Dun-dun… DUN!

Rinaldo paused. Was there *any* truth in it? Galia seemed to buy it, hook, line, and sinker. And sure, they had some Void tricks, like those given to them by Daud. But Daud had never harped on about destiny and revenge and a higher purpose.

Anyway, what he'd heard pretty much confirmed his own suspicions, namely, that Galia knew as much about the big plan as Rinaldo did. Which was to say, she knew nothing at all. Zhukov had a hold on her, something that made her believe him.

What was it? Galia was smart—one of the smartest people Rinaldo had ever known. Back in the old days of the Whalers, he'd been a master, and she was just a novice. But he'd seen the potential there, the talent that grew and continued to grow, right up until Daud's disappearance.

Galia would have been a master one day. Of that, Rinaldo had no doubt. And sure, the years afterward had been hard. He'd found Galia at the Golden Cat, but spending nearly every waking moment pickled in liquor. Then she'd got better and, he had to admit, this guy Zhukov had finished the job that Rinaldo had started. Since moving into the old slaughterhouse, Rinaldo hadn't seen her touch a drop of the Old Dunwall.

She'd done what she had always wanted to do—got the Whalers back together. Then again, it had been with the helping hand of a freak in a big coat and very stupid hat, who liked to tell tall tales about the snows of Tyvia.

Yeah, right. Still… something was going on. Something about revenge, and restoring balance.

Huh. Sounded strange.

Rinaldo turned back to the rail and leaned over, his eyes drifting across the slaughterhouse floor and to the stairs that led to the basement. He hadn't been down there—nobody had, as far as he knew. It was probably flooded, given the state of the building. Except… that was exactly where Zhukov was leading Galia. Which meant he was keeping something down there.

Rinaldo now knew where the answers lay.

In the basement. Down the stairs.

But it was too risky, for now. He wasn't sure what the basements were usually used for back when the slaughterhouse was running—storerooms, probably whale oil storage tanks? He would need to scout it out, take a look when the coast was clear.

Rinaldo crouched down in the shadows, and watched the stairs. Galia and Zhukov would return at some point, and Rinaldo was patient. But he wanted to see what was down there. He wanted to know what was going on—what Zhukov was planning.

What Galia had signed them up for.

Galia stepped back and didn't stop until she felt the cold steel of the storeroom door on her back. She took a breath, tasted bile in her throat.

She shook her head. Wanted, desperately, to turn around, to look away from the horror in front of her. Instead, she gulped, and lifted her chin again, a familiar tick that gave her courage, strength, confidence.

It worked, too.

She'd seen things, back in the day. Daud's Whalers had been ruthless. Galia, too, she told herself. Perhaps the years drinking herself to death had changed things, softened her. Or maybe it was moldering, graveyard stench, the decay and the rot, the worms and beetles and things that *slid*.

"You have all of... *this*," she said, gesturing with one hand at the contents of Zhukov's basement workshop, while trying not to look at any of it, instead focusing on his red shining goggles that glittered in the sticky yellow light of the whale oil lamps. "So I still don't understand what you need *us* for."

Zhukov turned back to his workbench, his fingers playing over the brass cogs and wheels of the large device that sat on it, some kind of instrument that wouldn't have looked out of place in the Academy of Natural Philosophy.

Of course, Galia had never seen the place *herself*, but Daud had made cryptic mentions a few times. Growing up, Galia had heard plenty of stories about the strange place, a monument to the hidden secrets of the cosmos, where bizarre practitioners dabbled in dozens of fields of natural philosophy, mixing modern processes with ancient alchemies.

Some said that they had built machines to predict when rain would fall, or where new silver veins could be found beneath the mountains of Serkonos, while other stories told of men attempting to reanimate dead tissue using electricity. Galia wasn't sure if any of that was true, but then again, she'd never thought the stories *weren't* true, either.

The machine on the workbench certainly matched the kind of thing she imagined would have come out of the Academy, anyway. The rest of the... *material*... that lay on the benches?

Well, she wasn't so sure about that.

"You and your Whalers have been of great help to me, Galia," Zhukov said. "And now you have seen the source of the power I grant you, yet this is not enough. I have promised you more, and you shall have it—we all will. But to that end I still require your help a little further."

Galia swallowed, and nodded, perhaps to Zhukov's back, perhaps to herself.

"Tell me what to do."

Zhukov spun around and approached her. She didn't

feel afraid—in fact, she felt sick—but the metal door was cold on her back as she pressed herself into it, its wheel digging painfully into her backbone.

Good. That's good. Galia pressed harder and it hurt more. It was something to focus on, something to keep her mind clear.

"I want revenge," Zhukov said, his red eyes bearing down on Galia, "and I will get it—not just against the rulers of my country, the High Judges, but against the people of Tyvia itself. My betrayal was wholesale and absolute. And for that, they will all pay."

Zhukov turned back to the table and leaned over his instrument, one gloved hand making fine adjustments to the wheels and levers that held the complex array of lenses in place. Galia couldn't see what was under the lenses, and she didn't want to look.

"I knew I needed help," Zhukov continued. "I also knew that there were once others like me, those who carried the mark. I had heard stories of a man called Daud, so I sought him out. I traveled far, but I could not find him. But I also heard about the reputation of his lieutenants—of Thomas, Billie Lurk, and other names. None of them could be found. But Galia Fleet—that was another name, one who was quick to learn, who knew Daud, and his secrets. One who would have taken her rightful place at his side, so some said, had the world not lost its balance all those years ago."

Galia felt her heart leap into her throat.

"I sought you out at the Golden Cat," Zhukov said, "because I need you to help me restore that balance. In return, I can restore the balance within *you*. I have promised you power, and you will have it. But not like this, not this *twilight* power. You have felt it yourself— the more you use this power, the weaker you become, and the greater the *desire*, the *need* you feel."

He turned and walked back to Galia, slowly. She stared at the red light shining in his eyes. She felt dizzy, light-headed, like she'd had too much Old Dunwall.

"I can give you all the power you want, and it will be yours *forever*," Zhukov said, his voice a low whisper. "I will give you the power to take over the whole city. Think of it. Dunwall will be *yours*. You will have the power to lead the Whalers to conquest. Daud didn't dream big enough for you, did he? I can see it in your mind. He had *potential*, but he was limited. You… you will go farther. Much, much farther, with my help. In return, I only ask your obedience, and your assistance."

Galia swallowed the lump in her throat. She thought back to what she had seen in the Golden Cat—the dream Zhukov had shown her, almost as if it had been plucked out of her head.

The Whalers—not a gang, but an *army*, with Galia its general.

Dunwall would be theirs.

And Dunwall would be just the first…

Galia fought the dizziness that threatened to overcome her.

She would do anything for Zhukov.

Anything.

"Tell me," she whispered.

Zhukov hissed behind his scarf, and he reached out, long, gloved fingers, taking Galia's sharp chin. He lifted her head, and she let it be lifted.

"Good," he said quietly. "Good." He dropped his hand, and at once Galia felt the absence of his touch, a strange, cold hollow feeling, somewhere deep inside her.

"My plan requires some very special preparations, for which I need you and your Whalers. You have found me the perfect facilities, but there is more. I need you to steal something for me. It will be difficult—the object is not valuable and it is not guarded, but it will be hard to reach."

Galia allowed herself a small smile. She was beginning to feel more like herself.

"With your power, Zhukov, we can go anywhere."

"Hah, yes," he said, "and you will need that power for the next task. To carry out this... let's call it a *heist*... I need to create something much more powerful than what you see in this room. The bones of the old merchants will suffice for now, but they are of comparatively limited use. I can carve them, animate them with my power, but what we need for the next phase are the bones of those infused with their own particular form of magic."

Galia frowned and pushed off from the door. She moved to the worktable, and, taking a breath, finally forced herself to look down at the items scattered across it. Then she turned, quite deliberately, and viewed the contents of the room—the contents she'd been trying so hard to ignore.

Now she saw things differently. In the room were raw materials, nothing more. Like the whale oil that had once been stored in the tanks nearby. But she frowned as she ran Zhukov's words through her mind. She turned back to him, confidence welling inside her.

"Me and my boys are at your disposal, Zhukov," she said, "but I'm going to need more to go on than just that. Just cut to the chase—tell me what you need, and we'll go get it."

Zhukov nodded. "I knew you wouldn't let me down," he said, and at that Galia smiled, feeling as if the simple compliment was lavish praise. He stepped back to her.

"What I need is at Brigmore Manor."

Galia's jaw went up and down before she found the

words to reply. She knew the location—she knew it well.

And its former inhabitants.

"Ah… Brigmore Manor?"

"Yes, Galia," Zhukov said. "Tell me, do you know the truth about a woman called Delilah?"

A thousand thoughts crowded Galia's mind. Yes, she knew Brigmore, and she knew about its former inhabitant. She knew *all* about Delilah. Galia didn't speak, but Zhukov nodded.

"Yes, the Brigmore Witches," he said. "A seat of awful magic."

Galia shook her head. She never wanted to go back to Brigmore. Not now, not ever.

But she had promised Zhukov loyalty, and he had promised her the world.

"What I need," Zhukov said, "is for you and your Whalers to break into the crypt."

Galia gasped. She couldn't help it.

"I want you to steal their bones," Zhukov continued. "The bones of the Brigmore witches, from which we can carve our destiny."

7

"The best sartorial designers from across the Empire were lured to the boutiques of Drapers Ward, where they found themselves freed from the need to solicit patrons. In fact they were elevated to high society, courted and pampered. The powerful and influential began to frequent the new Drapers Ward, paying any cost to be seen in the latest styles."

— THE HISTORY OF DRAPERS WARD
Excerpt from *The Districts of Dunwall*, a recent book

The days and nights passed quietly and for Emily, far, far, too slowly. The guard escort Corvo had assigned her quickly became annoying, although she knew her father had nothing but the best intentions for her.

She spent nearly the whole of the second day trying to shake off her escort around the palace. It worked, too.

On day three, she found that her escort had been expanded from one guard to two.

As a result, all she could do was wait for news. It felt as if nothing was happening, that she was locked away in Dunwall Tower while events raced ahead of her, outside in the city. She didn't go out at night, not while the hunt for the gang was on—it was too great a risk, not from the grave robbers, but likely from her own forces. The City Watch and the Wrenhaven River Patrol had boosted their numbers, calling in plenty of men for some well-earned overtime as they increased their surveillance of the city, and, with the Overseers, kept close watch on the city's cemeteries and burial sites.

While Emily knew she would have been able to get around the uniformed branches of her Imperial forces without too much difficulty, the anonymous secret agents of the Royal Spymaster were the real problem. How many Corvo had sent out—how many he even *had*, come to think of it—Emily didn't know, but what she did know was that they would be good. Very, very good. Under Corvo's leadership, they had the most advanced and formidable training in the whole Empire. She knew that because it was the same training *she* had received.

So the chances of being seen—of being caught—were exponentially higher. Her nights, for the first time in weeks, were spent in Dunwall Tower.

During the day there was work to do, of course. The duties and demands placed upon an Empress were constant. The ship of state, as her chamberlain was fond of reminding her, needed a captain at the wheel.

So there were documents to sign, dignitaries to meet and greet and with whom to share tea. Already, diplomatic overtures had arrived from the Duke Luca Abele, ruler of Serkonos. The Duke was proposing an official state visit sometime in the next year or so, perhaps to coincide with the annual day of remembrance for Emily's mother, Jessamine. The Serkonan officials had brought her a gift, too—a journal, bound in the finest hand-tooled leather their country could produce. Emily had been genuinely pleased at such a personal touch, and she promised to make good use of it.

She accepted her responsibilities without complaint, burying herself in the work. Anything was better than sitting around doing nothing. For once in her life, being the Empress was a welcome distraction, as was the company of Wyman.

Of Corvo himself she saw little, and when they did meet it was for official updates on the search, shared with High Overseer Khulan, Captain Ramsey of the City Watch, Commander Kittredge of the Wrenhaven River Patrol, and her friend and advisor, Jameson Curnow.

Not that there was anything to report. There had been, so far, no suspicious activity around the cemeteries, and life in the city went on as it always had. News of the desecration of the old merchant graves had reached the public, despite the best efforts of Corvo to keep it out of the pages of the city's newspaper, *The Dunwall Courier*.

For three consecutive days the paper ran a feature, complete with crime-scene etchings showing the dug-up graves, but with no progress in the investigation and no repeats of the crime, the reports quickly ceased. Emily had hoped the coverage would fade away, so she was not displeased, but the suddenness of the shift was surprising. Perhaps Corvo had gone down and had a word or two with the editor.

Whispers continued around the Imperial Court and nobles of the city for a little while longer, before conversation began to settle on a far more interesting and exciting topic. The most important social event in the Dunwall calendar was approaching—the annual Masquerade Ball at the Boyle Mansion.

*

Four days after the incident with the grave robbers, Emily sat with Corvo and Wyman at breakfast in the Empress's private apartments. Wyman delicately sipped tea while Corvo drank short shots of strong coffee, the thick, viscous black liquid lightened only slightly with honey-sweetened goat's milk.

The pair were talking about something exceedingly dull—the regional spice and food festivals of Karnaca—and Emily half-listened while she went through the pile of the day's correspondence that had been delivered to the table in a red leather valise. The cluster of letters was fat, but there didn't seem to be anything of particular urgency or importance. The chamberlain could deal with it all, as was his duty.

Then she stopped, midway through the stack of papers. She had come to a large envelope, the stiff paper a brilliant scarlet, the edges trimmed with gold, the front addressed to the Empress of the Isles in a huge, spidery hand.

She recognized it at once. She had received an identical letter on this day each year for the last thirteen years. Initially, she had received it as it was intended—hand-delivered by a coiffured page, bringing the letter directly from the desk of the person who sent it while the ink was still drying on the envelope. By long-established tradition, the Empress of the Isles was the first person in Dunwall to receive the annual invitation to the Masquerade Ball.

And by long-established tradition, the Empress was also the first person to decline.

After five years of this, Emily had instructed the chamberlain to collect the invitation at the Tower Gates, taking it from the page and slipping it into her correspondence box. The formality of receiving the stupid red envelope was ridiculous, given that she could never attend.

She frowned at the envelope, and slipped it out of the pile, holding it up to the light.

Corvo and Wyman stopped their conversation and turned in her direction.

"That time of year again, I see," Corvo said. He smiled as he emptied yet another tiny beaker of coffee in a single gulp.

Emily crinkled her nose as she turned the envelope around, reading the address of the sender that, like the writing on the front, covered nearly the entire back of the envelope in a hand that was barely legible. The last remaining Lady Boyle was getting old, she supposed. How many years had it been since Emily had seen her?

Wyman leaned forward. "Aren't you going to open it?"

She sighed and tossed the envelope onto the breakfast table, one gilded corner landing in a plate of pickled redjawed hagfish eyes.

"What's the point?" she asked, slumping back in her chair. "Every year the Empress—or Emperor, take your pick—is invited to the Boyle Masquerade. Every year, the Emperor—sorry, *Empress*—has to decline." Emily shook her head.

"But that's the tradition," Wyman said.

Emily raised an eyebrow. "Tradition is an *ass*."

"Says Emily Drexel Lela Kaldwin the First, of the House of Kaldwin, Empress of the Isles," Corvo said from somewhere behind the rim of his coffee beaker.

"You know what I mean," Emily said, folding her arms. "I'd have liked to have been able to go, even just the once. I would have, of course, if my mother was still alive. As an Imperial Princess and heir it would have been my introduction to Dunwall society, after all."

Corvo *hrmmed*. "You wouldn't like it," he said.

Wyman grinned, turning to the Royal Protector. "You've been?"

Corvo frowned. "Once."

"And?"

Corvo shrugged. "It didn't go so well."

Wyman laughed, then turned back to Emily. "What happened to the famous Boyle sisters, anyway? There's only one living at the mansion now, isn't there?"

Emily nodded. "Yes, just one left now," she said, picking the envelope up again, shaking the vinegary liquid from it, and finally opening it with a bread knife. She slid the card out, cast her eye over it, then passed it across for Wyman to take a look. Wyman took the card and read the text aloud in an exaggerated, formal accent.

"The Lady Esma Boyle requests the company of her most illustrious Imperial Majesty, Empress Emily Kaldwin, for a masquerade ball to take place at the Great Hall of the Boyle Estate, on the Fifteenth Day of the Month of Darkness, 1851."

Corvo reached his hand out and Wyman handed the card over.

"Lady Esma Boyle," Corvo said quietly. "Last of the three."

"Lady Waverly is still alive, isn't she?" Emily asked.

Corvo nodded. "Yes, but she's not in Dunwall. She hasn't been since that business with Lord Brisby."

Wyman looked from Corvo to Emily and back again. "I'm sorry, you'll have to fill me in on that one. Who's Lord Brisby?"

"A criminal, is what," Emily said. "And Waverly too."

Wyman's eyes widened in surprise, but Emily didn't say any more, her features set. Wyman turned back to Corvo, who sighed.

"Well, Brisby was a lord in the court of Empress Jessamine," Corvo said. "He was obsessed with Lady Waverly Boyle, kidnapping her on the night of the Boyle Masquerade of 1837. He took her out of the city, back to his old family estate on an island somewhere. She hasn't been back since."

"Good riddance," Emily said. She folded her arms.

Wyman glanced at Corvo.

"And…?"

Corvo frowned, then continued. "And Waverly Boyle was the mistress of Hiram Burrows."

"Oh? *Oh!*" Wyman said, quickly disappearing behind a raised teacup.

"Yes," Emily said. "*Oh.*"

"A few years later," Corvo said, "Lord Brisby himself disappeared—apparently he left on a ship heading back to Gristol, but he never got off the boat when it docked. There was a rumor that Waverly arranged for his disappearance, in order to take over his estate."

"And did she?" Wyman asked.

Corvo shrugged. "Have him killed? Nobody could find any evidence. But yes, she had his estate. She's still up there, on her own. Doing quite well, I imagine, given how rich Brisby was."

Emily stood from the table.

"Excuse me," she said. "I need to take a walk."

She spent the day wandering around Dunwall Tower. With Corvo in the palace, she was finally free of her constant escort, and savored the isolation.

As she stalked the halls, she passed courtiers who bowed and curtsied as she went by, turning to face the Empress as a matter of respect, the conversations suddenly snuffed out by her presence. Emily acknowledged them all, but it did little to help her mood, because she knew what they were all talking about. Some had even been holding their own red envelopes in their hands.

The Boyle Masquerade.

Eventually she found a quiet alcove and stood for a moment, gazing up at a larger-than-life portrait of one of her predecessors. She peered at the nameplate at the bottom of the frame.

"Empress Larisa Olaskir, 1783 to 1801," she read. "Huh. No masquerade ball for you, either." Then she lowered her voice, adding a rasp in a vague, mocking impersonation of the Royal Protector. "*But don't worry, you wouldn't like it.*"

She stood there for a moment longer, silently screaming in her head.

After that she felt better.

Then, on a whim, she headed for the Great Hall, and upon arrival instantly regretted it. The large space—usually reserved for grand events thrown for visiting dignitaries—was dominated by a table that ran the entire length of the chamber, big enough to seat two hundred people. But, as was tradition once the famous red envelopes arrived, for the next two weeks it would be turned into a tailor's showcase and haberdashery.

Half of the massive table was buried under acres of cloth from all over the Empire—bolts of colorful shot silk from Karnaca, rolls of heavy, dark velvet from Tyvia, woven woolen cloth from Morley with its characteristic fine-checked patterns. A half-dozen seamstresses and three male tailors—at least half of whom were contracted from Dunwall's famous fashion district, Drapers Ward—bustled about the room, fussing over the fabrics and patterns. As Emily entered, they fell silent and turned to bow to her.

She gritted her teeth, gave them a smile, and told them to carry on. She moved to the other side of the table and walked along it, her eyes drinking in the fabulous display.

Beyond the cloth and fabrics she found a set of large,

leather-bound folios, lying open. Emily wandered over to them and began leafing through the pages, her eye moving over the patterns for elaborate costumes—golden lions, purple peacocks, multicolored birds of paradise. Each design page was beautifully engraved with a color illustration of what the finished masquerade costume would look like.

Beside the folios, at the far end of the table, were the masks. It was just a selection of what was possible, a demonstration of the fine craftsmanship—no courtier would ever wear a ready-made mask. On the contrary, the Boyle Masquerade was the chance to *really* show off, to go all out with a fanciful, custom-made outfit.

Emily sighed as she picked up an elaborate headdress of a lion, holding it up to eye level. The face was a patchwork of yellow and orange corduroy, and the shaggy mane was shot through with gold thread.

The ball would be magnificent.

She knew that. She'd never been, but it was the same every year—two weeks of preparation at the court, and then for two weeks after the ball was over it was the only topic of conversation.

And each year it drove her crazy. One annual event, one glamorous night of music and dance, a chance to relax and mingle with the nobility of the city.

And she couldn't go.

She stared into the fake glass eyes of the lion—the real eye slots hidden in the folds of yellow beneath.

She couldn't go.

Or… *could* she?

Emily glanced down at the other masks on the table. There was a bear, a frog, a fox, and something with bulging, multifaceted eyes and long antennae that might have been a butterfly. There were also two bird masks—a blue and red creature with a long, curved bill that stuck out at least a foot from the nose of the wearer, and a smaller, more compact mask, a mask with iridescent black feathers and a stylized short beak. It looked like a black sparrow.

A thought flickered into life. A thought she liked. She fanned its flames a little, feeling it grow in her mind.

She *could* go to the masquerade, because it was exactly that—a masquerade. Everyone would be in elaborate outfits of all kinds, from simple half-masks or token efforts right up to the more complicated constructions on display here—masks that covered the entire *head*. Of course, she would have to keep the mask on the whole time, but if she did… nobody would know it was her.

Would they?

Emily sighed. No, it wouldn't work. She would have no invitation. They were all personalized, and each one needed to be presented to the footman on attendance at the door.

Unless she could come to some arrangement with Lady Boyle? Perhaps the host could be in on the secret, and she could be let in… discretely.

Corvo. He knew Lady Boyle better than anyone, and as Royal Protector, he would need to know, too. In fact, he could come with her as her escort, in a costume of his own. At least that was what Emily told herself. And the more she told herself, the more logical the plan became.

She left the Great Hall at a trot, ignoring the bows of the seamstresses and tailors as she headed for Corvo's chambers.

$\underline{\overline{8}}$

GREAVES AUXILIARY WHALE SLAUGHTERHOUSE 5, SLAUGHTERHOUSE ROW, DUNWALL
11th Day, Month of Darkness, 1851

"Bonecharms, a sailor's blessing, they say. The carving itself is a practice from long back, passed from salty-dogs to greenhorns still getting their sea legs. In old times, sailors cut into the tusks of ice seals and into the arm-long fangs of bears that roamed the islets north of Tyvia. Once the whaling trade began, the practitioners began engraving the bones of those great beasts, rendering charms that sing in the night and grant some small boon, increasing a lover's vigor or providing defense against pregnancy."

— *BONECHARMS*
Excerpt from a book on sailing traditions and scrimshaw

Rinaldo crept down the stairwell that led to the slaughterhouse's basement storerooms, grateful that these stairs were stone, not the rattling, rusting ironwork of the galleries that ran a tracery above the factory floor. Here, at least, he could move without risk of being heard.

He'd waited a few days before investigating, in the

meantime working with the other men to clean out the biggest of the old whale oil vats, all the while keeping an eye on Galia and the Boss. The pair seemed to spend most of their time away from the others, either up in the old control room or down in the basement toward which Rinaldo was heading. He had watched them carefully and, picking his moment, had managed to steal an old set of keys from the control room cupboard. He only hoped that one of the myriad keys on the ring would work when he needed it to.

He continued down the stairwell.

Rinaldo really didn't get it—who the hell was the Boss anyway, and what kind of hold did he have on his old friend? Galia seemed to be under his spell, unaware how plain *creepy* the man was, like a walking scarecrow. And to make matters worse, the man in the hat was revealing nothing—and Galia had the gall to defend that.

For the other men, it didn't matter much. They were hired mercenaries—this wasn't exactly the greatest incarnation of the Whalers that had ever been assembled, but they did the work and took their coin and didn't say much about it. Although they shared Rinaldo's view of their strange new boss, they wouldn't go near him. It wasn't much of an issue, though—most of the time the Boss just stood behind the big windows of the control room, motionless, staring down at them. It was impossible to tell if he was watching the gang at work, or if he was even awake behind the scarf and goggles.

Maybe he was moonstruck, Rinaldo thought. *Or maybe there was no "maybe" about it.*

But for Rinaldo, see, things were different. He wasn't in it for the money.

Well, no, scratch that. He *was* in it for the money. In fact, he knew full well that was what motivated *everyone* in the world—coin. But he was also doing this for Galia. He owed her, and it was a debt he didn't mind servicing, not one little bit.

She'd found him, picked him up—hell, saved his life, of that he knew full well. And sure, he, in turn, had helped her. Their reunion after all those years had been the saving of them both—if he hadn't wandered into the Golden Cat that random night, he would be nothing but a whisper in the Void now, doomed to wander it forever.

So he was doing this for Galia, but she was giving him nothing, *nothing*, in return. No information, not a single notion about what was going on. She was just sticking with her new friend in the coat and the hat, telling Rinaldo to trust her, while slowly, surely, cutting him out of the picture.

She'd changed. It was that man. That *thing*, he had a hold on her. Some kind of hold. What, and how, Rinaldo had no idea.

But he was going to find out.

He reached the bottom of the stairs and entered a short subterranean passage. The cement was damp and crumbling, and the door at the end of the passage, thanks maybe to subsidence or just general neglect, didn't quite fit the frame—certainly not as well as it had when the factory was a hive of activity, the whale oil harvested hot from the living carcasses of the great beasts as they swung in their cradles above the overflow vats.

Rinaldo slid up to the door. It was steel, with a wheel lock in the center, more like the door from a ship. Beyond, Rinaldo guessed, would be storage vats, and the metal door was designed to seal the room beyond in case of leakage. It was crooked, and there was an inch-wide gap between the frame and the middle hinge. Rinaldo slid up to the gap and looked through.

He tried—and failed—to suppress a shiver as he saw what was inside the storeroom. Because Rinaldo was many things, and he'd done a lot he'd regretted, things of which he wasn't proud, but, that was the life he had chosen. It was too late now to turn a new leaf, even if he wanted to.

But grave robbing. That was… well, it was pretty low. Give him a knife, give him a target—give him a *mission*—and Rinaldo would carry out his orders to the letter. That was how it was supposed to work. As a Whaler, he had a purpose, something meaningful. But this? Looting the dead? Dragging their corpses back here for the wraith in the coat to do… whatever it was he was doing?

That was pushing Rinaldo a little too far. Perhaps if he knew *what* they were doing, what they were working toward, then maybe he'd understand. Maybe he'd even be able to be more help than just being another one of the gang. Galia should know that.

Had she really changed so much?

No, she hadn't. It was *him*. The Boss. The black-coated weirdo with his red glasses.

It was time for answers.

Unfortunately, as Rinaldo stared with ever-growing horror at the scene behind the door, he wasn't sure he was quite ready for what he was going to find.

The pressed steel door was nearly off its hinges, but it was still locked, the pressure wheel in the middle unmoving under Rinaldo's hands. He stepped back, frowned at the mechanism, then reached into his tunic for the key ring. He extracted it, holding the jumble of keys with his free hand to keep them still and silent. Then he began to try them out.

The second one worked. *Well, that was easy.* Rinaldo smiled and carefully stowed the ring back inside his tunic. Then he spun the wheel, and pulled the door open, careful not to make a sound. It was heavy and leaning, and it was difficult to move it without the thing squeaking. The Boss was up in the control room, but while Rinaldo had assumed that Galia was up there, too, he hadn't actually seen her in a while.

One thing he didn't want to be was *caught*.

The storeroom was lit dimly by the bluish glow of an electric oil lamp. The space had been cleared, the debris and detritus piled against one wall. At the far end of the long, low space were two huge, bullet-shaped pressurized tanks, studded with rivets as big as dinner plates, capped with giant wheel locks and covered in a mind-boggling array of valves and pipes.

But this wasn't what held Rinaldo's eye. He stepped into the room, letting the heavy door swing closed behind him, and he looked down at the boxes on the floor. Four of the six coffins they'd brought in from their little graveyard raid lay in a line. The other two were up on trestles, and from his position by the door, Rinaldo could see that both were open. Curiously, there was little smell in the room—anything malodorous emanating from the caskets was hidden under the suffocating, dusty scent of decaying cement and wet metal.

Between the two great oil tanks, three long tables had been built out of more trestles. The tables were piled with bundles of something that looked, in the blue light, to be cloth, and next to those, long shards that looked almost ceramic, pale in the light and apparently arranged in some kind of order. In the dim light, it was impossible to make out any details, and Rinaldo cursed himself that he hadn't thought to bring a hooded lantern.

On the far left table sat some kind of mechanical apparatus, with a series of concentric circles mounted on a brass frame, with a collection of levers spaced all around it. It was a lens of some kind—perhaps the tools of a clockmaker. Rinaldo hadn't seen anything like it before.

He frowned, and tiptoed up past the coffins to the trestle tables, his eyes drawn all the while to the two raised, open caskets. As he reached them, he took a breath and looked inside. The first was empty, save for a layer of sticky dust.

The second, however, was still occupied.

At least… it was *partially* occupied.

Rinaldo grimaced as he moved around to the second box. There was a body inside, all right—a desiccated cadaver in clothing that was opulent but faded, antique and dusty.

But the body had been disturbed. It was *incomplete*, missing both arms, one leg… and the head. As he watched, a beetle, its carapace shining wetly, emerged from the mummified neck and crawled away under the body.

He shuddered, unable to tear his eyes from the sight, wondering what had happened to the man. Some kind of accident that had torn off his limbs and head? He supposed it was possible. Surely the Boss hadn't removed them. That was just… it was just *wrong*.

Then Rinaldo turned his attention back to the tables. Up close, he could see what the bundles were, what the ceramic shards were.

The bundles were body parts, brown and wet and oozing, the old, dead flesh looking more like moldering bread. There was a pile that looked like butcher's offcuts, and in front of this, an arm, intact from shoulder to hand. The arm was pinned to the table, the forearm sliced lengthwise with more pins holding back the crumbling, soap-like flesh. Normally there were two bones in a man's forearm, but there was only one remaining in this specimen.

And the ceramic shards weren't pottery, but bone. Human bones, most likely the skeleton from the first corpse, the inhabitant of the now-empty coffin. The bones were neatly disassembled and arranged, so that ones of similar sizes were grouped together. At the back of the table sat two skulls. One was intact, the other had a large circular piece missing from the cranium—in fact, nearly the entire top of the skull had been sliced clean off.

Rinaldo breathed out slowly as he looked over the remains. The Boss—what, was he some kind of natural philosopher? That would make sense. They worked with bones, didn't they? The way the skeletal remains were arranged, it was obvious they had been sorted. For study, perhaps?

He moved to the third table, where the complex brass instrument sat. It was scientifical. Had to be. Rinaldo frowned at the device, then moved to stand behind it and looked down, through the concentric array of the lens.

The device was trained on an ivory-colored object about the size of Rinaldo's palm, which lay on a brass platform on the table. The object looked like it was made of several long pieces of bone, bound together to form an octagonal shape. The inside corners were joined by other bone fragments, like a crazy wagon wheel, the whole thing held together by shining copper wire.

Rinaldo ducked his head around the apparatus to look at the object with unaided eyes. As he examined it, he noticed more of the objects stacked around the table— perhaps a dozen, all more or less the same size and shape, although he could see there was some variation in the bones that formed the internal "spokes."

What the ivories were, Rinaldo had no idea. They looked like something you might find in one of those ancient shrines that were still scattered around in inaccessible places, altars which were supposed to be offerings to some mythological nonsense.

With a sickening feeling in his stomach, he understood why the Boss had wanted the bodies. He was carving these… these things, these *trinkets*, from the bones, and assembling them down here, on the table. The thought made Rinaldo uneasy.

Death was nothing new to him, and he'd seen sights far more gory than the mummified remains of decades-old dead. But using the bodies to make these things? That felt… wrong. That was interfering in something that was supposed to be left alone. He couldn't quite explain the feeling that grew in his stomach, a ball of cold, rolling and rolling.

It was time to have a little chat with Galia. She'd been down here, she'd seen all this, and still she hadn't said anything, not even to her old pal Rinaldo.

Well, maybe it was time she did.

Rinaldo cast an eye over the small stacks of carvings, and, careful not to topple them, he slid one from the bottom of a stack. As his fingertips touched it, he felt a spark, and he gasped, but then the feeling was gone.

With the weird bonecharm thing in his pocket, Rinaldo retreated from the storeroom, re-locking the door behind him.

$\overline{9}$

"It is said that the Office of the Royal Spymaster has existed for as long as there have been Emperors and Empresses. However, in the earliest days of the Empire, this position existed in secrecy."

— THE ROYAL SPYMASTER
Excerpt from a historical record of government positions and ranks

Emily knocked on the door of the chambers that now served as the dual office of the Royal Protector and Royal Spymaster, but there was no reply from within. She knew Corvo didn't really like being stuck there, behind the desk, frequently complaining that he was supposed to be at the Empress's side, not pushing paper.

If only he was bloody well at my side now, she thought.

But when the two Imperial offices had combined, the nature of his job had changed. He was no longer simply her protector. As Royal Spymaster, he had a network of agents to coordinate. With the combined titles came more responsibilities, and *more* of the hated paperwork.

And sometimes that meant he needed to sit behind

a desk, much to his annoyance. However, the office was empty. The door was locked.

Checking that the corridor was clear, Emily reached down into her collar and pulled on the silver chain around her neck, at the end of which was a key—a skeleton master that would open any door in Dunwall Tower. She didn't really like using it—and she rarely did—but the key came with her rank, and it had proven useful on more than one occasion.

That didn't stop it feeling like she was breaking and entering.

As she turned the key in the door, she shook her head and took a deep breath. Emily was the Empress of the Isles, and Dunwall Tower was her personal property, and she could go where she bloody well wanted.

At least that was what she told herself as she opened the door and stepped inside. She just hoped that she could find something—a schedule, perhaps—that would tell her where Corvo was. She didn't want to have the palace guard running after him, if they didn't have to.

The office was a large, L-shaped room, the space dwarfing the furniture that sat in it. There was a big oak desk set at an angle against one corner, two deep armchairs in front of it, a high-backed chair behind. The desk was framed by bookcases on one wall and a huge landscape painting on the other which showed a bustling port city nestled at the base of a vast mountain, the rocky peak of which was split into two uneven triangular shards.

The city of Karnaca, capital of Serkonos—Corvo's reminder of home.

On the other side of the room, opposite the desk, sat Corvo's bed, normally hidden behind a set of ornate folded wooden screens. These screens had been moved and arranged more or less in the center of the chamber, shielding the spot where, Emily remembered, there was normally a table and couches.

Emily glanced around, then moved to the desk. Corvo kept his workplace tidy, and what little was on the desk didn't seem of much interest—some papers that looked like requisition orders, a letter from the High Overseer informing the Royal Spymaster that there had been progress in preparing something that wasn't actually specified. It also apologized for a delay, again without identifying the topic.

Well that's not exactly helpful, Emily thought.

She hesitated before checking the drawers, but she pulled them out anyway. More papers, but not much. Nothing that looked as if it had been touched in a while. Closing the drawers, Emily stood with her hands on her hips. She looked around the room, and her eye was caught again by the wooden screens.

She walked over to them, then around them. She'd been right. The table was still there. Next to it were the long couch she remembered, and another couple of deep armchairs. Emily took a step closer.

No, this *wasn't* the table that was normally there. That one had been pushed away and sat over by the far wall, on it nothing but an audiograph player and a candelabra. Corvo had brought another table in from somewhere, a huge square thing that looked to Emily at least ten feet on each side, if not more. She looked down on it, and her jaw dropped in awe.

On the table was a map of Dunwall, laid out in fine detail. She wasn't sure of the scale—there didn't appear to be any writing along the edge, or a helpful legend like in an atlas—but as she leaned over it she could see that every street, alley, and building was marked—even individual message boxes and horse posts.

The map was breathtaking, a work of art. It was by far the most detailed, the most accurate map of the city she had ever seen. There were markers on it—little discs of carved wood, each about the size of an old penny. They were stained in four different colors—red, blue, green, and black—and were distributed around the map at specific points, with red and green tokens at city cemeteries, blue along both north and south banks of the river, and black scattered apparently at random.

It didn't take Emily long to figure out what they represented—they were the various Imperial forces working in the city—red and black for the Overseers and City Watch keeping discrete vigil at the cemeteries and graveyards, blue for the Wrenhaven River Patrol down by the water, and black, Emily guessed, being Corvo's royal spy network. She looked up from the map, impressed, and blew out her cheeks. Her breath caught in her throat when she saw what was tacked to the back of the wooden screens.

More maps and charts, showing different parts of the city at different levels of detail and scale. She stepped closer for a better look, recognized maritime maps of the river harbor, showing in closer detail the various islands and outcroppings at the river mouth. There was a map of the neighboring city, Potterstead, although far less detailed than the great map of Dunwall on the table.

One in particular caught Emily's eye. She peered closely at it, then had to step away and look over the whole parchment to understand what it showed. She realized it wasn't a map, but a plan—a schematic of a large, symmetrical house. A mansion, clearly… something grand, but under repair.

The plan was marked in two colors, showing the layout and proposals for repair, and the sheet was stamped along the bottom with permits from the city planning office. Emily peered at the stamps, trying to figure out the location of the house. It was somewhere in the Mutcherhaven District, outside the city walls, along the course of the Wrenhaven River.

Casting her eye over the plans, she noticed there was an audiograph card pinned to the top corner of the board, along with a note in a handwriting that Emily didn't recognize.

BRIGMORE SURVEILLANCE REPORT
10th Day, Month of Darkness, 1851

Of course. Brigmore Manor—the old estate, several miles outside of Dunwall. Emily knew that the place had been long abandoned, but she wasn't sure if it was even still standing. According to the permit stamps, though, something was left, at least, as the estate and house had been purchased in the last year or so and was being repaired.

She glanced at the audiograph again. The note pinned to it was dated just yesterday. Intrigued, Emily took it and went over to the audiograph player by the wall. She slotted the card into the machine, then looked about again, walking around the wooden screens so she could see the rest of the chamber, instinct telling her to double-check that nobody—like Corvo, for example—had come in while she had been snooping behind the screens.

She went back to the audiograph and hit play. The voice that rang out surprised her.

"Jameson Curnow reporting on the situation at Brigmore Manor. It's as we thought—there's word going around that something big is going down at the house in just a couple of nights. We've got men out in the key taverns—the Randy Whaler, the Seven of Bells, even the ruins of the old Hound Pits Pub. Also at the Golden Cat. Plenty of chatter there—seems there's a new group looking for more members—they're offering good money, perhaps trying to attract those who were in the old street gangs, pull them out of the woodwork.

"We don't have any names yet," Jameson continued, "and we don't know what they plan to do, but talk is this gang had hit a graveyard, so we're fairly sure it's the same lot. The Wrenhaven River Patrol have done a good job—some suspicious activity has been seen at one of the old, abandoned whale processing plants on Slaughterhouse Row—the Greaves Auxiliary Slaughterhouse Five, to be precise. We have surveillance planned, but I advise caution—we don't want them knowing we're onto them. As you've suggested, let's watch them and see what they're up to. There's got to be more to it than just robbing graves. If we catch them in the act, maybe we can learn what their real plans are.

"I'll file another report after I meet with Commander Kittredge again. They're doing their best, but they're not spies, that's for sure. They get any closer they may as well just walk up to the slaughterhouse door and ask if anyone's at home.

"I remain your loyal servant, Jameson Curnow."

The audiograph clicked and the card poked out of the bottom of the machine. Emily looked at it, thoughts running through her mind as she considered what was going on.

She was angry, but she was also excited. She'd made a number of discoveries. The first was that Jameson Curnow was a member of Corvo's spy agency. He was her friend, her trusted advisor, but he also stuck to Corvo's side, constantly.

Well, that explained that.

Had they really located the gang's headquarters? There were plenty of hiding places in the city, given that there was so much construction and demolition still going on, even this many years after the Rat Plague. That they were using an abandoned slaughterhouse didn't surprise her, although they must have chosen it for a reason. Did they need the space, perhaps?

The longer she stood by the audiograph, however, the more she fumed. Jameson's report was a day old. In that time, she'd had two status meetings with Corvo, Jameson, the High Overseer, and Ramsey and Kittredge. None of them had brought anything to report, and Corvo had said that they were no closer to discovering the gang's location.

That was patently untrue, Emily knew that now. Corvo and his spies—including the oh-so-innocent Jameson Curnow—had known about the gang all along.

That was it. Emily was furious. She swore, loudly, her voice echoing in the chamber. Then she paced the room behind the screens, rolling her neck, her hands on her hips.

She closed her eyes, trying to figure out what to do. She stopped pacing, and when she opened her eyes she found she was looking again at the plans of Brigmore Manor.

Brigmore Manor. Jameson himself said they had it under watch, and Corvo's plan—whatever that was—was going ahead.

So... that was out. Too much of a risk, and Emily didn't have enough information. Wandering around a construction site outside the city seemed like a waste of time without knowing what she was looking for.

She turned back to the audiograph, and thought a moment. She slipped the punch card from the bottom, fed it back into the top, and played the message through again.

There. Greaves Auxiliary Slaughterhouse 5, Slaughterhouse Row.

She knew where that was. And that was where the grave robbers were.

It was time to put a stop to this—to act where Corvo apparently wouldn't.

Perhaps it was her anger pushing her, and as she stalked from Corvo's chambers back to her own apartments, part of Emily knew it. She had been cooped up in the Tower for too long, the boredom and frustration driving her out of her mind. She knew this, too.

But… she was capable. More than capable. She needed to find out what was happening in her city, and Corvo and his agents needed all the help they could get. Emily had seen the grave robbers, had taken their measure.

She knew she could beat them.

Which meant it was time to go out on an investigation of her own. To Slaughterhouse Row. To Greaves Auxiliary Slaughterhouse 5.

It was time to get some answers.

10

GREAVES AUXILIARY WHALE SLAUGHTERHOUSE 5, SLAUGHTERHOUSE ROW, DUNWALL
12th Day, Month of Darkness, 1851

"The Greaves Whale House grew rapidly, absorbing rivals until it dominated the trade. At its peak, the operation employed over 300 workers, not including the children who filled minor, and often tragic, roles. Those associated with the refinery were recognizable by their head-to-toe industrial leather uniforms and the masks they wore to protect against fumes."

— THE GREAVES WHALE HOUSE
Excerpt from a book on well-established
companies in Dunwall

Emily reached Slaughterhouse Row without much difficulty, thanks to her rough knowledge of the positions of the City Watch, the Wrenhaven River Patrol, and Corvo's spies, all courtesy of the big map in the Royal Spymaster's chamber. When she encountered patrols, however, she was forced to double-back and take alternative routes, to duck and hide, high up on the rooftops as the searchlights thrown from the boats played across buildings on each bank.

As a result, it took longer to reach the district than she would have liked.

The Greaves Auxiliary Whale Slaughterhouse 5 was a huge building, as tall as it was long, occupying roughly the same acreage as a city block, its name and number a fading stencil painted high on the side. The back of the huge edifice protruded over the river, the facility possessing its own wharf and boat dock, allowing the whales to be maneuvered directly into the factory through a pair of massive double doors. Once they were inside, the oil would be extracted, slowly—and painfully—from the creatures who were still alive, their skin drying as they hung suspended in the frames above vast overflow vats.

The thought did not please Emily, and, although she could never say so as Empress, she was secretly pleased that the whaling industry was slowly dying out. New power technologies were coming on line, thanks to the work of Sokolov and Piero, the two old scientists forming a reluctant and fractious—if rather successful—partnership at the Academy of Natural Philosophy.

The industry's decline was also responsible for the slow disintegration of Slaughterhouse Row. As she looked up at the towering side of the building, the once-proud company name now a dim palimpsest, Emily wondered how long it had been empty. Ten years? Maybe even longer. The place was intact, but decrepit.

And insecure. Easy enough to sneak into.

Ever cautious, she chose to enter via the river side, jumping the wall that ran along the embankment and clambering over the rusting girders that supported the underside of the wharf. Here it was near total darkness, and the going was difficult, but eventually she reached the giant dockside doors, grateful not to have fallen into the river.

The main doors were closed. There was a smaller door set into the wall for factory workers to use, and as Emily clambered up to the top side of the wharf and got closer, she paused to reconsider her options.

Because the factory was *not* empty.

Closer now, she could hear from within the sounds of work—hammering, metal on metal, and chains being dragged. The factories were, as a matter of course, insulated for sound, not so much because the process of whale oil extraction and processing itself was loud, but to save nearby residents from the terrible whistles and screams of the poor animals as they were harvested.

Emily moved up to the small inset door and pressed her ear against it. There were *lots* of people inside, working.

What in all the Isles is going on?

That ruled out entering through the small door. She looked around for another option, her eyes falling on the nearby fire escape, the metal framework of which spiraled up and up the flat side of the factory, platforms at intervals corresponding to the internal floors of the building, each with a door. The lowest platform was high above her head, the bottom rungs of the retractable ladder tantalizingly out of reach.

Then Emily spied fat iron pipes coming out of the wall just a little farther along, running horizontally along the length of the building and disappearing into the darkness. Waste pipes, perhaps.

They would do nicely.

Steeling herself, she ran, heading toward the pipes. She jumped, planting a foot on the topmost pipe to propel herself higher, stretching to catch the bottom edge of the fire escape ladder. She grabbed it with her padded gloves, but the ladder remained resolutely where it was, rusted in place.

Swinging in mid-air, Emily wasted no time. Hanging from both arms, she twisted around to face the factory wall and began to rock herself back and forth to gain momentum. Then, judging the timing, she released her grip, kicked off the factory wall and turned in the air, grabbing the platform above her and—momentum on her side—pulling herself up onto it.

From here the going was easy. She swung around onto the escape stairs and headed up, not stopping until she reached the door leading to the very top floor, a dizzying height above the street.

The door was jammed but, under steady pressure from Emily's shoulder, it eventually shuddered open, and she went inside.

Once she was inside the noise was surprising, as was the heat. She had emerged high up on a gantry near the ceiling. It formed a railed gallery that orbited the entire periphery of the slaughterhouse, with black iron stairs branching off at intervals, leading down to a lower platform that ran around the edge of the slaughterhouse offices, themselves a large, multistoried block that rose up from the factory floor, with windows on three sides through which to observe work.

Glancing across, Emily could see no movement behind the windows of the offices. She dropped to her knees, then to her stomach, and slid along the gallery until she was at its lip. She peered over the edge, wincing as the heat from the factory floor rose up, squinting against the bright yellowy-orange light. Sound echoed up from below. She pulled her hood back a little and looked down.

The factory floor was a hive of activity. In the center of the floor was the largest of the overflow whale oil vats, a rectangular pool that must have been a hundred yards on the longest side, by perhaps thirty yards across. This was the source of the heat, and the light.

The vat was filled with a glowing liquid that rolled heavily, like molten glass. Around the edge of the vat stood a number of men, silhouetted by the reddish glow, each holding a long pole that they worked through the thick, roiling substance. Occasionally a bubble broke the surface, the liquid spitting like lava, and revealing a hotter, brighter interior. The men seemed to be wearing protective masks and hoods.

There were others working on the factory floor, assembling a rig adapted from one of the whale frames that would have hung over the oil vat. The frame had been partially disassembled, the cradle and chains separated and laid out as the men dragged pieces of it around, cutting the chain and metal struts into new sections and reassembling the whole thing into something else entirely.

Emily counted twenty men at work. Too many to tackle, even for her.

Then she felt vibrations through her body as she lay on the platform, and glancing across to her left she saw two other men slowly walking along the iron gallery two levels down, deep in conversation as they watched the work below. They were dressed like the rest, although up here their masks hung loosely from straps around their necks, their hoods pulled back. One of the men drank from a canteen, then handed it to his companion.

She couldn't take out the gang, but what she *could* do was gather information. It was clear this wasn't just grave robbing. It was a large operation, far bigger than she had anticipated finding. Anything she could learn would be helpful to Corvo.

Emily pulled back into the shadows against the wall and slipped silently along the gallery, heading toward the stairs and the two men on the platform below.

*

As she approached, she could hear their conversation. Grateful for the deep shadows cast by the light of the boiling vat below, Emily padded forward, then ducked into a corner by the stairs to observe, and to listen.

The second man sucked back on the canteen, then wiped his mouth and handed it back to its owner, who shook it, then turned it upside down. Only a few drops fell out.

"Yeah, thanks, that's just great," he said, screwing the cap back on and swinging it over his shoulder so it hung at his hip.

"Hey, you said I could have a drink. This is bloody hot work."

"I said you could have a drink, yes," the other said, "but I didn't say you could *finish* it."

His friend leaned over the railings, apparently ignoring the other's protests.

"How much longer do you think this will take?"

The other adjusted the canteen strap, and shrugged.

"As long as possible, my friend, as long as possible."

"What?"

"Money, my friend, money. The longer they want me, the more I can collect."

His friend laughed. "You're crazy. The heat has got to your head."

"Nah, you forget, I'm from Karnaca. You think this is hot work? I used to work in the silver mines there. Now *that* was hot. And the dust! You wouldn't believe the dust. Y'know Karnaca has a Dust District? I'm serious. There's a whole quarter of Karnaca buried in the stuff."

"Uh-huh," his friend said. "The imagination of you Serkonans knows no bounds. Dust District? Do me a favor."

The pair laughed.

In the shadows, Emily frowned. The banter wasn't informative, and she was wasting valuable time. What she really needed to do was get down onto the factory floor and take a close look for herself. And to do that, she needed a disguise.

A hooded, masked uniform would work well.

She studied the two men standing at the rail. The one with the canteen was too big—a full head taller than she was. But his shorter, slimmer companion would do—as would his clothes. There was something about that uniform, about that mask, that reminded Emily of something, but she couldn't think what, so she pushed it out of her mind to focus on the task ahead of her.

She waited a moment, watching for the best approach, when her patience was rewarded.

"Here," the man with the canteen said. He slipped the strap over his head, and held the bottle out to his companion. "You drank it, you fill it." He tapped the bottle against the man's shoulder. "Take it from the rain cistern. Should be full after last night."

"Yeah, fine," the smaller man said, taking the bottle and turning around. He headed toward Emily's hiding position by the stairs. She held her breath, tried to make herself as small and as still as possible in the corner. Just feet away, the man grabbed the rail of the stairs and turned his back to her as he began to climb.

He didn't get far. Emily pushed off from the wall, approached him at a fast crouch, and just as the man went for the first step, she wrapped an arm around his throat and squeezed.

A strangled grunt, and the man was out in seconds, his unconscious body slumping against her. She bent over and, with a heave, slid the man across her shoulders. He was heavy—very heavy—but she didn't need to go far. Buckling under his weight, Emily turned and moved back to the corner by the wall. Laying the man down against it, she got to work, undoing the buckles on the leather straps that crisscrossed his tunic, her nose nearly pressed against the mask that hung around his neck.

Then Emily froze.

She glanced up, then jerked her head back as recognition finally dawned. She *had* seen the uniform before. And the mask—yes, the mask... that was etched into her mind forever. She'd been so focused on the moment that she'd somehow not realized who these men were.

The gang were Whalers. The most secretive, the most dangerous, criminal cartel in Dunwall. No mere street gang, the Whalers were mercenaries, assassins-for-hire.

Emily's fingers fell from the man's tunic. Her heart thundered in her chest and she felt a hot, hard lump materialize in her throat.

The Whalers had killed her mother. They had ended her life, right in front of Emily's ten-year-old eyes. Acting on the orders of Hiram Burrows, then the Royal Spymaster, they had helped instigate the coup that had toppled Empress Jessamine Kaldwin, starting a reign of terror that had only ended when Corvo had killed Burrows himself.

She forced herself to breathe, breathe, *breathe*. She didn't have much time. She was here to investigate the gang, to take that information back to Corvo. She was the Empress now, and she was determined to protect her city to the best of her abilities. Yet her eyes felt hot and wet. She inhaled deeply, closed her lids, willed her hands to stop shaking.

Whalers. Back in Dunwall. Now, here, today.

Emily opened her eyes and exhaled slowly, counting the seconds away in her mind. Then she gritted her teeth and redoubled her efforts on the unconscious man's buckles.

Yes, Whalers. She'd made one discovery already—and if anything, the fact that it was this group only strengthened her resolve.

She would not let the Whalers get the better of the Kaldwins, ever again.

The man leaning on the rail stood tall as the footfalls approached him, but he didn't turn around.

"That was fast," he said. When there was no answer, he turned around.

There was nobody there.

Huh. He was imagining things. He looked up, trying to see where his companion had gone. He couldn't have even reached the rain cistern yet. He looked down, then turned around with a start.

His companion was standing right behind him. For some reason he had donned his mask again.

"Hey! Stop creeping around like that," the man at the railing said. "Did you fill the canteen?"

A shake of the head.

"Well, what are you waiting for, an engraved invitation from the Empress of the Isles?" He waved his friend away, then turned back around to the railing.

Suddenly a small but very strong arm encircled his neck and squeezed. The man grabbed at the arm, pulling with both hands as his trachea was forced shut. His knees were kicked out and he could do nothing to stop himself being dragged backward, along the platform, into the shadows.

Satisfied that the man and his friend would sleep for a long while, safely trussed up and locked in a factory office, Emily adjusted the straps of the Whaler's mask around the back of her head to ensure they were secure. She took a deep, rubbery breath, and headed down to the slaughterhouse floor.

Loitering in the shadows, she watched the men at work. Lower down the heat from the vat was impressive, her cheeks burning even behind the thick rubber and leather of the mask. None of the men were speaking, each engrossed in his appointed tasks. Besides, it was too noisy for conversation.

This was no good. Emily wanted to learn what was going on, but with nobody talking, there was nothing here on the slaughterhouse floor that she couldn't have seen from the safety of the iron galleries above.

She considered her options, and didn't like any of them.

Perhaps there was something up in the factory offices. Emily turned and headed back for the stairs, grateful that she hadn't yet been picked out as an intruder.

"You there!"

She stopped, her foot on the bottom stair, and looked up. On the platform above was another of the Whalers, this one wearing a jacket that was a dirty red, instead of the browns and greens of the rest of them—including Emily's borrowed outfit. This Whaler was a woman, the only one in the gang, as far as Emily had been able to tell. She was youngish, maybe in her thirties, the bags under her eyes suggesting that she had led a tough life. She had short blonde hair that looked as if it hadn't been washed in a long while.

Emily held her breath and curled her fists. She could take out one, perhaps, but it would be pointless. There would be a slaughterhouse full of others on top of her in an instant.

She was stuck.

The Whaler rattled down the stairs and came up to her.

"Upstairs," she said. "Now." She stepped around Emily and bent down to grab a discarded section of pipe from the big framework that was under construction. Walking back to the stairs, she began banging the pipe on the iron rails to get the attention of the others over the din of their work.

"It's time!" she yelled, and she waved at the workers to come with her. Then she turned and walked back up the stairs, ignoring Emily, who hadn't moved.

Emily turned and followed, her heart racing as she found herself at the head of the group, following the red-jacketed leader into the office on the second gallery level. The room was big and empty, whatever furniture had been in there long since vanished. The red-jacketed Whaler stepped out to the front and turned around, her arms folded, as the members of her gang assembled before her—with Emily front and center.

Then the door at the back of the room opened and a man walked in.

Emily blew out her cheeks. Her eyes—safely hidden behind the mask—widened in surprise. The man wasn't wearing the Whaler's uniform—in fact, he couldn't have been more different, dressed as he was in his huge, heavy woolen greatcoat. But more remarkable was the face—or rather, the way it was hidden, not by a respirator mask but by a thick fur scarf that must have been wrapped around four or five times. Above the scarf, a huge pair of protective goggles, their circular lenses tinted a bright red. Topping the outfit off was a black hat with a large circular brim.

The man had to be baking in the heat of the factory, yet he showed no signs of discomfort. He stood in front of the group, looking the Whalers over, although it was really impossible to tell where his gaze went. Emily found her own eyes drawn to his goggles, to the curved, fish-eyed reflection of herself at the front of the group.

For a moment her head spun and then…

She sees,
*   A throne.*
*   A knife.*
*   A storm raging over Dunwall Tower. Lightning flashes silently.*
*   All she can hear is laughter, and the laughter is her own.*

Emily blinked and rocked on her heels. She tasted bile at the back of her throat. The vision…

But it was gone. It was never there. She blinked again, focusing on the man who was speaking. It must have been the heat, the sick rubber smell of the mask, the adrenaline pumping through her body.

"The work progresses with great speed," the man said, his voice deep, dry, muffled only a little by the scarf. "The plan proceeds to schedule."

Emily blinked again. The room swam a little, but the feeling was passing.

"We're ready for the next phase of the operation," the man continued, "and for this we need more materials."

There was a muttering from the workers. Beside Emily, a couple of the Whalers—their masks now lifted from their faces—turned to each other and gave looks that didn't seem particularly happy. The red-jacketed leader took a step forward, her hands on her hips.

"Enough!" she yelled. The workers fell silent. "You're being paid more than you're worth, so you'll do just what the Boss says, okay?"

At that she turned to the man in the coat. He merely nodded at her. Then the Whaler turned to face them again, and continued her address.

"We need more materials, so we're going to get them. I'll be leading the expedition, with Rinaldo. It'll be an easy job—straight in, straight out. We'll be hitting a crypt at an estate outside of Dunwall. The place is derelict and abandoned, has been for years, so there won't be anyone to disturb us. But be prepared."

The room fell silent again, all eyes—and masks—turned toward the strange man in the big coat. The red-coated Whaler paused, then nodded.

"Yes," she said, quietly. "We must be prepared."

Then she looked up into the man's red-glassed eyes and she seemed to sway on her feet, just a little. Emily glanced over at the man. She looked into his goggles, and she felt her body sway too, and…

She sees,

The throne room. Dirty. Dusty. The floor is the wrong color. It is wet. It shines in the flashing lightning, like the roof is missing, like the palace is in ruins, open to the night sky.

She sees,

Corvo. He grins. He grins as the man he holds with an arm around the neck struggles and struggles. The prisoner is speaking, waving his arms, but Emily doesn't hear him. All she hears is laughter.

Her laughter.

Corvo grins again and he slits the throat of the prisoner—the High Overseer. The body falls to the floor and his blood spills out onto it, joining the blood spilled from the bodies that line the walls of the throne room, the entire Imperial Court slaughtered by the Royal Protector.

And his Empress.

All she hears is laughter. Her laughter.

The lightning flashes and—

Emily swallowed, the sensation hot, her throat on fire. She didn't feel sick, as such, but... dizzy, disoriented. The world sounded like it was underwater. She was hot. She wanted to pull the mask off, to get a breath of air that was fresher, cooler than the air pulled through the respirator. But she couldn't.

So instead she swallowed again and worked at calming herself, willing her heart to stop racing in case it burst out of her chest. This time she remembered what she saw.

She blinked, snapping out of her reverie as the Whalers began milling about, the leader in red and one of the others, his mask pulled up to reveal a black man with a big grin and chinstrap beard, starting to organize the gang into groups. Emily didn't quite know what was going on— how much of the talk had she missed?—but she shuffled along with the rest and soon found herself in a group of about twelve.

Feeling better, her head clearing, she glanced around and saw that the man in the coat had gone. Emily was relieved. There was something about him she didn't like. It wasn't just his appearance. It was as if there was something *emanating* from him, an aura, or a power. The man had a halo which made Emily sick and made her... see things.

She licked her lips. It was ridiculous, wasn't it? It was the heat, the chemical smell of the respirator. But still, she felt relieved that the man didn't appear to be coming with them.

A few moments later, the Whalers began filing out of the office and back down onto the slaughterhouse floor, then into a storeroom that ran parallel to the main workspace. The storeroom was filled with weapons. The gang moved through, selecting their tools, sheathing knives and strapping small crossbows to their wrists. Emily followed suit, taking a small crossbow.

Be prepared, the man had said.

Prepared for what? The house—Brigmore, Emily knew—was empty and abandoned. Yet the man in the coat, he suspected resistance, didn't he? Did he know about Corvo's plan to meet the opposition there, at the house?

It was too late now. Emily was part of it. But at least now she'd find out what the gang was doing.

As the Whalers headed out of the factory, she flashed back to the man in the coat and to what she had seen in the curve of his goggles.

The vision of Dunwall in ruins, of herself not as Empress, but *tyrant*, and of Corvo, not as Royal Protector, but Royal Executioner.

INTERLUDE

UTYRKA, TYVIA
Month undetermined, 1848—1849

"I do not fear the Void, nor am I concerned with the spiritual sanctity of the weak. For I am now His herald, His chosen, having seen His sublime vault, where eternally He feeds upon the substance of the Void."

— *CALL TO THE SPHERES, VOL. 3*
Excerpt from a work of fiction, final chapters

The tunnel was long, and low, and pitch black save for the faint yellow light that danced ahead. It was far below the earth, a passage cut deep into the permafrost of the Tyvian tundra plateau.

Zhukov squeezed forward, pulling himself through with his elbows, trying to find purchase with the toes of his worn-out boots. He was not a small man, but the passage, on the other hand, was tiny. Barely big enough for him to fit through. The thought that there was two hundred feet or more of ice and rock pushing down on him from above did little to improve his mood.

A shower of debris hit him in the face and he stopped, spluttering, unable to quite pull his arms around to wipe the stinging salt out of his eyes. Blinking through the tears, he glanced up to see the boots of Milosch pushing at the passage walls ahead of him.

"Hey!" Zhukov called out. His voice didn't carry far at all, and it sounded like he felt.

Trapped.

He was just thankful he wasn't claustrophobic. Because crawling in the ice tunnel, in the dark, wasn't for the faint of heart.

Milosch called back to Zhukov, but Zhukov couldn't

work out what the man had said. In fact, Milosch hadn't said much at all since they'd started the journey. All Zhukov knew was that Milosch had found something, and that he thought Zhukov would want to see it.

Zhukov waited for his guide to get a few feet ahead of him, hoping to save himself another face full of gritty, salty ice, and then set off again. For a few seconds he couldn't move—he *was* stuck—but he breathed in and felt the walls of the passage ease around him. He pushed forward and moved a little. He breathed in again, acutely aware that there wasn't the space for his ribcage to expand back to its normal size. The farther they went, the shallower the breaths he was able to take.

He wondered how long it would be before their absence was noted. It felt as if they had been crawling for hours and hours, but the camp far above their heads was asleep.

The two of them had been working in the salt mine at Utyrka for more than a decade. Even before he had been sent here, Zhukov had heard of the mine. Everybody in Tyvia knew about it, by reputation at least. It was the hardest of the labor camps, the destination of the worst, the hardest, criminals. Mass-murderers and serial killers, some of whom, it was said, were cannibals, too. And people like him—traitors, those who had committed perhaps the worst crime imaginable.

Treason.

And here in Utyrka, the harshest of the camps, they would be worked to death in the salt mine, in the close darkness, deep below the tundra.

Except Zhukov actually *liked* the work. Yes, it was dark, but he liked the dark, and in reality they had ample light for their task, hewing the halite from the walls of the mine with nothing but a hand pick and drill. The salt was as solid as rock, of course, but Zhukov didn't mind the labor.

He used the work to keep himself strong, fit and in shape for when the time came.

The time to leave.

The salt mine was also claustrophobic, but that didn't affect Zhukov either. It wasn't so much the confined spaces—there were plenty of those, but the mine itself was mostly a series of huge caverns, some with ceilings so high they were completely invisible, disappearing into the darkness hundreds of feet overhead.

Yes, Zhukov liked working in the mine. He had worked in it for years, patiently chipping away at the walls while those around him were broken, their bodies destroyed by the work, their minds destroyed by the feeling of entrapment, of the world crushing down, of the darkness closing in.

Milosch had arrived at the mine a few months after Zhukov. After a few months more, he and Zhukov were the only two of the original mining gang left. Together they worked for years, and years, and years.

And then, a few months ago, Milosch said he had found something. He and three others were sent to sink an exploratory shaft in a new area of the mine.

When Milosch had returned, he had been alone. He reported to the camp leaders that the area was unsuitable and unstable, his two companions lost to a rock fall.

The camp leaders had accepted his word. To Zhukov, he told a different story—the story of a tunnel, and not a natural one, either, but a passage carved out of the salt by hand, hidden at the back of a huge cavern. Zhukov didn't ask what had happened to his companions, and Milosch never said.

And then they waited. Two months. Three, just to be sure. When they were certain the camp leaders really had no interest in the shaft, Milosch led the way. They left their barracks at night, walking through the biting, deathly cold, to the mine. They went down, Milosch leading the way to his cavern, to the passage. It was, as he said—man-made, a square doorway cut into the salt. The passage beyond was broad, but soon it got smaller, and smaller, ending in a tunnel that was barely wide enough for a man to squeeze through like a snake.

But Milosch was insistent. He had said there was something on the other side. Something he wanted to show Zhukov. Of course, it could have been a trap, but there were easier ways for Milosch to have gotten rid of him.

Zhukov was known in the camp—he was *famous*, even. He had been there for years, longer than any of the camp leaders shipped in from the military academy to run the place. Some prisoners said he had been a Hero of the State, but none really believed that. The whispers, though, the stories. They were enough. The others left him alone, deferring to his seniority, if not to the legends that orbited the man.

Except for Milosch. He was the same age as Zhukov, or perhaps a little older. He and Zhukov had formed, if not a friendship, then a kinship. Milosch never asked who Zhukov was, what he had done to end up in Utyrka, and he never told Zhukov what he was here for, either. Zhukov never asked, because he didn't care—whatever Milosch told him, Zhukov wouldn't have believed him. He knew how the camps worked.

It was entirely possible that the man was a plant, an agent sent by the High Judges to kill Zhukov, to eliminate someone who was seen as a problem, an embarrassment, even hidden away here in the tundra. Zhukov was a problem because he was a *survivor*. He already suspected he was the longest-serving prisoner of any of the labor camps, possibly in the whole history of Tyvia. That was a problem. The High Judges were watching, and they were nervous.

They were afraid.

But, as he crawled through the tunnel, Zhukov decided that perhaps he wasn't so sure. Maybe Milosch wasn't an agent. Maybe he had been sent to the camp because he was a cannibalistic serial killer, and hadn't killed Zhukov out in the open because he wanted to eat Zhukov's brains in private.

Or maybe he really had found something. Perhaps he wanted to show this wondrous discovery to the only man in the camp he could really trust.

Zhukov.

There was a shuffling, and another shower of ice and grit, and Zhukov felt a waft of cold, cold air in front of him. A moment later there was another face full of salt, and this time a gloved hand reaching to help him.

Zhukov accepted the aid and, with Milosch's help, he emerged from the passage. The chamber beyond was small, the light from Milosch's whale oil miner's lamp crackling blue as he turned the current up. The light reflected off sheer walls of ice and rock on three sides, the walls almost close enough that Zhukov could stand in the center and touch them with outstretched arms. The ceiling was invisible—Milosch pointed the light up and muttered something, but Zhukov wasn't listening. Above them was just darkness. It could have been the open night sky, for all he knew.

His attention was caught by the opposite wall.

Milosch's words trailed off as the man realized his companion wasn't listening, and he clapped a heavy hand on Zhukov's shoulder.

"I told you, my friend, I told you," he said, then he dropped his hand and he stepped toward the wall, the light of the lamp playing over the surface. "I had heard of such things, but to find one here—*here*!—of all places. It's amazing. Truly amazing."

Zhukov stepped toward the light.

The opposite wall of the small cavern was salt, and it had been carved by hand into two tall, fluted pillars positioned on either side of a shelf. Its surface was perhaps six feet wide and cut another four feet into the salt. The shelf, like the pillars, was elaborately carved and decorated with intricate scrollwork. The work was remarkable, the salt sculpted like the finest stone that graced the People's Citadel back in Dabokva. How long the shrine had been here, Zhukov had no idea. Down here, in the dark and the cold, it could have been carved yesterday or a thousand years ago.

Sitting in the center of the shelf was something even more remarkable—a knife. It was bronze, and had twin, straight blades, each twelve inches long. Under Milosch's light the blades glittered, the glare they reflected catching Zhukov's eye. He blinked, confused for a moment. It was a trick of the light, had to be, the way the reflected light wasn't blue but a deep, fiery red, the way that when he closed his eyes there were shapes that moved behind his eyelids, that couldn't possibly be afterimages, echoes of the light.

Zhukov stepped up to the shelf and ran a fur-lined gauntlet over the surface of the icy salt. He could feel the cold, even through the layers.

Abruptly he both heard and felt a rushing in his ears. Blood, pumping, like the sound of an ocean far away, a sea he hadn't looked at for fifteen years.

The knife glinted red, glinted yellow, glinted red again.

The sound of a great fire burning, the roar of an inferno from across the endless gulfs of time.

"Don't you see, friend," Milosch was saying, but it sounded as if he was talking behind a door, behind a hill, a thousand miles away, shouting into the wind. "This is an altar to him—the Outsider! That means his followers were here, once, and they're not here now. There must be more tunnels, leading out, away from Utyrka." Milsosch glared at him. "*Hey*, are you listening to me?"

Zhukov nodded, the pressure inside his head reaching a crescendo as his hand reached for the knife. As soon as his fingers touched the handle, the noise stopped. It was so sudden, the silence so profound it *hurt*, rocking him on his heels.

"There's another way out," Milosch said. "Listen, if we can find the other tunnels, maybe even through the mountains, we can escape. Traveling underground we'll be able to get past the bears and wolves, and it's warmer down here—only just freezing."

"Warm, yes," Zhukov whispered. Not taking his eyes from the knife, he lifted his hand and pulled his glove off, then he reached again for the handle, his bare fingers curling around it. It was hot, and the heat traveled up Zhukov's hand, up his arm, and flooded his whole body. Warm. Blood heat.

"Zhukov?"

He turned and Milosch backed away. Zhukov looked down and found himself holding the knife. It was warm. As he watched, he saw blood trickle out from between his tightly clenched fingers.

Then, a whispering. Somewhere, over his shoulder. Someone standing there, behind him, a presence looming. A voice in his ear, a whisper, a song.

Milosch frowned, holding his hands up.

"Are you listening to me? I said there's a *way out*. Zhukov? Zhukov, are you listening to me?"

Zhukov nodded, and tilted his head, listening to the song, watching the fire dance in front of his eyes.

The voice whispered. The *knife* sang to him.

Told him everything.

Told him what to do and how to do it.

"Yes," Zhukov said, nodding again. "Yes, there is a way out."

He took a step forward and plunged the knife into Milosch's stomach. The other man's eyes went wide, and he staggered, his legs going out from under him. Zhukov stepped closer, pushing the blades forward, holding Milosch upright. He brought his face close to Milosch's, until their noses were touching. Zhukov stared into the other man's eyes, watching the reflection of a fire from eons ago, watching the shadows dance in the flames, watching the form, the presence, standing at his shoulder.

Milosch spluttered, his jaw working as Zhukov moved the blades inside him, twisting them, pushing them. Milosch coughed, spattering Zhukov's face with blood.

"Yes," Zhukov said again. "Yes, there is a way out."

Then he stepped back and pulled the knife out. Milosch collapsed to the floor of the ice vault and didn't move. His fingers released the lantern, which began strobing as it hit the floor at an angle, partially dislodging the small whale oil tank within. In the flickering light, Milosch's dying eyes stared up at Zhukov, his mouth open in an expression of surprise and of fright.

Listening to the whispered song in his head, Zhukov knelt by the body and got to work.

PART TWO

THE WITCHCHARMS

11

"The adjacent streets are another matter. Bottle Street in particular, and the Old Dunwall Whiskey distillery, are currently controlled by Slackjaw and his Bottle Street Gang. Not much is known about Slackjaw, except that he has been particularly active during the plague crisis. As part of his illegal business revolves around the distribution of anti-plague elixir, the Watch has been slow in cracking down on the operation."

— SLACKJAW'S BOTTLE STREET GANG
Excerpt from a report on thuggish gang activities

Corvo leaned on the windowsill and scratched at his chin as he looked out onto the grounds of Brigmore Manor.

The night was cloudy, the rains thankfully staying away, and had that strange warmth that sometimes came to the city at this time of year, the last gasp of a good fall clinging on before the snow and *real* cold arrived. As the clouds swam above, moonlight occasionally broke through, casting an eerie pale light over the overgrown, swampy land that surrounded the house. Old trees, their twisted branches heavy with moss, crowded what open space there was, and here and there was the evidence of a once majestic formal garden left to rot—statues and balustrades poked out from thick, tangled ivy, while ornate bird feeders and low columned walls revealed the outlines and layout of perfectly symmetrical gardens now lost in the undergrowth. Wisps of fog drifted through the ruin.

Corvo sighed. The terrain was rough, the grounds of Brigmore Manor offering plenty of places to hide and approach the house unseen. And while this played in Corvo's favor—plenty of places to hide meant he had been able to secrete his own agents all over the estate—it also meant that their enemy had the advantage of cover, as well.

"Nice night, eh? Eh?"

Corvo turned to the man leaning on the window next to him. The room was lit by the moon only, revealing an empty chamber, the place stripped out in preparation for a rebuild that had already begun. New, pale floorboards had been laid down to replace most of the old rotting timbers, reflecting that moonlight back up into Corvo's eyes and into the droplets of moisture caught in the bushy silver handlebar mustache of his companion.

The mouth underneath that mustache was smiling, revealing big tombstone teeth. The man had eyebrows to match his facial hair, but his scalp was bald, save for an orbit of silver the man had grown long at the back, wearing it as a long plait that reached halfway down to his waist.

The man winked, and then nodded at the view of the grounds.

"I said it's a nice night, Corvo," he said. "What's the matter, you deaf, lad?"

Corvo smiled. "I can hear you just fine, Isaiah," he said quietly. "And I suspect everyone in the garden can, too, so if you don't mind?"

"All right, all right," the man said, not lowering his voice in the slightest, before realizing his mistake and waving Corvo an apology. "And it's 'Azariah,' not Isaiah," he whispered. "How many times does a man have to say it to get it through that thick head of yours, eh? Too many knocks to the brow, that's what it is."

Corvo's smile grew. "Sorry, *Azariah*." He turned back to the window. A moment passed. "And less of the lad. I'm nearly as old as you are."

Azariah snorted. "If that's the case, then I want to buy your secret and bottle it for sale in my distillery."

The Royal Protector snickered and shook his head, returning his gaze to the view of the gardens. The two men stood in silence for a while, listening to the croak of frogs and the slow chirp of nocturnal insects enjoying the overgrown state of the place.

Corvo pursed his lips. "Azariah," he said slowly.

"Eh?"

Corvo smiled. "Just trying it out. Suits you, actually. A lot better than your old nickname, anyway."

Azariah laughed, then waved an apology as Corvo gave him a stern look to keep quiet. "Ah, yes. Now there was a name for the ages, eh? But, I'll tell ya, that man died a long, long time ago, and old Azariah Fillmore doesn't know a thing about it." He coughed, then repeated his name a few times, rolling his tongue around it thoughtfully. "Azariah Fillmore." Then he nodded. "Azariah Fillmore. Aye, does the trick, my lad, does the trick."

He stepped away from the window and took a fob watch from the pocket of his embroidered velvet waistcoat, holding it to catch the moonlight.

"But look, Corvo, time's ticking on. How long have we been here now, eh?" He peered at the timepiece, then frowned and turned it to Corvo. "Bah. Help an old man out and feast your eyes on the dial, and tell me what secrets it tells you."

Corvo glanced down at the watch with a shake of his head.

"What's the matter, Isaiah? You got somewhere else to be?"

"Now look, Corvo," the other said, "I'm helping you out here, letting you and your men march in and make themselves at home in my shrubbery. And more than that, too—I've had to take me own boys off the job and put them under the will of that young fella… what was his name?"

"Jameson."

"Right. Jameson. Nice boy, too. But listen, I'm glad to help. And I'm glad *for* the help. I've spent hard-earned coin rebuilding this rotten pile, and I ain't going to let no one take that off me, oh no sir." The old man huffed in the night air.

"And," he added, "it's *Azariah*, not Isaiah. For pity's sake, Corvo. I've got a cover to maintain here. No good you getting me name wrong all over the show. I've spent too many years turning the wheel of me ship around for you to come and run me aground, my lad."

"And it sounds like you spent too long at sea, *Azariah*." Corvo grinned, and now Azariah seemed to notice the expression. He huffed a second time, finally realizing his friend had, perhaps, been getting his name wrong deliberately, just to annoy him. Then Azariah's face broke into a grin, as well.

"Ha! Maybe I did, Corvo, maybe I did—but I tell ya, that's where I really belonged. I got the call, I did. That's where I found meself, honestly and truly."

Corvo's gaze flicked across the night-shrouded estate. Still nothing.

"Two words I never thought I'd ever hear you say," he said.

"Eh?"

Corvo glanced at his old acquaintance. "'Honestly' and 'truly.' I'm surprised they even feature in your vocabulary."

"Well now, isn't that nice?" Azariah said, taken aback. "I've been busy, Corvo, busy ever since you saved me from Granny Rag's casserole. Changed me life, that did. Set me on a new path." The man looked down at himself in the moonlight and pulled at the bottom of his waistcoat. "Where do you think all this came from, eh? And this?" He waved at the empty room. "Eh? *Eh?*" Then he rubbed the fingers of one hand in Corvo's face. "Honest graft, that's where. I'm not who I was, you know. You're in the house of Azariah Fillmore, distiller of exotic liqueurs and exporter of the very same, and what's more—"

Corvo held up a hand.

"*Shh!*"

He leaned out the window, looking around.

On the far side of the gardens was a large, long stone building, the pitched roof supported by a ring of white columns that glowed in the moonlight. The old Brigmore mausoleum. And, as far as his agents had been able to discover, the *target* of the raid tonight.

There was a flash from the trees in the far distance, then closer, two more. Then another, all of them directed toward the house. Signals from Corvo's spies, stationed out in the gardens. The enemy had been sighted.

Corvo stood and turned to Azariah.

"This is it," he said. "They're coming. Go downstairs and get your men ready."

Azariah stood tall and gave a mock salute. "As the Royal Protector commands." He paused and added, "Or should that be Royal Spymaster now?"

Corvo rolled his eyes and waved the old man away. Azariah frowned, then turned and headed for the stairs. When he reached them, he stopped and turned back around. In the moonlight streaming through the windows he gave Corvo a wink, his smile flashing under his huge mustache.

"Hey, Corvo, just like old times, eh?"

Corvo allowed himself a small smile, but there was no time to waste.

"Come on, Slackjaw, go. *Go!*"

"Okay, I'm going, I'm going," the old man said. "And it's Azariah Fillmore, you bleedin' idiot. Honestly, how many times…"

12

"As a coddled generation has grown more accepting of heresy, even taking delight in the tales of witchcraft found in lurid adventure stories, this is the result: Now even those with no real connection to the Void are attempting to devise their own disgusting rituals and talismans. Such corrupted bonecharms and fractured runes could be even more dangerous than the original artifacts, as impossible as that might seem."

— WARNING ON CORRUPTED CHARMS
Excerpt from an Overseer's report on
black-market occult artifacts

It had taken a couple of hours to reach their destination, the old Brigmore Manor, north of Dunwall, beyond the city walls. The estate was itself surrounded by a huge stone wall that was at least partially ruined, the main gates completely missing. The information the Whalers had was correct—the estate was deserted, and, Emily imagined, probably had been ever since the Rat Plague.

Or at least it *seemed* deserted. She knew otherwise.

Corvo's agents were near, watching the place. Emily was ready to keep her head down and make a quick escape if things turned… difficult. She couldn't risk having her presence discovered—not by the Whalers she now found herself a part of, and not by any Imperial agents, either.

The Whalers, masks in place, approached the estate through the undergrowth that skirted the main drive, hidden by the night and by the thick fingers of fog that seeped out of the swampy, mossy woodland that surrounded them. The whole place was overgrown and tangled, the air full of a rich, earthy, wet smell. When they got to the gates, the gang stopped and split into their two pre-assigned groups, Rinaldo leading one and the red-coated Whaler—Galia, their leader—taking the other. The two groups, each consisting of twelve Whalers, headed along the outside of the walls of the estate, going in opposite directions.

Emily had been assigned to Galia's group, and she followed at the back, creeping along with the others in silence over the rough terrain. The Whalers were good, very capable in the art of stealth, and she was grateful she possessed at least a similar set of skills.

They walked for probably twenty minutes, skirting the crumbling wall, until they reached a portion which had partially collapsed, its demise hastened by the huge fallen bough of an ancient tree, the cradle of roots sitting perpendicular to the ground on the other side of the wall. Galia led the way through the breach, picking a careful path over the rubble. Emily followed after the others.

Once through she could see the house, just, the clouds clearing enough to cast the estate in pale silver moonlight. It looked as if they were around the back of the estate, the main block of the mansion far ahead, one rear corner closest to them. From here they would have to pass the remains of a formal garden, the fountain dry and choked with debris and weeds, and on one side, the vast iron skeleton of what must have been an impressive glasshouse, the hundreds of panes long gone.

Galia led the group forward to a low, semicircular wall that surrounded a large raised area, in the center of which was the old fountain. Abruptly she waved them down, and they all ducked out of sight quickly.

Then Emily saw it—a flash of light, a reflection of the moon on something, in the darkness on the far side of the formal garden. Someone was there.

Corvo's agents.

The group sat in their huddle for a few minutes, listening for any movement. When none came, Galia carefully scouted farther along the wall, vanishing out of sight for a few moments. Then she crawled back to the others.

"The crypt is on the other side of the old hothouse," she whispered through her mask. "I'll let you in—you know what you're looking for, so grab it and get out. Don't waste time looking for anything else. There's nothing in there but bones. Those are what we want, and as many as possible."

The others nodded and shuffled their positions.

"But it looks like we have company," Galia continued. "Hard to know who it might be. Jaxon, Clem, head east. There's a couple of lookouts in the trees. Take them out before they can get word to the main house. When we get to the crypt, I'll let you in, then Devon, Finn, you're coming with me up to the mansion."

Emily couldn't help herself. "I thought you said the estate was empty?"

The others turned to look at her. Galia didn't answer at once.

"There was always a chance it wasn't," she said finally. "Weren't you listening back at the factory… what was your name again?"

Emily thought fast. "Lela," she said.

"Well, Lela," she said, "we've got the city after us, so we have to be prepared for anything." Then she paused. "You're coming with Devon and Finn."

"I… what?"

"If there are more at the house, I'll need help to clear a path, so I can get in and get out cleanly."

"You're going *into* the house?" Emily asked.

"Are you up to the task, Lela?" Galia tilted her head, her respirator exaggerating the movement. "You seem to have been asleep when instructions were given."

"Ah… no, no, I'm fine, really. I'm fine."

Galia grunted. "You'd better be." Then she lifted herself up and peered over the wall. "Okay. Jaxon, Clem, go. The rest, with me."

The pair of Whalers split off, heading east. Galia scooted around the rest and led them east.

Toward the ruin of the old hothouse.

Toward the crypt.

The crypt was smaller than Emily had imagined, its white stone catching the moonlight where it wasn't encrusted with moss. With Galia at the head, the group quickly passed from the undergrowth that surrounded the building to the columned frontage that concealed a flight of wide stone stairs that led from the surface down to a subterranean door.

Of course, Emily thought, *that was why the building seemed small*. It was merely a folly to be admired from the house. The crypt itself was an underground vault, probably much larger than the footprint of the building above.

As they moved closer, she saw that the door to the vault wasn't a door at all. It was a solid block of stone, carved merely to *look* like a door, complete with inset paneling and even a stone-carved doorknob with escutcheon. Emily wasn't sure how they were supposed to get inside. The vault seemed well and truly sealed.

Galia ran her hands over the fake door while the others pressed themselves against the cool walls of the sunken stairwell, staying in the shadows and out of the shaft of moonlight that illuminated half of the space with surprising brightness.

Then Galia placed the flat of both hands against the stone and stood with her legs apart, as if she was going to just push the giant block out of the way. She glanced over her shoulder.

"Two minutes," she said. The others nodded. They seemed to know what was going on, even if Emily didn't.

Galia turned back to the block and bowed her head. She might have been whispering something, but Emily wasn't sure, as just then a stiff wind sprang out of nowhere, twisting into a strong eddy that whipped around the stairwell, dragging in dead leaves and dust.

Emily heard—or perhaps she felt—a click, and a tingling sensation. She watched as Galia lifted her head and…

She was gone, the space where she had been occupied for just a second by a swirling, inky-black substance that looked like smoke, but which was gone in an instant, seemingly dispersed by the wind—which just as suddenly died to nothing.

Emily gasped. She'd seen that before. Fifteen years ago, the terrible day her mother was killed. The Whalers— the *assassins*—had appeared out of nowhere, blinking in and out of view as they raided the gazebo and murdered Empress Jessamine Kaldwin.

The others in the group didn't move or show any sign of surprise. Of course they wouldn't.

Two minutes passed, Emily counting the seconds in her head. It felt like forever, but eventually there was a hollow scraping sound, and then the giant stone block tilted back at the top and forward at the bottom, the whole thing pivoting on a spindle at the middle. Beyond lay darkness, but in that darkness she could see Galia standing near, pulling on a chain which went up to a pulley, allowing the vault to be opened.

Only from the inside, of course.

With the slab open, Galia held the chain and motioned for the others to enter.

"Yeah, I don't think so, somehow."

The others turned, looking up the stairwell. At the top, silhouetted in the moonlight, were three men aiming pistols at the Whalers. One of the men motioned with his weapon.

"Come on, up," he said, "and lift them hands up too, while you're about it. I wouldn't like to see you try anything you might regret."

The gang shuffled. They were effectively trapped in the stairwell, cornered with nowhere to run. And at the wrong end of three pistols, fight was impossible. So they obliged, holding their hands up. Emily joined them, moving up the steps with the others and then stepping out into the moonlight. At the top, she turned around, following the twitching gestures of the gun barrels.

The men weren't City Watch or Overseers. They might have been Corvo's agents in disguise, but Emily wasn't sure. They were dressed like laborers—dirty and scuffed leather jerkins and pants, shirts with billowing sleeves that, a very long time ago, would have been the purest white. The man giving the orders was bald and had a big beard that reached halfway down his chest. The other two were younger, a man with close-cropped hair and stubble on his cheeks, a red kerchief tied around his neck, and the third with long blond hair crammed under an old top hat.

They looked like members of a street gang—the blond from the Hatters, the others perhaps from… the Bottle Street Gang? Emily frowned behind her mask, her hands in the air as the two younger men waved their pistols again, signaling the group to move away from the crypt.

There were still gangs in Dunwall. Emily knew that—she was frequently updated by Captain Ramsey—but things had changed from the days of the Rat Plague, when whole areas of the city had been under control of the gangs. They had carved Dunwall up between them into separate fiefdoms, driving citizens out from areas that weren't already overrun with the rodents.

Organized crime and gang warfare were still a problem, of course, but now the gangs were fewer both in number and membership, with a large proportion now serving their time in Coldridge Prison. Those who evaded capture had moved on to legitimate employment, mostly around the docks and wharves, or had left Dunwall, even Gristol, altogether.

So what were members of the old Bottle Street Gang and the Hatters doing here, on the grounds of an old, crumbling estate outside of the city? Emily's thoughts were interrupted by the big man with the beard.

"Hey you, get your ass up here, nice and easy."

He was standing at the top of the stairs, waving his gun at Galia, who Emily could just see was still standing in the doorway of the tomb, holding the stone portal open by the chain.

"Unless," the man with the beard continued, "you feel like joining the crypt's residents in what you might call a permanent arrangement?"

The Whaler next to Emily stiffened. The pistol-waving gangsters didn't notice, too busy chuckling at the sparkling wit of their boss.

"I think I'll take my chances," Galia said.

She let go of the chain.

"Bloody cheek!" the bearded man said. As the stone portal crashed down, he fired his gun, the bullet ricocheting in a shower of sparks from the stonework.

That was all it took. His men were distracted, and the Whalers were ready.

They moved in silence, and at speed. The bearded man was the first to die, his side filleted by a long knife even as he cursed at the closed vault door. The blond in the tall hat wheeled around as two Whalers jumped toward him—he got a shot off, but it flew wide, and by the time he had cocked the hammer of his gun for a second, he was tackled by the two assailants, his neck severed to the spine by another assassin's blade.

The surviving gangster gave a shrill whistle as he raced for the undergrowth. The Whalers spun to face him and give chase—and then they paused, as from the bushes came more men.

Lots more men. The same as the others, former members of the Dunwall street gangs, wearing a ramshackle collection of work clothes, some armed with pistols, others with knives and clubs. The two groups faced each other for a few seconds, both sizing the opposition up. And then, with yells from both sides, the two gangs charged.

Emily ducked down, rattling off in her mind the defensive moves her father had spent more than a decade drilling into her head as she allowed the Whalers to stream past her, racing in for the attack. Shots rang out— one, two, three, four, then Emily lost count. At the back of the skirmish she quickly dove behind a tree, the front side of which then exploded as a fusillade of shots peppered the wood.

She dropped onto her stomach, and waited, playing

dead. Counted to ten, and when no one seemed to be coming to take a closer look, she moved away from the sounds of the conflict, crawling flat on her stomach. Reaching an overgrown, broken wall, she pulled herself over it, then curled up and risked taking a look back.

The fight in the clearing was brutal, violent. Blades flicked in the moonlight and the foggy tendrils from the swampy woodland mixed with acrid clouds of black smoke from the gunfire. The body count was already high, and climbing.

The Whalers were losing. They were good fighters, but this wasn't *their* kind of fight. They were masters of stealth and assassination—or had been when Daud had led them—but this? This was an open, dirty brawl. Perfectly suited to their opponents. The Bottle Street Gang, the Hatters, the Dead Eels. It seemed like every faction of Dunwall street gang was represented, the men—and women—working together to take out those who had dared intrude.

Then, a snap of branch, a rustle of bushes, somewhere behind Emily, away from the action, toward the main house itself. She turned, pressing her back against the wall, to look.

There. Someone running toward the house. It was hard to see in the broken darkness, but the hooded jacket was a dull red color.

Galia. She'd escaped from the vault, using the same trick as she had used to get in.

Emily jumped up and ran after her.

13

"You want the chinwag on Slackjaw? What he was like when we was young, before he got his name? Oh, he's got a cool head now, but it weren't always like that in the days before he was boss of the Bottle Street gang. Time was, young Slackjaw wasn't such a reasonable man."

— EARLY LIFE AND CRIMINAL RECORD: SLACKJAW
Excerpt from a series of letters sent
by a member of the Bottle Street Gang

Emily kept on Galia's trail, the leader of the Whalers seeming to be unaware she was being followed, uncaring of the noise she made as the gunfire and cries of the fight by the crypt echoed out across the foggy darkness of the estate.

Ahead of them was a bright light that cast long shadows in the woods and reflected awkwardly in the goggles of the mask Emily realized she was still wearing. She yanked it off and dumped it, and reveled in the cool of the night air against her face.

The woods reached close to the house but stopped short, leaving a gap of perhaps fifty yards. Galia came to a halt behind the broad trunk of a tree, the branches of which reached out to gingerly caress the upper floors of the old mansion. Emily dropped into the hollow formed by an ancient tree root, and looked out over the edge.

One room on the ground floor of the mansion had massive glass doors, which opened out onto the weed-choked remains of a large patio—the perfect place, once upon a time, for an aristocratic garden party. The doors were open, and the room beyond was brightly lit now. With her first proper view of the house, Emily could see that it wasn't derelict at all, despite the state of the grounds.

The huge room beyond the glass doors—a ballroom, perhaps, or possibly one end of a long gallery—had been stripped, the walls showing the bare carcass of the house interior, while there were some large shapes under dirty white sheets. Farther along the exterior, the side of the building was partially covered with scaffolding. As she had learned from the permits and plans in Corvo's office, the house was being restored and repaired, and the work had already begun in earnest.

As Emily watched, some of the allied gang members appeared from the darkness and headed across the ornamental patio, dragging captured members of the Whalers between them. It was hard to see, but this was a different group of defenders, and other Whalers. Rinaldo's group had been caught, too.

Two men appeared in the light of the ground floor room. Emily gasped.

The first man was older, maybe in his late fifties or sixties. His head was bald but he had a long gray plait of hair trailing down his back and an impressive mustache decorating his upper lip, the bushy sideburns curling up to join what was left of his hairline. As he folded his arms, Emily saw his biceps bulge. He was old, but in good shape— perhaps, she thought, a veteran of the old street gangs.

But it was the man standing next to him who caught Emily by surprise. He was as tall and as broad as his companion, and he wore a hooded tunic crisscrossed with belts. Beneath the hood, the metal and leather of his skull- like mask shone in the night. It was a mask Emily knew well.

A mask from so many years ago—the mask she knew the Royal Protector secretly donned when he was involved in matters far from his official duties, a part of his life unbecoming his formal role in her court.

Corvo.

Then she felt the electric tingling again, the weird pressure behind her eyes. She glanced to her left, to where Galia was standing behind the tree, watching the proceedings.

Where Galia *had* been standing. All that was there now was the puff of inky-black nothing that faded and was gone.

Emily frowned, and crept forward. The huge tree was ideal cover, and the way its branches actually touched the second floor of the mansion—a second floor that was half ruin, half construction site, the entry points numerous and easy—just as useful.

Emily began to climb.

Slackjaw—*Azariah*—grinned and took a breath, then swung his fist again. That fist—and the brass knuckleduster wrapped around it—connected with the face of the man tied to the chair, sending both the bound prisoner and chair sprawling sideways and an arc of blood and spit spattering over the bare floorboards.

As Slackjaw stood there, bent over, both hands on his knees as he caught his breath, one of two lieutenants stationed in the room reached down and pulled the prisoner back to the upright position. The prisoner moaned, his face a blackened, bloody mess, his hair slick with sweat and stuck to his face. On the floor beside him was the discarded mask of a Whaler.

Standing at the back of the room, Corvo watched from behind his own mask, his arms folded, as Slackjaw tried his own interrogation technique. Corvo didn't approve of the methods, but he wasn't going to intervene, not yet. They needed information, and, despite everything, this was Slackjaw's house, these were Slackjaw's men.

Which meant he had to play by Slackjaw's rules.

The old gangster stood up and whooped at the ceiling. Then he turned and laughed at Corvo.

"You know, there was a time when I would have said this kind of work was behind me, and what I really needed to do was buy a little vineyard and spend most of my time napping in a cushioned rocker," he said breathlessly, "but lately I've come to change my position… somewhat."

Then he turned around and punched the prisoner again. The legs of the chair rocked, but the strike wasn't as strong this time. Bending over and gasping for breath again, he waved away a lieutenant who reached to lend a hand. Eventually Slackjaw stood and shook his head, the grin still on his face. He ran his non-punching hand over his mustache.

"This kind of exercise is good for the heart and soul, it is," he said. "Must say I've missed it. Nothing else like it to get the corpuscles flowing so."

Corvo was glad his mask hid his grimace of distaste. Of course Slackjaw hadn't changed, and it was foolish to have ever thought otherwise. He was older, for sure, and his business interests might have shifted sideways, turning the Bottle Street Gang and the distillery into a legitimate enterprise, but he was still a crook and a thug.

The Royal Protector glanced at the two lieutenants in the room. They were young men, built like brick privies the pair of them, and they were enjoying the evening's events just as much as their boss.

So, no, nothing had changed.

"Hey, boss, this one's no good."

Slackjaw, still puffing, turned back to his men. One of them was leaning over the prisoner, peering into the man's face as he held his head up by his hair. Slackjaw wandered over and squinted at the bound figure. He nudged his shoulder with the knuckleduster, then stood up and shook his head.

"Huh," he said. "They don't breed 'em like they used to. Used to be tough, the Whalers. You never wanted to meet one in a dark alley, else you'd likely not be coming home for yer supper." He straightened and nodded to the other lieutenant. "Bring the next one in, let's see if he's any better."

He walked over to Corvo, working the brass knuckles off his hand. He paused by one of the sheet-covered pieces of furniture and grabbed the edge of the cover to wipe his hand. Then he flexed his fingers and shook his hand loosely from the wrist. Even with the knuckleduster, Corvo could see the man's hand was red raw.

"Hey, you want to take over?" Slackjaw asked. "This old man needs a nice sit down, and a slug or two of the good stuff."

Corvo turned, watching as Slackjaw headed to the fireplace. On the mantle was a bottle of whiskey, which the old man took. He unplugged the stopper and tossed it into the empty fireplace, then upended the bottle into his mouth.

Slackjaw's Adam's apple bounced as he drank nearly a quarter of the bottle before coming up for air. He then offered the bottle to Corvo.

Corvo remained unmoving, his arms tightly folded.

Slackjaw laughed. "Guess you don't want to be taking that fancy mask of yours off, oh mysterious man of mystery."

"This isn't working," Corvo said.

Slackjaw stopped, the bottle halfway to his lips. He grimaced, as if he had stepped in something he would rather not have.

"What do you mean? We caught the bastards, didn't we? Isn't that what you wanted?"

"Yes," Corvo said, pushing off from the wall. As he got closer to Slackjaw, the old man lifted his chin in defiance. "But what we also need is information. We need to know who their boss is, and what they're doing."

"Yeah… and? Isn't that just exactly what I'm doing for you?" Still holding the bottle, Slackjaw gestured to the blood-spattered floorboards as another of the Whalers was led in through the big doors. It was an older black man with a chinstrap beard.

"We're not going to find out anything," Corvo said, "if you keep killing the prisoners."

Slackjaw frowned, then worked his mouth up and down, as if he hadn't really considered the matter until now.

The prisoner, meanwhile, was pushed down into the chair by one thug while the other tied his hands. The Whaler's gaze moved from Slackjaw, to Corvo—his eyes going wide at the sight of the skull-like mask—before settling on the body of his former companion, now lying on the floor in a growing pool of blood.

Slackjaw smiled at the prisoner and gave a bow.

"And a good evening to you, sir—a warm welcome to me humble abode." He stepped closer, sipping at his bottle, then he leaned down, sticking his face right in the other man's. "Now, let's get straight to it. The night is no longer young, and nor am I. I've enjoyed me exercise, but I need me beauty sleep, and me friend over there says I've been going a bit too hard on you all."

Slackjaw glanced down at the body by the chair, and he laughed.

"Maybe he's right. Thing is, this is my house. Maybe you and your friends didn't know that. I gather you were wanting a little souvenir from the old crypt. Well, that crypt is *also* my property, and when you steal from Azariah Fillmore, you make a very, very big mistake indeed."

With that he walked back to the fireplace, replacing the whiskey bottle on the mantle. Then he turned, took the knuckledusters from his pocket, and slid them back onto his hand, wincing at the discomfort.

"So, I've got a question for you," he said, walking back to the prisoner. "You look like a fine fella. You look like you've seen a thing or two, right? Not like your friends. The youth of today, eh? Believe me, I know what it's like."

Slackjaw glanced at his two lieutenants, who looked back at their boss, each with an expression that was slightly confused and annoyed at the same time.

"Anyway, to the question," he continued. "Well, one of many, but let's start with the basics. I want you to tell my friend in the corner there, the one with that scary old face, what you were all doing down at the crypt, and what you're planning on doing with all these bones you've been stealing."

The prisoner didn't say anything, his big eyes merely flicking between Slackjaw, his lieutenants, and Corvo.

Slackjaw sighed, then he cleared his throat and rolled his shoulders. He winked at Corvo.

"Well, I'll tell you now, lad, I'm going to be sore in the morning."

With that, he drew his fist back for the first punch.

And then the prisoner spoke.

"Yes!"

Slackjaw dropped his arm.

"Ah… yes? Yes, what?"

"Yes, I'll talk. I'll tell you what you want to know."

Slackjaw stared at the prisoner. He smiled, and then the smile flickered and went out and he slapped his punching arm against his side.

"Ah. Well then. Blow it all, I was hoping for a little more resistance than that." He glanced at Corvo. "Y'know, makes it more satisfying, like."

"Any more satisfying and he'd be dead, too," Corvo said. He unfolded his arms and stepped toward the prisoner. As he did, the man's mouth twitched into a smile at one corner, and he nodded slightly.

Corvo didn't like that expression.

"You got something to say?"

The prisoner nodded and the smile got bigger, showing yellow teeth again his dark skin.

"I know you," he said.

"I doubt it," Corvo said.

"Back then," the prisoner said, jerking his head to one side as if "back then" was someplace just over his shoulder. "Back when Daud was around. You knew Daud too, didn't you?"

Corvo frowned. "What's your name?"

The man's smile vanished. "Rinaldo. Rinaldo Escobar."

Corvo almost said *"from Karnaca too?"* but he kept his mouth shut. Instead he asked, "So what do you want to tell us?"

Rinaldo shifted in his chair and tried to lift his arms up, but the bonds holding him were firm.

"Untie me," he said. "I've got something to show you."

Slackjaw laughed. "I'll bet you have, son."

Rinaldo looked at the man with one eyebrow raised, then turned to Corvo and nodded.

"In my jacket pocket. Take a look."

Slackjaw glanced sideways at Corvo, his lips pursed. Corvo considered. There was no danger. Rinaldo was tied up. Slackjaw and his lackeys were rather keen to mete out another round of bone-crunching, and were unlikely to let Rinaldo get very far if the Whaler tried anything.

So he moved around behind Rinaldo, and felt the pockets of the tunic. Nothing in the first, the second. Then, moving up to the breast pockets.

There. Something small, hard.

Corvo reached in, then hissed behind his mask as he got a shock from something. He pulled his hand out quickly. At the movement, Slackjaw's two men had their knives at Rinaldo's throat. Corvo watched a bead of blood trickle down the prisoner's neck.

But Rinaldo wasn't scared. He was looking at right at Corvo.

"I know. It does the same to me. Try again."

Corvo watched Rinaldo with narrow eyes, then he crouched down and reached into the pocket again. His fingertips prickled at the contact with... whatever it was, but it was better, this time. He curled his fingers around it and drew the object out. Slackjaw drew close, breathing out a lungful of whiskey-flavored air.

"What in all the world is that?"

Corvo stared at the object in his hand. It was small and fitted into his palm. It was octagonal, crafted out of copper wire and what looked like bone that was white, but slightly charred at the edges. It was warm, and not just from being in Rinaldo's pocket.

He knew exactly what it was.

A bonecharm—but not like one he'd ever seen before.

He looked back to Rinaldo.

"Where did you get this?"

Rinaldo smiled. "Untie me and I'll tell you everything I know."

14

"The true weapon of the enemy is their eyes, because with their eyes they can see where you are, they can see what you are doing, they can see how you can be defeated. You must use your own eyes first, and act so that the enemy cannot. The art of spying is as noble as the art of war itself."

— A BETTER WAY TO DIE
Surviving fragment of an assassin's treatise,
author unknown

Emily lay on the bare floorboards of the room above the long gallery, peering down at the interrogation through a small gap in the floor. The room she was in hadn't been stripped yet, and was old, musty, and rotting.

She had watched as the old man with the knuckledusters had gone too far with his interrogation, killing two Whalers in a row. She had watched as Corvo stood by, impassively. At first she'd been shocked at how her father was just letting the other man dispense out such brutality. But Corvo hadn't taken part himself, and then Emily witnessed the argument about it between the two men.

She felt better. Not a lot, but she felt better.

It looked as if they were getting some answers from Rinaldo, who seemed very keen to cooperate. And whatever Rinaldo had had in his pocket, Corvo seemed to know what it was. She thought she could hear something else in his voice, a change, husky and echoing from behind his mask. It wasn't fear—the Royal Protector was *never* frightened—but something else. A quiet, but deep, concern.

Whatever the little thing was, it was important.

There was a creak from somewhere above. Emily looked up. The upper levels of the mansion seemed to be just as rotting as this floor, which made sneaking around difficult. Even for someone as experienced as her.

As experienced as Galia.

The boards above were broken and gappy, and in this part of the house the roof itself had partially collapsed, allowing moonlight to stream in. Moonlight, which cast a brief, flitting shadow that moved across as Emily looked up and watched Galia hopping across the gap.

Trying not to put a foot through the rotting floor herself, Emily stood and began to look for a way upstairs.

The upper floor of the house was even more difficult.

The room she had been in, with the collapsed ceiling, was easy enough to navigate, the moonlight providing ample illumination as she skirted the holes in the floor. But beyond, the next room was in darkness, almost as though something—a large tree, perhaps—had fallen onto the roof, plugging any gaps and blocking the windows on the moonlit side of the house.

Emily began to pick a path around the edge of the

room, then discovered there was a door in the wall. It led to a smaller room that looked mostly intact and was, importantly, better lit. Here the window was free of debris—and of glass—and the moonlight streamed in, almost as bright as day.

The room was square and empty, save for a series of old packing crates piled around the space, and what seemed to be a painter's easel folded against one wall, along with a high stool. Perhaps the room had been used as a studio of some kind by the house's previous owner. The easel didn't have anything on it, although down by its legs there rested an empty rectangular wooden frame, the canvas that once stretched across it long having succumbed to the elements.

Emily had no idea what had gone on at Brigmore in the past. All she knew were rumors and whispered stories from years ago, none of them remotely believable. But the fact that the house had been abandoned for so many years suggested that, perhaps, people were more than a little wary of its history.

She cautiously stepped into the room, aware she was well lit by the moon, aware that the corners of the chamber were comparatively dark, the spaces behind the packing crates very handy spots from which to launch an ambush.

As though confirming her thoughts, there was a sound.

Emily spun around and saw a puff of inky nothing evaporating before her eyes. Then another movement, in the corner of her eye, the tingling sensation running up and down her arms. She spun around again, and was rewarded by a puff of darkness on the other side of the room as Galia blinked around the periphery.

Toward the window.

Emily didn't think, she just acted. She flicked her wrist and the ingenious foldable crossbow she'd taken from the

Whalers armory unfolded into her hand. She lifted it, bringing it to bear on the naked window frame just as the image of Galia briefly solidified from nothing.

Emily fired, the crossbow bolt thudding into the wall. Galia was gone, only to puff back into existence on the other side of the chamber. Emily spun to see the Whaler shoving the lid off one of the packing cases and yanking something out—a sheaf of old, damp papers.

Emily fired again, in rapid succession, studding the packing case and the wall behind it with the small, deadly bolts. She was too slow—Galia had moved already, and fast.

Feeling a rush of air around her, Emily turned on the balls of her feet, firing the crossbow until its bolt quiver was empty. Galia was doing it deliberately, she realized, blinking once, twice, three times around the room, trying to disorient her opponent.

Then something hit her in the stomach.

Emily doubled over, her throat filling with a hot and bitter liquid, the air escaping her lungs. She staggered and collapsed into a sheet-covered armchair that shattered under her sudden weight, the crumbling wood turning to splinters. She looked up, coughing, to see Galia crouched in the window, her face still obscured by the mask, the papers sticking out of her tunic as she surveyed the ruined garden.

Then she turned. Emily tried to pull herself upright.

Galia was gone.

Emily scrambled to the window. The garden was still lit by the bright light flooding out of the interrogation room on the ground floor. She saw the form of Galia, sprinting into the woods and vanishing into the darkness. The leader of the Whalers had a head start, but Emily had a fair idea of where she was going.

Emily retrieved the crossbow bolts from the walls and the packing cases, and reloaded the quiver. Then she left the room, heading back out, returning to the garden and the woods via the branch of the great tree growing into the structure of the floor below.

The Whaler's base of operations was deserted and quiet, the entire company of gangsters having gone to the raid at Brigmore. Emily didn't know if any had survived their encounter with the united street gangs, or had managed to escape capture, but none had yet made it back to the slaughterhouse.

Except for Galia.

Emily had caught up with her easily as she skipped across the rooftops of the city. Galia, to her surprise, stuck to the streets, avoiding patrols and citizens alike by hiding in the shadows, using her conventional stealth abilities rather than her supernatural ability to transverse across space.

After trailing her quarry for a while, Emily knew why. Galia appeared to be sick, or hurt, or both. At one point, she did use her blink ability, crossing from one shaded part of a narrow street to the other in order to avoid a couple giggling in the doorway of a tavern. Almost as soon as she had rematerialized, the Whaler had bent over and yanked her mask up before vomiting in the gutter.

She didn't blink again, after that.

The heat of the factory floor was still intense and surprising. Once inside, Galia pulled her mask off and threw it to the floor as she headed for the metal staircase. She yanked her hood back and ran her hand through her thick thatch of greasy blonde hair.

Emily ducked behind a big metal cauldron on wheels, and watched Galia climb up to the control room. Glancing up, she saw the strange man in the coat standing by the windows. He seemed to be watching the empty factory.

She headed along the factory wall to another set of stairs leading up to the multi-level gallery, across from the control room. She had to get closer, though. Climbing to the office level, she padded along the grating on her toes, her progress silent, undetectable.

And then she stopped.

Across the factory from where she now crouched, the man in the coat came out onto the gallery in front of the control room. He moved to meet Galia, who was now making slow progress, pulling herself up the multiple flights of stairs with some difficulty.

For Emily, the only way forward was the metal walkway, yet between her and the factory office was an open section that was far too well lit. Standing as he was outside of the office, facing her direction, the man in the coat would see her, and easily.

Galia reached her boss and the pair began talking.

Emily looked around for options. There were higher gallery levels, and more stairs that led up to the same fire escape door she had come through before. That gave Emily a choice. Looking up at the slaughterhouse ceiling, Emily saw it was supported by a crisscross lattice of girders that stretched across the entire building, built to support the sliding cranes that moved the whale frames around.

The metalwork looked passable, but dangerous—one false move, and she would plummet two hundred feet to the factory floor below. But she could reach it from the topmost platform. All she needed was to jump across a ten-foot gap, and then she could move across to the control room. In fact, she would be right above it.

Time was pressing. She took a deep breath and headed up. Within a few moments she was at the top platform, roughly level with the ceiling's framework. She looked down over the gap—the factory floor was a *long* way down, and there was little room to get a run-up. In any event, that would have been too noisy on the rattling metal gallery.

Emily rolled her neck, rolled her shoulders. She remembered her training, the hours—the *years*—of practice. This was what it was all for. She took two steps back, and then darted forward, throwing herself across the gap.

Her hands met the edge of the girder.

She pulled.

One hand slipped off. Emily swallowed a gasp and, for a second that stretched into an eternity, she swung out over the gap, supported by only the fingers of her right hand, her legs wheeling through nothing.

Grimacing, she pulled with all her might, lifting herself just a fraction, but enough for her other hand to find purchase. Then she pulled with both arms and slid forward onto the girder on her stomach, twisting around so her body was parallel to it. The girder itself was perhaps a foot wide and the same deep, but it was solid and unmoving, and didn't rattle like the stairs and platforms.

She clung onto the girder, counting the seconds in her head, feeling the sickening thud of her heart in her chest.

Ignoring the height, she lifted herself up and looked ahead and down, toward the control room a couple of hundred yards ahead of her and a hundred or so feet below. The man in the coat and Galia were still talking, the Whaler kneeling in front of him.

Emily got up. The girder's span was about ten feet before another girder intersected it at a right angle, forming a larger—*safer*—platform. Emily was short on time, but she thought she could make it across fairly quickly.

At a half crouch, arms out only a little for balance, she ran to the first frame intersection, paused, then headed to the next. In a few short moments she had crossed the factory floor and was nearly directly above the pair talking on the gallery. She fell back into a crouch and leaned forward to listen to what they were saying.

"They were waiting for us," Galia said.

"How many?"

"Enough. *More* than enough. We matched for numbers, but…"

"But?"

Galia shook her head. "They weren't City Watch. They looked like a street gang—one of the old ones, back from the days of the Rat Plague. The Bottle Street Gang, or the Hatters. Maybe both." She rubbed her face. "The Dead Eels, too. Oh, I don't know."

"No matter."

"No matter?" Galia pulled herself to her feet. "What about all this? You just lost your entire workforce."

The man in the coat tilted his head, like he was thinking it over.

"You escaped."

"Yes, but…"

"Others got away. They will return soon."

"How can you possibly know that?"

"Do you trust me, Galia?"

"What? Trust you? After all this, you ask if I *trust* you?"

The man in the coat ignored her. "Did you get what I needed?"

At this, Galia paused. "They were exactly where you said they would be." Then she pulled the documents out of her tunic and handed them over. The man in the coat took them with one hand, and he held the other out, palm up, as if he was waiting for something else.

Galia swung her shoulder bag around from her back and pulled open the flap. She paused, then reached inside.

"This isn't going to be enough. We were supposed to empty the entire *tomb*."

As Emily watched, Galia pulled out a skull. It was missing the jawbone, but was otherwise intact. It looked old, dusty. She placed it in the man's open hand. He lifted it, turned it around to look into its empty sockets.

"No," the man said, his voice a sibilant hiss from behind his scarf. "You have done well, Galia. You have done *very* well."

"Is… is this enough?"

"It is, it is," he said. "More would have been better, but there is enough material here to craft the charm I require, especially as I now have these parchments from the house. The previous occupant knew much about sorcery that will be useful."

Then he dropped his hand and he jerked his head up, his red-glassed eyes scanning the ceiling.

Emily stifled a gasp and ducked down, flattening herself against the iron girder. Had she been heard, or seen? She held her breath, her ears alive for any sound.

"What is it?" Galia asked, following his gaze.

Emily could hear the man in the coat breathing heavily behind his scarf.

"Perhaps nothing," the man whispered. "Or perhaps something else entirely."

Emily stared at the black metal of the girder. She heard the two move on the gallery below, and then the man spoke again.

"You have done well, Galia. We can proceed."

Galia muttered something. Emily took the chance and peered around the girder. The two below had turned, their backs to her, and were talking in low voices.

Then Emily felt the blood rush in her ears. She felt her heart kick. She felt awake, alive, ready for action. She could take them. It was *perfect*. They had their backs to her. There was ample space between the girders to drop down, right on top of them. They wouldn't even know it was coming.

She could stop this. She could stop this *right now*.

Emily pulled herself into a crouch and slinked farther along the girder. The crossbow was no use to her now, but the Whaler's uniform she had borrowed had come with something else.

She pulled the knife from her belt. It couldn't have been more perfect.

And then…

And then she hears laughter and she hears screaming and the lightning flashes.

And then she sees Corvo separating High Overseer Khulan's head from his body and the warm blood arcs across the throne room.

And then she hears someone call out, asking for more, more, more.

The voice belongs to Emily, Empress of the Isles. She commands and Corvo listens and now he has another in his grip.

The Royal Executioner looks up and grins at the Empress, and the Empress laughs and the lightning flashes and the blade in Corvo's hand flashes as he runs it across the throat of the screaming noble in his grip.

The noble is Wyman. Dead.

And Corvo laughs.

And Emily, too.

Emily stood up on the girder. The slaughterhouse disappeared in a collapsing tunnel of darkness as she passed out.

She toppled sideways, falling, falling.

15

"I have postulated here that time itself is an illusion, not so much the inevitable decline of a system from order into chaos, but merely an additional aspect of space, the nature of which is not immediately obvious. If a solid object is said to occupy a space by virtue of its length, breadth, and volume, can the same object be not said to likewise occupy the measureable dimension of 'duration?'"

— THE HUNGRY COSMOS
Excerpt from a larger work on the movement
of the spheres by Anton Sokolov

When Corvo saw Emily fall he was down on the floor of the slaughterhouse, examining the chains of the huge frame that had been welded and bolted together next to the churning vat of what looked like molten glass.

He'd seen her running through the woods from Brigmore Manor, recognizing his own daughter immediately—the way she moved, the way she leapt down the big tree that touched the house and then sprinted into the woods—despite the Whaler's outfit she appeared to be wearing. He had followed her, leaving the cooperative Rinaldo in the safe hands, not of Slackjaw and his men, but of Jameson, with instructions to get him straight back to the Tower.

The strange bonecharm was still in Corvo's pocket. That, he couldn't let out of his possession. He needed to study it, examine it. And he would need the High Overseer's help in figuring out just what kind of weird charm it was.

On the way to the slaughterhouse he'd kept out of sight. That Emily had left the Tower was not a surprise—but that she was dressed as a Whaler certainly was.

And she was following a trail, chasing something. Something that had to be important.

He had watched from the shadows of the slaughterhouse as Emily climbed the gantry and jumped up onto the girder framework suspended from the ceiling. That had been sloppy. Emily must have known it, because after nearly missing the jump, she then crossed the roof supports carefully and with cautious ease.

From down on the floor, Corvo could see the two targets—the Whaler and the man in the coat. Emily was a lot closer to them than he was.

Good. She was learning. True enough, Corvo knew he should be angry with her, but he felt a pride within him— that she was out there, using her training, the Empress working hard to defend her own city, like no ruler before her ever had.

And then she had fallen.

Corvo acted instinctively. He leaped forward, the Mark of the Outsider burning on his hand as he called on the Void to rush into their world, the swirling eddies of two different, incompatible dimensions allowing time itself to be frozen, just—from Corvo's point of view—for a few short moments. The effort was immense and he couldn't keep it up too long. He had three vials of Addermire Solution with him, but that was all.

Emily's body froze in mid-air, the whole factory suddenly rendered in flickering black and white. Corvo gritted his teeth with the exertion, then blinked up to the platform above his head to reach the second level of the factory.

He spun around, sighted the girders in the ceiling. Too high. Instead he focused on the next gallery level above. Level three. Good enough for now.

He blinked, then gasped for air as he materialized on the gallery. He already felt heavy, slow. He turned to check on Emily. She was still suspended, a butterfly caught in amber, but already he could feel the drain. Any moment now he would need to release his hold on time and she would hit the factory floor.

Corvo relaxed his mind, relaxed his body. He blinked to the next platform up, to the ceiling framework, then down to the gallery.

He turned back to face Emily. He felt the Mark burn on his hand and he felt his own strength ebb, his limbs becoming heavy, his reflexes slow, his concentration slipping along with his grip on the power of the Void.

Time sped up and reality snapped back to normal.

Emily fell.

Corvo turned, and jumped, and blinked.

He materialized with his arms wrapped around her. They twisted, tumbled, fell. He reached out and blinked again, the tether linking his mind to the gallery across the factory, moving and slipping as he fell through the air.

He was going to be too late.

He had no target, no destination. No hope.

Corvo closed his eyes, pushed all other thoughts aside, and just blinked.

They hit the metal decking of the gallery with a thud, Emily rolling on her side. She was breathing and her eyes moved rapidly behind closed lids. She was alive, but unconscious. Something had happened to her up on the framework.

The sounds of voices rose from below.

Corvo sucked in a long breath of the hot air of the factory. He turned, expecting to see the leader of the Whalers materializing right behind them. But they were high up, and—thus far—alone.

He lifted Emily across one shoulder, and headed for the fire escape door straight ahead.

Outside the cool of the night air was a shock, but it was a good one. It woke Corvo up. Balancing Emily carefully, he reached inside his tunic, his fingers wrapping around a vial of Addermire Solution. He drank it in one gulp, and immediately felt the benefit, the ache of his body fading, the burning of the Outsider's Mark on his hand fading to an electric prickling.

He turned, checking through the door. There appeared to be some confusion inside—certainly more than two voices were now arguing. Some of the Whalers must have returned from the failed raid. Galia's voice stood out, instructing them to capture intruders they hadn't even seen.

As the Whalers piled up the gallery stairs, Corvo could see the man in the greatcoat standing outside the control room. He was facing Corvo, and even at this distance, the red glass of his goggles shone brightly, like two lamps.

A wave of nausea swept up Corvo's body, and he felt instantly cold, as if he had been plunged into the river. He felt dizzy, felt like he was going to be sick, and the factory began to swim in front of his eyes. He squinted, trying to focus on the only thing that seemed to be fixed in his vision—the man in the coat, his red glass eyes shining.

Corvo gasped and turned away, heaving in a breath of cold air. Already, dawn was approaching, the clouds gathered along the eastern sky colored as red as the man's goggles by the rising sun.

There was nothing left to be done here. His priority was getting the unconscious Empress back to the Tower. He looked down over the fire escape railing to the building that stood opposite—a pub, the Lost Cause.

Grimacing at the establishment's unfortunate name, Corvo tightened his grip on Emily and swung over the fire escape railing, blinking as he fell, reappearing on the tavern roof.

And then he ran back to Dunwall Tower, carrying Emily with him.

16

"I was asked, should we not tolerate the possession of simple bonecharms among the populace? Surely this is a trivial matter, merely a cultural practice seen across the Isles? Not as terrible as the creation and coveting of more complex occult runes? Such an insidious question."

— THE BONECHARM SITUATION
Excerpt from a report to the Office of the High Overseer

High Overseer Yul Khulan raised an eyebrow as he looked around the maps and charts tacked to the back of the wooden panels in Corvo's chamber, the screens forming a temporary—and slightly more private—operations center separated from the rest of the room. He steepled his fingers and pursed his lips.

"Most impressive, I'm sure."

Corvo stood by the map table. He looked up and folded his arms.

"I'm glad you approve, Yul."

The High Overseer laughed, still looking around.

"Well, let's not get away with ourselves."

Corvo raised an eyebrow and Khulan's laugh died fairly quickly in his throat. He coughed, and moved over to the map table.

"What is it you need to show me, anyway?"

Corvo stroked his chin, and stepped over to a painting hanging on the wall, one of Empress Jessamine. A reminder of another place, another world.

He swung the portrait open like a door. Behind it, set into the wall, was a safe. Entering the combination, he spun the handle, opened the safe, and reached in to take out a small linen-wrapped object.

"I called you in here," he said, "because I don't want this to get out of this room. It's too much of a risk." He placed the object on the map table, and unwrapped it. The High Overseer moved to his shoulder.

"What is it?" he asked.

"Take a look for yourself," Corvo said, folding the last of the linen wrap open.

"By all the Isles," the High Overseer whispered. His fingers gingerly reached for the object, then he snatched them back before they made contact, as if the object was hot.

"Where did you get it?"

Corvo folded his arms and looked down at the strange bonecharm. Already the white bone had charred even further, the entire surface now blackened and crisscrossed with a fine tracery of cracks. The linen in which the charm had been wrapped was burned where the fabric had touched it. The apparent disintegration of the object—and the heat that it produced—was curious.

"From one of the Whalers we captured at Brigmore Manor," Corvo said. "His name was Rinaldo—he knew Daud, back in the day. He had this on him."

"And where did *he* get it from?"

"That's where it gets interesting. He says he found it in the basement of a slaughterhouse, where the Whalers were regrouping." Corvo paused, thinking back over his own experience at the factory two nights before. Emily was fine, but exhausted, and had given Corvo a half-hearted story about being taken ill. She clearly didn't remember how she had got back to the Tower. Corvo was content to leave her with the belief that the strange disorientation he had seen her experience at the slaughterhouse had simply clouded her memory, and that she had made her own journey back home.

He had to keep his own involvement a secret from his daughter, so he played the innocent, accepting her claim that she was simply under the weather.

Corvo's thoughts turned to the strange man he had seen. He remembered the glowing red eyes, and shuddered.

"It seems that the Whalers have a new leader," he said, "a man who wears a winter greatcoat from the Tyvian military."

"A Tyvian agent?" the High Overseer asked, his eyebrows dancing on his forehead. "Do you think they're planning something against the Empress?"

Corvo scratched his stubbly chin. "I'm not sure, but it doesn't feel like it. I think this man is some kind of independent operative. He's revived the Whalers, with some of the old guard back in place. According to Rinaldo, a woman called Galia has become the stranger's right hand. She and Rinaldo were in the original Whalers together, back when Daud was operating in Dunwall."

"You don't think this stranger could be Daud?" Khulan asked. "Who knows what happened to him over the last fifteen years."

"I suppose it's possible," Corvo said. "I didn't see his face. Rinaldo says the man has powers, like Daud used to have—and he's shared them with Galia. That means it was she I encountered at the cemetery in the New Mercantile District. She was leading the raid. According to Rinaldo, this man in the coat never leaves the factory.

"And I saw how Galia could move," he continued. "Transverse, like the Whalers used to be able to do."

The High Overseer frowned. "Then it *is* Daud?"

Corvo looked down at the bonecharm. Was the man in the coat Daud? He was disguised, but he was bigger than Daud was… wasn't he? Did Corvo really remember?

Yes, of course he remembered. Daud was the man responsible for the murder of Jessamine. It didn't matter that it had been on the orders of Hiram Burrows. The blood was on Daud's hands.

Corvo should have killed him when he had the chance. The thought had come and gone throughout the last fifteen years. If only there was a way of doing more than just stopping time. Of turning it back…

The High Overseer leaned over the bonecharm. He reached out for it again, but Corvo stopped him, resting a hand on Khulan's forearm.

"Careful. It's hot—look at the way the linen is charred."

Khulan nodded. "Yes, I see what you mean." He took a white glove out of his red velvet coat and pulled it on, then he carefully prodded the charm with a covered finger. Even as he did so, the charm cracked across the middle, the two halves splitting and crumbling like spent charcoal. Khulan snatched his hand back and frowned.

"Well, if this is a bonecharm, it's like none I have ever seen before." He stood back. "It is clearly unstable. Perhaps the power it holds decays the structure over time, causing this instability."

Corvo nodded. "That's my guess. It would give it a limited lifespan, too." He rubbed his chin again. "I haven't seen a charm like this before, either. It's human bone, we know that—most likely taken from the cadavers lifted from the merchant cemetery. Rinaldo says the man in the coat has a whole workshop set up under the factory, and has been carving the bonecharms day and night.

"If they *do* have a limited lifespan, then—whatever he needs them for—he would need to make as many as possible. Perhaps their decay accelerates when they are worn, as their power is taken up by the wearer."

"Heretics!" Khulan said, shaking his head. Then he composed himself and continued. "That doesn't explain the power you saw at the cemetery. Bonecharms are not in the same league as that. If this Galia has been given the gift of transversal, then that's a higher magic all together."

"I agree."

"Have you elicited any other information from this Rinaldo character?"

Corvo nodded, and, unfolding an arm, he pointed to a spot on the map table.

"Rinaldo says that Galia and the man in the coat haven't yet finished. They're working on something— something big—and to finish the job, they need one more component."

The High Overseer peered at the map, then he looked back at Corvo, a shocked expression on his face.

"But that's… that's…"

Corvo tapped the map. "The Boyle Mansion, yes."

"But the masquerade is in just a few days. You're not suggesting—"

"I don't know, but it seems to fit. There is something at the masquerade they want. Whoever they have left from the raid at Brigmore, they're going to hit the party."

"Can't we stop them? We know the location of their base. We can send in the City Watch, the Overseers! I know the Music Boxes weren't tuned in time for you to take them to Brigmore Manor, but they are ready now. We can put a stop to this before any more damage is done."

Corvo shook his head. He pointed at the bonecharm. "The man in the coat has more of these things. Dozens of them, according to Rinaldo. Until we know just what they are capable of, we can't risk a frontal attack. Music Boxes don't have any effect on the power of bonecharms, remember."

"Then what do you suggest?"

"Stealth," Corvo said. "Subtlety. Let me do this the way I know how."

Khulan snorted. "So says the Royal Spymaster."

"Royal Spymaster *and* Protector, Yul. Don't think I take threats to the Empress lightly. However, we need to know what the man in the coat is planning. The more information we have, the better. He's dangerous, and powerful—in fact, we likely have no idea just *how* powerful."

"And what do you propose?"

"We let the masquerade go ahead."

"What? You can't be serious."

"Never more so," Corvo said. "The masquerade goes ahead. I'll fill the place with agents. Nobody will know, and nothing will change."

The High Overseer blew out his cheeks and shook his head. "I don't like this, Corvo. It goes against my grain."

Corvo nodded. "I understand, Yul, but it makes sense. Listen. The man in the coat never leaves the factory. The Whalers lost most of their men at Brigmore Manor. If they're going to hit the masquerade, it'll be Galia and the scraps of her crew."

Khulan raised an eyebrow. "I think I see," he said. "With the Whalers at the masquerade…"

"The man in the coat will be at the factory, alone, yes,"

Corvo said. "We wait at the masquerade and grab Galia and the others. Meanwhile, with the factory clear, we'll have that surrounded—as many of the City Watch and as many Overseers as we can muster. I'll take the Warfare Overseers to the masquerade. The Music Boxes will stop Galia using her powers, and I'll have enough agents among the guests to detain her and her men before they cause any trouble."

The High Overseer hissed. He stepped away from the table, and began pacing behind the screens, steepling his fingers again and tapping them against his lips.

"I don't like this, Corvo," he said. "It's a risk. A huge risk! You're using the masquerade—and the guests—as bait."

"It's a calculated risk, Yul, and the guests will be protected. I have more than enough agents at my disposal."

"And what about the Empress?"

"She'll be in the safest place possible," Corvo said. "Right here, in Dunwall Tower. The Empress is invited to the masquerade each year, but never attends. Protocol and tradition forbid it."

"So the Empress will be safe."

"Yes, absolutely."

"Even without her protector at her side?"

Corvo raised his hands. "Yul, listen. This is our one opportunity to find out who these people are, and what they are doing."

"By putting the people of Dunwall at risk, Corvo," the High Overseer said, waving around the room as if to indicate the general population of the city. "The elite of the Empire will be at the masquerade, and you intend to allow this gang to walk among them."

"We will be there, Yul. *I* will be there. No harm will come to any of them. You have my word."

Khulan frowned. "Very well, Corvo, but on your head be it—and on the head of the Empress."

Corvo nodded and walked over to his friend. He held out his hand, palm up. Khulan looked down at it with a grimace, but then he shook it anyway.

"On your head be it," the High Overseer repeated, and then he turned away and headed for the door.

17

DUNWALL TOWER
14th Day, Month of Darkness, 1851

"This leads to the most common critique of the Office of the Royal Spymaster, that actions are taken and deeds committed that even the Emperor or Empress is not aware of. This lack of oversight or accountability is a commonly debated topic during Parliamentary sessions, but those who hold the position of Royal Spymaster insist that in order to function the role must exist outside existing bureaucracy or law."

— THE ROYAL SPYMASTER
Excerpt from a historical record of
government positions and ranks

Corvo found Jameson waiting, as arranged, out in the gardens of Dunwall Tower, by the gazebo that overlooked the water lock, and together the pair headed for the throne room. It was late morning on the second day after rescuing Emily from the slaughterhouse, bringing her back to her own secret safe room, into her private apartments, and Corvo had hardly slept since. He had much to think about, and much to plan.

Now that he'd at least got the High Overseer to agree, it was time to put those plans into action.

Daylight dappled the pair as the Royal Spymaster and his chief agent headed toward the Tower foyer. Corvo blinked in the light. So much of his work was confined to the night, to the darkness, but not now. Sleep was for tortoises. There was no time lose.

On the way up to the throne room, he briefed Jameson on his plans, the two of them discussing which agents to disguise in the elaborate costumes required for the Boyle Masquerade. Corvo was pleased—in Jameson he was grateful that he had a faithful, loyal agent. Whatever Corvo wanted, the man would deliver, no questions asked. And if he wanted Jameson's opinion on his plans, he would ask for it.

He didn't.

At the throne room, the two guards on duty came to attention and swung the doors open. Corvo stepped through, then came to a halt. He frowned. Something was going on. Something he didn't know about.

Empress Emily Kaldwin was sitting on the throne, dressed in her usual black trouser suit with high white collar, looking none the worse for wear after a day of rest, and nobody in the room apart from Corvo—not even Jameson—had any idea that she had narrowly escaped death just two nights before.

Assembled in front of the dais were Captain Ramsey of the City Watch, Commander Kittredge of the Wrenhaven River Patrol… and High Overseer Khulan. As Corvo and Jameson approached, Khulan stuck his tongue in his cheek and gave Corvo a glance, as if to apologize for being summoned by the Empress. But that look told Corvo all he needed to know—the High Overseer hadn't betrayed his plans. A summons by the Empress of the Isles was simply an order one couldn't ignore.

Corvo bowed to the throne, then to the High Overseer. The Captain and Commander, meanwhile, saluted both him and Jameson. He turned back to the dais.

"I'm sorry, Your Majesty, I wasn't aware we had a meeting scheduled. Have I missed something?" He looked at her with narrow eyes, and wondered what she was planning.

"Lord Protector," Emily said, greeting her father in the customary, formal tone she reserved for those she commanded. Corvo bit his tongue to stop himself betraying his thoughts. "I've summoned you all here to issue an Imperial edict," she continued. "The city of Dunwall is to be placed under full lockdown until the grave robbers have been caught."

Corvo cocked his head. He exchanged a look first with Jameson, who clasped his hands behind his back and bounced a little on his heels, knowing well enough not to venture an opinion. Then Corvo glanced at the High Overseer. Khulan was trying very hard to keep his attention on the Empress, but he glanced at Corvo, as well, from the corner of his eye, and his lips twitched.

"Ah, on what grounds, Your Majesty?" Corvo asked.

The others in the throne room all turned to look at him. Only the Royal Protector would dare question the Empress like that.

"New information," the Empress said. "That is all you need to know."

Corvo cleared his throat. Of course, Emily was protecting her secret, not realizing that he knew all about her nighttime adventures. If she'd seen him at Brigmore Manor, then she knew he was on the trail of the Whalers.

Except she couldn't admit that fact.

Corvo allowed a small smile to creep up the corner of his mouth. "I understand, Your Majesty," he said, picking his words carefully. Emily would think she had the upper hand—believing that Corvo didn't want to reveal his own actions at Brigmore Manor.

The Captain of the City Watch cleared his throat.

"Begging your pardon, Your Majesty, my Lords, but the City Watch is stretched pretty thin as it is. We already have a liaison in place with the Abbey of the Everyman, to keep watch on the city's burial grounds—" He gave a bow to the High Overseer. "—and with the cooperation of the Wrenhaven River Patrol, we can redouble patrols around Dunwall, but a full lockdown will require more soldiers than I can muster. Unless the Royal Spymaster can offer any assistance?"

The Captain turned to Corvo. Corvo pursed his lips, then slowly shook his head.

"My agents are my own," he said flatly. "And you know better than to ask. They operate independently, and in secret. Anything else would jeopardize their anonymity and the security of the empire."

Captain Ramsey sighed, and turned back to Emily. "Yes, that was the answer I was expecting. Your Majesty, if a full lockdown really *is* your intention, then we would need to recall the Gristol army from their barracks at Whitecliff." He paused. "And, dare I say it, I'm not sure the good people of Dunwall would like the idea of troops moving in, to keep them locked in their homes."

"Even recalling the army would take time," Jameson said, interrupting the Captain with a small bow. "Forgive me, sirs, but this is time we do not have."

Corvo nodded at his companion, then turned to Emily.

"I have an alternative."

Emily licked her lips. "I'm listening."

"Do nothing."

At this, Captain Ramsey and Commander Kittredge

spun around to face him, their eyes wide in surprise. High Overseer Khulan looked at the floor. Corvo ignored them all, his gaze instead fixed on the throne.

The Empress stood and stepped down from the dais to join the group on the red carpet. She lifted one black eyebrow.

"Do *nothing*?"

Corvo nodded. "Precisely that."

Emily shook her head. "I don't understand. What does that achieve? What does it even *mean*?"

Corvo folded his arms. "It means, we do nothing— outwardly. The City Watch and Overseers will continue their watch on the cemeteries. But the Boyle Masquerade is fast approaching. Let it take place. Let the city go about its business and its pleasure as though nothing is happening."

The Captain of the City Watch lifted his jowled chin. "And how are we supposed to capture the gang if we do 'nothing,' as you suggest?"

"I have my own information," Corvo said. "My agents are working around the clock, believe me, but we need to set a trap."

At this, he outlined the plan he and the High Overseer had discussed, leaving out any specifics which might expose the extent of his secret spy network. When he was finished, Ramsey and Kittredge looked first at each other, then back at Corvo, both of them with their faces screwed up in disbelief. Ramsey opened his mouth as if to say something, then he sighed and turned back to the Empress.

"Your *Majesty*," he said, "this is pure folly. You leave the fate of the city's elite in the hands of one man? Corvo is the Royal Protector, your own bodyguard, but if he fails, consider the consequences. The city's most influential citizens will be in attendance."

That was all Corvo needed. Emily's loyalty to him was

absolute, and she trusted him implicitly. Any suggestion that he or his agents were somehow not up to the task would touch a nerve in the young Empress, and would only serve to reinforce his own position.

She shook her head.

"No, he won't be alone." She turned to her father. "How many agents do you have ready?"

Corvo smiled and gave a small bow. "Enough, Your Majesty."

"Very well." Emily smiled back. "You may proceed with your plan."

Commander Kittredge spluttered while Captain Ramsey exhaled, long and slow.

"Your Majesty, this is a terrible risk. The nobility of the city will be in the hands of your Royal Spymaster."

Corvo nodded. "And they will be safe, Commander." He turned to Emily. "As will the Empress, here in the Tower. I will double your personal guard, as well as the guard on the Tower gates. I'll also have agents stationed to keep watch." He paused, and smiled. "Besides, with recent events, a quiet night with Wyman sounds like just what you need."

Emily smiled. "Well, if you put it like that." Then she turned around to the others. "This audience is over. I place the City Watch and the Wrenhaven River Patrol under the Royal Protector's direct command. That will be all."

Ramsey and Kittredge snapped their salutes to the Empress and—with perhaps the tiniest hesitation—to Corvo, and then marched out of the throne room, leaving Emily with Corvo, Khulan, and Jameson.

As the throne room doors swung shut, Emily turned to her father, her arms folded and her head shaking.

"I hope you're right about this, Corvo."

"Trust me, Emily. Trust me."

Emily frowned. "You know I do."

Corvo gave his daughter a bow, then gestured to the High Overseer and Jameson.

"Gentlemen, let's get to work."

18

DUNWALL TOWER
15th Day, Month of Darkness, 1851

"The alchemy of war is a curious thing. If an enemy sleeps, they are already defeated, and if they wake later after victory is yours, they may never even have seen your hand in their defeat. The crafting of certain reagents to induce sleep is a necessary school to master, as is the development of immunity against such mixtures by the slow titration of self-administered doses."

— A BETTER WAY TO DIE
Surviving fragment of an assassin's treatise,
author unknown

The next day at Dunwall Tower passed quickly and uneventfully. Corvo was absent, busy arranging plans for the Boyle Masquerade that evening, while the Imperial Court was quiet as the nobles of the city retreated behind closed doors, ready to surprise their friends with the amazing and elaborate costumes they had prepared in secret.

The Masquerade Ball, the society event of the year,

would go ahead as scheduled. The revelers would be safe under the watchful eye of Corvo and his agents. Nobody would know anything was happening.

Meanwhile, the Empress was locked in her Tower, safely out of danger, while the Royal Protector did his job, defending the throne and the Empress who sat upon it.

Emily repeated those facts to herself over and over all through the day. Yes, the plan was risky. But she trusted Corvo. Not only that, she knew there was far more to the gang's activities than mere grave robbing, and she knew that *he* knew that, too. She'd seen him at Brigmore.

But there was also the information she had gathered herself—information she felt was important, and that she knew she couldn't tell Corvo without revealing her own secrets.

Emily entered her private apartments and paused. She'd come to her decision.

She was duty-bound to help, in any way she could.

She locked the apartment door then headed over to the opposite wall, where Anton Sokolov's secret lock was hidden in plain sight. She lifted her hand and pressed her signet ring against the keyhole that looked like nothing more than another delicate decorative embellishment. The ring mated with the finely balanced mechanism, and there was a click as the hidden wall panel unlocked and opened.

Emily stepped through. Once in her safe room, she headed straight for a secure footlocker that was against one wall. She spun the combination lock and opened the lid. Inside, nestled on levered shelves, were the various bolts for her wrist crossbow. Emily reached in and swung the top shelf out, revealing the second shelf beneath. The crossbow bolts there were different, the body of each a long, thin glass tube filled with a green, faintly luminescent liquid.

She picked out a bolt and took it over to her

workbench. Holding the bolt upright, she began carefully disassembling it, removing the flight and the arrowhead until eventually she had freed the vial of green liquid. She held it up to the light, and frowned. She really didn't want to do what she was planning—and she wasn't entirely sure it would work, anyway—but she felt she had no choice.

Not if she was to protect her secret.

Checking that the vial was carefully stoppered, she slipped it into her pocket and headed back into her apartment, closing the secret door behind her.

Emily found Wyman waiting for her in the Great Hall, smiling as she entered. Her step faltered for just a second, but Wyman didn't seem to notice before she moved in for a polite, formal kiss.

As they broke off, Wyman turned and waved at the room.

"Isn't this amazing? Every year, they outdo themselves."

Emily looked around. The Great Hall had been done up in colorful bunting, with flags hanging from the hammer beam roof high overhead. The great banquet table, which days earlier had been covered with the costume materials, had been separated into two halves, each set up on the opposite side of the room. Against the west wall, the table was covered with a veritable feast of exotic finger foods, while on the east wall about an acre of glassware was laid out in front of a forest of bottles filled with interesting liquids.

She sighed. Wyman was right, it did look incredible—the traditional pre-ball reception, held in the Great Hall of Dunwall Tower for the members of the Imperial Court to mix and mingle before the train of carriages took them all off to the Boyle Mansion. As per the tradition, this was as far as the Empress ever got.

Emily reached out and took Wyman's hand.

"M'lady!" Wyman gave a theatrical bow.

Emily laughed, but she couldn't help feeling sour to her stomach about what she was going to do.

"You're not unhappy to miss the masquerade this year?" she asked.

Wyman laughed and looked up at the flags of the nobility hanging from the ceiling. "Not at all. It's not my thing really. Never has been—and besides, who would I go with these days? My sister?" More laughter. "Believe me, there is no place I would rather be than here, locked away in Dunwall Tower with the Empress of the Isles."

Wyman squeezed Emily's hand. She smiled, but the smile faltered again. This time Wyman did notice.

"What's wrong?"

Emily blinked, then laughed, rather self-consciously.

"Ah… oh, nothing," she said. "It's just that one day I think I'd like to take you to a masquerade ball."

"What?" Wyman asked, hand pressed to chest, face an exaggerated expression of shocked outrage. "But, m'lady, people would *talk*!" Wyman's eyes rolled up as though a faint was imminent. "The scandal. Lords and ladies, the scandal!" Laughing, Wyman collapsed into Emily's arms and she spun, dragging them both around playfully until she was facing the doors of the Great Hall.

Over Wyman's shoulder, she cast a watchful eye. There wasn't much time. The first of the costumed revelers would be arriving any minute now.

"Time to get started," she said, pushing herself away, then leading the way over to the drinks table. Wyman's expression flickered in confusion at her words, but Emily quickly covered. "Time for a *drink!* As Empress of the Isles, I get to start first." Then she turned to the table, keeping her back to the room, hiding the glasses that rested immediately in front of her.

She was in luck. As well as Tyvian wines, there was a liqueur from Karnaca, the liquid a deep green, the aroma a heady mix of spices and peppermint. Selecting a tall glass, she slid the vial out of her pocket and upended it into the glass, then quickly filled the remainder with the liqueur. Replacing the empty vial in her pocket, she grabbed the drink and turned around.

Wyman was over at the other table, selecting something to eat.

"*My Lords and Ladies*," Emily said, mimicking Wyman's earlier pretentiousness. She held out the tall glass of green drink, bowing low.

"Well, well, served by the Empress herself. My, see how low the mighty have fallen." Wyman took the drink and peered suspiciously at the contents. "Uh... Serkonan spiced... something something?"

Emily nodded. She pressed her lips together.

Just bloody drink the stuff, she thought.

"I'd rather have some bubbly," Wyman said, looking expectantly at the drinks table before holding up Emily's offering. "You've got the right glass for that at least... I would have thought Serkonan spiced liqueur was drunk out of a small round cup, not this." Wyman gave the drink a sniff and frowned some more. "Oh, this isn't spiced... what's in it?"

"I made it with my own fair and beautiful Imperial hands," Emily said.

"Yes but *what* did you make with those fair and beautiful Imperial hands?"

"Ah... my own concoction. Let's call it, Emily's Elixir. Now just drink the bloody thing, and tell me what you think." She tried hard not to sound too annoyed.

Wyman was about to take a sip, then he paused before lowering the glass and looking at the Empress.

"You're not joining me?"

"No," Emily said. "I mean, yes, but I wanted to see what you thought first."

"So now I'm a test subject?"

"You could say that, yes."

Wyman sighed and lifted the glass to the light to observe the sparkling green liquid. The pompous voice returned, the elocution pitch-perfect, the r's rolling like thunder on the horizon.

"An experiment was carried out in the laboratories of her right Royal High and Mightiness." Then Wyman laughed. "Roll up, roll up, and take a snifter of the remarkable Emily's Elixir, guaranteed to cure what ails ya, and more besides!"

Wyman glanced sideways at Emily. "If my hair falls out, you're buying me a hat made of solid gold."

"Deal," Emily said.

"Bottom's up," Wyman said, before swallowing the contents of the glass in a single, long gulp. Wyman paused, jaw open, tongue dancing, then nodded. "Actually that's not bad. There's something sweet in it, sort of like... I mean... I think... maybe..."

Wyman dropped the glass.

Emily caught it before it hit the floor.

Then Wyman followed the glass. Emily, her own glass in one hand, managed to hook her other under the young noble's armpit, arresting the fall and letting the limp figure sink gently to the floor.

"Sorry, my love," Emily whispered, "but I know Corvo asked you to keep an eye on me."

Time ticked on. The guests would arrive at any moment. Looking around, she quickly darted over to the curtains at the end of the table and hid the spent glass behind it, then she ran back to Wyman and lifted her companion over her shoulders.

Bent under the weight, she shuffled to the back of the Great Hall and kicked at the curtains to reveal a wall of fine, dark wooden panels with an elaborate, carved border running along the top. She squinted as she searched along the upper edge of the border, until she saw what she was looking for—bird in flight, wings outstretched.

Balancing Wyman carefully against her, she reached up and twisted the carving. There was a click, and the wooden panel swung inward, revealing one of the Tower's many secret passages. Emily slid sideways through the opening, careful not to knock the sleeping young noble's head on the woodwork, then closed the panel with her foot.

The passageway beyond was short, and in just a few moments, she emerged from behind another panel in the corridor behind the Great Hall. The coast was clear but Emily paused, listening for a few seconds to make sure before carrying her unconscious burden off toward one of the guest apartments.

If she had judged the dose of sleeping elixir correctly, Wyman would sleep for hours, and Emily was already concocting a story in her mind to explain how her companion had come down with a sudden chill, and had been put to bed.

In the meanwhile, she had work to do.

The makeshift workroom and haberdashery was dark and quiet, the tailors and seamstresses long since retired for the night. Emily appeared from behind a curtain in the dark room, having stolen down the hallway past a lonely night-shift maid.

The large chamber was lined with shelves, on which were stacked hundreds of bolts of cloth—the same cloth which had been laid out in the Great Hall, the *very* same cloth from which many of the masquerade costumes had been crafted for members of the Imperial Court.

She crept to the back of the room, past the shelving, to where rows of finished and half-finished clothes were hung on long racks. Just behind these were the sample masquerade costumes, ready to be placed back into storage until they were needed next year.

Emily looked over the costumes. She needed something that was a complete disguise, with a mask that would cover her whole head, yet something that was still practical—as much as it could be. Butterflies with huge wings were no good, nor the lions and tigers with great trailing tails, their masks large and top-heavy. She had to be able to move when she needed to.

One costume came to mind as she fumbled through the racks in the semidarkness. She remembered it from the Great Hall display, and she quickly found it.

It was relatively modest, a black trouser suit inlaid with shimmering blue-black sequins and black metallic feathers, while the large collar of the jacket was embroidered with silver and gold ribbon. There were no awkward wings, and the mask itself was small and close-fitting, but still offered a complete disguise without being impractical.

Emily pulled the components of the black sparrow costume off the rack.

Yes. This will be perfect.

This year, the Empress was going to the Masquerade Ball, and nobody would know a thing about it.

INTERLUDE

"To know your enemy is to first know yourself. To this end, every day must present a challenge, every moment an opportunity, to meet the person that you are. To search for your limits and to step beyond them. Only then can you be ready to face what may come, because only then will you know that of which you are capable."

— A BETTER WAY TO DIE
Surviving fragment of an assassin's treatise,
author unknown

Empress Emily Kaldwin walked into the throne room, then paused, and looked around.

Something was wrong.

The chamber was huge, long and vaulted like the main hall of the Abbey of the Everyman, lined with cabinets showcasing the wealth of the Empire, with artifacts from every corner of the Isles. There was even, in one case, a small black piece of driftwood that looked more like it was the last survivor of a fire. As fragile as anything, it was supposedly a relic from the Pandyssian Continent. The idea had entranced Emily since childhood and, she had to admit, continued to do so to this day.

She stopped, halfway to the silver throne that sat on the raised, red-carpeted dais at the end of the chamber. The Imperial Court was not in session, and although she had been the Empress for some eight years now, she had to admit she disliked using this room. It was too—well, it was too *regal*. She had accepted her life as Empress, but she was determined not to sink into the soft leather of the throne and rule without a thought for her Isles, her cities, her people.

If only she could actually go out and *meet* her subjects. Learn about them and their lives as they struggled to rebuild Dunwall after the reign of the Lord Regent.

Perhaps she would, one day—free from the ever-watchful gaze of her guards, of her courtiers. Of her father, the Royal Protector. Today was her eighteenth birthday. Perhaps today could mark a change, if she *made* it so. At eighteen she was no longer a child.

She sighed, and stood, tapping her foot. She was here now because a request had been made. The Captain of the City Watch had requested an audience, with some urgency.

And yet... the throne room was empty.

The Captain hadn't arrived yet, and there was something else, too. Because even when not in use, the throne room was guarded—there had been two guards on duty outside, who had saluted her and swung the doors open for their Empress. But the two who were supposed to be on duty on the inside of the door were strangely absent. With the doors now closed, Emily found herself alone.

The hairs on the back of her neck stood up. She curled her fingers into fists, and instinctively she bent her knees, ready for what she sensed was about to come.

There was a creaking sound from behind her.

She spun.

Two men appeared from behind the thick curtains that were gathered on either side of the throne room doors. They were dressed in brown, mismatched leathers, their tunics crisscrossed with belts. Each man was hooded, his face hidden behind a black cloth mask tied around his head.

They approached slowly, shoulders rolling, their eyes on the Empress. They seemed to be unarmed, but one of them cracked his knuckles loudly.

Another sound, and Emily turned to face the throne. From behind it stepped two more men, the same as the others.

Four men, four intruders. Thugs, all here for one very particular reason.

Emily's eyes narrowed. She gritted her teeth, and glanced around the men as they closed in on her from all sides.

There was nowhere to go.

Nowhere to run.

Emily was alone.

All she could do was *fight*.

Corvo kicked at the body by his feet, then looked around the throne room. There were three more bodies stretched out on the floor, scattered like cut flowers. There was a lot of blood, but the men were all breathing. They would be sore when they woke up.

Emily sat on the edge of the throne, head tilted back as she held a cloth to her face in an attempt to staunch the flow of blood from her nose.

Corvo lifted an eyebrow at the Empress.

"I'm amazed," he said. "You've done well. You need to be congratulated."

"What I *need*," Emily said, "is a long, hot bath, some ointment, and for my Royal Protector to explain how in all the *Isles* a gang of assassins manages to penetrate not just Dunwall Tower, but the *throne room*."

Corvo pursed his lips, nodding. He placed his hands behind his back and carefully stepped over a groaning thug as he approached the throne.

"Mercenaries," he said, "not assassins. And they did pretty well, all things considered."

Emily's forehead creased in confusion, and she pulled the cloth away from her face. She looked down at her father.

"*They* did pretty well?"

"Yes. Pretty well." Corvo ran a finger along his bottom lip, then nodded. "Maybe... seven out of ten? How's the nose?"

"Sore and probably broken."

Corvo nodded. "Make that *eight* out of ten."

"Wait, are you saying what I think you're saying?" Emily stood and jogged down the dais steps, wincing as she did so.

Corvo shrugged. "Your Majesty?" he said, feigning ignorance.

Emily curled a fist and slammed it into Corvo's chest. He staggered back a little, and coughed.

Yes. Most likely he deserved that.

Emily kicked one of the mercenaries at her feet.

"*You* sent them!"

She looked up at Corvo. He looked at her with wide-eyed innocence. Emily's eye twitched with anger.

"What, this was some kind of test?" she asked. "You sent a gang of mercenaries to kill me as some kind of *test*?"

"You might very well think that, Your Majesty," Corvo said, "but the office of the Royal Protector is ignorant of such matters and cannot possibly comment."

"I... I..." Emily fumed, then she growled and kicked the nearest mercenary again. The poor man moaned and rolled over. "I could have been *killed!*"

Corvo smiled. "No, you couldn't. I was watching."

Emily spun around, then she lifted her head to the ceiling and let out a yell of frustration. She turned back to Corvo.

"You're moonstruck!"

"And you were very, very good. Don't forget that."

Emily opened her mouth to yell something else at her father, then she stopped, and sighed.

Then she smiled. Just a little.

"Was I?"

"You were."

She glanced at the carnage around her. "I guess I was, wasn't I?"

Corvo smiled, and turned on his heel. As he strode toward the doors, he called out over his shoulder.

"I'll talk to the Captain of the City Watch, and help him clean up."

Then he stopped, and turned back around.

"Oh, and happy birthday, Your Majesty."

He closed the throne room doors behind him. Emily stared at them. She was confused, sore, her nose was bleeding, and there were four unconscious men lying in the throne room.

Yes, she had done well, hadn't she?

With a grin, Emily headed for her private apartments, eager to take that long, hot bath.

PART THREE
THE MASQUERADE

19

"The late Lord Boyle and his lovely wife perhaps best epitomize this privileged class of citizens. Their annual costume ball is the talk of high society, creating ripples throughout Dunwall when one family or another is excluded from the guest list."

— THE ESTATE DISTRICT
Excerpt from a historical overview of the Estate District

"I must say I'm flattered by the attention," the old lady in the brilliant-scarlet trouser suit said to the snarling bear in the green cape, standing tall beside her. "To have the Royal Protector lending his services to my humble masquerade is something of an honor!"

The bear in the cape turned to the red lady and gave a small bow. Her face was hidden completely by an oval mask, on which was painted the grimace of a laughing jester, and she wore a red hat with the brim curled up at the front, which was pinned to a bouffant of gray curly hair.

The pair stood on the balcony landing of the broad double staircase that overlooked the grand ballroom of the Boyle Mansion.

"Thank you for your cooperation, Lady Boyle," Corvo said, his voice muffled under the bear mask. "My agents will be discrete—you won't even know we're here."

"There, young man, you may be correct."

Lady Esma Boyle turned her garishly painted mask toward the revelers milling around the ballroom, each clad in a brilliant, multicolored costume, their faces hidden behind a variety of disguises ranging from simple half-masks to full, face-covering ones like Lady Boyle's. At the extreme end of the spectrum were the more elaborate constructions like Corvo's bear mask, which covered the entire head.

Even so, some of the revelers could be easily identified—Corvo had already spotted Lord Curran and his wife, the pair dressed in antique finery of the last century, with big hats with curly brims like Lady Boyle's, only their eyes covered behind black domino masks. Tradition insisted that the guests remain anonymous and equal, the two footmen manning the door—one of whom was an agent of Corvo's—announcing each and every arrival with a simple, "Lords, ladies, and gentlemen, may I present a most honored guest!" No names.

It was all a game, of course—most people knew and recognized one another. The conversation that bubbled up from the hall was lively and loud from the start. Directly underneath the balcony a string quintet played light chamber music, amplified through a square speaker that hung over their heads, covered in red cloth.

The device was part of Corvo's plan. While it worked well to amplify the traditional music of the quintet, that was in fact its secondary purpose. Hidden away deep in the mansion was a Warfare Overseer, diligently cranking one of the Music Boxes unearthed from the stores of the Abbey of the Everyone. A flick of a switch and the speaker would cut from the quintet to the ancient, magic-suppressing music of the Overseer's device.

Corvo just hoped he wouldn't have need for it.

He leaned over the balcony rail and glanced to his left. Down below, two men in half-masks glanced up at the bear, and raised their glasses. One wore a ridiculously curled fake mustache that stuck out at least six inches on either side of his face, the other an innocuous mask that nevertheless hid his face well. It had been the best they could acquire on such short notice.

All were in place. Corvo had seeded twenty of his finest agents throughout the room, and there were more outside in the gardens. At least a hundred guests were expected at the masquerade, the attendees spilling out from the halls and ballrooms to enjoy the formal gardens, gazebos, and summer houses, lit and heated by electric whale oil lamps.

A murmur grew among the partygoers, who began gravitating toward the ballroom doors. Corvo watched the crowd.

Right on time. Next to him, Lady Boyle laid an elderly, but elegantly manicured hand on his sleeve.

"Oh, the carriages from the palace have arrived," she said. "I can't wait to see what the tailors of the court have come up with this year!"

As she spoke, the footmen began announcing more "honored guests," and within moments a procession had formed leading from the ballroom doorway over to the left-hand side of the stairs that led up to the balcony. Tradition further dictated that each new arrival make their way up to greet the masquerade's illustrious hostess.

The costumes were remarkable, Corvo had to admit. Glittering parrots and peacocks, multicolored foxes in jeweled waistcoats, tigers with rainbow-striped jackets. Some courtiers had come as insect life, too—butterflies with six-foot wings, and one man as a monochrome moth, the remarkable outfit rendered entirely in shades of gray.

In turn, each of the new guests made their slow way up the stairs and, once in Lady Boyle's presence, took her hand in their own and lowered themselves in a curtsy or bow as their hostess inclined her head in acknowledgement, the feather in her huge curly-brimmed hat bobbing back and forth. Corvo kept to himself at Lady Boyle's shoulder, his hands clasped under the green cape, nodding at the guests only if they acknowledged his presence. Discretion was the order of the night.

At the end of the line was a young, slim woman in minimal, even austere costume of black feathers and sequins, her head enclosed by a close-fitting bird-head mask. As the line of greeters drew closer, Corvo noticed the woman looking out over the ballroom. Whoever she was, she was apparently alone.

He studied her as she came closer. One of Emily's friends, perhaps. When the woman in the black sparrow costume reached Lady Boyle she paused, the beak of the mask pointing first at the host and then at Corvo, and then she gave an awkward curtsy, her hand resting on the top of the hostess's.

His eyes fell on the young woman's hand. It was youthful, the skin pale, and smooth. But, unlike every other woman who had paid their respects to the host, this woman's fingernails were clipped short and were unpainted.

He thought he recognized those hands—the nails kept short for sparring—but it was the ring that was unmistakable. It was silver, with a large diamond-shaped stop on which were four interlocking keys positioned like the hands of the compass. The ring was subtle and elegant... and one of a pair.

The twin of the one he wore on his finger.

The other belonging to the Empress of the Isles.

Corvo wasn't sure if Lady Boyle recognized the ring, or even noticed it. If she did, she didn't give any indication. She merely nodded, and released the hand. Emily stood tall, nodded again at Lady Boyle and then at Corvo, before moving along the balcony to head down the stairs on the other side. She disappeared into the crowd.

He waited a few moments as Lady Boyle continued greeting the new arrivals. Glancing down at the main doors, Corvo saw that the line of new arrivals now extended out past the footmen. Lady Boyle was going to be meeting and greeting for quite a while yet. So he laid a hand on her shoulder, bringing his bear mask close to her ear.

"If you will excuse me, Lady Boyle," he whispered. "Would you like me to get you a drink?"

Lady Boyle laughed behind her mask.

"Young man, you read my mind."

Corvo nodded and, making his excuses, cut through the line of people. As he headed down the stairs, Lady Boyle called out after him.

"And make it a strong one!"

Corvo lifted a hand over his shoulder to acknowledge he had heard her as he trotted down the stairs.

He needed to tell his agents that the party had an unexpected guest.

He spotted Emily from the big double doors that led out to one of the enclosed, "secret" gardens that surrounded the Boyle Mansion. The garden here was on two levels—a large area with fine enameled garden furniture, from which a curve of steps led down to a long, rectangular area which was used for archery and croquet. Already, both were scattered with costumed guests enjoying the warm, pleasant glow of the whale oil heaters.

Corvo scanned the area, his agents in play—four out here—discretely ignoring him. Emily herself stood alone by the balustrade that separated the upper garden from the lower. She had a tall glass in her hand, filled with bubbling wine.

Ducking into the doorjamb, he watched as Emily, ignored by the other guests locked deep in conversation, glanced around, her black sparrow mask turning this way and that, then quietly tipped half of her drink out into the shrubbery. She then raised the glass close to her mask, her elbow balanced on her other arm, and watched the crowd.

Corvo frowned, then ducked back into the ballroom. He made his way over to a man dressed as a white lion. Passing by, he leaned his bear mask in closer.

"Black sparrow in the garden," he said. "Keep watch."

The white lion muttered something which might have been "Right, lad," but it was muffled behind the elaborate and heavy mask. By the time Corvo had walked through the crowd and had reached the other side of the room, the white lion had vanished.

He frowned again beneath his mask. Having Emily here was far from ideal, but at least it meant he was near her side.

20

BOYLE MANSION (CLOSED WING), ESTATE DISTRICT
15th Day, Month of Darkness, 1851

"All there is in my mind is meat, death, bones and song. The terrifying songs, they come to me in my sleep now."

— MEAT, DEATH, BONES AND SONG
Excerpt from a Butcher's journal

The corridor was long and wide, paneled in a rich brown wood studded with ornate chandeliers in escutcheons down its entire length. But the passage—a long gallery— was dark, the chandeliers unlit. Instead, what light there was came in through the large windows set high in the walls on either side of the gallery, the bright moon illuminating a square area at one end of the gallery in a pale, monochrome light.

A woman danced in the light. She wore an elegant trouser suit of silver and white, the sleeves puffed from shoulder to elbow, the neckline low. The woman's hair was the same color as her clothes, and was long and straight, reaching nearly to her waist. She was barefoot, and she spun in the light, her arms outstretched as though to hold a dance partner who wasn't there.

She spun again, one way, then the other, her hair trailing like a comet's tail as she snapped her head this way and that. On her lips was a melody only she could hear.

Then she closed her eyes and she laughed, dropping her arms before giving her imaginary partner a deep bow. She muttered something, a string of words with no particular meaning, then turned and smiled into the moonlight, looking up at the windows as though she was an actress standing on a spotlit stage. She took another bow, and then another, and she smiled to her left and her right, acknowledging the applause of the audience inside her head.

Then she stood, swaying a little, the melody returning to her lips. The tune was familiar, it was her favorite, it had been ever since she was a young child, one of three sisters who played together in the long gallery and who sang the song together, over and over, holding hands in a circle as they spun around and around until the gallery went sideways and they went sideways with it.

Dragging her feet on the soft carpet, the woman in silver and white slowly drifted over to the wall. She held her hands out and dropped her fingertips onto the paneling before drawing her body in and pressing it against the wood. The wall was cool, it was solid, it was *real*. So little was solid and real anymore. The woman in silver and white closed her eyes and pressed her head to the wood.

There. She could hear it. The low rumble of conversation, punctuated by laughter and the clink of glass on glass. Beyond the wall—in the part of the house she hadn't set foot in for years—the Boyle Masquerade was in full swing.

And the music. Oh, the music. It ebbed and flowed like a tide, and as the woman in silver and white smiled it reached a crescendo, growing louder and louder and louder until she could bear it no longer. Still smiling, she pushed herself from the wall, her hands clapped to the side of her head as she squeezed and squeezed, the music becoming the infinite roar of the ocean in her ears.

She fell to her knees, her eyes screwed shut.

Sometimes the music, it *hurt*. It was so loud she couldn't think, so loud she had forgotten who she was and where she was and what she was.

Then it was gone, the silence as sharp as a gunshot.

She opened her eyes and on her knees looked up at the window. The moon was bright, a blaze of silver light that filled her eyes.

"My lady."

The woman turned toward the voice—a man's, echoing softly down the long gallery from the far end, the end drenched in shadows as black as ink. The woman in silver and white frowned, her lips moving soundlessly as she repeated the phrase over and over.

My lady... my lady... my lady... my lady...

Then she snapped her head around. On the wall next to her was a picture, a portrait of an old-fashioned man in old-fashioned clothes. The woman in silver and white stared at the picture.

"Was it you?" she asked.

If the man in the painting heard her, he did not reply.

The woman pulled herself to her feet. Next to the first portrait was a second, and then a third. Suddenly, or so it seemed, the walls of the moonlit gallery were lined with paintings, the ancestors silently watching her from across the years.

Had they always been there? Or had they all just appeared, in an instant?

Both possibilities seemed equally as likely to the woman in silver and white. She stood and moved from one to the next.

"Was it you?"

No reply.

"Was it *you?*"

Silence.

"My *lady.*"

The woman turned toward the voice, louder now, her lips repeating the phrase again. There, in the shadowed end of the gallery, stood a tall man in a black greatcoat. He was nothing but a shape, a shadow himself, but as he stepped forward she saw his eyes glitter then ignite in brilliant red. She stared at them as he came closer, unable to drag her gaze away.

His eyes were the red of her blood. They were the red of the hate and the anger that burned inside her.

And the red light moved. It flickered, wavering, the light of a fire that burned millennia ago, the light of the fire that ended one world and created another. She saw a figure in the flames. A woman in red, with long red hair, her skin red, her eyes red. She smiled in recognition, and the image of the woman smiled back.

And then she remembered.

Oh, Lady Lydia Boyle remembered.

The man in the coat stretched out a gloved hand. Lydia looked at it, blinking away the purple spots that danced in her vision. She reached out and took his hand, a hand that was as cold as the ice, as the howling winds, as the snowbound tundra.

She tilted her head, staring at her hand in his.

The memories flooded back like a freezing, surging tide. As the cold spread through her body, she felt a veil lift from her mind. Suddenly, sharply, the anger returned. Rage, hot and red.

She tore her eyes away from her hand in his, and looked around. The long gallery of the Boyle Mansion was dark, cobwebbed. Abandoned.

Like her.

She remembered what had happened. She remembered the rage and the anger and the shouting. The sadness at the fate of Waverly, the lost sister, descending like a pall over the mansion. The days—weeks, months, years—that she and her other sister, Esma, spent locked inside, trying to escape from the outside world.

For Esma, the solitude was healing. She found herself, her purpose. The annual masquerade balls were her lifeline, her connection to the world around her, a tether she used to drag herself back.

For Lydia, the sadness, the anger, were too much.

She remembered the shouting. Remembered the screaming. Remembered being dragged away, bound in a straitjacket. Months of isolation, locked in a room somewhere, a white room with soft walls and the smug, bearded face of Sokolov as he tended to her. The admission she overheard, that he couldn't do anything.

Her mind was gone, moonstruck.

Being brought back to the house by a carriage at night, bound again in the straitjacket. Being locked in a room on the other side of the mansion, and then being let out, only to find that her prison had merely enlarged to include the entire closed wing of the house.

She had not seen anybody for years. Not even Esma.

Oh, she could *hear* them. Doors opened and doors closed. Food was laid out, her bedchamber made each day. She spent days chasing ghosts, but she never caught them.

Lydia turned back to the man in the coat, and blinked under his gaze. She saw now that his eyes weren't red, he was wearing red-tinted goggles, and they didn't shine, they merely reflected the moonlight coming in through the high windows.

She felt cold, so very, very cold. She wrapped her arms around her body and she sank to the floor, shivering.

The man in the coat said nothing. Lydia looked up at him.

"Are you here to help me?" she whispered.

The man cocked his head, regarding her as though she were an insect pinned beneath a lens.

"Lady Lydia Boyle," he said. His voice was deep and it bounced around the wooden panels of the long gallery. "Do you remember your name?"

Lydia nodded. "I remember everything." Her expression twisted into a snarl, and she bared her teeth at the stranger, as if she was a cornered animal.

"Tell me," he said.

Lydia hissed. "My sister. Esma. She did all of this."

The man nodded. "Yes."

"She put me in here. Locked me away."

"Yes."

"Pretended I didn't exist. Pretended I never existed."

"Yes."

"I… I…" Lydia frowned. What had she been talking about again? She felt momentarily dizzy, then she looked back into the man's red eyes and her mind cleared.

"You hate her, don't you?" the man asked.

"Yes."

"She put you in here. Locked you away."

"Yes."

"She said you were moonstruck, that there was nothing that could be done for you."

"Yes."

"That this was for your own good."

"Yes."

"And while you are her prisoner, she has taken control. Not just of the house, but of the family. The famous Boyle dynasty, the fulcrum on which the fortunes of Dunwall turn. First Lady Waverly. Then you. Now Esma Boyle is alone, and she has it all."

Lydia stared into his eyes. Was that true? Was any of that true? Esma was her sister. A sister who loved her, who looked after her, who was doing this for her own good.

Wasn't she?

The man's red eyes flashed and Lydia blinked.

Esma, the conniving, plotting harpy. Esma the *betrayer*. The sister who wanted it all, if only her siblings were out of the picture.

"I… *yes*," Lydia whispered. "Yes, I see it."

"Tell me, Lady Boyle," the man said, "what would you do if you could change the past? What path would you take? What would you become if the world was struck on a different tangent?"

Lydia's lips moved, but no words came. She gazed at the man and he seemed to fade, and in the back of her mind she could hear music and laughter and she could feel the warmth of the fire as people danced and danced and danced.

And then silence, sharp and cold and awful.

The man in the coat returned, and held out his hand again. This time Lydia took it, and allowed herself to be pulled up.

"I can help you, Lady Boyle," the man said. "I can change it all. I can restore the balance that was taken so cruelly from you."

"Yes?"

"To do this, I need your help."

"Yes."

"Beneath this house is a vault. A chamber built to hold a secret."

Lydia frowned. A vault? Was there a vault? She

struggled to remember. One had been built, perhaps… not so long ago. The memory was fuzzy, but it was there.

"Ah… yes, yes I think so."

"I need you to take me there," the man in the coat said. "There is something there that I need."

Lydia nodded. "And what will you do when you have it?" She stood on her toes as she gazed into those shining red eyes.

The man chuckled quietly. He squeezed Lydia's hand until she thought her fingers would break.

"Why, Lady Boyle," the man in the coat said, "I will save the world, and save you along with it."

Then Zhukov laughed again, and Lady Lydia Boyle found herself laughing with him.

21

BOYLE MANSION, ESTATE DISTRICT
15th Day, Month of Darkness, 1851

"They came at once, out of the dark, out of the shadows! Silence was their skill, murder was their art! The history of the Empire was determined in that great room on that fateful night, the night the Mask and his Companion revealed themselves and saved the City of Appolitis with nothing but the force of their fists and the sharpness of their wits!"

— *THE MASK OF APPOLITIS*
Extract from a lurid gothic novel,
allegedly based on true events

Corvo made what must have been his twentieth lap of the Boyle Masquerade. Or was it more? He had lost count, but it had been *hours*. The house was huge, as were the gardens, and with this many guests, his progress was slow. But with his network of agents at the party, he was confident they had the whole event covered.

So far, nothing had happened. Nothing at all.

This is good, Corvo kept telling himself. The masquerade —perhaps the biggest in recent years—seemed a raging success. There was music, and dancing, and laughter. As he returned to the balcony overlooking the ballroom, he looked out over a multicolored sea of costumes and masks as those who occupied the upper echelons of Gristol society passed the night away in their revels, unmolested.

But it was a setback. Corvo couldn't deny it. Here was the chance to capture at least half of the Whaler's leadership, with the other taken, he hoped, at the factory, in a single, coordinated action. But no such opportunity presented itself.

Perhaps the information had been wrong. Perhaps it had been unwise to listen to the man, Rinaldo—he was too eager to cooperate, to help out. Perhaps he should have left the Whaler to the tender mercies of Slackjaw and his men.

Corvo frowned under his mask. *Perhaps not.*

And then there was the strange bonecharm. It was real enough, and there was no reason for Rinaldo to have handed it over—to have taken it in the first place— if he hadn't had doubts about what the Whalers were doing. About the man in the coat they now looked upon as their leader.

No, Rinaldo was telling the truth. It was just that—

Corvo turned, his eye caught by a masquerade guest standing just next to the ballroom doors. The man was standing alone, apart from the other guests. There was nothing particularly remarkable about him—he wore a black cloak, and he had his head bowed, his face hidden by a large curly-brimmed black hat. Corvo watched him, and found himself willing the man to lift his head and show his mask, but the man didn't move a muscle.

Moving along the balcony, Corvo headed for the stairs. He wanted that man checked out by his agents. As he walked, he looked up.

The man was gone.

Corvo stopped, and scanned the crowd.

Down on the ballroom floor, the guests participated in a formal dance, male and female partners lined up opposite each other. The dance itself was a relic from an earlier age, a whole lot of bowing and arm waving and walking around in circles, the appeal of which was completely baffling to Corvo. Back in Serkonos, dancing couldn't have been more different, an expression of movement free of formal rules and steps, the couple's bodies held close against one another. But he did have to admit, up here on the balcony, looking *down* on the dance, he could see there was a pleasure in its symmetry, and in the synchronized movements of dancers.

As he watched, Corvo caught sight again of his quarry. The man was standing to one side of the dance floor, but he still had his head lowered, the hat obscuring his face. He had one arm hooked inside his cloak, out of sight.

Then the man turned away and moved quietly along the side of the room, then disappeared through one of the doors that led out into the gardens.

Corvo wasted no time, jogging toward the stairs—and found another man standing in his way. This guest was also dressed in the voluminous black cloak and large black hat. He had his head bowed so the brim hid his face. He bowed. Corvo paused, and bowed in return.

The man didn't move out of the way. Instead, he lifted his head to show his masquerade mask. Leather and metal and rubber, two circular glass eyes, a cylindrical respirator hanging from the front.

A Whaler. They were here.

Corvo began to lunge for the man when a cry rang out from the ballroom below. He spun around at the sound.

The dancers had paused, and the musicians had fallen silent, all turning toward the garden doors as there was another cry. Then a group of masqueraders flooded in from the garden in a hurry, running from men in long black cloaks. The faces of the newcomers were hidden behind Whalers' masks.

The attack had begun.

Corvo turned back to the man he had met on the stairs, and found that he had fled. Cursing himself, Corvo pushed his way through the masqueraders on the balcony. They were now trying to head for the stairs on the other side in one heaving, chattering group.

Then he felt a hand on his shoulder. He turned, fists ready, to find himself staring into the mask of the white lion.

"The whole house is surrounded, lad," the lion whispered. "The bleeders are everywhere."

Corvo nodded. "Order your men to take their positions. My agents will follow." He paused, then added, "Find Emily and bring her to me."

"Right you are."

The white lion took off, pushing through the crowd.

There were more cries from the ballroom. Corvo moved back to the balcony to see the dancing couples backing into each other as the Whalers formed a tightening circle around them.

There are more of them than we suspected.

Then, as if following an unseen signal, they shed their unwieldy cloaks and hats, revealing the buckled leather tunics and hoods, pistols and knives at hand. They began herding the guests to each side of the gallery, clearing a space in the middle.

From the far end of the room stepped a masquerader in a simple costume—a big cloak that shone in brilliant gold and the mask of a cat, the metallic fur shimmering and shaking as the newcomer walked forward. The Whalers parted the crowd in front of her.

Then the golden cloak was pulled off, revealing red, buckled leather. Finally the mask came off, and was dumped on the floor. The woman standing in the middle of the room ran a hand through her short, greasy blonde hair.

Galia.

Corvo sped into action. Pulling off his own cloak and the bear mask, he vaulted the balcony rail and landed in a crouch on the ballroom floor, eliciting shrieks from some of the guests, who scattered out of his way. Behind him, the musicians cowered against the far wall.

He stood and stepped toward Galia. The woman was smiling, her eyes not leaving his as he walked forward. Around the room, the Whalers held the guests at knifepoint. Silence fell on the Boyle Mansion.

Corvo glanced around. His agents—and the men in the employ of the white lion—were all over the room, indistinguishable from the guests. They hadn't made any moves yet. They were waiting for Corvo's signal.

Good.

Galia's smile broadened as he stopped in front of her. She held a long knife, which she tossed casually from one hand to the other. She was confident, cocky, even.

It was time to put a stop to the charade.

"Now!" Corvo yelled.

In the alcove under the balcony, one of the musicians— one of Corvo's agents—reached behind a curtain to a hidden switch, and flipped it.

Immediately the room was filled with a harsh, metallic grinding, so loud as to be deafening. All around the room the masqueraders—and their captors—staggered under the assault of noise as the Ancient Music, played by the Warfare Overseer from his hidden room, echoed out across the ballroom.

As the Whalers staggered in surprise, Corvo's agents

moved into action, shedding cloaks to reveal their own weapons—knives, swords, pistols. In the confusion the tables turned, and within moments the Whalers found themselves at the mercy of the Royal Spymaster and his men.

To her credit, Galia only winced a little at the sound, her eyes darting around the room as she watched her gang get rounded up. She turned back to Corvo, one eyebrow raised, the grin still playing softly over her lips.

"Very impressive," she said, raising her voice to be heard over the Ancient Music. "A neat little trap."

Corvo lifted his chin. The game was up. The strange, discordant melodies had robbed him of his own powers—the burning of the Outsider's Mark on his hand was a painful reminder of that, as the power fought against the interference, slowly but steadily draining Corvo's own strength and mental focus. But he could stand it a little while longer, and it was worth it, because it meant that Galia was also powerless.

The balance was very much in his favor.

"Give it up, Galia," Corvo said. "You've lost this one. We've got your men at gunpoint. At my signal your base on Slaughterhouse Row will be raided and your mystery friend will be in custody. It's over. Drop the knife and I'll make sure you're well treated."

Galia pursed her lips, but otherwise her expression didn't change. She stopped tossing the knife from hand to hand, and instead held it firmly in her right, adjusting her fingers to get a better grip.

"Yeah, somehow I don't think this is going to go how you'd like it," she said, and she took a step forward. Corvo reached out, ready to grab her, to block the final, desperate swing of the knife.

He found his hand clutching at an inky, smoky nothing.

Galia was gone.

He spun around, too late. The Whaler was standing behind him—*close* behind him. It was impossible—she had transversed, blinked, despite the interference of the Overseer music.

Galia snarled, and stabbed forward with the knife.

22

"What are you doing? Leave this house! Go back to your frozen wasteland, pale rascal!"

— *THE YOUNG PRINCE OF TYVIA*
Excerpt from a theater play

With a cry that could be heard over the Ancient Music, Emily leapt out of the crowd, the black sparrow mask still in place.

On the ballroom floor, Galia appeared in a puff of blue-black nothing, standing behind Corvo's back. Her face twisted into a grimace even as Corvo spun around. In Galia's hand, the long knife stabbed quickly toward the Royal Protector.

Emily was quicker.

She kicked out, striking Galia's knife hand. The woman's grip on her weapon was firm, but she staggered under the impact. Emily pushed herself between the two of them, and ducked as the Whaler brought the knife around again, then swung a right at Galia's chin and was rewarded with a spray of blood and spittle as her opponent's head snapped backward under the blow.

Moving with her target, Emily took a step closer, punching in low. Galia doubled over and Emily swung up with her other arm, cracking the Whaler under her chin with an elbow. Then she swept her left leg out, catching Galia behind the knee. The woman fell backward, using an outstretched hand to stop herself hitting the floor. Emily went in for a kick—

And struck nothing.

A cry behind her, audible above the weird music. She turned, but too late. Galia appeared between Emily and her father and kicked the Empress in the small of the back, sending her to her knees. Emily spun on the floor, twisting to avoid Galia's fist, blocking two more attacks with raised forearms. Then she stood, swung, and missed as Galia ducked, then Emily threw out a kick.

Galia twisted to avoid it, then pulled her right arm back, the blade in her hand flipped around, ready to slice.

Corvo grabbed her arm from behind. She looked over her shoulder, snarling again, as he wrapped his arm around her neck.

Emily recovered and swung a punch at Galia's stomach.

Again, there was nothing there to hit. Overbalanced, the punch thrown too far with nothing to stop it, she fell into Corvo. He caught her and immediately pushed her off, allowing her to be ready for the next attack while he whirled around, calling out to his agents.

They were already at work—all around the ballroom. As Corvo and Emily had struggled with Galia, the Whalers had got the upper hand against the costumed agents. And as Corvo watched in confusion, he soon saw how they had done it.

They were all in trouble.

The Whalers could *transverse*, blinking despite the

torrent of grinding, discordant music that filled the room. There were more agents than Whalers, but they were no match for an enemy with supernatural powers, opponents who merely blinked out of reach of fist and knife alike, reappearing in new locations to take the agents by surprise. Several men lay dead on the floor, their costumes staining with blood as the Whalers slaughtered them. The screams of the guests were lost under the wail of the Ancient Music as they tried to flee the ballroom.

Corvo spun around. Emily was fighting Galia, but it was hopeless. The Empress swung at thin air, her enemy blinking and blinking again, leaving a series of still afterimages as she spun around and around in a haze of black smoke, leading Emily around with her, disorienting her, tiring her out.

Corvo rushed forward to help. He had to get the Ancient Music stopped—with it off, he would have his powers back. It would mean revealing them to Emily, but there was no time to be concerned about that now. Under the balcony, the musicians were at the mercy of the Whalers, the violinist—Corvo's agent—attempting to protect them. Crucially, he stood too far away from the concealed switch.

As he raced toward them, Corvo was aware of a popping in his ears, then he was grabbed by two Whalers who appeared on either side of him, a third materializing and clubbing him on the back of the head. Corvo gasped and felt his legs go out from under him. He hung between the two Whalers, who dragged him forward to where Emily was kneeling, Galia's knife at her throat.

Then, above the grind of the music, Corvo heard someone clapping. It was slow, mocking. From where he knelt, Corvo looked up to the balcony, as the man in the coat appeared, walking toward the railing. He looked out like a conquering ruler, and gripped the rail with both hands.

"My lords, ladies, gentlemen," he said, above the noise. "I bring greetings from the north!" At this he laughed, seemingly at his own words. Corvo glanced at Galia, and saw the woman looking up at the man, a broad smile on her face.

"Tonight you are guests of the Lady Boyle, heir to one of the greatest dynasties this wonderful city has ever produced." The man looked around, then stood to one side. "Please, give your regards to your hostess."

The crowd gasped. Behind the man stepped an older woman with long silver hair, dressed in a white and silver trouser suit, with one hand wrapped around Lady Esma Boyle's thin arm. In the other, the woman in white and silver held a small knife against Esma's throat.

The whisper swept around the crowd. Corvo knew who the woman in silver and white was. The whole room did.

Lady Lydia Boyle.

The *deceased* Lady Lydia Boyle.

Kneeling beside him, Emily struggled against her captor. Corvo turned to her, ready to tell her to relax, to focus, to not give them any excuse, when he found his eyes drawn back to the balcony.

The man in the coat was looking directly at him, the gaze of his red goggles suddenly bright, sparkling, like looking into a fire. Corvo felt his limbs grow heavy, his vision flashing black and blue at the edges as he felt a strange pressure at the back of his skull. He tried to blink it away, but when he closed his eyes he saw shapes move behind his lids.

It was a similar feeling to the one that had struck him back at the slaughterhouse, when the man in black had peered at him there, but here it was stronger, closer.

And then the feeling was gone.

Corvo screwed his eyes tight shut, reveling in the blackness, and then he opened them, and saw that the man was looking down at Emily. Corvo turned to the Empress. She was still wearing the black sparrow mask, but he could see the rise and fall of her chest as she sucked in air.

"Interesting," said the man in the coat. He brushed past Lydia and her captive sister and headed down the sweeping stairs to the ballroom floor, the Whalers pushing masqueraders out of his way.

Or keeping their own distance, Corvo thought.

The man stepped over to the kneeling pair, his attention on Emily. Corvo focused, tried to concentrate, but the Ancient Music sucked at any reserves of energy he had left—the power of the Void, channeled through the Mark of the Outsider, slipping further out of his grasp the more he tried to concentrate on it.

Instead, he turned his attention to the man in the coat, and the Whalers. They were using bonecharms, they had to be—strange, unstable charms, the likes of which neither he nor the High Overseer had ever seen. Charms that decayed over time, burning themselves up as they channeled powers that were far stronger than he thought was possible. Powers like transversing. The Whalers could blink, despite the Ancient Music, which suppressed magic—but not the supposedly minor boons granted by bonecharms.

Except the strange, charred charms, like the one Rinaldo had found, were different. That was why they were unstable. They granted far too much power, burning out in the process. Nevertheless, in using the bonecharms, the man in the coat, and Galia, and the Whalers, were all immune to the Ancient Music.

Corvo was not.

As the man in the coat got closer, Corvo could feel the disorientation, the burning cold that welled up inside him. Some kind of aura, a halo of confusion, of disorientation surrounded him like a protective field. The effects of another bonecharm.

The man in the coat stood over Emily and cocked his head, the big circular brim of his black hat exaggerating the movement.

"Well now," the man said, "I must say, this is an unexpected pleasure." He reached down, grabbed the beak of the black sparrow mask, and pulled it roughly up and off.

Emily blinked, blowing her hair off of her face as it billowed out from inside the mask.

"Good evening, Your Majesty," the man in the coat said.

A gasp went around the crowd, which quickly turned into a jabber of conversation. The Empress of the Isles was here, at the Masquerade Ball. Years of protocol, of tradition, shattered. Even held at knifepoint, at gunpoint, the nobility of Dunwall sensed a juicy royal scandal.

Emily's expression was firm, her mouth tightly closed. The muscles at the back of her jaw worked as she ground her molars, and her nostrils flared as she sucked in air. Her eyes were watering, but they were not tears. She wasn't afraid—she was anything *but*. Instead, she was defiant, brave, bold.

And she was *fighting*. The man in the coat took her chin in his hand and tilted her head up as Emily swayed on her knees. His eyes. She was staring into his eyes, caught in that same weird disorienting aura.

Then her eyelids fluttered and she opened her mouth, letting out a breath that was more like a sigh, and she collapsed onto the floor.

The crowd gasped again.

Galia stood before her master, the long knife hanging from her hand.

"What's going on?" she demanded. "You never said the Empress would be here." She moved over to the collapsed form and reached down, lifted Emily's head up by her hair. Corvo saw his daughter's lips move, her eyes darting around behind the closed lids, but she didn't wake up.

Then he jerked forward as Galia brought her knife to Emily's throat, but he was pulled back roughly by his two guards.

Galia's mouth twisted into a sneer as she looked over her shoulder at the man in the coat.

"Shall I kill her, Zhukov?"

Zhukov tilted his head this way and that. Corvo wondered what was behind the scarf, the goggles. Wondered what the man looked like, who he was. How he had managed to create—how he had even *learned* to create—his special bonecharms.

"No," Zhukov said. "I think the Empress will be most useful in the next phase. Bring her."

He turned on his heel, the tails of his great coat spinning as he walked back up the steps. At the balcony, he gestured to Lady Lydia Boyle, who still held at knifepoint the whimpering form of her older sister.

Galia pulled Emily up and lifted her across one shoulder, carrying the slight form of the Empress up the stairs without much difficulty.

On the balcony, Zhukov bore down on the two Lady Boyles.

"Leave her, Lydia," he said. "I need you to show me the way."

Lydia dropped the arm holding the knife. Lady Esma Boyle gasped behind her red mask, and slumped to the floor. Zhukov and Lydia ignored her.

Instead, Zhukov lifted both hands to the sides of Lydia's head. Lydia stared up at the man, into his red eyes.

"Show me, Lydia. Show me the way to the vault."

Lydia swayed on her feet. Corvo could see her lips moving, mouthing something over and over. Galia came up behind Zhukov, Emily still slumped over her shoulder.

"Show me the *way*!" Zhukov bellowed.

Lydia screamed. There was a crack, a puff of black inky nothing, and the balcony was empty.

Zhukov and Lydia, Galia and Emily, had vanished.

23

THE VAULT BENEATH THE BOYLE MANSION, ESTATE DISTRICT
15th Day, Month of Darkness, 1851

"It is in this dim luminosity that I can see them. The leviathans. The great whales. Here, in their domain, they move with grace and elegance. With purpose. They have approached the sphere repeatedly now, one almost touching the portal with her great eye. As I stare into the orb, it is clear to me that the thing is not mindlessly searching for prey, it is—observing me. It is curious. One by one they approach and peer in my window. There is an unnerving sense of intelligence in that gaze, devoid of malevolence. For a time they examine me, my predicament, and allow themselves to drift off to trace the broken cables along the sea floor."

— THE DEEP WATCHERS
Excerpt from a natural philosopher's journal

Galia opened her eyes and found herself, not on the balcony overlooking the ballroom, but in a dimly lit passageway made of old stone, the ceiling high and vaulted. Just a few yards in front of her stood a set of big double doors in heavy, dark wood, barely visible in the gloom.

She felt dizzy, sick, disoriented. Weak.

The Empress was a dead weight on her shoulder. Galia adjusted her grip. Then she took a slow, measured breath, willing her head to clear, willing the strength to return to her limbs.

"Where are we?" she asked, looking around. Zhukov and Lydia Boyle stood over by the doors. Lydia was singing, her arms outstretched as she danced a circle with an imaginary partner. Zhukov walked up to the door and laid a gloved hand against it.

"The Boyle Vault," he said, not turning around. "Lady Lydia, you have done well, but your task is not yet complete."

Zhukov pushed at the door, but it remained unmoved. He turned to face the woman. She stopped dancing, bowed low, then reached into her tunic and extracted a key with a long silver shaft.

Zhukov took the key and slipped it into the lock. He turned the key left and right and left and right, each time pushing the shaft further into the mechanism. As his gloved fingers touched the door, there was a final click. Zhukov withdrew his hand, leaving the key in place, then pushed at the doors with both hands.

They swung open and he stepped inside, Lady Lydia close behind. Galia readjusted the unconscious weight slumped over her shoulder and followed.

The subterranean vault was an immense, rectangular chamber, crafted from pale stone that had been carved into fluted gothic columns, which reached up to a high, fan-vaulted ceiling. Where tall windows would have been, had the building been above ground, there were merely stone archways, the mock windows filled in with stone of a different hue.

The architecture was epic and ostentatious, the room clearly designed to impress. Nevertheless, to Galia, it felt close, despite the cavernous space. The air was too still, the space too quiet. It felt more like a mausoleum, a tomb for the single, huge object which occupied the chamber, suspended from the ceiling by a series of iron chains.

Her jaw dropped as she stared up at the prize exhibit.

It was a whale skeleton, perhaps two hundred feet from nose to tail, the bones the same pale color as the stone of the vault. In life, the creature must have been impossibly large, longer even than the most impressive of the whaling ships that made their home in Dunwall harbor. The creature's vast, flat skull formed a huge sloping wedge, itself forty feet long and fifteen high, while beneath this, the two halves of the lower jaw were two gargantuan, curved beams of ivory, thirty feet in length each. The crest of the animal's spine arced up, the spinous process rising from each vertebra like a sail made of bone, the two symmetrical transverse processes sweeping out horizontally like wings. The pair of front flippers drooped down from the body, the tip of the finger-like bones nearly touching the floor of the vault.

Galia struggled to take in the sheer size of the thing. It was so big, it almost didn't seem real. This was no ordinary whale.

"And so the Deep Watcher sleeps," Zhukov said. He spread his arms out to the skeleton, then trotted down the short, fan-like curve of shallow steps that led from the main double doors to the floor of the vault. "A creature of myth and legend, leviathan of the boundless depths. A creature of *power*." He turned around to face the others. "And a creature of *magic*."

"Where did it come from?" Galia said breathlessly. She couldn't help it—she was fascinated by the object. She knew about leviathans. She'd even met someone, years ago, at the Golden Cat. He was a natural philosopher—a First Researcher, whatever that was—who claimed to have gone down in a diving bell and encountered huge creatures, monster whales far larger than anything known to science.

So he had said, anyway. Galia had heard a lot of things at the Golden Cat and knew that the tales told to the courtesans late in the night were often tall, but that one had stuck in her mind.

Perhaps he had been telling the truth, because here were the bones of just such a beast.

"Oh, this old thing?"

Lydia weaved her way to the skeleton, dragging her feet on the floor. When she was close enough, she reached up and laid a hand on the tip of the skeleton's flipper. "It was a gift from the Lord Regent to his mistress, dear old sister Waverley. The story is that it was caught by the ESS *Keeper* on some terrible expedition, when they lost a bathysphere. There was a fellow in it, and he went down too far and the chains broke. As the men in the ship tried to rescue him, something came up from the depths—something very big and very angry. Perhaps the bell had gone down too far, and had disturbed that which should not have been disturbed, and now the things that lived down there were coming up to teach them all a lesson."

Lydia looked up at the skeleton as she spoke, a smile playing on her lips, her eyes moving along the great beast.

"They harpooned it, but that wasn't enough. It pulled the ship along for days, farther and farther out. The whalers say it took them so far out they could see the shores of Pandyssia, though nobody believes that. But the ship was very nearly wrecked. When it came back to Dunwall, the whaling frame was missing, torn off by the high seas. Not that it would have been big enough to hold the leviathan. They had won their struggle in the end, and had dragged the beast behind the ship, the body so heavy the ship was taking water in."

Galia frowned. "I don't remember hearing about that."

Lydia's head snapped around to face her. Her expression showed anger, then the old woman's features softened and she shrugged.

"Well, not many did, did they? A signal was sent ahead of the ship, that they'd caught something big. The Lord Regent heard about it and instructed them to come in under cover of darkness. I think he wanted to keep the creature out of the hands of the Academy of Natural Philosophy. He wanted this prize for himself, the centerpiece of his own private collection. To show his generosity he gifted it to Waverly, a priceless artifact to be the envy of all the aristocracy. He even paid for this vault to be built. The first grand design of his private collection."

Lydia's shoulders slumped. "Then the regency was deposed and all the plans came to nothing. This beast has been sitting here ever since." She looked up at the skeleton. "Perhaps Esma liked to keep it as a reminder of our beloved sister."

Galia sniffed loudly. "So what does this have to do with us?" She walked up to Zhukov, who stood silently at the foot of the steps, his head tilted upward. "You said you needed my help to steal something that was locked away in the Boyle Mansion vault. Well?" She waved at the room. "Look around, boss. This is the vault. We're standing in it. So how about we cut with the history lessons and get down to business. What do we need to take?"

Zhukov turned his red eyes to his acolyte, and his laugh once more sounded from deep within his scarf-covered face.

"Have you heard nothing, Galia?" he asked. "Open your eyes." Then he turned and pointed at the giant skeleton. "I need you to steal *that*."

Galia blinked at her master, then laughed, and walked up to the skeleton. She reached up and slapped the flipper bones. Maybe she hit it too hard, because her fingers tingled afterward.

"Are you moonstruck like your friend here?" she said, casting a sour glance at Lydia, who stood smiling on the other side of the artifact. "I don't know if you've noticed, but this thing is a little *big*. It must weigh bloody tons! And all you got is me, an unconscious Empress, and an old woman with no shoes who doesn't even know what day it is."

"Don't worry, Galia," Zhukov said. "I don't need all of it. Just one of the jawbones will serve my purpose."

Galia walked to stand underneath the skull, and craned her neck to look directly up.

"Oh, well, that's fine, why didn't you say so?" she muttered sarcastically. *Just a jawbone. Right. Just a thirty-foot curve of ivory currently suspended twelve feet from the floor.*

Zhukov pointed to the chains that held the skeleton up.

"See if you can bring the front of the skeleton down," he said. "Then you can work on removing the jawbone."

Galia frowned. "You're serious about this?"

"Never more so."

She glanced up again. The individual components of the skeleton were held together by iron bolts and plates... If she could work out how to lower the skull down on the chains, it didn't look as if it would be too much trouble to get one of the jawbones loose. But the thing was still the size of a boat. There was no way they'd be able to carry it out, even if they could lift the thing between them in the first place.

Galia made her thoughts on the matter known to Zhukov, but her words trailed off as, for the first time that she had seen, he began to unbutton his greatcoat.

"I have prepared for this," Zhukov said. "This is why I had you steal from the crypt at Brigmore, and retrieve the parchments from the house. I have a method by which we can transpose the jawbone, and ourselves, back to the factory."

With his coat unbuttoned, Zhukov pulled one lapel aside. Galia caught a glimpse of the corroded bonecharms—the ones she had seen down in the basement workshop, back at the slaughterhouse. They hung on the inside of the coat, stitched into fabric.

And… were they smoking?

As she watched, she was sure she saw fingers of gray smoke slowly waft up. A moment later they were gone.

From inside the deep pockets of his coat, Zhukov pulled four short, fat candles, their surfaces pockmarked as though they were beeswax, though each was bright orange in color. As well as the candles, he was carrying a stick of white chalk.

Buttoning his coat up, he knelt on the floor, chalk in hand, and began to write on the stone flags. Galia frowned as she watched, but she was unable to read or understand what Zhukov was drawing.

There were geometric shapes, circles and squares and triangles, each overlapping the other or connected by arcs or tangents. Zhukov's hand flew as he inscribed the sigils on the floor. After a few minutes, one complex section was complete, so that triangles and circles intersected with mathematical precision to form a central, five-sided shape, surrounded by a mass of inscriptions.

In that central point, Zhukov placed the first of the candles. Then he stood and moved around to the side of the leviathan, ignoring Galia, stepping around Lydia as the old woman began another slow, circular dance in the silence.

Galia cocked her head. "What's with the drawings?"

Zhukov didn't look up as he worked. "I told you, I can transpose the jawbone back to the factory." Then he paused and looked up. He pointed at Lydia with the chalk. "I will need to carve some extra bonecharms. The witchcharm from Brigmore will help stabilize the transfer, but I had hoped to carve more. I will need all the extra power upon which I can draw."

Galia pursed her lips and glanced at Lydia.

"Ah… okay?"

Zhukov returned to his work and he didn't look up again.

"For bonecharms I need the raw material—and there it is." He raised a hand quickly to indicate Lady Lydia Boyle again.

Suddenly Galia realized what the boss was talking about. Her lips curled into a sneer, and she nodded.

"As you wish."

She drew her long knife, wiping the ten-inch blade on her leg. Then she raised it up, and turned it over in front of her face, as if she was checking to make certain it was up to the task.

And then, as Lady Lydia Boyle danced and sang to the music in her head, Galia stepped up to the old woman, taking her hand. Lydia was startled, but then she smiled, and the two of them circled and swayed for a turn or two.

Then Galia smiled and drove the knife into Lydia's chest, the blade sliding easily between the ribs, and pushed as hard as she could.

24

"Throughout the natural world there are ripples that we can barely perceive with our senses, an Ancient Music permeating everything as a fundamental structural rule. Through it, you can work wonders without violating the natural world or begging favors from unfriendly spirits. Throughout my studies I have found a seventeen-note scale derived from this phenomenon, and with the right equipment those notes allow for astonishing effects. Not the least of these is the ability to calm the turbulence originating in the Void, which we attribute to the Outsider."

— THE ANCIENT MUSIC
Excerpt from a longer work

Corvo lifted his head and glanced at the white lion held at knifepoint beside him. His guard noticed the movement, and used it as an excuse to push his prisoner's head down and stretch his arm painfully back. Corvo gasped. A moment later the guard got tired, or bored, and relaxed his grip.

Sucking in a breath, Corvo tried to focus. The

discordant music rolled around the room and the Mark of the Outsider on his hand burned with electric fire as it fought against the interference that cut it off from the Void.

They'd lost, and lost badly. They hadn't been outnumbered at the masquerade, but they had been out-maneuvered. The Ancient Music that Corvo had planned on being their salvation, preventing the Whalers from using their powers, had turned into their downfall. Using the power of Zhukov's corroded bonecharm, the Whalers had easily overcome their opponents while Corvo himself had been unable to use his gifts, the power locked away from his mind.

Zhukov and Galia were ten steps ahead of them. Whatever they were planning, they were getting close to realizing their goal. And more than that, they now had a hostage.

Emily.

Corvo closed his eyes and cursed himself for being so stupid. What they were being kept alive for, Corvo didn't know, but for the moment he was grateful. Whatever it was that Zhukov was doing, however, their time was almost up. When the man got what he came for, he'd likely give the order to slaughter everyone in the mansion.

"Young man, would you please turn that racket off."

Corvo opened his eyes and slowly looked up. After her sister had vanished with the others, the Whalers had dragged Lady Esma Boyle downstairs, but they at least had the decency to save the old woman from lying on the floor.

Underneath the balcony, the musicians had been pushed out to make room for her. She'd been allowed to sit, perched on a red velvet sofa that had been dragged out from the side of the room. A Whaler held a pistol on her.

Her mask was off, as was her hat, her mass of gray curls cascading down around her face. It was bruised purple on one side, a trickle of blood drying at the corner of her mouth. But despite her ordeal, the matriarch of the Boyle dynasty sat with her back perfectly straight.

Dignity under adversity.

The Whaler standing guard didn't give any indication that he was listening to her. The Music Box was the key— it was keeping Corvo from using his powers. There was no way the Whalers were turning it off until they were good and ready—if they could even find the man who was operating the box.

Corvo shifted on his knees. This time his guard didn't pay him any heed.

What he needed was a distraction. It didn't have to be big. It didn't need to buy him much time—two seconds, maybe three. After the chaos of the fight, the Whalers had left Corvo and the others unbound, confident that keeping them on the floor with blades at their necks was enough to keep the prisoners subdued.

Lady Esma was giving the man standing over her the evil eye, her chin held high, the elderly skin at her jowls drawn tight.

Corvo cleared his throat—loudly—and was rewarded with a short, sharp shove on the back of his neck. But as his head bounced up, he shot a glance at her.

She looked right at him.

Good.

Corvo waggled his eyebrows, and, with an exaggerated movement of his eyes, tried to indicate Lady Boyle's guard. Esma frowned a little, her eyes moving between Corvo and her guard. She adjusted herself on the sofa, but didn't do anything more.

No one had noticed, so he took a chance. He mouthed

the instruction at Esma, while rolling his eyes at her guard. He *really* hoped she would get the message.

She did. Her nostrils flared and she gave a slight nod, then she looked up at her guard again.

"Do you have any idea who I am, young man?"

The Whaler ignored her.

"I am Lady Esma Boyle. My family have owned half of Dunwall since your wretched great-grandparents were tilling the soil in the little inbred village where they met."

Nothing. Corvo wasn't sure if that statement was true, but it didn't matter. Esma was just getting started.

"In point of fact, my family name is even older than that of the Kaldwins." The color began to rise in her cheeks, her pale, thin skin taking on a hue not dissimilar to the scarlet of her silk trouser suit. "And you dare to come into this home and molest my guests so?" Her voice was raised, to be heard over the cacophonous screech of the Ancient Music, and she ramped the volume up even more. "I don't know what you ruffians are planning on doing in my house, but I demand that you leave at once!"

The Whaler shuffled and glanced back at the others. Corvo could hear the creak of leather as the guard behind him shifted position.

"At once, do you hear me?" Lady Boyle stood up and, to Corvo's amazement, she actually stamped her foot. "At once!"

"Shut up and stay put!" The Whaler gave her a shove. Lady Boyle tipped back onto the sofa, bouncing on the cushion, and used that momentum to get back onto her feet.

"How dare you lay lands on me. The Empress shall have your entrails decorating Kaldwin's Bridge before the night is over, you scoundrel!"

The Whaler shoved her again, harder, and this time Lady Boyle cried out and fell, missing the sofa entirely, landing awkwardly on one elbow. She rolled on the floor, her face contorted in pain.

Come on, come on, come on.

Corvo's luck was in.

As Lady Esma's guard walked over to her prone form, his guard stepped out to join his companion. Corvo wasted no time. In one second he was on his feet. In two, he lunged and grabbed the gun hand of the guard standing over the white lion, wrenching the pistol out of the surprised Whaler's hand before throwing an elbow into the man's face, sending him careening backward.

The room broke out into chaos, the Whalers springing into action, the two men over by Lady Boyle spinning around, weapons at the ready. Corvo leapt sideways, reaching the left-hand staircase and, in one fluid motion, bringing the pistol around to bear on the two guards by Lady Boyle.

He fired.

The speaker suspended below the balcony swung on its cord, the wooden lattice front shattered by Corvo's shot. The Ancient Music stuttered, then stopped altogether.

The Mark of the Outsider pulsed on his hand as the interference faded, the power flowing through him like sap flowing in a tree, returning from the Void. It was like being plunged into a warm bath—blood warm, body warm. For a second he couldn't tell where he ended and the world began, as clawing fingers from elsewhere reached out and caressed the Mark of the Outsider that blazed in blinding blue glory behind Corvo's closed eyes.

He stood. He blinked behind one Whaler, took him out with a twist that snapped the man's neck. He blinked again, and again, crisscrossing the hall, crisscrossing the Void as he stepped between the seconds of the clock. Time running as slow as treacle, he dispatched the Whalers one by one.

However, he didn't have much energy to call on—he'd spent many, many minutes under the spell of the Ancient Music and his reserves were down. The more he used, the weaker he became. There were four vials of Addermire Solution in his tunic, but he didn't want to use any of them until the last possible moment.

He blinked again, once more, and his vision began to spark with black dots. Time came crashing in like a concussion wave, knocking him to his knees. He opened his eyes and looked up.

And found he was not alone. With the Whalers in disarray, his agents released themselves and overpowered their captors, the masquerade guests cowering and screaming in the corners of the hall as the two groups fought hand to hand.

Then a Whaler appeared in front of him, materializing out of the air, a gun in his hand.

A gun pointed at Corvo's face.

He watched as the Whaler's finger curled on the trigger. And then he watched as the Whaler staggered, the gun dropping from his hand as the tip of a blade appeared in the center of his chest, pushing through in a spray of bright, arterial blood. The Whaler dropped to the floor and the white lion stepped forward, holding his hand out.

Corvo took it and allowed himself to be pulled to his feet. The White Lion released his hand then yanked his mask off and tossed it to the floor. Slackjaw blew his cheeks out, his face flushed.

"Thanks," Corvo said.

Slackjaw gave a breathless nod, and looked around the room. "Looks like we've got this. You need to get after the Empress. Here, take this. As much as I'd love a little swig, I think it'll do you more good."

From somewhere inside the white lion costume, Slackjaw brought out a glass vial filled with a blue liquid. Addermire Solution.

Corvo took the vial thankfully, pulling the stopper off with his teeth and draining it in a single gulp. The effects were immediate, his strength returning, a warmth spreading out all across his body. Even his vision seemed sharper, brighter, his thoughts somehow clearer.

He was ready, and his own reserves of restorative elixir remained untouched.

"Thanks, Azariah," Corvo said. "I'll remember this."

Slackjaw gave Corvo a tired slap on the shoulder. "Now I really am starting to think about that little vineyard again," he said with a laugh. "You go get 'em, lad. And hey, you remembered my name for once. Wonders will *never* cease."

Corvo squeezed Slackjaw's forearm, then turned and headed over to where Lady Esma Boyle lay on the floor. She had managed to bring herself up to lean on the wall, but she looked pale and was breathing heavily. She cradled one arm in the other. Corvo had seen the way she had fallen, cracking the elbow.

"Lady Boyle," Corvo said, crouching down, "I need your help. Can you hear me? Esma?"

Lady Boyle opened one eye and sniffed loudly. "Of course I can hear you. What am I, deaf?"

Corvo couldn't stop himself smiling. "Zhukov said he needed Lydia to lead them to a vault—do you know what they were talking about? Do you know where this vault is?"

Lady Boyle gulped and nodded her head. "Yes," she said, her thin tongue wetting her lips. "They must be talking about the vault under the house. It was built to house Hiram and Waverley's private collection. Nobody has been down there for years though."

Corvo frowned. "Private collection of what?" He wracked his brains, trying to think of what Zhukov could possibly want to steal from the house.

Lady Boyle laughed dryly. "At the moment, a private collection of nothing much. The only thing down there is the bones of an old leviathan. Biggest one ever caught, so I'm told. Can't stand the sight of it myself. You get to my age, old bones cease to hold much interest."

Corvo felt a chill crawl up his spine.

Old bones, and not just any. The bones of a leviathan— the legendary deep-dwelling whales that some people didn't think existed. Creatures that were said to possess natural, magical powers all of their own.

He glanced down at Lady Boyle. Leaning against the wall, she looked like what she was—a tiny, old woman with a broken arm and maybe more broken bones besides.

"Can you tell me where it is?" he asked.

Esma laughed. "Sure, get me some parchment, I'll draw you a map."

Corvo frowned. "I really need your help. They have the Empress."

Esma nodded, the humor evaporating from her face. "I know. It'll take too long to describe the path. I'll have to show you." At this, she held her breath and pushed up from the floor, but she made little progress. Corvo moved to help, but she waved him away with an annoyed hiss. Then she dropped back against the wall and sighed.

"Okay, you'll need to carry me."

Corvo needed no further invitation. He slid his hands underneath Lady Boyle and stood. She was small and light, impossibly light, as if there was nothing inside the scarlet trouser suit. He couldn't help but remember carrying another Lady Boyle on the night of another masquerade, more than a decade ago.

"Ready?" he asked.

Esma nodded, then she pointed through the double doors set under the balcony.

"It's that way."

Corvo called out for his agents, and at once Jameson appeared from the crowd, dressed in a once-immaculate white suit now stained with blood and dirt.

Together they headed deeper into the house.

25

THE VAULT BENEATH THE BOYLE
MANSION, ESTATE DISTRICT
15th Day, Month of Darkness, 1851

"There are some depraved rituals which not even the
most adept can describe, the very act of recording
the atrocity of their nature enough to corrode the
mind of they who dare approach the task. It is said
that even the whispering of such eldritch spells
weakens the tether that links this world to the Void,
the very connection that we draw upon in order to
command the magicks of the ages."

— THE METAPHYSIKA MYSTERIUM
Excerpt from a longer, banned,
work on supernatural ritual

The Boyle Mansion was a maze and while Esma's
directions were perfect, the need to carry her slowed
them down.

The doors of the vault were open. They were too late.

Corvo led the way in and gently settled Esma on the
shallow stairs that led down to the main chamber.

The skeleton of the leviathan dominated the room,
suspended from the ceiling by chains. Only the back half

of the specimen was supported, however. The entire front of the skeleton, from the front flippers to the enormous skull, lay on the floor. The skull sat at an angle, with half of the gargantuan lower jaw missing. Beside the skull were scattered a collection of black iron bolts and angled plates.

Something else caught Corvo's attention.

The floor around the skull was covered with writing and drawings, a spider's web of lines and symbols rendered in white chalk. Positioned at intervals were four orange candles, extinguished but burned nearly down to the flagstones, their wicks still smoldering, the remnants of blue smoke drifting upward and smelling sickly sweet.

In front of the skull lay a bundle of something soaked in a red liquid that pooled out across the floor. The skull was lying in the liquid, and as Corvo got closer he could see that the bone had begun to take it up like a wick, while the white chalk lines on the floor remained uncovered. It was almost as if the drawings were somehow repelling the liquid.

It was blood. A lot of blood. The thought registered in Corvo's mind, followed quickly by another.

Emily!

He ran over to the bundle, crouching down in the blood. He reached out, then paused. It was the body of a woman, but whoever it was, she had been wearing white and silver, not black. Corvo rolled the body over, only for the arm to come away in his hand. He stared at it for a single, incredulous moment, then placed it on the floor next to the body. He reached over, rolling the body, feeling the way it moved in ways that it shouldn't. When it was lying face up, he peeled back the long, red-stained hair that adhered slickly to the corpse's face.

The wide, dead eyes of Lady Lydia Boyle stared up at him. Her lips were frozen in a small smile.

Corvo stood. She had been partially dismembered—

one arm severed at the shoulder, the other still attached, but missing everything from the elbow down. The killer had gone to work on the torso, too, partially dissecting it, the flesh and organs cut and pushed to one side, the ribs cracked and pulled open like a door. The breastbone had been cut out, and on the right side of the body there was only one rib remaining.

Corvo wiped his hands on the front of his clothes as best he could, but the blood had stained his skin. He kept his back to Jameson and Lady Esma.

"Are you going to just stand there feeling sorry for yourself, young man, or are you going to let us in on the news? Do we still have an Empress or not?" Lady Esma Boyle's voice was strong and loud, but Corvo could hear it crack, just a little. The Boyle Matriarch was doing her best, while her world fell apart.

He stepped away from the body and turned to her, ready to tell her what he'd found. But as he looked up, Esma pursed her lips and nodded.

"That thing isn't Emily, is it?" she said. "It's Lydia." She paused. "Or what's left of her."

Then Lady Esma Boyle dropped her head, tucking her chin into her chest, and she didn't speak again. Corvo sighed as Jameson came to his side, his gaze fixed on the gruesome remains. Jameson took a deep breath.

"What did they do to her?" he whispered, leaning close.

Corvo frowned. "Bones. They wanted her bones." He turned and walked over to the complex web of chalk drawings on the floor. The whale's skull was sitting in the center of the space, but in front of it, Corvo noticed another, smaller drawing—an octagon, formed by the intersecting lines of triangles and squares. In the center of the octagon, the stone flags were blackened, and there was a charcoal-like residue on it.

Dropping to his knees, he picked up the largest piece. It was light, fragile, the burned-out remains of more bone. The corroded bonecharms Zhukov was able to carve were potent, yes, but their power was fleeting, ephemeral. They were limited, the highly unstable objects disintegrating after use.

The crumbling, carbonized shards fell to the floor, and, wiping his hands, he stood. He glanced over at Lady Esma Boyle, who was huddled against the column, her shoulders shaking, her face buried behind her gray curls.

"Look after her," Corvo said. "Call back the agents from the slaughterhouse. They're needed here. I need you to make sure that everyone at the masquerade is attended to—see to any injuries, and get everyone home, where they belong. The man in the white lion costume—his name is Azariah. He's an associate. He'll help, and he has agents of his own here.

"I also need you to spread a counter-narrative—that it wasn't the Empress who was here tonight, it was one of her chambermaids. A lookalike. Leave no room for doubt. We need full deniability. I'm sure you can come up with something."

Jameson nodded. "And what will you do?"

Corvo lifted his hands, flexing his bloodstained fingers.

"I'm going to get Emily back," he said. "And I'm going to finish this, once and for all."

INTERLUDE

"While people in the lower city of Caltain share much with their nearest neighbors in Morley, most Tyvians are a breed apart, shaped by generations of life in the inhospitable cold. Austere and regal, Tyvians are proud of their customs, food, and history, and have little concern for the Isles to the south."

— *THE ISLE OF TYVIA*
Excerpt from a volume on Tyvian geography and culture

Zhukov strode into the People's Chamber in the Citadel of Dabokva, the vast, domed building that sat at the heart of Tyvia's capital.

The room was huge, the walls a dark gray granite, the stone flecked with gold that caught the light from the globes held at the end of outstretched bronze arms that lined the room. The bronze arms were exactly that—gargantuan sculptures of men's limbs, the muscles bulging as they cradled the light. The effect was one of epic grandeur—of strength, not just of purpose, but of the body itself. The design of the chamber said that Tyvia was a harsh land, but the people who made it their home were made of even sterner stuff.

Zhukov smiled, pleased with the way his boots hammered loudly against the smooth, hard floor, announcing his approach to the Presidium as they sat at the large, circular table that occupied most of the room. It was situated directly beneath the circle of the citadel dome high above—nearly two hundred feet, in fact, the entire design of the People's Chamber designed to diminish those who met within it, emphasizing the unimportance of individuals, reminding them that the world was big and that they were insignificant.

In Tyvia, all were equal.

Some, however, were more equal than others.

Beyond the Presidium's table, the far wall of the People's Chamber was different from the rest of the room. It was a giant panel bordered on each side by columns in a bright red stone, richly veined with sparkling gold and silver threads. These represented the riches of Tyvia, locked away in the hard stone of the country, while the red represented the blood which was given by the people as they wrested control of this wealth, carving out their own destiny in the Empire.

The portrait that filled the space between the two columns dominated the People's Chamber, demanding attention. It stood one hundred feet high, and was half again as wide. It wasn't a painting but a mosaic, hundreds of thousands of minute colored tiles forming the head, shoulders, and upper torso of Tyvia's first Hero of the State, Karol Topek. He was resplendent in his black-and-red military coat, his stern, bearded face gazing importantly into the middle distance, his right hand clutching his belt, his left raised as he pledged allegiance to his beloved country.

Zhukov smirked at Topek's image. True enough, he was a great hero, a founder of their nation-state. But he was long, long dead.

It was time for Tyvia to worship another idol.

"Gentlemen," Zhukov said, sweeping off his hat and bowing before the Presidium. The circular table was full, the assembly of councilmen complete. This was an unusual occurrence—while the Presidium had absolute power over the affairs of Tyvia, the *real* power actually rested in just the three most senior members of the council—the *High Judges*—seated at the side of the table under the looming image of Topek.

The rest of the Presidium had to turn in their seats to

greet Zhukov, but the High Judges remained unmoving, their eyes fixed firmly on the newcomer.

There was a moment of silence. Zhukov kept his expression flat but pleasant, even as he considered each person seated there.

Fools, all of them. Eleven men and five women who sat in the big cold room, saying nothing but "yes" to the three High Judges. A council of sixteen who were supposed to represent the people of Tyvia, but who did nothing of the sort.

Certainly, their election to this chamber was democratic, and voting was compulsory for the entire adult population of their vast island. But given that there was only one political party, however, which fielded only one candidate in each of the districts, the result was always a foregone conclusion.

There was silence in the chamber for a moment, then a shuffling as the members of the council turned back around in their seats, all eyes now back on the High Judges.

Zhukov replaced the hat on his head and raised his left hand, mirroring the gesture in the great portrait of Karol Topek. Zhukov gave the pledge of allegiance, as was customary when invited to the Presidium, while his eyes moved from one High Judge to the next.

First there was Secretary Cushing, an old man whose days were surely coming to an end and whose voice had never once been heard at any meeting Zhukov could remember. In a way, this made him more worrisome. That he was one of the High Judges meant that he possessed real power, and clearly he had the ear of his comrades. But the fact that he never spoke, either in public or at these closed meetings, made him unreadable, inscrutable.

Seated next to Cushing was Secretary Taren, the one member of the group who could claim lineage from the great Karol Topek. She was younger than her colleagues, but not by much, and in her watery-blue eyes there burned a light, the fire of passion, of dedication. Of the knowledge that she had power, and she could wield it. Taren was outwardly fierce, her expression as stony as the granite walls.

Finally, there was Secretary Kalin. As with the other High Judges, there was nothing to distinguish him from the rest of the Presidium council. No special insignia, no unique uniform—like the others, he wore the simple black-and-red, high-necked tunic that marked his rank merely as "Secretary for the People of Tyvia." And there was nothing at the circular table either that indicated he, or his two comrades, were of particular note.

But Zhukov knew the secrets of the People's Chamber, and the way the Presidium worked. Secretary Kalin was seated directly under Topek's left hand. The hand raised in allegiance. Secretary Kalin's position—his authority—was very, very clear.

"Friend Zhukov," Kalin said, gesturing for him to step closer to the table. "Thank you for coming at such short notice. The Presidium knows how important your work is across the great nation-state of ours, and we know that this work can only be interrupted for reasons which are themselves of equal or greater importance.

Pompous ass. Typical Kalin. Never used one word when ten would do. *The Presidium should serve a nice Tyvian red with their meetings*, Zhukov mused. He couldn't imagine sitting through an entire session without a drink to take his mind off things.

Aloud, he said, "I thank the Secretaries," and he gave another bow. "I am here only to learn how I can better serve Tyvia."

He'll like that. Kalin was justly proud of his country,

and equally proud not just of its legacy and history, but its *ideals*.

Oh yes. Kalin was a true believer.

The Secretary's lips twitched into a small smile.

"I'm afraid I must deliver bad news to you," Kalin said. "You have been traveling for days, so will be a little… out of touch, shall we say."

Zhukov shifted on his feet.

"News, Friend Kalin?"

Kalin nodded. "We have had a dispatch from Dunwall. There has been something of a… scandal."

"Ah," Zhukov said. *Scandal?* Interesting, perhaps, but idle gossip was hardly something that caught the attention of the Presidium. He glanced around at the others.

Taren shifted in her seat, pulling down the front of her tunic to smooth it. Then she linked her fingers together and leaned on the meeting table.

"Empress Jessamine Kaldwin has been killed— murdered by her own Royal Protector," she said. "Hiram Burrows, Royal Spymaster, has been elevated to Lord Regent for the moment, given that the heiress to the throne, Emily, has not yet come of age. The heiress has been moved to protective custody until this crisis is brought to a satisfactory conclusion."

Zhukov felt the air leave his lungs. He managed to suppress the resulting cough, instead lifting a trembling hand to his mouth as he cleared his throat.

Kalin was watching. This time his smile grew in size.

"A tragedy, I'm sure you'll agree, Friend Zhukov."

"I… yes," he said. "A tragedy indeed, Friend Kalin."

Kalin pursed his lips. "While the Empire of the Isles includes Tyvia within its domain, we have been very fortunate to enjoy a… *special* relationship with Dunwall, a certain autonomy granted as a consequence of the Morley

Insurrection. The Empress, and indeed the Emperors before her, have always viewed Tyvia as a friend and ally."

Zhukov lifted his chin. His throat was dry. He licked his lips.

Still Kalin watched him.

He knew. He *knew*.

Kalin lifted an eyebrow. "Well, Friend Zhukov? Don't you agree?"

Zhukov bowed his head. "Indeed, Friend Kalin." He paused. "Forgive me, I'm... well, I'm appalled by this news. When did this happen?"

"Yesterday," Secretary Taren said. "The news has not been officially announced, but we learned through our spies in Dunwall mere hours after the event."

Spies in Dunwall? This was news to Zhukov. News that merely helped confirm his suspicions. The Presidium wasn't here to tell him that the political landscape of their neighbor—and technical ruler—had shifted.

No, they had summoned him for another reason.

He could leave. He could walk out. The People's Chamber was unguarded—the whole *citadel* was unguarded. That was the point. Nobody here had any power or was in any way important—theoretically. Anyone in Dabokva, anyone in *Tyvia*, could walk in and take up a seat at the table.

All were equal.

It was just that some were more equal than others, and anyone daring to enter the People's Chamber without invitation would find themselves leaving it in a box.

Zhukov cleared his throat again and bowed to the Presidium.

"Friends, thank you for summoning me to hear this tragic news firsthand," he said, keeping his voice controlled. "But if you will excuse me, I have my duties to perform in the service of our nation."

He could leave. Walk out. Then run. He could be at the docks, be out of Tyvia before the Presidium had a chance to make their move.

"We understand, Friend Zhukov," Kalin said. "But I'm afraid we must relieve you of those duties. You have served the People well."

Zhukov smiled faintly.

Was it his imagination, or was there a sound from behind him, somewhere out beyond the towering doors of the People's Chamber?

"As, I believe, you have served Empress Jessamine Kaldwin," Kalin added.

Zhukov barked a nervous laugh, his forehead creasing in confusion.

They knew. Of course they knew.

And now his ally—the Empress—was dead.

And he would be next.

"It is unfortunate that the murder of the Empress has spoiled your plans, Friend Zhukov, but you may rest assured that your actions had not gone unnoticed. Our spies have been watching you for a long, long time. We know about your plans with Jessamine—about her vision to bring Tyvia under more direct control. In fact, that was why we sent you to Yaro in the first place, to give us time to search your apartments."

Kalin raised a hand, as though to pre-empt an imagined interruption. Zhukov, however, remained silent.

"Yes," Kalin continued, "we know about your little hidey-holes. As I say, you have been watched for a long time. You are a Hero of the State. You are—you *were*—a valuable piece of property, and surely if you have valuable property, you would expect it to be watched, night and day. Watched, or locked away."

The charade was up. Zhukov turned on his heel and

ran for the double doors, then careened to a halt, sliding on the smooth floor as they swung open. The men who walked into the People's Chamber were dressed in featureless black, their faces hidden behind flat, opaque black metal masks.

Zhukov recognized them at once for what they were.

Operators.

Tyvian law stated that every citizen was equal, and that none could ever act against another—the perfect vision of an ideal that could never, truly, be accomplished. Yet it didn't stop the Presidium from trying. To sidestep the law, they used Operators—anonymous agents, their citizenship stripped, their identities concealed behind the flat black masks.

Operators were never seen. They came at night. They made people disappear. But here they were, standing in the People's Chamber. The Presidium was ready. Of course Zhukov couldn't run. That was a fool's dream.

He spun around and marched back to the table. He gesticulated toward the picture of Karol Topek.

"You can't do this," Zhukov spat. "I'm a Hero of the State. I am beyond the authority of this farcical council."

At this, Taren leaned in toward Kalin. On the other side, the ever-silent Cushing did likewise.

"See how he reveals himself," Taren said in a ridiculous stage whisper. Kalin smiled, nodding, while a murmur of agreement swept around the circle of leaders. "See how he speaks out against Tyvia."

Footsteps behind him. Arms on his.

The Operators held him now. Now they would make *him* disappear.

"Friend Zhukov," Kalin said. "We thank you for your service. You have given Tyvia balance, allowing the ship of state to ride turbulent seas, but we now hereby renounce your position as Hero of the State. For conspiracy against the people, we sentence you to a lifetime of freedom."

Freedom. Such a euphemism.

Such a farce.

"Take him away."

The Operators pulled at his arms. Zhukov pulled back. He knew where they were taking him.

To the interior, the seemingly endless icy wastes that formed the heart of the country.

To his "freedom"—freedom to work in the labor camps, freedom to die in the snow. There were no walls at the camp. Everyone sentenced to work there was officially innocent, pardoned by the state.

Because nobody ever returned.

"Freedom?" Zhukov asked, as the black-masked men began to drag him toward the doors. "You know nothing of freedom, *friends.* I was going to bring balance to this state. Do you hear me? *Balance!* I would have been more than a Hero of the State. I would be remembered. *Remembered!*"

Zhukov pulled against the Operators, but they were stronger than he was and their grip was firm. He had no choice—either he walked out with them, or was carried out. It made no difference to the Presidium.

He was dragged out through the giant doors, which closed after him, and the last he saw of Tyvia's ruling council was the portrait of Karol Topek, hand raised in allegiance, his eyes gazing toward a bright and hopeful future.

That would have been me, Zhukov thought.

That would have been *me.*

PART FOUR
THE BLACK MIRROR

26

GREAVES AUXILIARY WHALE SLAUGHTERHOUSE 5, SLAUGHTERHOUSE ROW, DUNWALL
15th Day, Month of Darkness, 1851

"Beware, for history is written, not by the vanquished, but by the victor."

— TYVIAN PROVERB
Excerpt from a volume on
regional customs and traditions

Emily blinked her eyes, and moved her head. It felt heavy and she felt hot and sick, so she let it fall back— smacking it smartly onto a surface that was both hard and wet. Startled, and now hot and sick and *sore*, she pulled herself up.

She was back in the whale slaughterhouse, lying against the rim of one of the disused oil vats on the vast factory floor. She pulled on her hands, quickly discovering that they were tightly bound behind her. She managed to drag herself up into a sitting position, her head throbbing. She squeezed her eyes tight shut, then opened them, willing herself to wake up and start taking notice.

The slaughterhouse was still hot, but it was relatively quiet, the only sound the ever-present rumble that came from the whale oil overflow vat, the red-orange contents of which rolled thickly, like lava, the surface punctuated occasionally by a bursting bubble.

The Whalers had made progress since her last visit. The giant metal and chain framework that had been built on the factory floor had been lifted into place, suspended over the main vat. Despite its size and weight, the frame swung gently in the hot air that rose from the churning liquid beneath it. Tracing the heavy chains down, Emily saw they actually disappeared beneath the surface of the intensely hot substance.

Standing on the thick rim of that vat was Zhukov. He had his back to Emily, and seemed to be looking down into the roiling, molten liquid. Galia was sitting on the rim, which formed a foot-high step, her elbows on her knees, her head in her hands, and she was watching Emily.

There were other Whalers in the factory—two over at the far wall, standing by a pulley system that had been jury-rigged from one of the whale frame systems, linked to the new assembly hanging over the vat. Emily glanced around, and saw a few others positioned in various places, but not many, perhaps five or six. They seemed to have lost most of their members—first at Brigmore Manor, then at the Masquerade Ball.

Not that it seemed to matter. Whatever they had been planning, it seemed they had achieved their goals.

Emily wondered what they were going to do with her. Her kidnap couldn't have been planned—nobody knew she was going to be at the event. No, the Whalers had struck the Boyle Mansion for some other purpose. As she looked around, however, she couldn't see anything—or anyone, for that matter—that might have been taken from the house.

What in all the Isles did they want?

Galia lifted her head, her lip curling into a lopsided, nasty smile. The Whaler's long knife had been resting across her knees, and now she held it in one hand. With her other she pressed the tip of her gloved finger into the tip of the blade, and she twisted the blade around and around on the makeshift pivot.

"Hey, boss," she said. "She's awake." Galia stood and took a few steps toward Emily, the smile growing wider the closer she got. Then she sighed and called out over her shoulder.

"I *said*, her majesty is awake."

No response. Galia turned on her heel and stalked back to the vat. She was impatient. Zhukov had stayed Emily's execution back at the house, but she could tell that Galia was very keen to have it resumed. Very keen indeed. A chance perhaps for a lower-class criminal to get one over on her upper-class oppressors—by killing none other than the Empress herself.

"Are you listening to me, Zhukov?" She stepped up onto the rim of the vat, pulling her head back a little and half-raising an arm to shield her face against the heat.

Zhukov didn't turn around, but he did, at last, speak.

"I hear you."

Galia shrugged, then pointed at Emily with her knife.

"So what are we waiting for? We've got the Empress of the Isles, right here, in our power. Don't you know what this means? We can get anything we want. *Do* anything we want. We can start *wars* with this."

Zhukov laughed, deep in his chest. He turned away from the vat and glanced over at Emily, his red eyes shining. As his gaze met hers, she felt the ball of sick appear somewhere between her chest and her stomach, her skin breaking out in gooseflesh despite the heat of the factory.

She blinked and she saw the outline of a man, his arm moving swiftly from left to right as he slit the throat of the prisoner in his grip and she heard the laughter of a young woman carried on a cold wind.

Then Zhukov turned his eyes away from her to look at Galia, his minion, and Emily snapped out of it. The factory lurched around her as the strange vision vanished and the heat of the place slapped at her body.

It was him. Had to be. There was something, some kind of power he possessed, that made her feel sick, that sent her head spinning, that—

That made her see things.

Emily cleared her throat, then spat onto the wet floor beside her. She knew about magic—everyone did. Few people saw it, however, and fewer still believed in it— but everyone knew about the sailor's scrimshaw, how it somehow tapped into the power that slowly decayed down the years from the Great Burning.

Whatever it was that Zhukov wielded, it didn't seem to affect Galia or the other Whalers. Or anyone else at the Boyle Masquerade, at least as far as Emily had been able to see.

Zhukov's amusement seemed to annoy Galia. She took a step toward her boss and lifted her knife—not exactly threatening him, but the point was still in his direction.

"What's so funny?" she asked. "Don't you get it? We have the Empress. We can make our demands. We can have the whole *city* if we wanted it."

"Oh, Galia, how little you understand," Zhukov said. "I want more than just this city."

The woman jutted her chin out as she snarled. "You said we would have power. You said you would give *me* power. Well, I've done my part. Now it's time for payment.

Call it my fee for services rendered, if you want, but I want what you promised.

"What you *promised!*"

Galia screamed out her last demand, her whole body shaking, the knife tip somewhere at Zhukov's neck, lost inside the fur scarf.

He reached out a gloved hand, and gently caressed Galia's cheek. She jerked at his touch, and looked up into his red glass eyes.

"Please," she said, her voice becoming a whisper barely heard over the dull roar of the vat. "*Please*. You promised me. You promised me everything."

Zhukov nodded. "Yes, Galia. You wished to be part of this, to share in my power and to share in my victory. I am a hero of Tyvia and a man of my word. You shall share my power, just as you desired."

Something flashed in Zhukov's other hand—a knife, the twin blades wicked, as shiny as a mirror. It threw red and yellow and, impossibly, blue light around the factory as he drew it out of the folds of his coat.

And then he pushed it into Galia's stomach, while his other hand still stroked her cheek. Galia's eyes went wide, searching Zhukov's hidden face. Perhaps for answers, perhaps for an explanation.

Emily didn't think she would find it.

Zhukov pushed again and twisted the blades, holding the handle firm—the only thing that kept Galia standing. She coughed once, twice, blood spurting from her mouth onto Zhukov's coat.

Then he let go of his bronzed knife. Galia fell, the blades still embedded in her, backward into the vat. The thick liquid spat as her body slid into it. There was a viscous cough, treacle-like rivulets flipping up into the air, as the Whaler's bleeding body finally broke the surface tension and sank out of sight. Within a moment, the liquid settled down.

But it was different now. Emily could feel it. The heat in the factory intensified, and she had no idea how Zhukov, in his strange getup, could possibly stand the temperature so close to the edge. The light changed, brightening, moving from red to orange to yellow. Emily glanced around again.

The brighter light cast longer shadows, and the figures of the Whalers stationed around the factory floor seemed bleached out, flickering, a blue buzz of light dancing in the corner of the eye. Whalers who were looking at each other nervously, surprised at the sudden death of their old leader.

Emily turned back to Zhukov, to the roiling vat, to the shining light, and then it was gone.

She tried to stand again, but with her hands tied it was difficult, and there didn't seem to be much point. But she managed to get herself up onto her knees. She lifted herself up, as tall as she could. Then she lifted her chin at the back of her captor, and—

She paused. A dozen thoughts ran through her head, a dozen things she could say to Zhukov—a dozen variations on *"what do you want with me?"* and *"what are you going to do with me?"* and *"you have to let me go!"*

But it was another question which swam to the surface of her mind, pushing the others aside.

She lifted her chin again.

"How do you think this is going to end, Zhukov?"

He tore his gaze away from the vat. He turned to look at Emily, then stepped off the lip of the vat and walked toward her. He stood over her, his red goggles boring holes into her head.

She didn't falter, although she felt weak, confused, a ball of cold nausea rising in her throat. She sucked in a breath, her nostrils flaring, the tendons standing out on her neck like the cable and chain holding the frame up.

I am the daughter of Corvo Attano and Jessamine Kaldwin, she told herself. *I am the Empress of the Isles.*

Focus. Focus. Focus.

She saw herself reflected in Zhukov's goggles.

There.

She focused not on him, not on his hidden eyes or his hidden face, but on *herself*. She watched the mirror image of Empress Emily Kaldwin I, defiant and strong.

The nausea passed, even if the feeling of tiredness did not.

"You ask an interesting question," Zhukov said finally. "One with many different answers."

Emily shook her head. "I am Empress of the Isles. Anything happens to me, and the might of my Empire will fall upon your head."

Zhukov laughed, then he turned away and went over to the vat again. She followed his back with narrowed eyes.

"Nothing will happen to you, Empress," Zhukov said, and then he paused, and turned to look at her over his shoulder. "Nothing will happen to you. *Ever.*"

He turned in the flickering, moving light and waved to a group of four Whalers standing over on the left side of the factory floor. The group were slow to move at first, perhaps afraid of getting too close lest they shared Galia's fate, but Zhukov waved his hand again and the group seemed to snap out of it, rushing forward to gather around a long, curved object covered in an oilcloth, sitting on the floor beside them.

Whatever it was, it was huge and awkward and heavy, requiring the strength of all four men to turn it on the floor so it rested on its curved side. Then, as two of the men held the object steady, the other two pulled the oilcloth off.

It was a bone, a giant, curved bone, something

belonging to the anatomy of a creature Emily didn't recognize. Was it a rib, maybe? Whatever it had belonged to, the creature must have been gigantic. Something like… a whale, perhaps?

That made sense, given where they were.

She watched, fascinated, as the four Whalers somehow managed to carry the huge arc of bone over to the vat. With careful positioning and a lot of silent cooperation, they set it down on the rim, balancing the thing on one end and pushing the other side up, so the bone stood vertically.

But only for a moment. Then its weight and gravity took over, and with a little helpful steering from the Whalers, it toppled over, into the vat, slipping into the thick liquid with a wet slapping sound.

Get him talking, Emily thought. *Get him to tell you something. Something important. Something that will help stop him.*

Something that will get you out of here.

"What was that?" Emily called out.

The Whalers retreated from the heat while Zhukov stepped back up onto the rim and looked down into the liquid. From Emily's position, he was just a black silhouette against the yellow-blue-white light shining from the vat.

"The final ingredient," Zhukov said. "The jawbone of an abyssal leviathan, a so-called deep watcher. Do you know those creatures, Empress? They live away from the world of man, in the farthest, darkest places of the world. There they weave their own kind of magic, channeling a power that comes from within their very bones, the current flowing through them like a living battery."

He turned around and stepped down.

"The final piece I needed, the final element of power," Zhukov continued. "I spent a year searching for something like this. I traveled to Morley, Serkonos. Every isle in your precious Empire, and even those beyond."

Emily lifted an eyebrow.

"Oh, yes, Empress," Zhukov said. "I even set foot on the shores of Pandyssia in my search."

Keep him talking, keep him talking.

Emily forced out a laugh.

"I don't believe you," she said. "Very few people have ever reached Pandyssia. Even fewer have made it back."

Zhukov shrugged. "What you believe is irrelevant. I found what I was looking for. The information did not come cheap, or easily, but those I interrogated were useful in other ways, even if they didn't tell me what I needed to know."

"What's that supposed to mean?"

"It means I filleted their flesh and took their bones." He paused, then continued. "I am a sick man, Empress. My time is short and my need to feed is great."

"What was the jawbone for?" she asked. "Shame you lost your fancy knife. Antique, was it? A souvenir from the old country."

"You could say that," Zhukov said. "Unfortunately, a sacrifice that was necessary. That artifact was from another time and place, a world that existed before this one, tethering me to it." He gestured to the vat. "It was a tool that served me well, and now its job is done. I needed to unlock its power and pull on that tether, bringing that world closer to this one."

Zhukov turned and clapped his hands together.

The four Whalers who had manhandled the jawbone into the vat moved around the other side, over to the wall, where the controls were for the pulley system—the one that held the frame. Unhooking the chain from the wall, one Whaler knocked a pin out of a geared wheel, while another grabbed the crank handle on the wheel and began to turn it.

The grinding of metal rubbing on metal, chains clanking and rattling, filled the factory as the frame hanging above the vat began to lift clear, pulling up whatever was in the vat. The thick white-yellow liquid clung to the object like honey, slowly sloughing off and falling back.

Emily squinted at the object, trying to work out what it was. It was huge, and perfect, a flat plane of bright brilliance, as clear as a window—twenty feet from side to side, the corners held in black iron clamps. The object was lifted high and it kept going, up and up and up, as if it would never end, as if the roiling vat was a bottomless abyss, as deep as the lair of the leviathan. Deep enough to hold the entire world.

As the object was raised, Emily stared at the reflection in its perfect surface. She saw the factory in reverse, she saw Zhukov standing beside her, she saw herself sitting, hands bound, against the other vat.

It was a mirror. A huge, flat, perfect mirror, the surface shining but somehow dark, black, like the reflection had a *depth* you could reach out and touch.

Zhukov nodded to himself, and then he began to laugh.

"Take a good look, Empress. Watch the world that *is* become the world that *was*."

Emily frowned. The image in the mirror... did it flicker? Did it move slightly, from left to right? One moment Zhukov was standing to her left, then on her right, then on the left again.

"Balance is restored," Zhukov said, "and revenge is mine."

27

GREAVES AUXILIARY WHALE SLAUGHTERHOUSE 5, SLAUGHTERHOUSE ROW, DUNWALL
15th Day, Month of Darkness, 1851

"Restrict the Wandering Gaze that looks hither and yonder for some flashing thing that easily catches a man's fancy in one moment, but brings calamity in the next. For the eyes are never tired of seeing, nor are they quick to spot illusion. A man whose gaze is corrupted is like a warped mirror that has traded beauty for ugliness and ugliness for beauty. Instead, fix your eyes to what is edifying and to what is pure, and then you will be able to recognize the profane monuments of the Outsider."

— THE FIRST STRICTURE
Excerpt from a work detailing one of the Seven Strictures

Emily forced herself to her feet. At once, a Whaler she didn't realize was there grabbed her arm, dragging her over to the middle of the slaughterhouse factory floor, where they pushed her down onto her knees again.

Zhukov said something, but she didn't hear it. She didn't hear anything or see anything other than the reflection in the mirror.

It flickered again, and changed. The factory was still reflected in its impossible surface, but the vast chamber was empty—she was gone, Zhukov and the Whalers were gone. The factory was dark, dead, weeds growing through cracks in the floor, and the rear wall—the towering rear wall that should have been behind Emily, as solid as ever, was a jagged ruin, like smashed teeth grinning at the city outside.

A city on fire.

Somehow she could see it all, as the cityscape stretched away into the distance. The famous Clocktower was nothing but a jagged, broken shard, and the Wrenhaven River was itself a mirror, reflecting the glow of the inferno.

Dunwall was a ruin, every house, every building a shell. As Emily watched, walls collapsed like wet sand, sending plumes of dust lazily into the air, mixing with black, thick smoke that swam like ink in water.

And she saw Dunwall Tower. Her home, the Imperial fortress, a symbol to not just the people of Dunwall, of Gristol, but to citizens across the Empire.

Except Dunwall Tower was a gap-toothed, abandoned pile, the walls cracked and collapsed. The fire hadn't reached it yet, but it would, soon. Already the only inhabitants remaining in the palace were making their fast escape.

Rats.

Thousands and thousands of rats. They ran and they swarmed, moving in a single, undulating wave, cascading over the rubble, over broken walls, through dead windows that looked more like the dead eyes of a dozen rotting skulls.

The Rat Plague had destroyed Dunwall. The Rat Plague had killed everyone, and now the city burned. Dunwall was dead, a footnote in history, a tragedy that rang like a funeral bell down through the ages.

"Balance," Zhukov said. Emily flinched at his words, and she blinked. Suddenly the image in the mirror flickered again and she saw the factory as it was. She saw herself, and Zhukov, and the Whalers, and…

No. It wasn't her. Somehow, in the middle of the factory, there was a throne—*the* throne. There was a woman sitting on it—an Empress—but she was older, her hair grayed and wild, her face drawn, the rings black and heavy beneath her eyes.

Emily recognized her. But it was not a memory, it was not the past. It was somehow *now*. The present. A present that had never happened, that could never have happened.

Because the woman on the throne had been murdered. Assassinated nearly fifteen years ago.

Jessamine Kaldwin I.

Emily's mother, staring with dead eyes on a broken throne as the city burned.

Emily shook her head and squeezed her eyes tight shut. Behind their closed lids she watched as the shadows of a fire danced and danced. With her eyes still closed she lifted her head and she screamed.

She screamed until her throat was shredded, every bit of air expelled from her lungs. Then she fell sideways, her cheek hitting the hard, damp factory floor.

Good. That was good. The floor was cold and her cheek hurt and she focused on that pain, willing herself to concentrate, focus on what was real, what was here and now. Not on the games of Zhukov.

He was laughing, and she opened her eyes. The mirror was still there—now it just showed the factory as it really was, the mirror acting like a real mirror. Yet as Emily watched it, she saw its surface ripple, as if it was still, deep water caught in a gentle breeze.

She pushed herself up with her shoulder. Her head pounded, and then settled. She looked up at Zhukov, standing next to her.

"What are you?" Her voice was a dry, croaky whisper.

"My name is Zhukov," he said, "and I am the Hero of Tyvia. For twenty years I served my country, and served it well." He lifted a hand, palm up, toward the mirror, and then he curled his fingers, as if he was pulling something in.

Pulling in the past to the present, for Emily to see.

She looked again into the mirror.

She saw,
Trees, hills, mountains, snow. Tyvia, a land of beauty and bounty, the coastal regions of plenty surrounding a frozen, unforgiving heart.

She saw,
People, villagers, going about their business. And then horses, galloping, men in black riding in, slashing with swords, throwing blazing torches onto straw roofs, trampling women and children under their hooves in the cold mud.

She saw,
A man in green, appearing from nowhere, leaping onto a burning roof. He moved like lightning, jumping onto the back of a bandit's horse, slitting the bandit's throat before throwing the body to the ground. Riding, fast and quick and agile, his knife moving with equal speed and dexterity.

One against so many, and he won. The village was saved.

She saw,

A man in green, moving along a torch-lit passage, the flames throwing flickering light that revealed his face—a handsome young man, his eyes blue and bright like the ice of his homeland, a black beard, trimmed to a sharp point. This time there was not a knife, but a sword. He crossed the passage, entered a chamber, a great hall.

There was a long table, at which sat a man in a uniform surrounded by men in the same uniform. The men laughed. On the table were documents. Perhaps a map, perhaps something else.

They didn't stand a chance. The Hero of Tyvia slipped into the room then slipped his sword through the neck of the nearest soldier. Before the others could even react, before the man could even stand, heads rolled on the wooden floor.

When the man in green left the room he left only the dead behind, the documents on the table curling with flames that soon lapped at the bodies then at the room, the curtains, the walls.

She saw,

A building—huge, like the Abbey of the Everyman, but wider, squat, like a fat spider sitting at the center of its web. An avenue, as straight as an arrow, led to the door. The avenue was laid with flowers—millions of them, in every color—and was lined by people cheering, clapping, applauding, while behind them, men in black-and-red uniforms watched, their faces expressionless, their eyes searching.

They were in the crowd, they were on rooftops, they were everywhere. Somewhere, at the back, on a quiet street, the men in uniform dragged people out of the crowd—people who weren't cheering or clapping or behaving like the rest, and beat them with long truncheons before throwing them into the backs of iron wagons.

And on the steps of the citadel, a line of old men, their faces hard, unreadable, their uniforms identical to all the rest. In front of them, a man in green, with blue eyes and a neat beard and on his chest a red ribbon—a small thing, a square of shiny cloth, nothing more— waving at the crowd while one of the old men stood by his side, whispering something, telling the man in green to keep waving and not to stop waving and that he was doing a good job.

Emily blinked and the image flickered, stuttered. She drew in a breath and looked up at Zhukov.

He took a step toward the mirror, still holding his hand out, watching himself. The past. Emily knew that. She recognized the Tyvian citadel at Dabokva. She recognized some of the men on the steps—it was their local governing council, the country allowed a measure of autonomy under the umbrella of the Empire of the Isles.

The handsome man in green was Zhukov, that was obvious. The red ribbon his reward for his heroism and courage and service to the people.

"What happened?" Emily whispered the question, her voice catching in her hoarse throat. She was about to ask it again, thinking he hadn't heard, but he answered first.

"The world changed, Empress," he said. "The balance was shifted, and the world teetered."

The image in the mirror changed again. Emily felt herself drawn to it, and then she shuddered, and felt cold and sick in the hot factory. She watched the images move in the mirror, playing out a scene she had replayed in her own mind, a hundred, a thousand, a million times over.

Dunwall Tower. The gazebo overlooking the harbor.

The day Corvo came back with bad news.

The day that her mother died.

Emily felt her chest tighten as she watched. She saw Corvo talk to the Empress. She saw the tears in her eyes.

She saw the Whalers appear, their murderous leader Daud with them. Saw their blades flash. Saw Corvo fight, and lose.

Saw them kill her mother.

Saw Corvo dragged away, beaten into unconsciousness.

Emily closed her eyes.

"I don't understand," she said, opening her eyes, forcing herself to look at Zhukov as he stared at the mirror. "What does that have to do with you and Tyvia?"

"It has *everything* to do with Tyvia." Zhukov hissed, the rage palpable. Emily jerked back.

He threw his hand toward the mirror and pulled back again, tugging on the strings of time to show something else. The image shifted, back to the citadel. The crowds of people cheering or being arrested. The council honoring their hero. And…

No. This was different. The council was missing more than half its members, including the sour old man who had been whispering. Zhukov was there, but he was not in green, he was in black and red—the military uniform, distinguished only from the others by the red ribbon pinned to his breast.

Behind him, escorted by members of the City Watch—the *Dunwall* City Watch, in their ceremonial uniforms—was…

"*No*," Emily breathed, not believing it.

Empress Jessamine. Looking as she had on the day she died. Young, vibrant, alive.

"A new dawn for Tyvia," Zhukov said. "This was as it should have happened. Tyvia was ruled by a council of cruelty, the people not governed, but controlled, a yoke of iron around their necks." Zhukov hissed and took a step closer to the mirror.

"It was criminal, and I saw it, so I became a criminal, too. I did what I could, working in the shadows, helping people where I could, but those who ruled—the so-called Secretaries of the People of Tyvia—they had spies watching me. Black-masked, nameless, stateless Operators, ready to act.

"They came for me in the night. But they did not take me to my death. They took me to the citadel, to the High Judges, the three who ruled. They recruited me. They said they understood what I was doing, that they had a plan to change Tyvia. Each of them had been forced to wait until they had reached their position, had acquired their power, before they could act. They told me they had been waiting their whole lives, working to enact change. They needed me to be part of that. To continue my work, fighting for the people.

"Tyvia was beset by bandits, by revolutionaries encouraged by the exiled princes who spent all their time and money in taverns, whispering, encouraging resistance to the movement that had toppled them from power. The people didn't understand, and the High Judges couldn't tell them, not yet. Revolution was the danger, anarchists the enemy.

"Oh, but the High Judges were on their side, the side of the people. Revolution was necessary. Change was required. The High Judges agreed with these dangerous ideas, supported them even, but they were working from the *inside*. In the meantime they needed me to keep the peace, to stop those who were plotting against them.

"Nothing could jeopardize the Great Plan.

"And I believed them. I was presented to the people as

a hero—the first among equals, just one man—one man—who could keep the people safe at night. I was feted. Celebrated. I worked for the High Judges for years—years of my life that, I realized later, had been wasted. I was being used—a tool not of freedom, but of oppression. The change they promised was not coming, was *never* coming.

"I was the distraction, a symbol on which the people would fixate, allowing them to dream of better days that would never come, while the iron fist of the High Judges gripped tighter and tighter."

Zhukov spun around to face Emily. The image in the mirror faded, and the surface rippled as it reflected the real world of the here and now.

"I was contacted by agents from Dunwall," he said, "servants of the Royal Spymaster. Dunwall, I was told, had seen what was happening in Tyvia, and wanted change—*real* change, not the false promises and charades of the High Judges. They saw me as the means to enact that change. I was on the inside. I had access, knowledge. I was to be a mole, digging my way through their secrets, gathering information and feeding it back to Gristol.

"And then I realized the possibilities. Dunwall was planning something—not a war, but something far more insidious. A slow takeover, retaking that part of the empire they had let fall too far from their control."

Zhukov balled his hand into a fist, and he beat his chest with it.

"And *I* was the key! Without me, they could do nothing. *Nothing!* I was the center, around which the balance of the world would spin. There would be none more important than me, none more worthy to take Tyvia from the people who had betrayed it. The Secretaries and their High Judges would be no more. I would lead the people, as was my *right*. I had fought for them. Tyvia was *mine*, and with

Empress Jessamine's help, I would take that country. *My* country." Zhukov's fist shook as he squeezed it.

Emily swallowed a hot ball of nothing. She nodded, realizing herself what had happened.

"But what you didn't know," she said quietly, "was that there were those plotting against my mother. Planning on taking power for themselves."

"Yes." Zhukov nodded. "The assassination of Empress Jessamine changed everything. With her gone, the Royal Spymaster lost his interest in revolution, now that he had proclaimed himself Lord Regent. Perhaps it was his arrogance, believing that the whole Empire was now his to rule, ignorant of the state of Tyvia."

Emily nodded. "They sold you out to the High Judges, in exchange for closer diplomatic ties."

Zhukov inclined his head. "I was granted the ultimate gift of the people of Tyvia—freedom!" Zhukov barked a laugh, a single, harsh sound. "Freedom! Freedom from responsibility. Freedom from duty. Freedom from liberty. *Freedom from freedom!* They sent me to Utyrka, to the salt mines."

Zhukov chuckled, calming down.

"But they did not expect me to return."

"Now I know you're lying."

"What?" Zhukov rounded on Emily. He stood over her, and at once she felt the pulsing, nauseating wave of dizziness sweep over her. She swallowed the taste of metal and forced herself to look away from his eyes. The feeling waned, but did not disappear.

"Nobody escapes the prisons of Tyvia," Emily whispered. "Everybody knows that."

"You speak the truth, Empress, but know that I am not lying."

Emily blinked hot tears from her eyes and forced

herself to look back up at the man, focusing again on her reflection in his goggles. It was a trick that had worked before, and it worked now.

"Then how did you get away?"

Dropping into a crouch, Zhukov knelt in front of her. She didn't take her eyes off the reflection, but, so close, she could feel the heat radiating off him. It didn't feel like heat absorbed from the vat—Zhukov hadn't stood near it for a while now. No, it felt more like heat coming from *within* him, somewhere in the folds of the scarf and greatcoat.

"I had a vision," Zhukov said. "It came to me, in the salt mine. A vision of fire, of a great burning. Deep under the glacier, where we dug the frozen earth, I found an artifact— the knife. A relic from another time, a relic filled with power and secrets. As soon as I held it, I heard its song. It whispered its secrets to me, and there, in the dark, I opened my eyes. It showed me the light, blazing across time."

Zhukov held his hands up, the fingers curling, moving as though he still held the knife, twisting and turning it— the knife now part of the molten mass in the vat.

"The blade told me how to carve bones—tokens of its power. It moved my hands, moved my mind, allowing me to craft charms that unlocked the power of the Void. At first, it was too much, this power. I was lost in it, swimming in it. I even tried to carve myself, cutting my own flesh, but when I awoke all I had carved was a symbol on the back of my hand—a crude image of the Mark of the Outsider, an echo of the knife's song, the song I heard in the cold darkness of Utyrka, of the boy whose life the blades had taken a millennium ago.

"After that, I turned my blades on others, carving charms from their bones. It was with these charms I made my escape. They unlocked a power that was already within me, a reflection of my own will. With that power, every mirror, every reflection became a corridor through which I could travel."

"And that allowed you to escape?" she said.

"The camp at Utyrka was surrounded by the famous blue glacial field, right at the center of Tyvia. The ice held many reflections." Zhukov shrugged. Emily could almost imagine him frowning underneath the scarf.

If only she could see his face. See what he was now. Because one thing she was sure of, the monster hiding inside the winter coat, the hat, the scarf, the goggles, it wasn't the handsome, bold hero of Tyvia who she had seen in the mirror.

"Show me your face," Emily said.

Zhukov laughed, and pushed himself to his feet. "I don't think you really want that." He walked away, holding his hands up, rotating them in front of him. "Transversing through the ice had certain… *effects*." He turned, and raised a hand. Emily thought he was going to relent, to unwrap the scarf at least, but then he dropped it again, and instead used it to point at Emily.

"Tell me what you saw."

"What?"

He pointed to the mirror. "There. Tell me what you saw."

"Ah… I saw Tyvia. Your life's work."

"No, before that! What was the first thing you saw?"

Emily frowned. Hadn't he seen it? The ruined, burning city. Empress Jessamine, alive but older, alone on a broken throne.

The rats. The swarming, shrieking rats.

Keep him talking. Keep him talking.

"I don't understand," she said.

Zhukov cried out in annoyance—the first time Emily had seen him lose control of his temper—and walked up to her. As he looked down, she felt the red eyes bore into her and the factory went fuzzy at the edges as a wave of disorientation hit her.

And then it was gone.

"Don't trifle with me, child," Zhukov said. "I carry charms which grant many different powers, and can cause you much more harm than merely casting an aura of disorientation." He pointed to the mirror again. "The mirror shows the past, the present, and the future—possible futures as the deck of the world is reshuffled, the hand replayed.

"So tell me, what did *you* see?"

Emily frowned, her forehead creasing in concentration as she put the final pieces together.

The vision of the city—of her mother, alive but condemned to a reign of torment—was the future. A future that might have been.

Like the visions of Emily on the throne, laughing as Corvo slaughtered the aristocracy of the city for her pleasure.

Possible futures—futures that would have existed only if Zhukov's plan had succeeded, fifteen years ago. If he had taken control of Tyvia, replacing one iron fist with another.

A future that would have existed if Emily's mother had not been murdered.

"I…" Emily faltered. What did Zhukov want? *What is this all for?*

"Tell me, Emily!" Zhukov roared. "Do I succeed?"

Emily screwed her eyes tight shut.

"I don't understand!"

"The mirror!" Zhukov said. He reached down and yanked her to her feet. With one hand he grabbed her cheeks, forcing her face around to the mirror, and with the other he pointed. "The past, the present, and the future are here, in this very room. All I need to do is find the right moment and step through." He released Emily, and she fell back to the floor. "Tell me the right moment, and I can save your mother! I can save her and history can unfold as it was intended!"

Emily blanched. *Of course.* He could travel through mirrors—through reflections. He had said that, for him, they were a corridor. And this mirror, this impossible, magical mirror, was…

A door.

A door into the past. To a day, fifteen years ago, when Corvo came home bringing bad news. The day Emily's world had ended.

The day her mother was murdered.

And—

He could stop it happening. Zhukov could do it. Step into the mirror. Travel back. Help Corvo fight Daud. Prevent the assassination.

Save her mother.

And—

And condemn the world to a future of death and of darkness, a future where Dunwall fell, where her mother ruled over a black empire, her daughter a raving maniac aided by her homicidal father.

Emily shook her head.

"No."

Zhukov took a step back, as if he'd been slapped.

"What?"

"I won't tell you."

"Listen to me, Empress," he whispered. "I am offering you the world. I am offering you a chance to correct what is wrong. To rebalance the world. I can save your mother."

Emily nodded. "I know."

"Then what…?"

Emily smiled sadly. "If you go back and save my mother, you will save yourself. You will take control of Tyvia. You will have the power you want."

"And your mother will be alive, here, now."

Emily shook her head. "In a world that is crumbling," she said. "Ruler of an empire of disease and fire. You will rule Tyvia, but only for a short while. The Rat Plague will spread, killing everyone. Dunwall will just be the first city."

"You lie."

"You asked me what I saw."

"You *lie*."

Emily said nothing.

Zhukov spun around, back to the mirror. "No matter. It is only one of many potentials. Your presence here was a boon, but it was not essential. I can find another moment. My plan will succeed, and I will gut the High Judges like the pigs they are."

Emily collapsed onto her haunches. She stared at the ground. She pulled at her bindings again, but they were tight, the leather straps digging into her wrists.

She felt helpless. *Was* helpless, alone.

Zhukov stepped up to the mirror. Its surface shimmered like water and changed as he searched for the right moment.

Emily looked up.

She saw something move out of the corner of her eye.

She heard a sound from the metal stairs. Zhukov, distracted, turned his red eyes to look.

And then Emily felt a breath in her ear.

"I'm here," a voice whispered.

28

SOMEWHERE NEAR GREAVES AUXILIARY WHALE SLAUGHTERHOUSE 5, SLAUGHTERHOUSE ROW, DUNWALL

15th Day, Month of Darkness, 1851
(…a little earlier)

"All conflict is deception and lies, for to defeat the enemy, he must be fooled—fooled into thinking you are far when you are near, that you are sleeping when you are awake, that you are still when we are moving. And the greatest ally of deception is darkness, for it is only in the darkness that we can truly see the path ahead."

— A BETTER WAY TO DIE
Surviving fragment of an assassin's treatise,
author unknown

It had taken longer to reach the old slaughterhouse than Corvo had liked, but the Boyle Mansion was a substantial distance away, and he was on foot. En route he blinked from rooftop to ledge to windowsill to rooftop, but he'd already guzzled one of his own vials of Addermire Solution and, not knowing what he was going to face at the factory, he wanted to save the last two.

Because he was going to need all his strength, all his power. Whatever Zhukov was doing, whatever his plan was, it faded from Corvo's mind as he rounded a corner and came to the riverfront and saw the factory looming on the opposite shore. There was just one thing in his mind now. One task at hand.

Rescuing Emily.

But as he got closer, crossed the river by blinking from the north-side wharves to the south—via the hulk of an old freighter anchored in the middle, he saw that Zhukov wasn't taking any chances. The Whalers must have been down to just a handful of men, but he'd placed at least three outside the factory, guarding the approaches. For all Corvo knew, there would be more on the other side of the building, and who knew how many inside.

He would need to move with cunning, with stealth.

Corvo clung to the rusting ironwork underneath the factory jetty as a pair of booted feet trod the old wooden boards over his head. He watched the Whaler pass, oblivious to his presence, then he swung himself up onto the wharf and jogged, half-crouched, toward the Whaler's exposed back.

The man never knew he was there. Corvo wrapped an arm around his neck and maintained the pressure until the man stopped struggling. Then he slid him onto his shoulder, ducking back down to the riverbank, and dumped the body out of sight.

One down. Two to go.

The factory had huge, hangar-like doors on the riverside, where whaling ships could dock, their frames hanging their precious cargo being slid directly into the building. There were two Whalers here, patrolling by the door, looking out into the night, toward the river.

Corvo ducked behind the jetty framework. There was no way in there. He would have to take the fire escape, up on the side of the factory.

He glanced up to the railing. It would be easiest to blink, and there would be time enough for the Mark of the Outsider to regenerate his power, pulling on the dark, electric force of the Void, before he got inside. That would save him one of the vials of Addermire Solution.

Judging his landing spot, Corvo reached out—then ducked back down, the Mark burning on the back of his hand in protest.

There was another Whaler, on the fire escape.

Corvo counted time, the precious seconds evaporating forever as the Whaler just stood there, enjoying the view. Emily was inside the factory, and Zhukov, and Galia, and time was running out.

He had to get in.

The Whaler moved. Corvo got ready... then cursed silently as the man, rather than walk away, just leaned down on the railing and got comfortable.

There was nothing for it, and no time for anything else. Flicking his folding sword out from its hilt, Corvo picked his destination, and pulled himself across the impossible gap. He materialized on the edge of the fire escape platform, on the outer side of the rail.

The Whaler started, jerking back at his sudden appearance, but before he could sound an alarm Corvo plunged his blade into his target's neck. The man gurgled, hands scrabbling for the weapon, his head thrown back as a torrent of blood spurted from the arterial wound. Corvo gritted his teeth and twisted the blade, and the Whaler's head dropped forward, the life leaving his body.

Refolding his weapon, Corvo vaulted the rail and dragged the body into the shadows, where it couldn't be seen from the ground. Glancing down, he saw that he was in the perfect position to take out the two Whalers at the main doors. He could do it from this angle. They would be dead before they even knew he was there.

Despite his profession, he regretted the loss of life, wishing there was time to take them out without killing them. But with the Empress's life in peril, the Royal Protector had to do what he was charged to do.

Corvo padded along the platform that skirted high on the factory wall, picked his spot, and blinked down to the ground. Arriving in front of the hangar doors but behind the two guards, he snuck up behind the first, killing him swiftly, his blade severing the man's neck nearly to the bone. Dropping the body, he spun on his heel, even as the other Whaler was still turning at the sound, and jammed his blade into the front of the Whaler's mask, piercing the leather and rubber like they were butter. The man shuddered, his arms stretched out as if he'd touched the live terminals of a whale oil tank, and then he was still.

Pulling out the sword, Corvo headed for the small rusting portal set into the left side of the giant hangar doors. Checking through a split in the old metal, he saw that the coast was clear.

Corvo opened the door, and stepped into the slaughterhouse.

He saw Emily. He saw Zhukov. Of Galia there was no sign. There was something very large and rectangular hanging from a framework over the vat of hot liquid, but there was no time for that now.

His first priority was getting to Emily.

The factory was unlit, and while the main oil vat shone brightly, providing ample illumination, the light blazed from a single, central point, casting very long shadows, throwing the periphery of the factory floor into a deep, inky darkness. And, thanks to the plethora of factory machinery, pallets, drums, and tanks that were scattered around the place, there was a lot of cover available too.

Corvo ducked and ran to the edge of a rusting drum that sat on a wheeled cradle, like a rail car. He peered around, and saw a Whaler ahead of him, his mask turned to the light.

Corvo blinked forward, then choked the Whaler out, dragging the body to cover behind the wheeled drum.

One down.

He checked again. Two more Whalers, a pair standing over by the stairs leading up to the factory offices. This was more difficult. There was no cover around them—if he blinked behind the pair, he would be in the light, and easily seen by Zhukov.

Those two he needed to save for later.

Corvo retraced his steps, and moved from the wheeled drum to a stack of wooden pallets to a low wall formed by a moveable tool rack. The rack still held harpoons and hooks and blades strapped on the end of ten-foot poles. Every tool needed for slicing into the still-living flesh of a whale as it hung, helpless, in the air.

There was a Whaler near the cabinet and just enough shadow behind him for Corvo to sneak up, cut off the man's supply of oxygen and dump the unconscious body behind the tool rack.

Two down.

Corvo glanced up. There were no Whalers that he could see up on the galleries or the ironwork platforms, unless they were skulking in the shadows, but there didn't seem to be any reason why they would be. Just to be sure, he picked a spot on the gallery opposite his hiding place, blinked, then rolled into the shadows high in the factory.

His limbs grew heavy as he expended his energy, but there was no time to wait for himself to recover naturally. He reached into his tunic and drank the second vial of restorative. That left only one.

Down below, Zhukov was saying something, talking to Emily, but Corvo couldn't make out the words over the steady rumble of the vat. He glanced to his left, and—

There.

A Whaler by the factory office platform. Corvo slunk along the gallery as far as he could, blinked up to the platform above the Whaler, then dropped down on top of the man, felling him without a sound.

This gave him a good view of the factory. He looked around. Still no sign of Galia. That was problematic, but Corvo put that thought to one side. There were no other Whalers that he could see, save for the two directly ahead of him, one flight down at the bottom of the stairs.

More luck. The two sentries were facing Zhukov, who was standing by the vat. Emily was on the other side of the factory floor, kneeling in front of the disused vat. As Corvo watched, Zhukov walked over to her. In a few seconds, his back was to the Whalers, who watched their master from behind their leather and rubber masks.

Corvo blinked.

He smashed the Whalers' heads together, then grabbed them under the arms and pulled backward, letting them drop down onto the bottom of the staircase. The attack had been awkward, and far from ideal. Not silent, either— but as it happened, the noise had been a useful distraction.

Zhukov turned his head in his direction, but in an

instant, Corvo blinked, reappearing behind Emily, severing her bonds without a moment's delay.

"I'm here," he whispered in her ear.

Zhukov wheeled back around as Emily and Corvo stood together. Corvo slipped a knife from his belt and handed it to Emily, his own folding sword raised and ready.Emily lowered her head, her eyes narrowed. One side of her mouth twitched up as she hefted her new blade.

Then Empress and Royal Protector, daughter and father, charged the enemy.

29

"From what we've gathered, the item possessed some occult power. It also seemed to come at a cost, however, afflicting the bearer in several unwanted ways as well. Whether the individual or cult responsible for the creation of the corrupted bonecharm made it that way deliberately, or whether their capabilities proved somehow inferior, is not something we know at this time."

— WARNING ON CORRUPTED CHARMS
Excerpt from an Overseer's report on
black-market occult artifacts

Zhukov backed away, raising his hands toward the oncoming pair. Emily was ready to fight—fight for her life, for her city, for Gristol and the Empire.

For her mother—a mother she couldn't save. History had to run its course.

Beside her, Corvo moved with fluid ease. This was what they had trained for. He was a master at arms, her champion, her protector. She trusted him to the ends of the world and back again.

Corvo fell first.

Emily saw him drop from the corner of her eye, and she turned to him, the world suddenly moving in slow motion, the factory floor bucking and tilting like a whaling ship on a high sea. Corvo stumbled, and fell to his knees, then he toppled sideways, stopping himself from hitting the floor with the hand that held his foldable sword. Then he stayed in that position, and didn't move.

That was when Emily realized she wasn't moving either. She was standing, or trying to stand, and she looked around, but her head felt as if it was made of solid stone, and when she *did* move it around, the world moved in an odd, sickening swinging motion. It was as if the factory had slipped its foundations and slid out onto the river, the top-heavy building listing as it began to sink and sink and sink and—

Emily hit the floor on her knees, the pain sharp and exquisite, an electric burst that cleared her mind for a moment, sweeping away the fog and the sickening dizziness. She whopped a deep breath, and heard Zhukov laughing.

He was walking backward, toward the mirror, still holding his arms out. Next to her, Corvo finally succumbed fully, his sword arm slipping out, letting his body fall sideways to the floor.

Zhukov's aura.

The bonecharms.

It was impossible to get *near* him, let alone attack him. There was nothing they could do.

Emily pulled herself up, staggered over to Corvo, then fell back to her knees. She reached out for him, glancing up at their enemy. He was at the vat now, his back to the mirror. Emily saw him, saw his reflected back.

Saw the smoke rising.

Not from the vat, but from *Zhukov*—and it wasn't because he was standing too close to the vat. No, the smoke was coming from him… or, more specifically, from inside his coat. It seeped out from between the double-breasted lapels, it rose in cautious fingers from under the collar, filtering through the tightly wrapped scarf to shroud Zhukov's goggle-hidden eyes.

Emily felt her stomach lurch, and the world flipped around. She collapsed on top of Corvo, the blackness behind her eyes spinning, spinning, spinning as Zhukov channeled his aura, stoking the disorienting energy until it washed over them. There was a crackle, and in Emily's spinning vision she thought she saw a flame lick the front of Zhukov's coat, as though using his power was burning him up.

That meant he couldn't keep the assault up forever. The question was, how long *could* he last? Emily could hardly think. Her body seemed to be a far and distant thing, a memory, the factory a dream.

She couldn't do it. It was too much. She wanted to die, and consciousness began to lose its grip on the world.

Then she saw it. Corvo's blade. He was still holding it, his sword arm trapped underneath him.

But the blade itself was free.

And within reach.

Emily sucked in a breath that seemed too hard to draw, and she reached forward. The blade was either very close or a million miles away, she couldn't tell, the way the slaughterhouse shifted and rippled. Her vision was surrounded by sparkling blue stars that roared in her ears with the sound of a forest fire, a cleansing inferno from time beyond time.

Her fingers touched something.

Cold. Sharp. Metal. Her fingers danced around the top, thumb hooking underneath. She squeezed, and slid her hand an inch along, and felt hot wetness and a dripping sensation.

And then she felt the pain. Her hand was on fire, lighting her whole body up like fireworks on the first day of the Month of Earth. She gasped and let go of Corvo's blade, holding her cut hand curled, unwilling or unable to work the frozen fingers.

She clamped her jaw and forced herself to close the hand into a fist, felt the blood ooze and squelch, felt the agony arcing across her nervous system in jagged, zigzagging bolts. She wanted to throw up.

Corvo's blade was sharp. She had cut deep—and that was exactly what she had wanted to do. Because there was something more powerful than Zhukov's aura of confusion, something that cut through the disorientation, the nausea. Something that overrode it—something primal, ancient. Simple.

Pain.

Emily stood, her head clear, her hand throbbing with every beat of her heart. She ignored both. She had to, and her body obliged, the adrenaline coursing through her system. She felt awake, aware, fast, agile, ready, like being dropped into an ice bath. Everything hurt, but everything was clear, pin-sharp.

Zhukov lowered his arms, faltering, perhaps seeing or realizing that something wasn't right. On the floor, Corvo groaned and rocked on his side. Zhukov's concentration had diminished, the power he channeled lessening.

Emily bent down, reaching underneath Corvo to yank his sword free, the blade streaked with her own blood. She spun around and lunged forward, sweeping the weapon out. Zhukov mirrored her movement, jerking backward, but not quite far enough. The tip of Corvo's blade unstitched the front of his coat, popping buttons and dragging one lapel from another.

Seeing that her opponent was unsteady, Emily lunged again, sweeping the other way. Another slice and the front of Zhukov's coat fell open, the ragged halves of heavy wool sagging with the weight of the small objects that seemed to be sewn into the lining.

They were roughly circular, like little pinwheels fashioned from bone and copper wire, and they were glowing, red and orange, like hot coals. A pall of smoke, trapped under the coat, rose up toward the factory ceiling.

Emily righted herself, stabbed left, but Zhukov was fast, sidestepping once, twice, keeping himself out of the blade's reach. He was unarmed, but as he moved Emily saw his hands cut gestures, carve sigils in the air.

A wave of nausea hit her.

She nearly doubled over, stumbling, her ears filled with laughter—*her* laughter, the laughter of an Emily who never was but that who might have been. She heard the snick of blade on flesh, the wet gurgle as another throat was cut for her entertainment by her murderous father, the Royal Executioner.

She squeezed the injured hand and her head cleared, although her throat was still hot and raw. She stabbed with the blade but it was awkward this time, off-mark. Zhukov avoided it by jerking his body out of the way, allowing the cutting edge to slice the flap of his greatcoat.

Twisting around, he pulled, tangling the blade in the thick fabric. Emily felt herself yanked forward, her sword hand trapped. Zhukov twisted again, pulling her sword arm around, and Emily had to go with the movement or have it broken.

Crying out, she twisted as well, falling to her knees

as Zhukov stepped over her. She could feel the heat from the glowing, corroded bonecharms, and she could smell something—something old, dusty, a mix of rotting vegetables and burning meat.

She let go of the sword, but wrapped in the coat she couldn't free her hand. She pulled, then grabbed at Zhukov with her injured hand. The sword clattered to the factory floor.

Grabbing handfuls of his coat, Emily pulled herself up. Zhukov was strong, and bigger than her, but she was no weakling. She was a fighter. She had been trained by the best for most of her life. She knew how to use an opponent's size, his strength, against him.

But Zhukov was a fighter, too, and while Emily was able to resist the disorientation aura thanks to her injured hand, it was exactly that—an *injury*—a bad cut that slowed her down, the pain clearing her head but distracting her mind, the hand itself burning and lacking any kind of strength or dexterity.

The fight became a struggle, the two wrestling beside the vat, the burning bonecharms clacking in Zhukov's open coat. Underneath she saw he was wearing ragged green leathers, worn and dirty, rimed with salt from the years the Hero of Tyvia had worked in the mine.

She forced Zhukov toward the vat, and he grunted as the backs of his legs caught the rim. Emily pushed again, but too late she realized that Zhukov had an advantage. He leaned away, then, using the vat itself as leverage, shoved forward, pushing the Empress off him. She fell, overbalanced, her hands scrambling at something, anything, to use as support.

Her fingers vanished into something soft and hot, her hand sinking into coils of something furry.

She hit the factory floor on her tailbone, pain shooting

up her spine, down her arms. She shook her head, and then looked at the scarf in her hands. Beside her, the broad-brimmed traveler's hat rolled a tight circle on its crown.

Zhukov roared as he bore down on her, hands reaching out, jaw stretched wider than was possible for anything other than a cadaver. Emily gasped in surprise and in horror at the blackened, crinkled skin, the puckered, tight black lips and the black teeth within the gaping, lopsided maw. His skull was bald, the dark, crusted skin stretched tight and thin. Only the goggles remained, two great red circles, the thick leather straps that held them in place passing around his head, passing ears that were no longer there.

The walking corpse that was the Hero of Tyvia screamed at Emily. It was an animal sound, a wet howl. He leaned over her, reaching for her throat, the open flaps of his greatcoat snapping everywhere.

Reaching out with her injured hand, she grabbed for the first corroded bonecharm she saw. The charm hissed and steamed as it touched her blood, and, with a yell, Emily pulled. It sprang free of the stitching that held it in place, and it cooled immediately, collapsing into charcoal in her hand.

Zhukov staggered, his blackened maw twisting in confusion. The hands that were reaching for Emily's throat were no longer as close as they had been. Then he snarled, closing his fingers into a fist.

The dizziness hit Emily like a runaway carriage, like a physical thing slamming into the side of her head. The room spun what seemed like a full three-hundred-and-sixty degrees and she felt as if she was falling, and falling a very, very long way.

She blinked her eyes, and looked up, her head roaring. She could see Zhukov—many Zhukov's, his image doubled, trebled, multiplied a dozen times, spinning around as if she was looking through a kaleidoscope, his disorientation aura at full effect, his bonecharms dancing with small, blue flames, his coat smoking.

Squinting, she willed the world to come back to an even keel. She saw that one bonecharm was burning more than the others, the red coal flaring into white heat like a beacon. The charm he was drawing on the most. The one that granted him the power of disorientation.

Emily closed her eyes and launched herself at it. She felt herself hit something, soft and yielding, enveloping. She felt heat, and the bonecharms seemed like scalding stones against her face. Then she fell, face down, and rolled on the stone floor, only stopping when she hit the factory wall.

Her injured hand blazed anew with pain. She grimaced against it, her hand squeezing almost involuntarily around the object in her palm. The object that cooled, and cracked, then crumbled under the pressure, as light and as fragile as dry, dead wood.

Turning over, Emily saw someone lurch up from the floor, roll his shoulders, his neck, bend down and pick up the folded sword. He flipped the hilt in his hand, and then raised it, the folding blade snapping out, pointing toward Zhukov.

He was Corvo Attano. He was Royal Protector.

He was father to the Empress of the Isles.

The disorientation charm destroyed, the spell was broken. Corvo was freed from its grip. He stepped toward their enemy.

"The story of the Hero of Tyvia ends here," he said.

At this, Zhukov laughed. He held his hands apart, and he gave a small bow to his opponent.

Then he turned his back to them, and he ran into the mirror.

30

GREAVES AUXILIARY WHALE SLAUGHTERHOUSE 5, SLAUGHTERHOUSE ROW, DUNWALL
15th Day, Month of Darkness, 1851

"The sun was setting, a bloody stain against the sky, silhouetting the charred ribcage of the slaughterhouse. The stench of burned meat—the flesh of men and whales—soured the air... [he] erupted from the ashes and timbers, his body wreathed in flame and rent with injuries that no mortal man could have survived. His shadow stretched out before him on the ground, and it revealed his true nature—a horned thing warped by heresy. A shape too terrible to put into words, my gentle readers. A sorcerer from the Void, without question... his heart... colder than Tyvian ice."

— THE KNIFE OF DUNWALL, A SURVIVOR'S TALE
From a street pamphlet containing a sensationalized sighting of the assassin Daud

Emily pulled herself to her feet, her good hand wrapped around the heavy chain that hung on the wall above her head. She glanced up. It ran up the wall to a pulley and gears, connected to another set of chains that hung across the ceiling, heading up to the top of the frame.

The frame that held the mirror.

She looked across at the vat. Zhukov was running toward the mirror. He had almost reached it. For him, it wasn't just a mirror but a door, a portal.

An escape route.

Moving quickly, on pure instinct, she unhooked the chain from the wall, knocked the locking bolt out of the geared wheel, and then let the chain go.

Gravity took over. Released from the lock, the chain shot up to the pulley mounted up on the ceiling framework, the gears screaming as they spun. The chains leading up to the top of the frame whipped tight as they were dragged toward the ceiling, then they ran off of the gears and licked across the factory in opposite directions.

Emily ducked just as one end flew toward her, cracking like a whip across the brickwork just inches above her head.

And then the mirror fell.

Zhukov slid to a halt, gaping as the huge surface dropped, sliding down into the vat. Behind him, Corvo ran toward his target, ready to make the kill. Then Corvo himself stopped, and leaped to one side as the mirror, off-balance, swung forward and *down*.

Zhukov bellowed something, but with the grinding roar Emily couldn't hear what it was. He remained where he stood. It was too late to move out of the way. The sheet of glass, metal—whatever magical substance it was—came down right on top of him. He raised his arms over his head, as if that would offer any kind of protection.

The mirror smashed, exploding across the factory floor in a million shards. Emily gasped and turned away, crouching tightly to avoid the flying shrapnel, the sound of the glass breaking as loud as the walls of Dunwall Tower crashing down in the visions she'd had.

The silence that followed was somehow louder, more shocking. Emily's head rang like a clocktower bell.

Then the ringing faded, replaced by a dull, low rumble. She lifted her head, and looked over her shoulder. The vat was still there, the contents softly bubbling, the surface thick, viscous like cooling caramel, lapping at the sides of the vat as it settled after the falling mirror had disturbed its convective churning.

"Emily!"

She turned fully around now. Corvo was walking toward her, brushing glass dust and tiny shards off himself. The pieces of the mirror, some as small as daggers, others as large as windows, lay across the factory floor, the smallest fragments glittering like diamonds. It was difficult for him to find a safe pathway.

Of Zhukov, there was no sign—he was somewhere under the largest pile of shattered mirror, in the space just in front of the vat.

Emily reached an arm up as Corvo drew close. He grabbed it and pulled, and she cried out. Corvo loosened his grip and ducked down to crouch beside his daughter, one arm reflexively moving around her shoulders, the instinctive gesture of a father to a daughter. Together they rose, Emily holding the hand against her chest.

"Are you all right?" Corvo asked, then he saw the blood trickling down Emily's wrist. "You're hurt. We need to get you back to the Tower, now."

Emily shrugged. "I'm fine, really. It's not bad."

She held her injured hand out, palm up, and uncurled the fist. It stung like nothing in the world, but she managed to move the fingers, waggling them a little to show her father that none were broken. Corvo winced as he examined the wounds, but Emily felt herself grin.

"I'll live."

Corvo smiled, then he turned to survey the wreckage in the factory. Emily stepped forward, carefully tapping at a large shard of mirror with the toe of her boot. The factory was still lit by just the glow of the vat, and the color was different now, the light dimming from the brilliant yellow-white to a warm orange glow. Emily stared down at the fragment at her feet.

"His body must be under there somewhere," Corvo said. "He looked pretty bad, like he'd been burned in a fire. He must have been in constant agony."

Emily frowned at the fragment. She tilted the edge of it with her boot, and found herself staring at her own reflection. She was dirty, bloody, tendrils of black hair floating free in front of her face. She reached up and tucked them behind her ears.

"Did he tell you what the mirror was for?" Corvo asked. "Or what he was planning on doing?"

Emily nodded. She had a lot to explain. She opened her mouth to speak, but at her feet the fragment of mirror seemed to flash blue, reflecting not the light of the vat but of something else.

She gave a yelp of fright, and jumped back. The fragment clattered back to the floor.

"What is it?" Corvo asked, moving to his daughter's side.

Emily sighed. "It was just a trick of the light."

It was, wasn't it?

"What?"

"For a moment I thought I saw Zhukov's face, over my shoulder."

Just a trick of the light.

"I'm not sure anyone could survive that," Corvo said, pointing to the pile of shattered glass.

A trick of the light.

Emily opened her mouth to answer, to tell Corvo about Zhukov's powers, about what he had told her of his plans, when there was a sound from the middle of the room—crystalline, bell-like, the sound of a wind chime floating out across the city on a hot summer evening.

Emily and Corvo turned around together. The rubble in the center of the room was moving, like there was something underneath, pushing up. As they watched, the shards began sliding apart, the largest pieces lifting up onto their ends, supported by some invisible force.

In the center, Zhukov raised himself up to his feet. He wore the tattered remains of the greatcoat, hanging in folds and loops of heavy cloth. His red goggles were gone, and in the flickering light of the factory it looked as though he had his eyes screwed tightly shut.

Emily took a step back. She couldn't help herself. Not when Zhukov raised his arms and the shattered remains of the mirror began to lift themselves off the floor, slowly, uncertainly, as if each piece was hanging on an invisible thread.

Corvo tensed beside her, his face a mask of concern, bewilderment, and amazement, his fists clenched by his sides.

In front of them, the mirror fragments, chiming like bells, slid up into the air. They didn't reassemble into the single, magical mirror, but instead formed a cylinder, no piece touching the other but each remaining in a fixed position in the air. The mosaic of fragments that began to turn around Zhukov, who stood at the center, his arms still outstretched, his eyes firmly shut.

The fragments flashed with light that wasn't there, but was shining from *within* them—the stars, the sun, the moon, all shining from the images in the shards, each piece showing something different to the next. Most of them were small, offering scant glimpses or flashes of light—but some were big enough to show clearly what was within.

She saw,
   Smoke rising from Dunwall Tower. She saw the city burning. She saw the rats swarming.
   She saw the gazebo in the morning sun, her mother sitting at the breakfast table. Emily herself running in the white trouser suit of an Imperial Princess. Hiding from Corvo as they played down by the old stone steps near the river.
   She saw her mother cowering in fear as the assassins dressed as Whalers appeared and killed her. Corvo led away on the orders of Hiram Burrows.
   She saw herself on a broken throne that crawled with rats as Corvo slaughtered Wyman for her enjoyment.

A wind whipped up. A wind from nowhere, howling from the moments trapped behind the floating mosaic of mirrors. Mirrors, Emily knew, that were really doorways, corridors leading to the past, to the present, to a thousand futures. The images were so real, so vivid, she felt certain she could just reach into them, plucking an apple from the breakfast table, a rat from the gutter, a stone from the crumbling walls of Dunwall Tower.

One shard caught her eye in particular. Something flashed inside it as it whipped past. Something brilliant, something golden—and then it was gone as the shard turned to complete another orbit. Emily kept her eyes on it, trying to track it among the countless other pieces that filled the air in the slaughterhouse.

Zhukov turned to face the two of them. He was the central point, the nexus of the tornado. The tattered remains of his coat caught fire, engulfing him in a blaze of blue flames that were pulled toward the fragments, connecting them all, the last remains of the corroded, unstable bonecharms burning to fuel this, his final act.

He opened his eyes. They were blackened hollows. At the center of each burned a star the color of blood, the color of a fire that burned a long time ago.

He gestured, and one of the largest fragments of mirror spun out of the mosaic and floated into position behind him. In it, a frozen slice of time—the gazebo, the message from Corvo, the final moment before her mother, Jessamine, was killed.

"So," Zhukov said, his croaky, wet voice somehow amplified, echoing above the sound of the unholy wind. "This was what you saw, my child. The end of the history you remember." He laughed. "But the beginning of a new one, of my making."

He turned and reached into the mirror. The surface rippled at his touch, and he plunged his hand into it.

The other fragment Emily had been watching drifted within touching distance, the blue energy from Zhukov spiraling into it like luminous smoke. She reached out for it herself. Corvo shouted something, but she couldn't hear over the wind. She reached out with her cut hand, plunging it into the mirror, meeting no resistance.

Her mind exploded with pain. It was all-encompassing, a thing that enveloped her body like a heavy blanket, a thousand hands pushing her down to the ground. She felt a heat grow within her, until she thought her heart was on fire, her whole *body* was on fire.

Her hand closed on something. Cold. Hard. The surface intricately engraved, the thing molded for a perfect grip.

Cold. Hard. *Metal.*

She pulled her hand back, falling backward.

She held the golden knife, Zhukov's twin blades. The knife—she knew, somehow, just upon holding it—that had spilled the blood of someone both important and unremarkable, thousands of years ago.

And she heard it whisper and sing, the blaze of agony in her mind flooded by the light of flames and the heat of an inferno and the forgotten song of another age.

She screamed. She fell, Corvo caught her, and as the world spun into fiery nothing she felt him take the knife from her, saw him run past her, saw him grab Zhukov around the neck as the cadaverous evil stepped into the mirror beyond.

Saw Corvo plunge the golden knife into his blackened carcass.

Saw Zhukov's body go stiff, the Hero of Tyvia frozen, just inches away from his escape.

And then she saw nothing at all.

31

"Sometimes when I sleep I dream, and in those dreams I am many things. I am an adventurer, a traveler. I am a hero and I am a tyrant, a beggar on the street, the ruler of the world. And sometimes in those dreams I see a light, bright and shining, red and golden white, the light of a fire that burned so very long ago, when one world ended and another began. And when I wake the dream is gone but the feeling remains, the echo of song ringing in my ears, the warmth of a winter hearth and the shine of light on a distant, unknown horizon."

— THE ASHEN VEIL
Extract from a private journal

Emily flinched at the light, then jerked awake. She gasped, and fell back.

Back into something soft and cool. She lifted her head. It was a pillow. *Her* pillow.

She frowned, and turned her head, the room coming into focus as she blinked into the daylight streaming through the window. Beside it stood a woman in a long white robe, with stiff, high collar and a white skullcap on her head. She thought she should recognize the uniform, but the effort was too much and she let her head fall back.

There were voices nearby, murmuring by the window. She opened her eyes again. The woman in white was talking to a man in a black leather tunic. He looked familiar, somehow. Short hair, gray at the temples, darker on top, his face peppered with a light stubble. He had his arms folded and she saw his biceps bulge under the sleeves of his tunic.

She remembered. The woman in white was a court physician—the *royal* physician, Doctor Toksvig, who had apprenticed under Sokolov. The soft pillow was hers, as was the room. And the man was...

"Corvo?" she asked, surprised at how quiet and weak her own voice was.

Her father turned to her and smiled. Then he unfolded his arms and moved to the bed.

"Emily," the Royal Protector said. "You're awake. How are you feeling?"

She frowned. How was she feeling? About what, exactly? She shifted in the bed. She felt tired, her head heavy. She moved again. She'd had a dream, a dream about a fire—

She jerked up, then winced as a bolt of pain shot up her neck.

"Ouch!"

Corvo stood back and chuckled softly. "Yeah, you'll be sore for a while."

The factory. Zhukov. The mirror.

It all came back to her.

"I feel like a building fell on me," she said, her voice louder, the strength coming back with every passing second, albeit slowly.

"Funny you should say that," Corvo said, laughing, "because you had a building fall on you. Well, part of a building, anyway."

Beside him, Doctor Toksvig loitered, clearly wanting access to her royal patient. Corvo stepped back to allow the court physician some room as Toksvig wrapped the arms of a pair of small circular glasses around her ears and leaned in. She asked a series of questions, some about how she felt, others about what year it was, what month, who she was, where she was. She frowned at these, but behind the woman's back she saw Corvo grin and give her a slight nod, so she answered the questions dutifully and without complaint.

The physician seemed happy enough, and she stood back and took her glasses off. The big wire loops got stuck behind her ears and she struggled to free them as she spoke.

"She'll be fine in a day or two, but I think rest is the best remedy," she said. "Perhaps a week at Heronshaw Lake would be in order. I think the Empire can survive without its Empress for just a little while." She paused, finally having got her glasses off, only to turn to Emily and put them back in place.

"But I must say, she's in good health," the doctor continued. "No bones broken, just some minor contusions. Nothing out of the ordinary, aside, of course, from Her Majesty's noteworthy physical condition. It never ceases to amaze me what garden walks, ballroom dances, and the occasional horseback jaunt have done for Lady Emily's health. More muscle than the average officer of the City Watch, I'd say."

With that, the physician stuck her tongue in her cheek and glanced sideways at Corvo, then gave Emily a deep bow and moved away.

Corvo sat on the bed as Emily shuffled to sit up. She swiped her hair out of her face with both hands, then dropped them to her lap, staring at the palms. Her hands were fine. *Both* of them. She lifted her left one, turning it over and flexing the fingers. There was no sign of the deep cuts she had given herself with Corvo's blade.

"The doctor says you can get up now, Your Majesty," Corvo said with a smile. Emily just frowned at him.

"How long have I been out?"

"Three days."

Emily blinked. Then she held up her hand again. Had she dreamed what had happened?

"Your hand is fine," he said. "Somehow it healed when you reached into the mirror and grabbed the knife."

"Right. Of course." Emily nodded slowly. "That makes as much sense as anything else."

Corvo just shrugged.

"What happened in there?" Emily asked.

Corvo tugged on his bottom lip. "After you passed me the knife, I knew I had to stop Zhukov—I don't know what he was doing, but he was stepping through the mirror fragment, somehow. I pulled him back and used the knife." He cleared his throat and for a moment Emily's eyes flicked down. She knew what Corvo was, what he was capable of doing, but it wasn't something she wanted to dwell on.

"And then what?" she asked.

"Well, we struggled a bit, he tried to get the knife out. The mirror fragments came crashing down, so I had to run. I grabbed him and pushed, and he fell into the vat."

Emily shook her head. "I don't remember that."

Corvo smiled. "No, you wouldn't, you were out cold. There was an explosion—the whole factory went up, then collapsed into the river."

Emily's breath caught in her throat.

"Don't worry!" Corvo laughed. "You're here, aren't you?"

"How did we get out?"

Corvo shrugged. "I ducked and ran, carrying you. I guess we were lucky, right?"

Emily sank back into the bed, shaking her head. *It was over. Wasn't it?*

"What about Zhukov?"

Corvo shook his head. "If there was anything left of him after he fell into his soup, we haven't found it. I have the Wrenhaven River Patrol trawling the riverbed. There's a lot of rubble to dig through, but there's no sign of his remains. Or of any of the mirror fragments."

"What about the knife?"

Corvo shook his head.

Emily sighed.

The two of them chatted for a while. She wanted to tell him about what Zhukov had told her, about his plan and his powers, but her father steered the conversation away, saying there would be plenty of time to go through all of that. They talked about the last three days, about court life, ordinary things.

According to Corvo, the initial shock of what had happened at the Boyle Masquerade had faded, replaced with a strange, whispered excitement about the drama so much of Dunwall society had experienced firsthand. Lady Esma Boyle was recovering, but seemed withdrawn now, and her nephew, Ichabod, was handling the family affairs.

There was a knock at the door.

Corvo stood to open it, and let Wyman in. The young noble nodded at the Royal Protector, then grinned at the Empress. Emily let out a breath.

"I'm bruised and unbathed, but you may approach."

Then she gave Wyman a wry smile. Wyman bowed, and the pair laughed, then Corvo clapped the noble on the back.

"Young Wyman, I'm glad you're feeling better."

Emily's eyes widened, and she bit her tongue. Her father was grinning, and Wyman nodded.

"Thank you, sir. I feel much better. I really don't know what happened." Wyman turned to Emily. "I'm glad you're okay, Emily. I feel awful—I had promised the Royal Protector to keep you in my sight, and then…" The words faltered, and Wyman shrugged. "Next thing I know I'm in one of the guest apartments, being tended to by Doctor Toksvig. Last thing I remember, we were together in the Great Hall, talking about… well, I don't know what."

Corvo put his arm around Wyman's shoulders. "Never mind, I'm glad you've recovered." He turned his smile on Emily. "Must have been something you drank."

She didn't say a thing.

32

"Why, Sir, you find no man, at all intellectual, who is willing to leave Dunwall. No, Sir, when a man is tired of Dunwall, he is tired of life; for there is in Dunwall all that life can afford."

— CONVERSATIONS OF A NATURAL PHILOSOPHER
Extract from a popular pamphlet

The night was cool and the gentle breeze was pleasant. Emily enjoyed the fresh air. Crouched on the rooftop, she pulled down the collar of her jacket and found herself smiling.

It was good to be out again. Heronshaw Lake had been nice, and she certainly had needed the rest, but she was glad to be back in Dunwall.

It was when she'd unpacked that she had found the black sparrow costume—part of it, anyway—in the closet in her apartment. She'd been wearing it when Corvo carried her back to the Tower. The mask was missing, abandoned somewhere in the Boyle Mansion, although Emily's memory of the events of that night was a little fuzzy still, and her full recollection of the struggle against

Zhukov seemed to be fading, as if something about it wasn't quite real enough to leave solid memories.

But it had given her a good idea. She'd been at the masquerade for hours, leaving no one any the wiser that their Empress had walked among them.

So, that night, when the Tower was quiet and sleeping, she'd stolen out of bed, and padded over to the closet. Dragging the black sparrow costume out, she carried it into her safe room and laid it out on the table. Then, taking a dagger, she began to cut, stripping the feathers off, making adjustments here and there. Then she folded the collar up and buttoned it. It covered her nose and mouth, leaving her plenty of room to see, but providing an excellent disguise.

It would do, for now. When she had time, she would have a quiet word with her royal tailor to come up with something a little more... customized. In her mind, she could see a smart jacket with asymmetric tails and embroideries in gold thread, and a high collar that could be raised, to cover the face...

But now she enjoyed the night, Dunwall spread out in front of her, sparkling like a jewel. Over on her left, farther down the river, the lights of the Wrenhaven River Patrol blazed as they continued their search of the Greaves slaughterhouse ruins. At least the river hadn't been blocked by its collapse, and some prime industrial real estate had become available. In fact, she was due to meet representatives of the Greaves Lighting Oil Company in the morning to talk about the building collapse and what it meant for—

Emily stood and sighed. That was for tomorrow, when she would return to her job as Empress. A job that was dull and boring.

Not like tonight. Not like *this*.

She flexed her muscles. She felt good. No, she felt *great*. Alive. *Electric*, and all around her the city slept, no one realizing what had happened, the fate that had almost befallen the Empire, in a future that might have been.

With a grin, Emily judged the distance to the next rooftop. She backed up, pulled the collar of her makeshift disguise up over her nose and mouth.

She ran, and she jumped, the city of Dunwall her playground, her home.

On another rooftop, another figure crouched, watching her leap, run, leap, roll, disappearing over the rooftops as silent as a shadow.

She had done well. *Very* well. She was ready.

After all this time, she was more than ready.

Corvo felt a swell of pride inside him. He stood, judging the best spot to which he would blink, to keep her in his sight.

And then he stopped himself. He thought for a moment, watching the Empress vanish into the shadowed eaves of a building, and then he lifted his hand. On the back, the Mark of the Outsider flared blue for a moment, and then was quiet.

"No," Corvo whispered. "Not tonight."

He turned and headed back into the Tower, leaving the city and Emily alone with each other.

EPILOGUE

DUNWALL TOWER
1st Day, Month of Clans, 1837

"At least [the Royal Protector is] likely to stop any immediate threat to her safety, but a strong arm is not what's needed against those who would undermine us. How will Corvo's sword stop a poisoned wine glass or an explosive delivered by courier? It will not. There are many threats around us."

— FIELD SURVEY NOTES: THE ROYAL SPYMASTER
Excerpt from the personal memoirs of Hiram Burrows,
dated several years earlier

Corvo jogged up the steps to the gazebo that stood overlooking the great ship dock at the waterside of Dunwall Tower. As he approached, he slowed.

There was someone in the gazebo—someone wearing a regal black trouser suit, with a big white lace collar, her dark hair coiled high on her head. She was standing with arms folded, her back to him as she looked out across the harbor.

Corvo blinked, his stomach pitching over. He stepped into the gazebo, and cleared his throat. The woman, startled, turned around, one hand at her breast. When she saw who it was, she relaxed, and laughed.

"My Lord Protector."

Corvo relaxed too, and gave a small bow.

"Callista."

She wasn't wearing the regal black trouser suit of the Empress—she was wearing the simple uniform that identified her as Emily's personal attendant. The lace collar was simply the fashion, and Callista's hair wasn't black, it was brown.

Corvo shook his head, cursing his own mind for playing tricks on him.

He was Royal Protector, Royal Spymaster. Emily had

been restored to the throne just a month before, and already the young girl was showing aptitude for the role, seemingly enjoying the work while he, Callista, and the new High Overseer, Yul Khulan, helped guide her hand.

There was no regency. There never would be.

Not again.

"Are you well, Corvo?"

He blinked, then rubbed his forehead.

"Ah, yes, sorry, Callista," he said. "I've just been busy these last few weeks. Burrows left the Tower in a real mess. It'll take forever to get things straightened out. Ah, how's the Empress? She sent me a note to meet her here."

Callista smiled. "The Empress is doing very well. It's amazing, the change in her. Ten years old, and already I can see a great future ahead of her."

Corvo nodded. "And for the Empire, too." Then he pursed his lips, and took his daughter's handwritten note from his jacket. "But I guess even an Empress needs to let off steam."

Callista folded her arms. "Hide-and-seek again?"

Corvo laughed. "Looks like it."

"Corvo! Come on Corvo! Come *on*!"

The young Empress's voice carried on a breeze from somewhere to Corvo's left. He turned, just catching sight of Emily as she darted down around the stairs that curved away from the gazebo, out of sight among the cliffs at the base of Dunwall Tower.

Corvo sighed, and made a point of neatly folding Emily's note and slipping it back into his jacket.

Callista laughed. "Good hunting, My Lord Protector."

Corvo gave Callista a deep and elaborate bow, then turned and headed toward Emily's voice.

*

Corvo stepped cautiously down the stairs as seagulls wheeled overhead. He looked around, almost nervously.

He hadn't been here for a long time. Not since that fateful day when he had returned to Dunwall after his tour of the Isles, the day he'd brought back news that the rest of the Empire was blockading the city, waiting to see if the Rat Plague would burn itself out. Jessamine had been devastated. Her authority had been questioned, her plans for the city laid to ruin.

The day everything changed, forever.

Corvo remembered these stairs well. Fresh off the boat, Emily had raced to meet him at the royal dock, and before he'd taken his report to her mother, the Empress, he had indulged the young girl in a game of hide-and-seek.

It seemed so... so innocent, so harmless. An indulgence, yes, but he had been away and he knew that things would get worse before they got better.

If only he'd had any idea of just how bad they would get. That, mere moments after playing with the heir to the throne, down by the stairs under the towering cliffs and sheer walls of the palace, their lives would be destroyed.

Jessamine, murdered.

Emily, kidnapped.

And Corvo, branded a traitor—imprisoned.

But they had survived it. It was hell, but they had survived it, and here he was, reinstated as Royal Protector—Royal Spymaster, as well, combining the two offices to ensure that no traitors could ever occupy such positions of power again. Not while he lived.

He had avenged the death of Empress Jessamine with his own hands, and had saved the life of Emily, the heiress—their *daughter*. Here she was, now Empress, playing hide-and-seek around the old stairs.

Corvo took the rest of the stairs at a trot. He looked

around, but there was no sign of his ward.

"Ready or not, here I come!" he shouted with a smile. As he reached the bottom of the stairs, he slowed, putting on an exaggerated, cautious approach, knowing she would be watching from some nearby vantage point.

He walked up to the wall ahead of him, and leaned out over it, gazing down at the steep rocky incline leading to the Wrenhaven River, far below. A whaling boat was making slow progress out to sea. The huge cradle, designed to hold its precious cargo, was empty, waiting for the ocean's bounty.

In front of it, traveling in the opposite direction, a small skiff of the Wrenhaven River Patrol sped back into the city, its pilot merely a silhouette in the bright morning sun.

Gulls squawked in the clear blue sky. Corvo glanced up. Savored the moment. The world was at peace, and the city was still, and the Empress—

He heard her coming. A grunt of effort, her feet sliding in the dirt, but he didn't register what she was doing until Corvo felt Emily jump onto his back, two legs wrapping around his middle, one arm grabbing him in a choke hold, the other...

Corvo turned and stepped away from the wall, carrying her to a more safe position. He grabbed at the arm around his neck—Emily was actually pretty strong and was squeezing for all she was worth, but it had little effect, especially with the thick collar of Corvo's uniform in the way.

What he was more concerned about was the weapon Emily had in her other hand. They'd dueled with wooden sticks before, but not like this. As she struggled to stay secured to her father's back, her free hand waved a wooden sword wildly in the air—a wooden sword with a decidedly sharp, wicked point.

"Hey!" Corvo cried out, his surprise only half exaggerated. "What in all the Isles is the Empress of the world doing? Is this any way to treat your sworn and loyal protector?"

Emily laughed. Corvo gave up on trying to free his neck, and instead grabbed hold of her knees. He felt her shift position, pushing herself up so she was sitting on his shoulders. Happy that she was more secure, he spun around on the spot as fast as he could. Somewhere above his head, Emily shrieked and laughed.

He came to a halt, puffing for breath, and found the wooden sword held vertically in front of his face.

"Do you yield, Hatter?"

"Ah... Hatter? What—"

"Yield or die!" Emily tightened her grip around Corvo's neck.

He chuckled and, not without some difficulty, reached up to pull the Empress off his shoulders. But she had her knees locked, and... well, she wasn't a small child anymore. Corvo leaned forward, trying to persuade her to climb off, but the more he moved, the more she clung on. Eventually he overbalanced, and he found himself on his hands and knees.

Only then did Emily jump off.

Corvo laughed, shaking his head, and looked up. Emily stood in front of him, peering down her nose with her chin raised, one hand on her hip, the other pointing the tip of the short wooden sword at his nose.

"You are defeated!" she cried.

Corvo lifted himself up off his hands, which he raised above his head, but he stayed on his knees.

"Yes, oh mighty Empress, I am defeated."

Emily's face dropped, along with the sword.

"Corvo, you're treating me like a *child*."

Corvo paused. "Ah, well, I regret to inform her majesty

that she is, in fact, a child, and I humbly point out that her majesty should really be studying with her governess right about now."

"Corvo, you don't listen. You never listen!"

"I... all right, Emily, what's this about?"

"Don't you remember?" She waved both arms—sword and all—around as she spoke. "I told you. I told you the day you came back. I said I wanted to be a fighter, just like you."

Corvo sat back on his haunches. Yes, that's what she had said. He remembered now. He also remembered that it was just the kind of thing an impressionable young girl like Emily said all the time.

She looked up to him. He was a role model and, he hoped, now that the throne had been restored, that life was getting back to some kind of normality, that he was, *would be*, a good one. But... he had to be careful.

This young girl—not even eleven years old—had been through more than most people in their entire lifetime. She was coping well.

But...

Emily dropped to her knees in front of him, and looked up into his eyes.

"I need you to teach me, Corvo. I need you to teach me everything about fighting. I have to be able to do these things for myself."

Corvo blinked. "What? Trust me, you don't want to be a fighter, Emily. You're Empress now. I'm your protector, and besides me, you have an entire army to command. You're safe now."

"*Now*," Emily said. "But you won't be around forever."

Corvo hadn't expected Emily—his own flesh and blood—to say something like that. Though, at his core, her words teased apart one of his deep fears, that someday their enemies would come for her, perhaps even after Corvo was gone.

"Emily, don't talk like that."

"See?" she said. "Treating me like a child again, Corvo. I won't have it!"

"Emily, listen—"

"No, you listen to me, Corvo. My mother died in front of my eyes, up there." Emily pointed in the direction of the gazebo, somewhere above them. "I was *there*. And maybe if you hadn't gone away, that wouldn't have happened."

Corvo felt the heat rise in his face. What was Emily accusing him of? Surely she didn't blame *him* for the death of her mother?

"Emily, I know you're still angry," he said quietly. "And listen, I know what it's like, believe me, I *know*. We can't change the past. I miss your mother as much as you do. Don't think that not a day goes past when I don't wonder what would have happened if she hadn't sent me on that errand around the Isles. What would have happened if I had stayed, if I'd… I don't know… been more observant, paid more attention."

As Corvo spoke, he saw Emily's eyes well with tears. To her credit, she held her expression firm, set, as she looked back at him.

"But I was doing it for her," he continued, "and I was doing it for you. I was doing it for the *city*, Emily."

"I could have done something." Emily's voice was a whisper.

Corvo placed his hands on her shoulders.

"No, you couldn't have. You couldn't have fought them off. They had orders to capture you, but who knows what they would have done if you'd tried to resist. And I'm here—right here, right now. I'm your protector, and I swear to you, I will never let you out of my sight. Not ever."

Emily said nothing. Corvo sighed, and went to stand up, when she spoke again.

"And one day you won't be here," she said, "and the only person left I will be able to trust will be myself."

Corvo slumped back, and gave his daughter a sad smile. Someone so young, thinking such things. She had seen too much of the world, too much of its darkness. And now she was Empress, and she was expected to *rule*. An Empress at ten years old.

"I want you to teach me to fight, Corvo," she said again. "I want you to teach me how to be *you*."

If only you knew, Corvo thought. *If only you knew.*

He sighed, and held his hand against his daughter's cheek. His hand was so big, the skin rough, against Emily's soft, pale face.

Maybe... maybe she was right. Who could she trust, really? Perhaps one day things would be back to normal— whatever "normal" was—but the next few years, they were going to be difficult. There would be many who saw the coronation of a child Empress as an opportunity to make a move.

"Well, I guess there's no harm in teaching you a few things..."

Emily's face lit up, and she stepped back.

"Here, today, a short lesson," Corvo said. "More later, in the days to come. I know a place along the old waterfront, just east of Drapers Ward. We can make it our practice grounds."

"Yes!" the girl said. "That sounds very good. Now, wait here!"

Corvo laughed, and shook his head as Emily darted away. A moment later she was back. In one hand she held her wooden sword.

And in the other, a second—the old sticks they used

to duel with, now whittled into something rather more dangerous. Corvo stared at it as Emily offered him the weapon.

"I made you one, too!"

Corvo laughed, taking the sword. He stood, and lips pursed, he hefted the weapon, seeking its balance as though it were a real blade of steel.

"The finest blacksmiths of Morley couldn't make a better sword, Your Majesty."

Emily gave Corvo a bow, then she straightened and held her own weapon out, her other arm raised for balance. She stood, knees bent, feet at ninety-degrees. The perfect *en guard* position.

Corvo watched her for a moment. Emily frowned and relaxed, straightening her legs and lowering her sword.

"I'm ready for my first lesson, Royal Protector. You may begin."

Then she returned to *en guard*.

"As you wish, Your Majesty."

Corvo dropped into position, and tapped the end of his wooden sword against Emily's.

Yes, this was a beginning, all right.

ABOUT THE AUTHOR

Adam Christopher is a novelist, comic book writer, and award-winning editor. The author of *Seven Wonders*, *The Age Atomic*, and *Hang Wire*, and co-writer of *The Shield* for Dark Circle Comics, Adam has also written novels based on the hit CBS television show *Elementary* for Titan Books. His debut novel, *Empire State*, was *SciFiNow*'s Book of the Year and a *Financial Times* Book of the Year for 2012. Born in New Zealand, Adam has lived in Great Britain since 2006.

Find him online at www.adamchristopher.ac and on Twitter as @ghostfinder.

THE GRIPPING NEW COMIC BOOK SERIES!

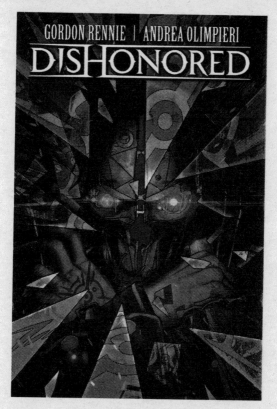

Comic series out now

Graphic novel on sale November 2016

WRITER GORDON RENNIE | **ARTIST** ANDREA OLIMPIERI

For more fantastic fiction, author events,
competitions, limited editions and more

VISIT OUR WEBSITE
titanbooks.com

LIKE US ON FACEBOOK
facebook.com/titanbooks

FOLLOW US ON TWITTER
@TitanBooks

EMAIL US
readerfeedback@titanemail.com